THE LAST TEACHER

For the Benefit of Humankind

by

George L. Fearns

Strategic Book Publishing and Rights Co.

Copyright © 2015 George L. Fearns. All rights reserved.

No part of this book may be reproduced or transmitted in any form or by any means, graphic, electronic, or mechanical, including photocopying, recording, taping, or by any information storage retrieval system, without the permission, in writing, of the publisher. For more information, send an email to support@sbpra.net, Attention: Subsidiary Rights.

Strategic Book Publishing and Rights Co., LLC
USA | Singapore
www.sbpra.com

For information about special discounts for bulk purchases, please contact Strategic Book Publishing and Rights Co., LLC. Special Sales, at bookorder@sbpra.net.

ISBN: 978-1-68181-262-5

To my wife Sylvia, for her patience and understanding, since she spent many lonely hours while I was writing *The Last Teacher*.

To Syd.
Relax, read and enjoy.
George L. Fearns.

The planet Earth had been under surveillance by the inhabitants of the planet Zel for millions of years, during which time they witnessed the slow development of a creature of apparently limited intelligence take place. As this appeared to be somewhat similar to their own beginnings in the mists of time, they resolved to assist this ape-like being to evolve more rapidly than nature intended. To this end, the Zellians embarked on a project to transform these monkey-like creatures physically and mentally into something more in keeping with their own image. The experiment began by landing small teams of biologists and genetic engineers on the planet, where they lived and worked for a number of years, carrying out research projects, encouraging the fittest and most intelligent to breed. Unfortunately, the Zellians were handicapped by their own inability to live on Earth for more than a few years due to the planet's stronger gravity, so they devised a method of training and selected a few of the native inhabitants to act as Teachers to the global population. They returned every five hundred years to observe what, if any, changes had occurred to the native species during their absence.

They allowed this process to continue for many thousands of years before concluding that nature was not going to be hurried, and therefore, drastic methods had to be used to accelerate the physical and mental development of these Earth creatures. After much argument among their scientists, they decided to genetically modify the species by artificially inseminating as many of the females as possible with the sperm of the Zellians in the research group. After this was done, they departed for another five-hundred-year hiatus during which some twenty generations of the native species were born. When the Zellians returned, they noted that changes had occurred in the stature and intelligence of the Earth creatures, but they had evolved far too slowly. This required the Zellians to repeat the insemination process many times.

Fortunately, the Zellians had a very long life span, more than one thousand Earth years on average, so it was possible for many of their scientists to observe the results of their experiments first hand. As time went by, they genetically modified this primitive creature until both male and female of the species resembled the Zellians themselves.

Finally, it was realised that nature had been given the boost to ensure that this emerging creature would not only survive but flourish. Therefore, it was decided that the time had come to leave Earth to develop in its own time, but over the ensuing millennia, the planet was not forgotten. From time to time, every five hundred years to begin with, a Teacher was provided to ensure that progress was maintained in the physical and mental development of what was now the dominant species on Earth.

During this time, climatic changes occurred throughout the planet, which affected the way of life of these primitive people, and yet they flourished. Teachers continued to be trained, mostly unaware of their purpose, and were placed in the different communities to continue the education process among their own people, and so it continued until the present day. Along the way, many scholars, artists, engineers, philosophers, and other wise men lived and passed on their knowledge before making way for others; they improved the way of life for their human counterparts generally, but it was still evident that their primitive origins were merely covered by the thin veneer of civilisation. Eventually their Zellian benefactors had to intervene yet again, and the search began for a Teacher endowed with the power to control the world.

Chapter One

As he gazed out of the observation window of his craft, watching the interstellar mother ship gradually recede into the distance, Captain Jara turned to the most junior member of his crew standing beside him, a young cadet—a female by the name of Lana. Indicating the progress of the mother ship, he said, 'Once clear of this moon's gravity and a safe distance from us, the commander will be anxious to leave this solar system and resume his patrol to another star system. Only then will he be able to activate the time and space line system, but in the meantime, he will accelerate gradually to interplanetary speed.'

Lana smiled her acknowledgement of this information; it was something she was already aware of since every cadet had to learn the basic concept of space/time travel very early in her career in addition to everything required to run the ship efficiently. Eventually, every crewmember had to be able to take command and operate as an individual; therefore, all control systems of this comparatively small spacecraft were already completely familiar to her. She was the most junior rank on board, and also the youngest, a mere eighty years.

Compared to her captain, she realised that, although physically and mentally mature, she had much to learn, but plenty of time to do so. After all, her race, her people, had a life expectancy of a thousand years; in fact, some had exceeded that by another hundred years or more.

Chapter One

For some time after the mother ship had completely disappeared from view, it was still visible on the screens of the control panels. Lana and Captain Jara remained at the observation window taking in the view of the moon's surface below them, Earth's satellite, a bleak and hostile environment. The surface was pitted with craters of bygone meteor impacts, some small, others very deep and miles across, and low mountain ranges, and everywhere, it was covered in thick layers of compacted dust, undisturbed until the recent landings of astronauts in man's attempt to take his first tentative steps toward space travel.

'You could very quickly become bored looking at this view, Lana,' Jara remarked. 'And while I have been here many times in the past, we have always remained in orbit since our sensors on the ship showed there was little in the way of minerals or water on this moon, thus we've had no incentive or desire to land. The Earth inhabitants have established a primitive base of sorts in the recent past, however, and who knows, they may return again someday.'

'Captain, at the moment we are docked on the blind side of the moon so far as Earth is concerned; is there any reason for that? If we were on the other side, we would have a much better view. At least Earth looks similar to our world, another blue planet.'

Jara smiled indulgently at the young cadet. 'A century ago, we could have hovered a mere hundred miles above Earth, and no one would have been any wiser, but in that time, humans have made technical progress in leaps and bounds, so much so that their military would no doubt be alarmed by our presence and attempt to attack us. Futile, of course, but as we have been observing and intercepting their communications systems for the last hundred years, we are well aware of the war-like attitude these people have toward each other, and undoubtedly, we would be regarded as an enemy, despite the fact that we have been their benefactors since they came down from the trees.'

Chapter One

Lana smiled at that observation. 'But didn't our race evolve in a similar way?'

'Yes,' Jara replied, 'but while it took us several millions of years to gain our present level of civilisation and culture, we did so without any help or interference from an outside source. As you know, we have assisted humans at different stages of their evolution without their knowledge, and now they have reached a point where they are almost ready to self-destruct.'

He frowned as he recalled how his own people, his own superiors, had monitored the wars and destruction taking place on Earth during the last thousand years, petty squabbles for the most part, but in the very recent century, the scale of conflict had increased in severity, causing the death of millions of people. With the development of nuclear fusion, the results of which had been observed from afar, the time had come once more for the Zellians to intercede for the preservation of humanity and Earth.

Now it was Lana's turn to frown. 'And this is the purpose of our visit to Earth? We're here to find another teacher to guide their governments and people to lead a life of peace and to address their understanding and technical abilities so that all may benefit?'

Jara smiled grimly. 'Yes, Lana, we are going to find yet another teacher and train him to educate his own people as we have done periodically over the past millennia.' At this point, he turned away from the observation window and sat down in front of a control console. 'We have trained and installed a teacher at five-hundred-year intervals ever since the first civilisations began to appear, some as early as four thousand years ago. They were called the Greeks and the Egyptians, and we were encouraged by their progress, but as ever, humankind's inability to live in peace caused these civilisations to founder and virtually disappear. They did leave a legacy for other people, however, and empires were forged and flourished, but they, in turn, were consumed in war and corruption and disappeared.' After a moment's reflection, Jara continued. 'At one point, a little

Chapter One

more than two thousand years ago, we tried a different type of Teacher, a young boy whom we managed to train secretly while he was growing up. We instilled in him a spiritual belief in a God and that he was the earthly son of that God. He tried to educate his fellow men to lead a good life based on existing superstitions of the past, but unfortunately, it was to no avail; his own people killed him in a barbaric manner.'

He shuddered at the thought. 'Thereafter, every two hundred years, we've been able to persuade certain individuals to become Teachers for the good of humanity. Some developed into politicians of note, changing the lives of many, and others became scientists. But the world was not ready for their advanced thinking at that time. There were several who developed art and beauty as a way of life, and while we have seen some actual improvement in humankind since those early beginnings, we are now seeing signs of retrogression, and if atomic warfare should be developed, and that is a possibility, the whole planet and its people will become extinct.'

As the captain leaned back in his chair, his eyes took on a faraway look as he thought of the challenge that lay ahead, to find the one man among millions who would be capable of doing what no man had succeeded in achieving, to bring peace and prosperity to the entire planet.

While he was considering this almost impossible task, Mort, his second-in-command, took a last look out of the observation window before activating the closure mechanism, in effect making the ship ready for departure from their temporary static orbit above the moon's surface.

'With respect, Captain,' he said quietly, 'now that the mother ship has departed, there is little reason to remain here. May I suggest we set course for Earth as planned? The Northern Hemisphere was your preferred area to begin our search for the Teacher, was it not?'

Chapter One

His reverie having been disturbed, Jara looked around the control room and gave an affirmative nod to Mort. 'Yes,' he acknowledged. 'The sooner we can go into orbit above Earth, the sooner we can begin our search.' He paused reflectively. 'On previous occasions, we've examined dozens of candidates before making our final selection, and he was indeed from the Northern Hemisphere. The people on that part of the planet seemed somewhat more willing to cooperate, although it has to be said that many of them just didn't have the mental capacity for the necessary training required.'

With due deference to her captain, Lana asked, 'How long did it take to find the last Teacher, sir?'

Although his mind was already contemplating the forthcoming search for a suitable candidate, Jara nevertheless answered readily. 'The planet had rotated some thirty times on its axis; that would equate to thirty days and nights, not a great deal different from our own planet, and we had to land in order to pick up each individual who was potentially suitable for questioning.' He smiled. 'While we can teleport to the surface of the earth and return quite easily, our human counterparts don't have that ability, which is why we have to land however briefly, but with any luck, we may be more fortunate on this occasion.'

Turning to his second-in-command, Jara said, 'Instruct Holt to set a course for Earth. As technical officer, he can give Lana the opportunity to take the con, under his supervision, of course.' He added quietly, 'We are not equipped with the space/time technology for these short trips, but as it is only a quarter of a million miles to travel, we should enter Earth's orbit in about six hours, according to real time on that planet.'

With each of his officers allocated to their respective tasks, Captain Jara relaxed in his chair and resumed his contemplation of the purpose of the mission. As predicted, it was some six hours later that they entered orbit a few miles above Earth, which was within

Chapter One

easy range of their surveillance equipment and teleport distance, and so the search began.

Chapter Two

With his eyes staring sightlessly at the scene outside the window, the young man's mind was in turmoil. *Am I doing the sensible thing, or am I throwing away a perfectly good career?* It was a profession he had always found interesting and rewarding until the events of the last few months following the death of his wife and two young children in a horrific car crash. Witnesses claimed that his wife had been to blame, overtaking on a bend at a high rate of speed that resulted in a head-on collision with a lorry, ending in instant death for all his family. The only consolation was that no one else was injured, although the lorry driver had been hospitalised for shock.

The sound of his name being spoken by the secretary of the airport director caused him to focus on his surroundings. 'Mr Bradburn, would you care to step into the office, please. Mr Thorpe will see you now.' Knowing the purpose of his visit, she spoke sympathetically and gave a gentle smile as she held the door open for him to enter the inner office. As he hesitantly approached the large gentleman sitting behind the desk, he sensed he was about to be given some kind of advice about his future prospects as a senior air traffic controller at the airport and the futility of terminating his employment. And such proved to be the case. Mr Thorpe talked very reassuringly about time being a great healer, and that it might be more helpful to immerse himself in his work to take his mind off his personal grief.

Chapter Two

Jon Bradburn was not prepared to be dissuaded from his purpose. Ever since that fateful day when he had been informed of the tragic accident—he had been at his post in the control room at the time—he had been unable to focus on anything, even daily mundane tasks, and certainly not on the important function of directing air traffic into and out of Manchester Airport, one of the busiest in the country.

Reluctantly, Mr Thorpe eventually accepted Jon's formal resignation, to take effect immediately on compassionate grounds, but not before assuring Jon that his position as a controller would be held open for him should he desire to return. That would not be an option, however, which neither of them knew at the time.

As he made his way out of the office complex and walked toward the car park, Jon's head was in a whirl. The deed was done; he was no longer committed to a career or a family. Living his life on his own was not a prospect he looked forward to. In fact, at this moment, he had no idea what he was going to do in the future other than to get away from his immediate surroundings and painful memories of the past. The loss of his wife and children had left him like a ship without a rudder, an aimless existence.

As he approached his car, an ancient Volvo Estate, he couldn't help the thought that passed through his mind. *Would they have survived the crash if they had been in this car?* But it was a futile thought, and he quickly dismissed it from his mind; life, however bleak, would go on.

Before his interview with the airport director, Jon had packed a few essentials into a bag with a vague intention of going somewhere, anywhere but Manchester. As fate would have it, shortly after leaving the airport, he found himself on the M6, heading north. *North, east, south or west, it doesn't matter. I'll just drive until I'm far away from home and everyone I know. Then perhaps I can have some peace of mind.*

Chapter Two

He drove relentlessly on, mile after mile, and crossed the border into Scotland. He continued north, stopping only for fuel when the need arose. Eventually, with the sun low in the sky, he realised that he was in the remotest area of the Highlands. *Well, I wanted solitude,* he thought, *and now I've got it.* It was at that moment that the engine of his ever-reliable Volvo died on him, with no warning whatsoever; his first thought was, *I can't have run out of fuel! The gauge is still reading half full.* When the vehicle coasted to a standstill, he gave a sigh of exasperation and got out of the car. 'Not a yellow van in sight' he muttered.

In fact, there was not a soul in sight for miles around.

However, not to be deterred, he lifted the bonnet of the car and systematically checked all the obvious causes of breakdown, starting with the electrics and ignition system. He had only been concentrating on the problem for a few minutes when he suddenly became aware of a presence nearby, and when he looked up, he saw two men standing just a few feet away. His first thought was, *Where did they come from, and how did they get so close without me hearing them approach?* It then struck him that there was something different about their dress and physical appearance, although he had no time to dwell on that thought as one of the strangers began to question him.

At least he thought they were talking at first, but then he became aware that the words were forming in his mind. He was vaguely aware that they were communicating by mental telepathy, a strange experience! The two men were taking turns questioning him. Some of the questions were of a personal nature relating to his family background, and to his surprise, his recent bereavement, and it was then that he realised they could read his mind and that he was unable to stop them from doing so.

After what seemed like a lengthy interrogation, the older of the two men, Captain Jara as it turned out, invited Jon to accompany them to their ship, a request he felt unable to refuse. *What ship?* He

Chapter Two

didn't have to wait for the answer, and to his astonishment, he looked up and saw a flying saucer. *So, they do exist!*

The craft didn't actually touch the ground, but appeared to hover a few inches above, while an area on the side of the craft shimmered briefly and then dissolved, leaving an aperture for entry, while a small set of steps then protruded making access easier. Without any further need for encouragement, and feeling confident of his own safety, Jon mounted the few steps and entered the vehicle, which, to his surprise, was far more spacious than he thought it would be. Appearances could be deceiving.

Captain Jara and his second-in-command, Mort, followed close behind, and as soon as they were all on board, the aperture closed without any visible trace. To Jon's surprise, he was greeted verbally by a young female crewmember wearing what he now assumed to be the distinguishing uniform of the ship's company.

'You may now take the ship into orbit, Lana,' Mort commanded, 'just about one hundred miles for the moment; we may have to return our passenger before long, unless he can be persuaded to become a Teacher.' Lana sat down at the control console, and with a few graceful movements of her hands, she activated the power to lift the craft off the surface of the planet. Within minutes, the saucer was in orbit.

Jon was astonished that there had been no feeling of inertia or gravity during their ascent, something Jara clearly expected him to be aware of as an air traffic controller. With a smile of assurance, the captain activated the observation window, beckoning Jon to come and look for himself. Although he had seen films shot from space by astronauts in the past, the view that met his gaze was breath taking. Although they were not far enough away to encompass the full sphere of the earth, it was sufficient to clearly define the curvature of the earth's surface, showing the land mass of Europe below with the Atlantic Ocean coming into view, and to the north, the polar cap.

Chapter Two

From time to time, weather systems moved across the surface of the planet, obscuring land and sea alike, huge masses of swirling cloud, but breaking up occasionally. 'Nice weather down there,' Jon murmured quietly to himself.

Waiting until he was sure that his guest had seen enough to satisfy his curiosity, Captain Jara then gestured that everyone should sit down; it was time for discussion.

As the senior member of the crew and the representative of his people, he gave Jon a brief history of the Zellian people, including their beginnings, aspirations, their involvement in cultivating the human race, how they had introduced Teachers into human society, and the resistance of modern people to change. The downward spiral into ever-increasing violence and wars made the outlook for progress or even survival bleak.

Jon had to acknowledge that everything Jara said was true, and had to concede that it would take some kind of super-politician to unite all the nations of the earth, but unity was something completely lacking among the people of the planet below.

'Which brings me to the reason why we have brought you here,' Jara said as he pursed his lips and frowned. 'We,' indicating his crew members, 'believe that you have all the qualities that would make such a super-politician, as you suggest, or Teacher as we prefer to call such a person. If you are willing to undertake this mission on behalf of your own people to bring peace and harmony to the planet Earth, which is a huge task, it undoubtedly will take many years of commitment to complete.'

'Me, a Teacher!' Jon gasped. 'I wouldn't have a clue as to how to begin. I have had no experience in politics or government. My job was an air traffic controller, a very demanding job on the individual, it is true, but it was something I was able to do well only after years of training.'

Chapter Two

It was at this point that Mort, the training officer, joined in the discussion. With a quiet laugh, he raised his hand in a conciliatory gesture. 'There is no man on Earth who, at this time, could do what we are asking you to do, and unfortunately, we ourselves cannot live long enough on your planet to complete such a task. The stronger gravity of Earth has a detrimental effect on our physical well-being. This is why we have always used native Teachers to bring about the necessary changes.'

'So, why do you think I could change the world on my own, when, as you say, there is no man on Earth capable of doing so?' Jon exclaimed.

'There is no other man at this moment in time, my friend,' Mort calmly replied.

Once again, Jara stood up and walked over to the observation window, looking down on the apparently tranquil scene below. 'Your planet is very much like our own; it has all the requirements to sustain life in its many forms. But unless humans can be persuaded to change their ways, to preserve the environment, to renounce nuclear weapons of destruction, to live in peace with their neighbours, then what I can see down there,' he gestured to the blue jewel below, 'will all come to an end.'

'I can appreciate what you say, Captain,' Jon replied, 'but how can I possibly bring about any change in the policies of so many different governments and cultures? So far as I'm aware, men have been fighting each other since the dawn of time, for whatever reason, be it food, territory, wealth, or . . .' He added with a wry smile, 'Women.'

At that comment, Lana smiled in amusement. 'It is hard to imagine the Zellian men behaving like that since there would be no logic for such behaviour.'

'Be that as it may,' Jara intervened somewhat hurriedly. 'I will let Mort explain what we can do to prepare you to become a Teacher, and then you can decide if you will accept this role or return to the world below to live your life as before.'

'Talking of which,' Jon said with a worried look on his face, 'what about my car sitting down there on the road? It will be dark now, and if anyone comes across it, they'll wonder where I am.'

Jara nodded in agreement. 'If you decide to return to your vehicle, you can always say that you tried to seek assistance—no need to mention that you met aliens. On the other hand, if you decide to stay with us, your disappearance will be another mystery to your people, like the *Marie Celeste* some years ago.

Jon made no comment on that statement, but turned to Mort to listen to what he was about to say.

'Before I begin, Jon Bradburn, let me reiterate our previous conviction that you have all the qualities in a normal human being to become a Teacher. You don't, however, possess the mental capacity or intelligence as yet to undertake the training that you will need, and your communications skills certainly would not meet the needs of your role.' He paused for a moment, studying Jon's face for his outward reaction to this statement as he probed deeply and telepathically into the mind of the potential Teacher for a true assessment of his feelings. Finding his search positive, he gave an affirmative nod to Jara, a nod of approval that everything so far was entirely satisfactory.

Mort then continued. 'The training or induction that you will be required to undergo, Jon, will take several weeks to complete, and its success will depend on how receptive and willing your mind is to your education, but before I go into any further details, I must ask you one very simple question. Can you see a future where you are a Teacher of your fellow humans, or if you like, a saviour even?'

As Jon struggled in his mind to answer this question, he thought of the very considerable time that it would require—months, or

Chapter Two

possibly years. He had no family and no commitments of any kind; he was a free agent. Who would miss him?

Mort could see and understand the emotions passing through Jon's mind, but waited patiently for the answer to his question.

After a comparatively short time, Jon was ready to give his answer. Looking at the captain then at Mort and Lana, he replied in a firm clear voice, 'Yes, I am willing to undertake this mission, assuming that you believe that I can be suitably trained. I have nothing left of my life on the planet below; therefore, I will wholeheartedly commit myself to learning the skills of the task you have in mind for me.'

Mort gave a quiet smile of satisfaction and laid his hand on Jon's shoulder as a sign of assurance. 'We are all glad that you have accepted, Jon; you have brought a long search to a close, and we can report that you are the new Teacher.' He again patted Jon's shoulder in a friendly manner.

Jara also expressed his relief that their search was over, the first in the last two hundred years.

Out of curiosity, Jon enquired, 'If I had refused to cooperate in this training program, what would have happened?'

Raising a quizzical eyebrow, Jara replied, 'The same as has happened to many previous candidates. We picked them up and questioned them, and since none of them were suitable, we erased their memories of their time with us and returned them to their original location, none the worse for the experience other than a blank in their memory for a few missing hours.'

Pressing for further information, Jon enquired, 'And what happens now, Captain? When does this training begin, and how long will it take?'

From his chair in front of the control console, Jara replied, 'First of all, we will move out of Earth's orbit; we have probably been observed by the military, who may be tempted to investigate our presence, and we don't want to embarrass them,' he added with a laugh. 'Therefore, as your training will involve a lengthy procedure, we will take up a docking position on the other side of the moon where we will be completely screened from view, visually or otherwise.' He raised his voice slightly again as he called, 'Lana, you will take the con and set course for our earlier location behind the moon.'

'Aye, aye, captain,' she replied. Glancing in Jon's direction, she said, 'This won't take long.'

The return trip to the moon was uneventful as far as the crew were concerned, but for Jon Bradburn, the experience was awe-inspiring. To leave the blue glow of the earth behind and enter the obsidian blackness of space, with the stars so bright and beautiful that it was almost painful to the eye, the infinity of space gave a whole new meaning to him, a meaning beyond description. All too soon the six-hour journey was complete, and as the spacecraft entered into a static orbit above the lunar surface, Jon could not but compare its dead, barren landscape below with the living, vibrant, and colourful surface of Earth. Truly, it was a jewel in the universe, and a world to preserve at all costs.

'Well, Jon,' Jara said as he came up behind him, interrupting his thoughts. 'This is where we will remain until such time as your indoctrination and training is complete, but as you have been through a severe emotional upheaval in recent days, we will delay the start of the procedure for another twenty-four hours. As I have much to attend to myself, may I suggest that you pass your time with Mort and Lana and ask any questions you like about your training, life on our home planet, their personal lives—anything that comes to mind. No doubt they will be equally curious about you.' And so, with occasional rest periods and sleep, the hours passed until at last, Mort beckoned Jon to join him at a door leading to a hitherto unexplored region of the ship.

Chapter Three

The room in which he found himself was surprisingly spacious, considering the overall dimensions of the spaceship. There was an array of electronic equipment, outwardly similar to his old familiar air traffic control room, and taking centre stage, a reclining chair with connections to a bank of what he presumed were computers. And then another surprise: Lana was already seated at yet another control panel, smiling serenely in expectation of his training programme. She was obviously going to assist.

Mort invited Jon to take a seat beside Lana then lowered himself into another convenient seat facing them. 'First of all, Jon,' he said, 'don't imagine that your training is going to involve weeks or months of studying in the way that your people have to learn. The subjects that you have to be taught involve many years of intensive study.' He smiled gently as he continued. 'For all that you are an intelligent man, Jon, you don't have the ability to assimilate the amount of knowledge required to perform the task ahead of you.'

'Then how can I be expected to learn all that you suggest I must know if I don't have the ability to do so?' asked Jon. 'To me, it sounds as though I've failed even before I have begun.'

Mort again smiled reassuringly. 'Lana is going to assist me with your preparation for your training programme, and as part of her own training, she will be monitoring your progress with her computers.' Mort could read the doubts and questions going through Jon's mind.

Chapter Three

'How long is all this going to take?' he enquired. 'How much exactly do I have to learn? Will I be able to communicate with the leaders and politicians on Earth? And here's the big question: Am I likely to survive what will be seen as interference in world affairs?'

Mort sat there, calmly observing the emotions flitting over Jon's face and reading every thought going through his mind. 'As I said a moment ago, you are an intelligent man, but not intelligent enough. We can address that as part of your indoctrination. This is something we have never done before. But for you to perform your function as a Teacher on Earth today, you will require not only super-political skills but many other powers in common with the Zellian people. In effect, by the time you are fully trained and prepared, you will have the mental capacity of any one of us, with the added advantage of your earthly strengths, which we shall also enhance for your future protection.'

As Jon listened to Mort's spoken words, he wondered what other powers he would share in common with the Zellians.

'I was coming to that,' Mort said in answer to his unspoken question. 'You'll find it an advantage to read the minds of the human beings you will be dealing with; they will not be able to lie or conceal information from you, and hence the need for you to become a telepath,' he added with a hint of humour. 'But you will have to learn to control your thoughts when associating with Lana.'

Point taken, Jon mentally replied.

'Another important function you will be able to perform when your training is complete,' Mort continued, 'is teleportation. As you no doubt remember, we intercepted you on Earth and brought you back to our ship by that means.'

'I was going to ask you about that,' Jon exclaimed. 'How far is it possible to teleport on your own, and can you always take someone with you if necessary?'

Chapter Three

Although it was not a question he was expecting, Mort answered with patience. 'For myself, so long as I have the coordinates of where I want to go in mind, distance is of no consequence, but if I were to carry someone with me, someone like yourself who is unable to teleport, for example, I would be limited to perhaps a hundred miles.'

'And no further?' queried Jon.

'Only in a series of short hops,' Mort replied. 'Inconvenient, but enough to get out of trouble.'

Jon could not help but grin as the conversation continued. 'So, I'm to be made more intelligent; that will be welcome! I'm to become a telepath, and I'll be able to teleport any distance. Why were all the previous Teachers not trained in the same way?'

Again Mort smiled. 'Had they been in possession of these powers even two hundred years ago, the natives would truly have regarded them as gods, and that was not necessary at that time. But there was one Teacher, two thousand years ago, who was said to be able to walk on water, a claim that was never authenticated as far as I'm aware.'

Feeling somewhat reassured by the information regarding the training he would receive to equip him for his future diplomatic endeavours on Earth, Jon felt quite relaxed as he jokingly enquired, 'More intelligent, able to teleport, physically enhanced, telepathic—is that all, Mort, nothing more?'

Appreciation of earthly humour was not a strong point for Mort, so, with a serious expression on his face, he continued. 'Yes, there is one more power that you may find useful one day, one that we rarely use, and that is telekinesis, the power to move objects at will. As you undergo your indoctrination training, all these powers will be further explained to you, and your newfound intelligence will cause you to use them wisely.'

Lana had been listening intently to the conversation, and although not invited to do so, she too had a question to put to Mort.

Chapter Three

'Will Jon be able to absorb all the training information that you have already mentioned, and will he learn how to fly and navigate this ship on his own when the time comes?'

Mort smiled indulgently at the question from one so young. 'Yes, Lana, that won't be a problem, but it will take much longer for Jon's brain to develop in intelligence than it would for one of our own kind. If we were to hurry the process, I'm afraid it would prove fatal to our prospective Teacher, but otherwise, he will know everything he needs to know, and the programming will be complete by the time Earth has rotated twenty-eight times on its axis.'

Then looking at Jon directly, Mort continued. 'There is also the small matter of communication with your own people. In the past, the Teachers only had to speak to people in the small area where they lived, so their own native language was sufficient, whereas you will probably have to travel to many different parts of the world to meet heads of government and councils, so an ability to speak the local languages will be advantageous, will it not?'

'It certainly would be,' Jon conceded. 'But while I speak French fluently, that's my limit, and outside Europe, that won't get me far.'

'That is no cause for concern,' Mort stated. 'We have monitored radio transmissions from Earth during the past century, and we are aware of the many languages spoken, but to make your task easier when dealing with your own people, you will be taught at least ten other languages of your choice.' Noting the look of dismay on Jon's face, he said with a smile, 'Don't worry; it will all be in the programming, and all the skills and knowledge you are about to acquire will seem to be naturally obtained, as though you had been born with them. Apart from that,' he continued, 'from time to time, we also use a portable translator if there is any difficulty on Earth and any other planets.'

Mort was aware of Jon's inner confusion and turmoil at the thought of the many changes he would have to undergo, mentally

Chapter Three

and physically, which was one aspect that had not yet been explained. Mort didn't try to impress on Jon the control of the mind over the physical body; it was something he would become aware of on completion of his programming.

Lana too was aware of the doubts in Jon's mind and sought to reassure him. 'This is the first time I will have assisted in the training of a Teacher, but with Mort supervising every stage of the procedure, you may be confident that you will be the most comprehensively prepared ambassador to arrive on Earth.' With a smile she added, 'One of the physical changes that you will benefit from, other than your muscular strength, is your longevity. What age would you normally expect to live to, Jon?'

After a moment's thought, he replied, 'I suppose a good average age for a man is about eighty years, if he's in good health.'

Lana giggled in amusement. 'I'm that age already!' Noting Jon's incredulous look and reading his mental observations, she continued. 'Although you may not live as long as our people, you can expect to attain a lifespan of several hundreds of years, five or six at the least.'

'So long as I don't become a decrepit old man and mentally feeble as I get older!' He laughed. 'Five or six hundred years—surely that should suffice to persuade humanity to live in peace?'

'One would hope so,' Mort gently intervened. 'But if your experience is anything like what has happened throughout human history, you may discover that at some stage, it will be necessary to use some forceful persuasion. But with this ship at your disposal and all its weaponry at your command, you will have more power than any or all of the combined military of any nation on Earth. The big challenge is how to use that power correctly or beneficially.'

'Even before I undergo my indoctrination program, my first thought is to follow the diplomatic route, to lead by example and persuasion, although I can think of several countries on Earth that would definitely benefit from a short, sharp show of force. But that can wait until I have decided on a coherent plan of action.'

'Whatever thought you have in mind at this moment, Jon,' Mort said quietly with his usual tolerant smile, 'you will probably view your strategy quite differently after your programming. No doubt we will discuss the important issues later.' He rose to his feet. 'First we must implement your education and training without any further delay.'

At this point, Lana took Jon by the hand and guided him toward the reclining chair in the centre of the room. 'Make yourself comfortable, Jon; this is where you will be during the next twenty-eight revolutions of your home planet.' She laughed gently at Jon's mental reaction to that statement. 'The time will pass without any awareness on your part, and on completion of the procedure, you will be a very different Jon Bradburn, citizen of Earth. You will be almost one of the Zellian people and ready to undertake your mission to save your planet and its people. Oh yes you will,' she contradicted as she read his mind again.

Mort also assisted in the operation of securing the safety straps holding Jon in the seat. 'Just a precaution,' he assured. With a final pat on the shoulder and a smile from Lana, the ship, the moon and the earth all ceased to exist for Jon Bradburn. Although the earth had begun its first revolution, there would only be twenty-seven more before the programming was complete.

Chapter Four

In the meanwhile, back on Earth, the activities of the spaceship had not gone unnoticed by various defence authorities across the Northern Hemisphere, the United States and Europe in particular. Each time Captain Jara had touched down to pick up a potential Teacher, his position had been carefully noted and logged. But as his stay had been invariably brief, there was little time to intercept his movements. Eventually, it was Jodrell Bank in England who was able to pinpoint the last known location as the spaceship lifted from the ground and headed out into space.

The director of the facility asked to be put in touch with the ministry of defence, a senior air vice-marshal and close contact with the prime minister himself. 'Sir Geoffrey, good news and bad news. We finally got a steady reading on your mystery flying object that we've been tracking these last few weeks.' Sir Geoffrey must have given a snort of disbelief. 'What do you think it is then, a flying saucer?'

As a man of science, the director had a very open mind regarding matters relating to UFOs, so he was smiling as he recounted the movements of what was undoubtedly an extra-terrestrial vehicle. 'Yes, sir, it may well have been such a craft, but its last known contact was a location in the northwest Highlands of Scotland where it remained at an altitude of some hundred miles for a few hours. Then, it accelerated at a phenomenal speed, heading in the direction of the moon, and that's where we lost contact with it.' The air marshal

Chapter Four

could be heard spluttering on the phone. 'Lost sight of it? Do you mean it landed on the moon, or did it go farther out into space?'

'As I said,' the director repeated, 'we lost sight of it as it went around the far side of the moon, although it may have been using the slingshot method to build up even more acceleration before heading out into deep space. We estimated the speed at the last count to be some forty-one thousand miles per hour, faster than anything we could put up there.'

'In which case, be a good chap and keep us informed of any further sightings,' said the air marshal as he rang off.

***

Captain Jara looked down at the recumbent form of Jon Bradburn, noting with interest the outward changes in his appearance, the effects of programming on his physical structure and undoubted mental changes. Whereas before he had been of good, if average physique, he now appeared more muscular, taller, and probably very much stronger than a normal human being, and certainly more powerful than any of the Zellian people.

Lana, of course, had been monitoring the procedure from its inception, fascinated by the gradual change in the appearance of the Teacher. 'Look at his physical structure; he must be capable of enormous feats of strength even by the standards of Earth men.'

Both Mort and Jara noted the tone of admiration in Lana's voice and smiled. 'Yes, Lana,' Mort answered, 'but it's possible that his physical abilities may prove to be yet another means of protecting himself from his own people.' Then he added with a touch of irony, 'Least of all, the women of his own race.'

Lana experienced a strange sensation, realising that Mort, at least, had briefly glimpsed into her mind and seen her innermost thoughts and her attraction to the Teacher. Changing the subject for a moment, she pointed out another physical change that had gradually occurred over the time the programme had taken to

Chapter Four

complete. 'His hair, Captain, has gradually changed from a dark colour like our own to a bright almost luminous, silver. Has that always happened before?'

Captain Jara had already noted this change in hair colour and concluded that while it was a superficial difference to himself and his crew, Jon Bradburn might think differently. Answering Lana's question, however, he said, 'No, this is a change that has never occurred before, but then again, no human being has had to be trained or educated for such a long period of time. Three or four days was considered normal, whereas Jon has been programmed for a full lunar month. Talking of which, Lana, your computer reading is showing that the program is now ending.'

While Mort loosened the restraining straps from the Teacher, the captain and Lana closed down the computer, and then they all stood around the now upright chair, waiting patiently for Jon Bradburn to regain his normal faculties, which was a process they expected to take several minutes at least, and so it proved to be the case.

For Jon, the process wasn't just a matter of opening his eyes and immediately returning to normality. His first sensation was the awareness of a blinding light, which caused him to close his eyes again. Then, a kaleidoscope of images passed before his eyes as he partially recalled parts of the training programme, voices in his head, the sounds of many different languages that had been installed in his subconscious mind, and finally with relief, his eyes focused, first of all on Lana, who was bending anxiously over him, and he was aware of what she was thinking. Finally, Captain Jara and Mort, both smiling with apparent relief, said, 'Welcome aboard, Teacher.'

At first, Jon made no attempt to answer, but sat quietly gazing around the room, taking in every detail, noting every piece of equipment and electronic apparatus, all of which he now found to have a familiar function. *Will this be the same with the rest of the ship, I wonder?*

Chapter Four

Captain Jara replied telepathically. 'Yes, Jon, you will now be aware of every part of the ship and its function, its power system, navigation controls, and weaponry. Although the occasion may not arise for some time for you to use your multilingual skills, you are now capable of communicating fluently in the ten different languages that you chose before your programming began. All you require is a stimulus.' He hastened to clarify this. 'If someone speaks to you, you will be able to reply in the same language.' With a smile he added, 'Your ability to communicate verbally is now far superior to our own; we would have to rely on the translator equipment in most cases.'

As Jon studied his companions and looked around the control room, he became aware of something very different from when he had begun training: he was naked except for a small garment about his loins. 'Where are my clothes?' he asked, not because he was embarrassed, but merely out of curiosity.

It was Mort who answered. 'You will find, Jon, that you have undergone what might be described as a metamorphosis, not a great one, but you are somewhat different to the Jon Bradburn who came aboard this vessel twenty-eight days ago.' He gave a smile of satisfaction as he described the changes that had taken place. 'Your physique has been improved in appearance, your physical strength has been greatly enhanced, and your mental abilities now far exceed any of your fellow men. In fact, it's not unlikely that had this transformation occurred several thousand years ago, you would have undoubtedly been hailed as a god among your people.'

Lana took the opportunity to explain to Jon that, as his physique became more muscular, his original clothing had to be cut away, and it was she who had done so. She smiled quietly at the recollection of the pleasure that had given her, but was careful to screen those thoughts from her companions. 'You now have a body that will be the envy of your fellow men,' she said.

'And the strength of some of your mythical gods,' added Captain Jara. 'It is just as well that your wisdom has been equally enhanced.

Chapter Four

Your people have a saying, I believe, Jon——with great power comes great responsibility.'

While Lana was quite content to gaze on Jon's nakedness, it was she who suggested that he should now be allowed to refresh himself and dress in Zellian clothing, if a uniform could be found to fit.

At the mention of freshening up, Jon felt his own face and the month's growth of beard. 'First thing is to get rid of this,' he said, running his fingers through his facial hair.

'I can do that for you quite easily,' exclaimed Mort. 'Removal of facial hair is something that is only required when Zellian males are quite old.' Laughing, he continued, 'You would still be regarded as an adolescent, but if you come with me . . . .' He beckoned Jon to follow. 'We will have your face perfectly smooth again and ready to face the world in no time.'

As they were about to turn away, Captain Jara laid his hand on Jon's arm, restraining him for a moment. 'There is now one slight difference in your appearance, Jon, and that is your hair. It may be a shock to you when you see it for the first time, although Lana assures me that she finds it most becoming. It gives you a more striking appearance, a description I would agree with, although it remains to be seen how you will regard yourself.'

Although forewarned of his changed appearance, it was still a shock to Jon when he saw his own reflection for the first time. Mort had removed all his facial hair but left his head untouched, and that hair was quite long and a silvery blonde. 'I hope blondes are popular where I'm going,' he quipped to himself. Lana's description was more accurate. His hair was a luminous silver in colour and shone like a halo about his shoulders. *Like a prophet of old* was another thought that came to mind, but with his smooth, unlined complexion and splendid physique, there was no mistaking that he was still a handsome young man, an opinion shared by Lana and every woman he was destined to meet.

Chapter Four

Before long, they rejoined Lana and the captain in the main control room, explaining that finding a uniform to fit Jon had proved to be a difficulty. What he was now wearing was stretched over his muscular frame 'as taut as a skin on a drum' was Jon's own description, but even so, it felt quite comfortable.

Jara lost little time in announcing that the mother ship was due to rendezvous with them in two days' time, the intention being that Captain Jara, Mort, and Lana would transfer ship, leaving Jon to begin his crusade on his own. He would be completely in charge of his own vessel, which he was now fully trained to operate. Jon felt apprehensive at the thought of being left entirely on his own, not having any clear idea as to how to begin the education of humanity. Jon's mission would be overseen by the new commander, senior to Mort and himself. Being sympathetic to the difficulty and loneliness of the command to be undertaken by Jon, he had a very un-Zel-like thought. *Let Lana go on the mission, ostensibly as a junior adviser, a good career move for her, and as a companion for the Teacher.* Having decided that this course of action would be of benefit to the success of the mission and the well-being of the two young people, Jara made preparations for the handover of the ship to Jon and to make out his report to the commander of the mother ship. He was confident that his decision to allow Lana to accompany Jon on his mission would be upheld by the commander, whose first concern would be that the Teacher had every incentive to succeed, and if the company of a junior adviser were to help, then so be it.

Now that he was refreshed and dressed comfortably, Jon asked Jara if he would accompany him on a tour of the ship as a means of familiarising himself with what was to be his command, a request that was met with some enthusiasm. He was conducted into every compartment of the ship, and while he had a latent memory of every aspect of its layout and controls, he nevertheless asked for confirmation of its armament and what it was capable of doing in terms of its firepower and defence systems. Jara was patient, pointing

Chapter Four

out, 'You already know all of these things, Jon; just look into your own mind. The answers are all there.'

'One thing I don't seem to have any knowledge of, Captain,' Jon queried, 'is the space-time control system. Was there any reason why that was omitted from my programming?'

'Yes,' Jara commented, 'for the simple reason that the system will not be required on your mission since this ship is not intended for interstellar flight. Interplanetary flight? Yes, it is capable of that, but for very long distances, craft like the mother ship would be employed. Even for the Zellian people with a lifespan of one thousand years, travelling at the speed of light means that we won't survive the journey between the stars since the distances are so vast.' He continued thoughtfully, 'It is only by accident that several million years ago our scientists stumbled on the secret of warping the timelines to bring them closer together, enabling us to pass through the time zones at a fraction of the time of conventional travel. By a series of compressions of the timelines, not only are we able to traverse time itself, but to travel light-years in a matter of hours. Unfortunately, the equipment required to do so cannot be contained in a small craft such as this, Jon; therefore, you will have to be content with having the fastest craft in the solar system.'

Jon was appreciative of Jara's attempt at humour, and smiled as he replied, 'As I shall be spending the next few years on and around Earth, this craft will more than meet my requirements.'

Having completed their inspection of the ship, Jara decided that it was time to inform Lana of his decision to allow her to accompany the Teacher on his mission—purely to further her training and career prospects, of course. Jon was gratified to hear this information, and Mort as well.

While they waited for the arrival of the mother ship, Jon held discussions with the crew regarding the various courses of action open to him in opening dialogue with various governments on

Earth, but as this was something beyond their previous experience, they could only make tentative offers of advice. 'You must know your own people,' they said, and left it at that.

Chapter Five

After Captain Jara and Mort had transferred to the mother ship, Jon the Teacher and Lana were left on their own, and as they once more watched the enormous bulk of the interstellar ship gradually accelerate out of the moon's slight gravity, they both wondered what life in the future would hold for them. Then their minds merged by mutual consent; there would be no secrets between them.

Even after the other craft had long disappeared from view, they remained at the observation window, taking a last look at the lunar surface below, possibly for the last time, but eventually Jon turned away, leaving Lana close to the viewpoint. 'Well, Lana,' he said, 'I have decided on the first phase of my strategy, and that is simple. I intend to make our presence known to the governments of Earth by orbiting the planet for several days, not doing anything, just orbiting. Then I shall spend a little time above several of the major cities of the world to test the reactions of the citizens. Will they be blindly aggressive or try to communicate? We can pick up their radio and television transmissions, of course, and that will tell us a great deal.'

With little reason to delay their departure from their static orbit of the moon, Jon smiled as he said, 'Now is the time for me to prove how effective my training programme has been. I'll take control of the ship myself, Lana, and set course for Planet Earth; this will be quite a homecoming for me!' He sat before the command console for the first time, and his hands moved confidently over the controls.

As Lana watched, she thought, *I think you will be able to teach me how to fly this ship, Jon. Will your mastery of all the other aspects of your training be equally impressive?* Without realising it, she had unconsciously tuned in to Jon's mind, and her question was quickly answered.

'I have every confidence in Mort's induction techniques,' he said. 'As I sit here, I feel as though I'm part of the ship, aware of its power and potential, and I look forward to trying out the craft in Earth's atmosphere.'

Deliberately avoiding telepathic communication, Lana again laughed as she said, 'You remind me of one of our children with a new toy.'

'But what a toy!' Jon exclaimed. 'By the time we have orbited the earth a few times and visited the cities I have in mind, I will feel confident to handle the ship in all situations.'

With a more serious expression on her face, Lana enquired, 'Will you feel equally confident in operating all the defence systems in the ship should we be attacked? And will you be prepared to use the destructive power at your disposal?'

Jon paused for a moment before answering. 'Our defence against attack is not a problem, Lana; the ship has a force field to protect it from any kind of missile attack. We can also outrun any kind of aircraft that the military might use against us, and as for our own weapons, I take it that you have never seen them used offensively.' Receiving a negative shake of the head, Jon continued, 'We have more destructive power available aboard this small ship than all of the military of any of the superpowers on Earth, but it is not my intention to use force to subjugate the nations of Earth. Remember, I am supposed to be a Teacher, and that is the path I intend to follow, to persuade by example that peace is beneficial to all, to talk with the representatives of governments, to provide new technology to assist the development of the poorer nations—in all, I hope to be a benevolent influence on the people.'

Chapter Five

'Very commendable, Jon,' Lana said, 'but from the history of your people in the past, do you think they will listen to what you say just because you declare yourself to be a Teacher, a force for good?' She frowned before continuing. 'I have no knowledge of life on Earth, but I have seen many other peoples on primitive planets, and they all seem to conform to a certain pattern of development; evolving from savages to civilised beings takes millennia. At what stage of evolution are the people of Earth?'

Jon hesitated before replying. 'Physically, we have evolved slowly over the last million years or so, with a little help from your people, into the beings you will see and meet quite soon, very much like Mort, Captain Jara and yourself. Mentally? Well, by Zellian standards, with a few notable exceptions, humans could be described as mental pygmies.' He didn't try to elaborate on that expression. His mental picture was sufficient.

'But I have every hope that over the next few years, they can be educated to live in harmony with each other and develop the social skills that will make that objective possible.'

Lana smiled sympathetically. 'So in other words, Teacher, you have a great deal to do before Earthlings can be accepted by the wider Confederation of the Stars. Such progress may require more than talk and gentle persuasion. A powerful river can be diverted by a few strategically placed barriers, and you may have to put such barriers in place to guide your people in the right direction.'

In his former self, Jon Bradburn might have been tempted to argue with Lana as to his proposals for dealing with the problems of humanity, but now, in his newfound wisdom, he conceded that while he would prefer the gentle persuasion approach, he might conceivably have to resort to a show of power to achieve his ends.

Jon was amazed at the mental harmony he shared with Lana. It was something he had never before experienced, not even in his former marriage, which had been a happy one, and as a result, the short journey back to Earth was quite fast, necessitating in him taking manual control of the ship. Again, Jon expressed his intention of selecting an orbit close to Earth. 'I want to make sure that we can be seen with or without radar or even telescopes,' he said. 'If the people on Earth are aware of our presence, no doubt the military and governments will not be able to exercise their usual propaganda and deny our existence.'

'And do you anticipate any hostile action when we are seen in the sky so close to Earth?' Lana asked. 'And if so, will you retaliate?'

'Definitely not,' he replied. 'Even at comparatively short range, their missiles will be completely ineffective against our energy shields, and hopefully our passive resistance will convince them of our peaceful intentions.'

Although she was convinced that Jon's experience of life on his own planet and the induction training he had received on board the ship would be more than sufficient to cope with any eventuality, she still wondered how and when he would make his first contact with his own kind. That thought was picked up telepathically, since she and Jon shared each other's thoughts as though they were one person. The prospects for the future were good!

Sitting at the control console, Jon had a clear view of the planet below, but at that moment, while in a very low orbit, they were only twenty miles above the vast expanse of the Pacific Ocean, and there was little to be seen through the cloud cover except the bright view of the water reflecting the sunlight. He was content to fly the ship at this low altitude and maintain orbital speed. 'We will remain on this course, Lana, for several days, during which time we will pass over much of the Northern Hemisphere. No doubt after our first circumnavigation of the globe, the whole world will be aware of our presence.' As he watched the monitor screens, he saw a land mass coming into view. 'Looks like the tip of northern Australia.' Again, his thoughts were shared with Lana. 'And as we continue, we will pass over the Asian continent, and eventually Europe.' Although he

Chapter Five

knew that his geographical knowledge was shared with Lana, he nevertheless explained that they were in a slightly elliptical orbit and would in this way pass over the more densely populated areas of the world.

'And having made our presence known,' Lana stated, 'assuming that we don't have a hostile reception, how do you intend to make our first contact? By landing and introducing yourself?'

Jon laughed at Lana's attempt at humour, but reminded her that the Zellians had been monitoring radio signals and intercepting television programmes for nearly a century; hence, their comprehensive knowledge of life on Earth and their ability to learn so many languages. 'That is how we will break our silence, by interrupting their broadcasts and projecting our images onto their television screens.' Knowing that Lana would respect his method of communication, Jon added that they would broadcast their message of peace and friendship at intervals as they circumnavigated the globe, and when they were sure that the people would not panic at the next phase—a close encounter— they would contact the United Nations in New York. As he further explained to Lana, these were the leaders of most of the governments on Earth, and their best opportunity to meet as many influential people as possible in one location. 'I'll wait until we have finished our broadcasts before I attempt to address that assembly,' he added with a certain irony. 'If they are prepared to listen to my lone voice calling for world peace, I shall be very surprised, but we must give them every opportunity to allow the different nations to live in harmony; otherwise, we may have to introduce a few strategic barriers as you mentioned, Lana.'

'If we were talking of a few thousand people trying to live together peacefully,' she said, 'that would be difficult enough, but how many people actually live on this planet?'

Jon shook his head in disbelief at his own count. 'Seven billion so far as I am aware and still rising.'

Chapter Five

To which Lana replied soberly, 'Then I would suggest that the people of your planet have a problem, a big problem. We, the Zellians, had a similar situation several million years ago, overpopulation, until a natural catastrophe overtook our people. However, I'm sure that is something that can be left for the future. In the meantime, you will have to organise your broadcasts and decide when you will arrange to meet the delegates of the United Nations.'

Chapter Six

'How do you intend to introduce yourself to your people, Jon?' Lana enquired. 'Will certain people still recognise you from your former life as an air traffic controller at Manchester Airport?' Lana was, of course, fully aware of every aspect of his life due to their union of minds, a fact that Jon was now fully aware of and content with. 'Which being the case,' she continued, 'would there be any difficulty in being accepted as a Teacher?'

Jon smiled. 'I'm well aware of the change in my appearance since I agreed to undergo the training procedure, the metamorphosis that occurred as Mort put it. I doubt my own parents would know me if I stood in front of them. In fact, even when I look in the mirror, I find it difficult to believe that I'm looking at myself. No, very definitely, I won't be recognised, so we can assume that I will be regarded as an extra-terrestrial like yourself. In fact, you are more like a human being than I am. You're tall and slender, but many European women are of similar build, whereas, apart from my enhanced physique, which I'm quite happy with by the way, my hair sets me apart from any race on Earth.' He grinned. 'It almost glows like an angel's halo, and its colour is striking, to say the least, even out of this world, you might say!'

Lana smiled at his humour, but the reference to an angel's halo was quite lost on her until she searched Jon's mind for clarification, then she laughed and said, 'If you could be mistaken for an angel, wouldn't that help your cause?'

Chapter Six

'So long as I'm not mistaken for Lucifer, the fallen angel, as that could add to my difficulties!' They both laughed, happy in each other's company before returning to the more serious business of searching the airways for radio and television transmissions. They wanted to find out what reaction their presence had evoked in the minds of the public and the military.

As they were orbiting the earth, the strength of the signals varied, and television transmissions tended to be somewhat garbled, so much so that eventually Jon decided the time had come to hover the spacecraft above various highly populated areas in the hope of picking up clear signals and the information he required. As it happened, the first city he targeted was Moscow, and the expected panic and blaze of transmissions from the media came as no surprise, but the lack of response from the military seemed odd to Jon. *Perhaps our passive presence has reassured them,* he thought, *or they are willing to play a waiting game.* After a short time, he decided to move on, giving the Russians a demonstration of the speed the spacecraft was capable of, static one moment and then travelling at the speed of sound within seconds. He would have been gratified to hear the comments from the military on the ground. 'Unbelievable, comrades.'

Having crossed over Europe, their next stop was Paris, and as it was late evening, it was obvious why it was called the City of Lights. On this occasion, Jon allowed the ship to sink into position a mere hundred feet above the Eiffel Tower. To the horror of the onlookers below, it looked as though the craft was going to collide with the tower, their national monument. Lana was controlling the communications system, monitoring the television output from the Paris station below, and Jon interpreted the broadcast on her behalf. It rapidly became obvious that the populace had been informed of their earlier visit to Moscow and that there had been no sign of aggression, which being the case, the streets of Paris were thronged by thousands of people gazing up at the spaceship hovering above

Chapter Six

the city. As Lana adjusted the viewing screens, the images were enlarged to the point where the faces of the people could be seen as clearly as though they were in the crowd with them, almost within touching distance.

The television commentator was clearly excited as he described this momentous occasion, the first authenticated visit by aliens from outer space. Clearly, there was no panic at their appearance, and after an hour or so of observation, Jon commented, 'I think the good people of Paris have seen enough of this flying saucer to satisfy their curiosity and to allay their fears regarding any hostile intentions, and again, there's been no intervention by the military.'

Lana's next question was, 'Where do you intend to make the next stop, Jon?' Without waiting for a verbal reply, unnecessary as ever, she agreed mentally. 'Ah yes, London; if I recollect the data from the education and factual information program, that city has more people than the entire planet of Zel.'

'That may be,' Jon replied, 'but even so, it is not the biggest city on Earth, as you will no doubt see. Population centres tend to be concentrated within certain geographical latitudes,' he explained, 'but not near the Polar Regions.'

Lana accepted that fact with a smile. 'Zel lost its polar regions more than one million years ago, and as a result, we have a benevolent climate over the entire planet. No doubt the same will happen here on Earth.'

'Given time, Lana, that is unless people destroy the planet before nature is allowed to work this miracle.' With a last look at the city below, Jon decided to make a more leisurely departure than they had taken from Moscow. *Give the people a show,* he thought. So he controlled their ascent very slowly but vertically until they were several miles high, then with the course set for London, he again boosted the speed to well over the speed of sound, disappearing from the view of the Parisians in a flash of light and a characteristic sonic boom.

Their flight was intentionally a leisurely one; it wasn't practical to cover the short distance at full speed, but even so, they arrived over London within fifteen minutes. Again, as they were travelling westward, they were chasing the sun, with the result that it was still quite light, late evening in the summertime, as they approached the outer areas of the city.

Lana opened the viewport and gasped with surprise at the panorama below. 'I can understand why we can see London from thousands of miles out in space, even from the moon!'

Jon felt gratified that Lana was impressed by the cities that she had seen so far. Despite Earth's problems, he was proud to show her his home. *But will she be impressed with the people when we make contact, I wonder?* He knew that with her telepathic ability, she would be able to see into the minds of those she met. *Unless she chooses to blank off her own mind, an option she might well choose to adopt rather than share the thoughts of some of the less desirable citizens of Earth.*

Jon hovered the spacecraft above central London at an altitude of several thousand feet. Their arrival had been no surprise since their approach from the continent had been traced on radar, and as soon as they opened their communications system, they were bombarded with requests to identify themselves. That, of course, was by the military, and they could hear the comments from the reporters on the television networks. They watched and waited, and soon they received the images on their own screens of what the public was also seeing, the spacecraft hovering above the city. Even as they watched, they noticed that they were illuminated by a number of searchlights.

As they looked at the images on the screen, the purpose of the searchlights soon became apparent. Commencing with warning

Chapter Six

lights flashing on her command module, Lana said quietly, 'We have company, Jon. We have two aircraft approaching at speed from the north; do you think they could be a threat?'

Without hesitation he replied calmly, 'Unlikely, Lana, but as a precaution, just in case they get too excited, raise the energy screens, range one thousand yards. For this situation only, I will break radio silence to warn them not to approach too closely; if they collide with the energy screens, they will be destroyed immediately.'

As a former air traffic controller, it only took Jon a few seconds to tune into the military wavelength frequency where he warned the pilots of the danger of attempting to fly too close, stating, 'My intentions are peaceful.' He then ceased transmitting and listened to the conversation of the two pilots. *Just like old times,* he thought as he noted the colourful language being used. Service personnel could be quite descriptive! However, after a time, the pilots must have been recalled to base as the spaceship didn't appear to be a danger to the city, and once again, Jon and Lana turned their attention to the television broadcasts.

The commentators were trying to out vie each other with their theories as to which planet or solar system the space travellers had originated from, and their purpose in being here on Earth. They also speculated on the appearance of their visitors; were they like the fictional little green men from Mars or grotesque monsters from outer space? It was with some amusement that Jon, in particular, listened to the broadcasts. 'A load of tosh,' he exclaimed.

Although not familiar with the expression, Lana could understand his meaning and agreed.

'When are you going to make yourself known to your people, Jon? Little green men indeed!' she protested indignantly. 'You are the most perfect specimen of man to walk on Earth, that is, when you do actually land,' she added with a smile.

Chapter Six

'We are going to make one more visit before I introduce myself, Lana,' Jon stated. 'My voice has already been heard by the pilots of those aircraft, and no doubt recorded by ground control, so it isn't going to be a surprise when I talk to the Americans in English. Yes,' he confirmed, 'that is our next stop, Washington, DC, on the east coast of America, but I intend to return to orbit, about three hundred miles out, and let the authorities calm down before our arrival over the Capital. The White House should be quite distinctive from the air.'

***

Meanwhile, the director of Jodrell Bank Observatory was in conversation with a certain sceptical air marshal. 'Now, sir, do you believe in flying saucers?' But the telephone call was short lived as the phone was slammed down.

***

They orbited the earth for a further twenty-four hours, alternately listening to the radio broadcasts in several different languages, many of which Jon was familiar with, and from time to time, they were also able to catch the television transmissions, although not always satisfactorily due to their height and speed. It soon became apparent that their presence was viewed with distrust or caution by all nations, and the military were being organised in the event that the spaceship proved hostile. As ever it was, the politicians were the most threatening. Their oratory was already inflammatory, rallying the masses to repel the invaders. And all this before the Teacher had spoken to the representatives of the nations.

This was a situation that Lana had never experienced, and as she had never undergone the training and education to cope with it, she was now reliant on Jon for guidance for their future actions. She was also apprehensive at the prospect of their first physical contact with any humans. From what she had already seen and heard, they were vociferous, violent, and not to be trusted. When she expressed

Chapter Six

this view, Jon tried to assure her that many members of the human race were sincere and reliable, and regarded the welfare of the people as sacrosanct, men and women whose principles were beyond question, but he also had to concede that there was always a possibility of treachery when dealing with his own kind.

'My first contact will be with the President of the United States, the most powerful man in the world. I will allow my image to be transmitted on their television network and introduce myself simply as Jon. I won't disclose that I am from Earth, and an Englishman at that. Diplomatically, that could be a disaster.' He smiled at the thought of the possible repercussions. 'From my physical appearance, if they conclude that I am an alien, I won't try to persuade them otherwise, and when I inform them that the ship has come from the planet Zel, no doubt they will naturally believe that is my planet of origin. I have no need to conceal the truth when it comes to you, however, Lana. Your beauty is of a kind quite alien to that found on Earth, although having dark hair may raise a few questions,' he said while pointing at his own silver mane.

Jon's description of her and the warmth of his mind pleased Lana, but she worried about his welfare and personal safety whenever he should meet the Earthlings. 'What precautions will you take for your safety when you are down there?' she asked. 'You may be superior to your fellow men in every way, but you could still be vulnerable to physical attack.'

Jon had already thought of that possibility and recalled the information received during his training with regard to self-defence. Touching her hand gently, he said, 'Don't worry, Lana, one important piece of equipment I shall be wearing at all times outside the ship is a personal force field. You've seen one before, haven't you?' She nodded briefly in reply. 'It looks like an ordinary belt around the waist with a few decorative buttons for the controls, but whilst it is worn, it is always activated. At the very least, the force field extends only a few inches, but it is impenetrable by any physical body; it can be extended in stages up to a distance of sixty feet, and is capable of absorbing a blast or impact from a missile, even a vehicle.'

Smiling with relief, Lana said, 'So long as you don't start a one-man war, I'm sure you will be safe; besides, if you get into real trouble, you can always teleport back to the ship.' Then as an afterthought she added, 'Another advantage of using the force field is that you can prevent people crowding in too close to you, like with a mob.'

'I'll bear it in mind should I get into that situation,' Jon said with a grin. 'As for the physical attack by other men, I could quite easily defend myself against any number, I should think. My strength and agility is now such that even three or four opponents could be brushed aside, but again, the force field should make that kind of confrontation unnecessary, just entertaining.'

After their predetermined time in orbit, Jon asked Lana to set the coordinates to bring them into position above Washington, DC, and in particular, in close proximity to the White House itself. 'Come in about five hundred feet directly above it, but come in slowly and deliberately, and while we are approaching, I will radio our intention that we come in peace.'

Lana calmly set about the task of piloting the craft down to a few thousand feet and then slowed the ship until it approached the city. Having the distinguishable White House on her visual screens, she edged closer until the spacecraft was hovering a few hundred feet above it, and hopefully, the president of the United States.

Jon, for his part, was trying to establish radio contact with someone in authority, but their approach had caused a state of alarm on the ground below, triggering a reaction, a standing order to scramble a detail of aircraft if anyone entered into the airspace above Washington. It was an order obeyed with alacrity, as witnessed by the arrival of a number of fighter jets. 'Raise all energy shields, Lana,

Chapter Six

I believe we are about to be attacked for having the temerity to enter their airspace uninvited.'

Lana carried out his instruction and said calmly, 'All shields activated, Jon.' Then the fighter jets closed in on them with their armament firing, air-to-air missiles and cannon fire. No doubt the pilots congratulated themselves on a quick kill, since it was a target too big to miss. But that idea was quickly dispelled as the energy shields deflected every missile that came within one thousand yards. One of the pilots, more daring or ambitious than the others, attempted to close to what he thought would be a more effective range, and as a result, he flew into the invisible force shield, with the result that the aircraft immediately disintegrated. The debris scattered over a wide area of the city below.

During the attack, the spaceship continued to hover, and as it became obvious that they were not returning fire or retaliating in any way, the pilots were ordered to withdraw from the one-sided conflict, minus one aircraft.

'Now they will realise the futility of attacking us,' Jon said, shaking his head with remorse. Within the next few minutes, a radio link was established with one of the military aides in the White House, who first of all apologised for the unprovoked attack, and then requested, very politely, that they identify themselves.

Jon kept his reply as brief as possible. He didn't intend to go into detail with anyone other than the president himself. 'We are representatives from the planet Zel, from another galaxy, and we come on a mission of peace. Despite your hostile reception, it is our wish to speak with your president.' He paused for a moment then continued deliberately. 'I will establish a video link with you, and two hours from now, I will expect him to respond.' He then cut off the contact. *It's always best to negotiate from a position of strength*, he thought.

Chapter Six

During the two-hour-waiting period for the video link to be established, which would give the president and his advisers time to organise this first meeting between humankind and representatives of an alien culture, Jon and Lana discussed how they should present themselves, singly or together. Whilst on the ship, Earth's gravity had no effect on Lana, but on Earth, she would feel its pull. 'But,' she stressed, 'I'm sure that for short periods of time, it will have no ill effect; after all, I have been on other worlds far bigger than Earth, and apart from tiring me more quickly, I could live and work quite normally.'

'Nevertheless,' Jon replied, 'our stay on Earth is likely to be extended to at least several months, possibly years, and I don't want your life expectancy to be curtailed by extended stays in Earth's gravity.' Noting the look of disappointment on Lana's face and her telepathic thoughts, he added, 'The initial meeting with the president I will do alone, but thereafter, we will stay together as much as possible.'

Being somewhat mollified by this promise, Lana conceded that the first encounter would probably be best served by Jon on his own while she remained on board where she had access to all the backup systems, computers, and weapons should there be any sign of treachery.

Jon said, 'I don't think the Americans would be so foolish as to attempt to interfere with me personally. They will think that I'm one man alone, but thinking of the ship hovering above the White House, and not having any idea of its capabilities, they will be cautious.'

With a smile of amusement, Lana said, 'If they knew your capabilities, Jon, they would be even more cautious. Perhaps you could arrange some kind of demonstration of your physical prowess for their benefit.'

'You mean a physical confrontation, as in a fight, or a demonstration of telekinesis?' He grinned in amusement. 'I will wait

Chapter Six

until the situation arises where such action is necessary. Remember, I'm the Teacher, a man of peace.'

Noting the time since the last radio contact with the White House, Lana again took her place at the control console. 'Are you ready for your first television appearance, Jon? It's almost time.'

'Yes,' he replied solemnly. 'I'm ready; punctuality is the politeness of kings, they say, and alien representatives. Let's hope the president shares that belief.'

As Lana established contact, the face of the president appeared, a sharp clear picture, the face of a middle-aged man who looked calm and relaxed, a man of intelligence. They also had the view of the area around his desk and several of his advisers close at hand, among them some men in uniform. How many others were in the room they could not see, but presumably there were more. *So, it will be one against many,* Jon thought, *but hopefully on a friendly basis.*

As for the president and the other people in the Oval Office, when Jon's image came on the live television screen, most were pleasantly surprised to see that they would be dealing with a man rather than some weird otherworldly creature, but what a man!

As the president gazed at Jon's image, he realised that he was looking on the face of a man who radiated intelligence, compassion and wisdom, and yet a young face, apparently younger than the president himself and most of his advisers, but the most outstanding feature of this representative of the planet Zel was his hair. It had not been cut or trimmed since Jon had agreed to remain on the spaceship, with the result that it was now almost shoulder length. On the television screen, it glowed with a luminosity resembling a halo. One thought was shared by many looking at the image on the screen: *Why does this man remind me of an angel?*

Jon, no doubt, would have been amused and flattered by such a description, but this was an impression that he would project to millions of people throughout the world, yet another Teacher to help humankind, but one whose powers far exceeded any who had come before. Now his task was to generate trust and understanding.

'Mr President,' he began, 'I bring you greetings from the Grand Council and the people of the planet Zel. I am their representative, and I come in peace. I hope that henceforth my welcome will include an opening of hearts and minds.' As diplomacy was required, he made no reference to the earlier attack and self-destruction of the jet aircraft.

The president was wise enough to follow the same line of diplomacy and was relieved at the opportunity to gloss over the earlier incident without having to admit that his security services had committed such a blunder.

'I accept the greetings and friendship of the representative of the Grand Council and people of Zel,' the president replied gravely, looking intently at the angelic face before him, but he thought, *I hope we don't have to be this formal all of the time.*

Jon had every sympathy with the president regarding protocol as a normal human being, albeit one who had been indoctrinated and educated by the Zel. He also felt stifled by this formality and decided that it would help matters if they could meet face-to-face in a more relaxed and informal manner, and to that end, he made a suggestion.

'Mr President, we have much to discuss, but before we go any further, may I suggest that we meet in a more informal manner, and with only your most senior advisers present. For my part, I will be quite happy to be unattended on that occasion, although you will undoubtedly meet my companion, my only companion, at some time in the very near future.' One other reason for Jon to request a face-to-face meeting was because he realised that telepathy was more practical when in close proximity, not hovering five hundred feet above the heads of the people he wished to scan.

Chapter Six

Without thinking, but relieved at the suggestion, the president immediately agreed to the meeting, not expecting Jon's next request.

'I would like to join you as soon as possible,' Jon said.

The president, not to be outdone, replied, 'You can join me as soon as you like.' Good old-fashioned American hospitality at its best, but even so, he was completely surprised and astonished by what happened next.

In the spaceship, Jon turned to Lana and said, 'This is my opportunity to make a grand entrance. You remain in charge here, and I'll teleport down to join the president. Here goes!' The echo of the president's words of invitation had barely died away when the teleportation exercise was complete, and Jon appeared in the middle of the Oval Office without warning, triggering yet another panic and security alert among the Secret Service personnel.

Guns were drawn and several shots were fired at the intruder before the president could order them to put their weapons away, revealing Jon still standing, wreathed in smoke, but smiling calmly at the discomfiture of the bodyguards and their futile attempt to gun him down.

'Mr President, may I suggest that you clear the room,' he said, 'with the exception of two of your most senior personnel, possibly your secretary of state and your senior military adviser. We may then be able to talk without further attacks on my person.'

Under the circumstances, the president was only too glad to clear the room of most of the people, and this gave Jon time to think. Once the room was cleared, with fewer confusing thoughts to unscramble, Jon was able to see clearly into the president's mind, an honest man, contrite at the actions of those around him. *Blithering idiots,* was the phrase he sensed was often repeated.

It was some time before order was restored and they all sat down, with the president making profuse apologies for the unacceptable behaviour of his security staff. 'We have had a number

Chapter Six

of assassinations of presidents in the past,' he explained. 'Not the kind of thing you've seen happen on the planet Zel, I'll wager.'

'That is something I've never seen,' Jon replied truthfully.

'I'm only glad that all those shots missed you, ambassador,' the president added. 'Although I don't know how, you must have a charmed life.'

Jon chose not to reveal that he was protected by an energy shield or how it worked. This was not the time to divulge any information or secrets about himself, Lana, or the ship. They still had a long way to go before that kind of trust would be established.

'The only excuse I can offer for my staff,' the president continued, 'was your sudden appearance, they didn't think, just reacted to a perceived danger.'

'I've no doubt my sudden appearance threw them into some kind of confusion,' Jon conceded generously, 'but all is well that ends well since no damage was done.'

As this first incident was passed over, Jon pointed out that this meeting was the first person-to-person meeting that he'd had with any world leader, although as a means of communication, he would welcome the opportunity to address a meeting of the United Nations in New York, if the president could arrange it. Many of the problems besetting the world would require the cooperation of the major nations and many of the minor ones as well as they were often the catalyst for outbreaks of minor wars, which then escalated to embroil some of the major nations. Trouble all around.

The presence of the secretary of state proved to be very beneficial. He was a man of great charm and persuasion and was obviously held in high regard by the president and was frequently called on for advice or to give an opinion on the several points of discussion that followed; whereas, the military commander present had little to say at this time, although in his mind he was thinking,

Chapter Six

I'll let these guys show their hand before I say anything. What is the real aim of this meeting?

During the course of the proceedings, Jon found it irksome to be constantly referred to as ambassador, which he was not, since he was a representative appointed by the commander of the mother ship, so he politely requested that he be addressed simply as 'Jon,' a request gladly conceded by the president and his staff. Informality was something they could readily accept.

After some time, Jon had answered some of the many questions from the presidential team, including the matter of teleporting into the Oval Office, and if this was an ability shared by all the Zellian people. 'Yes,' Jon affirmed, but he didn't elaborate on his own extra powers, powers beyond a normal Zellian citizen. Not wishing to disclose too much about himself or his own origins, he changed the discussion to why he was there, and was pleased to note the military commander's reaction. *So, now we are going to find out at last.*

That thought came through loud and clear, forcefully, in fact, thought Jon.

'Mr President, for years, your scientists and philosophers have been asking one question. "Is there anyone out there?" We know that they have been studying the skies and monitoring the radio waves emitted by the stars in the hope of picking up signals that they could interpret as being from alien but intelligent cultures. Well, the signals were there, but were not recognised by your people, whereas the Zellians have listened to your broadcasts on radio for more than one hundred years and picked up your television transmissions for the past sixty.' Noting the sceptical look on their faces, Jon smiled, but continued, 'All these signals were picked up and recorded by our ships when travelling in the solar system, which we do from time to time, because it takes many years for those same transmissions to reach the planet Zel, as the distance is so vast.'

Chapter Six

'And I take it then that that is how you can speak our language, Jon,' the secretary of state said. 'By listening and learning from everything you have seen and heard?'

Better than you can imagine my friend, Jon thought with amusement, *and many other languages as well.*

'In fact, you speak English more correctly than we do,' added the president with a laugh, 'which is quite often the case when foreigners learn a new language.'

'Suffice it to say,' Jon commented, 'that I will have no difficulty in speaking to the representatives of the United Nations when such a meeting can be convened, Mr President, and when that time comes, I hope to persuade all the nations to come together to live in peace and prosperity so that this planet may live for many more millions of years.'

The army general still made no verbal comment, but Jon scanned his mind to find out his true feelings and was not in the least surprised to read, *You've got no chance, brother, the human race always have and always will fight each other, ever since they came down out of the trees, lived in caves, even when they claimed to have formed the earliest civilisations. I guess they just enjoy a good fight.*

No surprise regarding the general's outlook on life, live by the sword, die by the sword, Jon mentally commented.

'It may take a little time to organise the meeting you request, Jon,' declared the president, 'when it is known what will be on the agenda and who will be the principal speaker, I guarantee you will have a full assembly. We have a full team of interpreters on hand at all times so there won't be any language barriers, although personal contact such as ours might have been beneficial in some cases. It gives you more of an 'edge' for the feelings of the other person, don't you think?'

Jon replied with a smile, 'I agree entirely, Mr President.' Inwardly he thought, *I will know.*

Chapter Six

Having spent several hours in the White House with the president, and feeling that there was little more to gain by his continuing presence, Jon stood up before the other three men, making them realise for the first time just how big and muscular this citizen of Zel was. *Wouldn't like to tangle with this guy,* the general thought, much to Jon's amusement.

As Jon looked at the other three men in turn, he was aware of their curiosity as to how he would take his leave, would he teleport from the Oval Office, walk out of the building first of all, or call down the spaceship to pick him up? They were going to get used to him appearing without warning, but hopefully by arrangement. On this occasion, they witnessed his disappearance after he bade them his formal farewell, but one thing the general, in particular, noted, none of them had made any physical contact with Jon. There had been no shaking of hands as a greeting. *Maybe these guys don't go in for that kind of thing,* he thought. The president and the secretary of state both had similar thoughts.

Jon, of course, was aware that if he were to attempt to shake hands before his departure, or as a greeting on any future occasion, the recipient of such a gesture would be amazed to find that physical contact was impossible. While Jon's energy force field was activated, there would always be a minimum of two inches between himself and any other person, until such time as he removed the control belt from around his waist, and that would only be when he was back aboard the ship with Lana.

To overcome this difficulty and to observe some form of protocol, he decided to salute, not as the general would have done, but as many soldiers in bygone days had done, by laying a clenched fist on his left breast. *Like a centurion of Rome,* he thought with a smile. Apparently, the president could accept this as a natural gesture; after all, he himself often saluted in a similar fashion, hand on heart.

'One more thing before I go, Mr President,' Jon said. 'During the time it takes you to arrange the United Nations assembly in New

Chapter Six

York, I shall take my departure for a time, for it is my intention to look at many other locations around the world. I believe there are many areas that would be described as war zones, and it is my intention to see that such conflicts are resolved as soon as possible. Whereas America is regarded as the guardian of law and order in the civilised regions of this world, the Zellian people try to uphold a similar role in the Federation of the Stars.'

With that, still holding his gesture of salute, he disappeared instantly from their view, teleporting back to his ship, which hovered five hundred feet above the White House.

'Well, ain't that something,' the general said with a grin. 'That's a trick we could do with learning.'

'Yes,' the president replied. 'I'm sure that if we had that ability, we could put it to some good use.'

Chapter Seven

'Now that you have talked to the President and his advisers, Jon,' Lana said solemnly, 'what will your next course of action be? Presumably, you will need more information regarding events occurring around the world affecting the lives of the people. We already know that there are some areas of conflict, strangely enough, though, they are isolated to some of what we believed to be the more impoverished countries with large populations.'

'Yes, it's as though they have a collective wish for self-destruction,' Jon replied. 'So, what I intend to do while we wait for this meeting in New York is to do a surveillance trip over the northern hemisphere of the world, which is strangely enough where most conflicts seem to occur. In the recent past, there have been two World Wars resulting in the deaths of millions of people, civilian and military alike, and as I said, it is the northern races who appear to be more aggressive.'

Lana acknowledged that statement with a nod of the head. 'Yes, over the years that we have monitored the radio and television transmissions, we have learned not only their languages and way of life, but that humans are reluctant to live in peace. It seems that conquest is a part of their nature, driven by their perceived need for more land and mineral wealth, and the only thing that we would understand, territorial gains in order to grow enough food to sustain their massive populations.'

'Well, if they carry on as they are doing at this time,' Jon remarked grimly, 'one of the more irresponsible governments will unleash

Chapter Seven

their nuclear weapons in the belief that, if they strike first, they will conquer. Sadly, that will only initiate retaliation from the other nuclear powers with the inevitable outcome of Armageddon—a religious prophecy,' he explained to Lana, who was frowning at the absurdity of such destruction of life and a beautiful planet.

'Surely the first step for you to take, Jon,' she said, 'is to rid the world of these nuclear devices before they can be used aggressively.'

'And that will be one of the issues that I shall raise when I address the United Nations, Lana,' Jon replied. 'But I have no illusions; to make them to give up their nuclear toys would be regarded as throwing away all their means of defence, and they will not cooperate with that suggestion.'

'So, what is the alternative then,' Lana enquired curiously. 'They won't give up their weapons voluntarily, so you will have to take them away from them, is that it?'

'You make it sound simple, Lana,' Jon said as he spread his hands wide in a gesture of mock surrender. 'No, I can't physically take away all their weapons, not even the nuclear ones. I can't even confiscate them, but I can destroy them. But first, I must locate the position of every nuclear weapon on the planet, and if my plea for peace on Earth should fall on deaf ears, then I shall systematically destroy every weapon. That is one of the purposes of this surveillance we are about to do.' He paused thoughtfully as he looked around the control room. 'We have here the means to detect by geological survey any type of minerals that may be contained within the mass of the planet, and that will, of course, also identify any fissionable material such as in a nuclear bomb. So although it is going to take some time to do so, we will overfly those countries most likely to possess these weapons. First of all, to locate the positions and enter them into our computers for reference, so if it's necessary, we can destroy the fissionable material without detonating the bombs.' He smiled as he said, 'If we were to detonate the arsenals of all the superpowers, I doubt that there would be much left of Earth.'

Chapter Seven

As Lana probed into Jon's mind, she could see that despite the levity of his voice, he was very much concerned for the future of Earth and its people. 'When will you inform this meeting of the nations of your intentions, Jon, or will you simply destroy their destructive capability without their knowledge?'

'I will try to persuade the leaders of the nuclear powers of the futility of holding so many weapons of mass destruction, but I can also appreciate their concerns that unless they have the means of retaliation, they would be at the mercy of a ruthless aggressor. The only safe situation is that no one nation will possess any nuclear weapons, and that is why we will survey every potential landmass on the planet.' As an afterthought, he added, 'And if we see any sign of activity of rockets of a military nature being launched, I will arrange for a suitable demonstration of our abilities.'

'Can you do that, Jon, without being accused of warlike behaviour yourself?' Lana's anxiety showed on her face and in her troubled thoughts.

'A timely demonstration against a weapon of war can hardly be construed as an act of war,' replied Jon. 'Besides, it would be a very foolish government to admit to launching a missile of that nature; its destruction and the ease with which we can do it will hopefully convince a hostile nation of the futility of a nuclear war.'

'I can see that your training programme must have been a comprehensive one, Jon, since much of what you talk about, the capabilities of this ship, I have never seen demonstrated. Was this what Captain Jara meant when he said that I should accompany you on this mission, to complete my training, to watch and learn from you?'

'Very probably, Lana,' Jon acknowledged. 'He probably wanted you to learn first-hand how to use the weapons systems on board, rather than as I did, by the indoctrination method. However, during

Chapter Seven

the next few days or weeks, my mind will be open to you, for you to share my knowledge of all things.'

The sincerity of Jon's words and the feeling of pleasure emanating from his mind evoked a similar emotion in Lana. *A strange but pleasant emotion,* she thought.

'But for the moment, Lana,' Jon said, 'we are going to leave the White House, the President and America behind. We will continue westward across the Pacific Ocean, the world's largest mass of water, and begin our quest for nuclear weapons over the continent of Asia first of all. But as we fly over the States, I will still note all their weapons sites, as no country will be excluded from our search. One unfortunate aspect of this survey is that we will have to reduce speed to sub-sonic levels in order for our instruments to pick up the tell-tale emissions that will identify fissionable materials, but no matter, time is of no consequence as I don't expect the United Nations could be assembled any time soon, and who knows, an opportunity may occur for us to demonstrate our capabilities.'

To the many people gathered on the streets of Washington, the spacecraft slowly appeared to rise vertically without any apparent noise, as though it were drifting upward on a breeze. After it had risen several thousand feet into the sky, with the sun reflecting on its saucer-like dome, the craft gradually, almost majestically, turned to the west, accelerating as it went and after a few minutes, it had completely disappeared from sight, leaving the White House strangely naked without its temporary ornament above. Meanwhile, the president and his staff wondered what events were to follow. However, the word was out, organise the meeting of the United Nations in New York.

In order to scan the maximum area of ground below, Jon allowed the craft to fly at an altitude of some twenty miles, high enough for a reasonable view, but sufficiently close for their detection instruments to function and detect the emissions from fusion materials. As he explained to Lana, 'We are already aware of the weapons silos from

Chapter Seven

previous surveillance surveys conducted by Captain Jara, what will be of particular interest to me now, will be new sites deep underground, sites where efforts have been made to render them invisible from the air, but not from our instruments. Once we have listed all the sites, I will then be ready to deliver the ultimatum, "give up your weapons voluntarily or have them rendered useless on their launch pads," and each will be a monument to their folly.'

Chapter Eight

As the hours passed on their westward flight, the on-board computers controlled the craft and the search pattern to confirm the location of the various launch complexes, and by the time they had cleared the Pacific coast of America, their instruments had recorded several hundreds of missiles ready to be deployed. 'Are they for defence or attack? If this is what we can expect to find in Asia as well,' Jon mused, 'plus whatever may be found in Europe, if a nuclear war were to break out and all these weapons were to be implemented . . . .' The mental picture he projected for Lana's benefit was one of total destruction of the planet, leaving nothing but a glowing radioactive cinder orbiting the sun.

'Then it's important that your mission succeeds, Jon. You must use every means at your disposal, even though you may have to apply a little forceful discipline, Teacher.'

Once over the Pacific Ocean, Lana set the course for the first landfall on their quest, Japan. Apart from the possibility of nuclear armed submarines, there was no previous record of nuclear activity in the Pacific itself, which being the case, Jon allowed the ship to gain altitude and speed. 'Altitude, one hundred miles, speed two thousand mph, that will allow us to reach some of the major cities of Japan quite quickly, but in view of the country's past history of nuclear devastation, I think it unlikely that we will have to look for missile sites, so a quick overflight will be sufficient for our purpose.'

As predicted, their survey of the country proved negative, and they had to come down to a lower altitude and speed to carry out

Chapter Eight

the emission checks. It soon became obvious that their presence had been noted, as a burst of radio signals flooded the airwaves. The military were the first to respond to the appearance of the UFO, but even though the spacecraft now travelled at a much reduced speed and altitude, it was still out of reach for conventional aircraft, and the authorities could only watch and wait. By this time, most areas of the world were aware of the presence of a flying saucer, largely due to the American publicity machine, but as no threat of aggression was forthcoming, the Japanese authorities decided on a observation only approach to their visitor to their airspace. What else could they do?

'I take it that you intend to continue our flight until we are over the mainland of China, Jon,' Lana enquired. By way of reply, he nodded as he looked at the observation screens in front of him, already looking for any telltale signs of emissions. After a time, he looked up for a moment with a rueful smile. 'With a country this size, it could take months to do a proper survey of the terrain from such a low altitude, so let's climb to, let me see, fifty miles. That will increase our scanning area considerably, but we will have to rely on visual screen information rather than our instruments.'

'Very well, I'll set the ship on an automatic search pattern.' Lana smiled as she altered the controls on her console. 'That will maintain our height and sweep from north to south until there are any possible sightings of nuclear activity, in which case we can then come down to close proximity with that area.'

'So, in the meanwhile, Lana,' Jon added, 'all we can do is wait patiently for any alarm to be raised by our surveillance instruments and be prepared to make a closer inspection with every means at our disposal.' He thought for a minute then continued. 'If and when we do reduce altitude, this is one of those countries in the world where we can expect some objection to our intrusion into their airspace, along with several other countries bordering with China. They will have a very strong military presence and are for ever sabre rattling,' Again, he didn't have to give a verbal explanation of this phrase, as Lana was already getting the picture loud and clear.

'Assuming that we do find it necessary to come down to a very low altitude,' she asked, 'and we are attacked by hostile aircraft, Jon, will you do as before over Washington? That is offer only passive resistance?'

'But of course,' he answered. 'They can do nothing to harm us; we are impregnable to their rockets and other weapons, and . . . .' he smiled grimly. 'I don't think pilots nowadays go in for kamikaze tactics.' Once again, he allowed Lana to see the image in his mind of the suicide pilots as in the Second World War.

Her only response was, 'Futile.'

Realising that to attempt to survey the entire land mass of China would be equally futile, Jon was satisfied to overfly those areas where rockets could possibly be located. Remote or mountainous areas, and in particular, he always looked for signs of roads capable of being used by heavy machinery, which ruled out the thousands of rural farm roads or tracks which crisscrossed the countryside below.

In due course, as they covered large tracts of the country, particularly in the northern regions, they found positive evidence of nuclear rocket sites, not visible by normal means, but on coming down to a low-level altitude, some two or three miles, their instruments gave a very positive reading of a concentration of missiles, enough to blow China itself off the face of the planet. As though to substantiate their suspicions, after only a few minutes in the vicinity, Lana calmly drew Jon's attention to what she could see on her observation screens. 'We have a large number of aircraft approaching from below, Jon. Do you want me to take evasive action or simply outrun them?'

'Try the passive-resistance technique, Lana,' he replied. 'We will just hover as we are and let them fly around us. They will soon find that, if they mount a real attack without provocation and we don't

Chapter Eight

respond, then while we may be trespassing, it is they who are the aggressors and not much good it will do them. They can't penetrate our force shields.'

Within a few seconds of sighting the aircraft, Jon counted about ten of them. 'Must be a full squadron,' he murmured, 'so there's definitely something down there that they want to keep away from prying eyes.' While the spaceship was in passive mode, the same could not be said for the military aircraft. After asking for formal identification of the lone craft, even after receiving acknowledgement from Jon, who explained in fluent Mandarin Chinese that their presence was of a peaceful nature, but who continued to hover as before, the squadron commander issued an ultimatum for their immediate withdrawal from Chinese airspace or suffer the consequences.

Jon once again gave an assurance of their non-aggressive intentions still in fluent Mandarin, which seemed to have a unsettling effect on the other pilot. *Who was he talking to,* he wondered? Nevertheless, as the spacecraft obviously had no intention of leaving, an attack was immediately forthcoming. And so over the next ten minutes, the squadron of Chinese aircraft lined up for attack, fisrt of all wheeling and diving with their air-to-air missiles, which were rapidly expended, and then they continued with normal cannon fire, which was lethal by any usual standards, but against the force field surrounding Jon's ship, as Lana had said earlier, was futile.

Once the activity of the assault had died down, it didn't take long for the smoke to get blown away, revealing the spaceship hovering serenely against a bright blue sky, untouched, and unscathed. The crew, Jon and Lana, quietly contemplated the squadron of aircraft still circling them. Was it aimless or useless to go around? To impress on their erstwhile combatants the futility of another attack, before withdrawing from the scene, Jon reminded the squadron commander that, 'We didn't retaliate because, despite the intensity of your attack, your weapons are completely ineffective against us, and again, we are on a mission of peace.'

'But who are you and who do you represent?' the pilot queried urgently. 'Are you one of our own countrymen, a dissident perhaps? You speak perfect Mandarin so you can't be a foreigner.'

Jon chuckled inwardly at that accusation. *That says a great deal for my own training programme,* he thought. *Wait until I show myself on their own television networks; I don't think they will ever have seen a Chinaman like me.*

Lana also shared his thoughts on the matter. 'None of your races have ever seen a man like you, Jon.' But she went to some lengths to conceal her true meaning; she may have been from the planet Zel, but she was aware that she had a growing feeling for this man from planet Earth.

As it wasn't policy to reveal their identity as yet, Jon courteously bade the squadron leader farewell, observing all the protocol of polite Chinese society, further enhancing the flyers' belief that he was talking to one of his own. Then, to further impress their audience, Jon requested Lana to 'Get us out of here.' Within a few minutes, they were many miles further south, heading for the Chinese/Korean border.

As they flew silently over the mountains between the two countries, Lana observed, 'This part of your planet is very much like my world, except our mountains are much higher and tend to be as green as those forests below. We also have many rivers to irrigate the land and make it fertile.'

'You make it sound like some kind of paradise, Lana,' Jon exclaimed with a smile.

'Of all the lands I've seen whilst I've been in the space service,' she replied wistfully, 'Zel is the most beautiful, although,' she added hastily, 'Earth is almost as good, except for the heavy force of gravity.'

Chapter Eight

Their respective planets and merits of each was not something they had talked about before, probably because the subject had never arisen. But now that they had time to spare from their duties—the craft was again on automatic search mode—Jon decided to improve his knowledge of his mentors' place of origin, the better to understand them, their thinking, philosophy, and way of life in general. Besides, he enjoyed being with Lana, being in her company and around her cheerful personality. After all, she was only a young girl, a cadet in the space service with much to learn, and he had to remind himself, *She's only eight years old.*

At the speed and height at which they were travelling, they very soon arrived over North Korea. In order to carry out the surveillance procedure efficiently, Jon requested Lana to bring the ship down to a suitable altitude and speed. They didn't have long to wait before their instruments began to register emissions from fissionable emissions below, masses of it. Neither was it long before the military became aware of their presence. No doubt they had been informed by their allies of the recent confrontation over the border in China, and the futility of using conventional aircraft against the spaceship. This time around, the Koreans decided to use ground-to-air missiles, which were much bigger and more powerful than the airborne type.

Again, it was Lana who remarked, 'Looks like they have launched a strike against us, Jon, but with only two missiles; they are due to impact in five seconds time or at least they will hit the energy screen.' No sooner had she uttered the words than the rockets exploded on impact with the shield. The glare as they ignited illuminated the vision screens in the cabin, but otherwise, no feeling of impact was felt, and there was little awareness of any noise either.

'This is an act of war,' said Jon quite calmly and deliberately, 'so I will try to communicate with them and express my displeasure, but this may also prove to be a further opportunity to demonstrate how we can neutralise their aggression. Can you find me their radio frequency, Lana, and put me in contact with their ground control?'

Chapter Eight

And in answer to her unspoken thoughts, he answered, 'Yes, I will speak again in Mandarin; I've no doubt they will understand that language being so close to the border of China.' Even while Lana was trying to establish contact, they could see on their screens yet another salvo of rockets approaching. Without waiting for them to hit the force field and subsequently exploding, Jon utilised one of the many defence weapons available, a neutralising device to render explosive compounds useless, so when the missiles hit the force field, the impact was barely discernible. This no doubt left the military on the ground wondering why they couldn't shoot down this solitary craft, which was, in effect, a sitting target.

Lana was able to establish contact with the ground radio crew, but as she had no knowledge of the language, she simply thought, *Over to you, Jon, but talk to them nicely.* She was developing a very earthly sense of humour.

Even as Jon began talking to the commander on the ground, he became aware of yet another salvo of missiles approaching, and he again neutralised them with the same result as before. He pointed out to the Korean commander that, 'You're wasting your time and effort in trying to destroy my craft. No matter how many missiles you fire against me, none of them will reach their target. I can eliminate them all.' Then, as a possible means of making the man listen to reason, he continued, 'You can continue firing on my ship for as long as you like, but that will achieve only one thing, you will be putting your government to a great deal of expense without any result.' Then he added with a touch of humour, 'Don't you know how much these missiles cost?' Whether it was Jon's bantering tone or the reminder of how much their failed aggression had indeed cost his superiors and his country, the commander could be heard ordering his men to stop firing.

The inevitable questions soon followed. 'Who are you? Who do you represent? Where do you come from? What kind of craft is that?'

Chapter Eight

Replying in impeccable Mandarin, a language apparently familiar to the military garrison in this northern region of Korea, Jon replied, 'This ship belongs to the Star Federation of the Zel people.' Knowing that he might just as well have proclaimed their arrival from the moon for all the difference it would make, he continued, 'We are, at this time, representing the United Nations.' Again, this drew little or no response' oppression was the routine practiced by the military in this land.

When the question 'what kind of ship is that?' was asked, again in a belligerent tone of voice, Jon felt inclined to simply reply simply, 'What does it look like?' But not wishing to appear sarcastic, he let the question go unanswered.

However, they had seen and been made aware of yet another country in possession of a limited number of nuclear and conventional intercontinental missiles, a country that appeared to be prepared to use them with little provocation, and therefore, a potential troublemaker and threat to peace. The thought did pass through his mind, and Lana's also, *This serpent needs its fangs drawn and soon.* There being little to gain from protracted conversation with the military commander, Jon gave a slight nod to Lana, indicating that it was time to go, and very shortly, the people on the ground saw the craft rise vertically into the air at first, then in a blur of movement, accelerate over and beyond the mountains, and then it was gone.

Chapter Nine

Over a period of several weeks, the spaceship traversed the highly populated areas of the world, and also some of the more sparsely inhabited regions, and it was no great surprise to discover some countries were in possession of illicit nuclear weapons, sometimes a single bomb, but sometimes three or four. *No doubt for their own protection,* thought Jon, *but all these weapons must be neutralised or destroyed. That is their best protection.*

By this time, they had travelled nearly halfway around the globe while doing their inspection and survey, mapping and recording the position of every known missile. So-called friend or enemy made little difference; every nuclear weapon would have to go. 'Will the different governments allow you to destroy their weapons, Jon, won't they object?' Lana enquired.

Although he was not aware of it, when he was deliberating a question such as this, Jon's face took on a look of profound peace reflecting his inner thoughts on the good of humankind. His silver hair apparently glowed ever brighter, and although Lana had no such concept to go by, he now looked more than ever like the proverbial angel in appearance, something that undoubtedly would stand him in good stead for his appearance at the United Nations assembly.

'I have thought about that for some time, Lana, and I'm quite sure that all the governments, even those who advocate peace, will be reluctant to give up their deterrents. They won't trust each other; such is the nature of humankind.' He smiled. 'I will, however, wait until the meeting of the United Nations and gauge their response to

Chapter Nine

my suggestion, and hopefully, we can reach a decision on disarming every country in the world of their nuclear weapons.'

'From what you have said many times before, Jon,' Lana said quietly, 'you are unlikely to succeed in persuading every government, every country, to destroy what they perceive to be their only guarantee of protection. As you say, your people have no faith in the integrity of their neighbours.'

Jon smiled as he replied, 'That's putting it mildly, Lana. Some of them would sooner hold the tail of a tiger than the hand of a rival politician.'

Lana laughed in disbelief as she picked up this mental picture from Jon's mind. 'Then, how do you propose to destroy the weapons arsenals of so many countries without their approval? Can it be done?'

Again, as he briefly contemplated that question, one that he had already given some thought to he replied quietly, 'Lana, I have no great expectations of convincing the delegates from so many different nations that the sensible course of action is so simple, destroy all nuclear weapons. They will raise every possible objection, the loss of security without a deterrent at their disposal, the cost involved to their governments, and the lack of trust as I've said before. One other aspect that some astute politician or military person may raise is, how do they destroy hundreds of nuclear bombs over a short period of time without blowing up the world itself?'

Looking intently at Jon and allowing her mind to merge with his in order to get a clearer picture of the answer she required for her next question, she asked, 'Did you not suggest some time ago that with the technology available to you on this ship, you could render all the fissionable materials in the bombs inactive, incapable of being detonated?'

'I did, Lana,' he answered with a smile playing about his lips. 'And that is what we will do within days of this meeting in New

Chapter Nine

York. I have no delusions as to the outcome of that worldly gathering. They may well say one thing, but disagree on others, but you can be assured that they will prevaricate for days, months, possibly for years, and quite simply, we don't have time for that.' Having made that statement, Jon explained further. 'While your normal life expectancy would be about one thousand years, Lana, any prolonged stay on Earth will drastically reduce that time, so it is my intention to clear up this situation on Earth before recalling the mother ship. No doubt your own people, Captain Jara in particular, will be happy to have you rejoin them.'

But I don't want to go back; I don't care if I only live for a few hundreds of years. I want to stay with you. These were the thoughts going through Lana's mind, which she carefully screened so as not to be interpreted by the man in her affections. *In the past there have been unions between the people of Earth and early Zellian visitors, so why not us?* Having successfully hidden her emotional thoughts, Lana resumed their conversation with regard to Jon's intended actions to dispose of the nuclear threat. 'How long will you wait after the UN meeting before you take any action,' she asked, 'and will you inform the president of your intentions?'

Again, Jon deliberated for a few moments before answering, 'I will only wait for one day, no matter what is decided at the meeting; and no, I won't inform the president of my intentions. I like the man himself, but he alone can't answer for all of his own people, the military alone would force his hand, and he is unlikely to persuade the other governments to reach a decision quickly either.'

'So, having waited for one day only,' Lana pressed the question, 'what are we then to do, tell the various governments that we are coming to destroy their weapons?'

Laughing at the humour of Lana's statement, at least he thought it was meant to be funny, he replied, 'Not quite, Lana, we have not yet completed the survey of all nuclear sites. I think that will take about another week, but when we have, when the time comes, it

Chapter Nine

will only take a matter of days to revisit these locations and immobilise every bomb. It will only take a matter of seconds to render the fissionable materials useless, and the carrier vehicle, the rocket, will be just one expensive firework.'

'And presumably,' Lana continued, 'as all these weapons are rendered useless over a period of a few days, and assuming that no hostile action takes place within that time, there will be no outward indication that the missiles have indeed been rendered useless and will be monuments to past military ambitions.'

Smiling in satisfaction, Jon nodded his agreement. 'Yes, they may launch their toys, but they will also find that the rocket fuel will not burn effectively, and the missiles will come down very quickly. They will probably do more damage to themselves than to some enemy, which being the case, they will soon realise that something is radically wrong. That is when I can inform them of the futility of nuclear warfare, and just in case someone slips through the net and can still threaten the remaining nations, I shall take it upon myself to destroy them personally, to teach them that they must conform to law and order.'

'With the action you propose, Jon,' Lana exclaimed, 'you may be able to bring peace to your people with a minimum of danger to ourselves and avoid the death of millions of your people. I have seen the results of such wars on several planets in the past and the outcome of them was, well, there were no winners. With the arsenal of weapons we have discovered so far, if they were all utilised over a period of a few hours, this planet would be uninhabitable.' To lighten the mood and to satisfy a personal thought, she asked, 'In which case, would you be prepared to live on Zel, Jon?'

Not wishing to be drawn to answer such a question at this time, Jon laughed gently. 'What other choice would I have, where else could I go?' But sensing that this was not the answer Lana wanted, he relented and said, 'Yes, Lana, I would be prepared to live on your planet if your people would accept me, and of course, if you would consider a life with an "alien." But the same situation applies to you at this moment, would you be prepared to stay here on Earth for the remainder of your life, despite the fact that you would only live for half of your expected lifespan?'

'Remember, Jon,' she replied, 'your earthly longevity has been increased to about five hundred years while mine had been reduced to the same level, so assuming that we can prevent humans from destroying this planet, we could be together for a long time to come.' While this was not a firm commitment for the future for either of them, nevertheless their mental bond was now much stronger.

As they touched hands briefly, they both smiled as they then drew apart. 'Then let's get down to business,' Jon declared, 'let's root out all the remaining missiles sites, those Jara has already located and those that are now all well concealed underground.' He pursed his lips as he speculated as to where next to search. They had already inspected a vast area of the planet. The automatic surveillance guidance system appeared to be taking them over the Indian subcontinent, and sure enough, their instruments were recording the presence of quite a number of nuclear warheads. 'No doubt we will be back for those as well,' Jon commented, 'but now we'll pass over the Middle East before long, the lands of oil and bloodshed, where human conflict has raged for centuries, and that has been without the bomb. What hope is there for their future?'

Lana was observing the instruments in front of her, recording the positions of any further launch sites as they passed over. 'Surprisingly, not so many in this part of the world, Jon.'

'No,' he replied rather cynically. 'The people down there,' he gestured at his viewing screen, 'in some respects are still living in a mediaeval society, and their concept of wealth is not measured in how many bombs they have stockpiled. Only a few privileged rulers are even aware of the outside world, no, they look upon the possession of grand palaces, luxury yachts, and cars, and the ability to travel the world with a grand entourage as a means to flaunt

Chapter Nine

their financial wealth. I doubt if we would be lucky to find many bombs in this region, but there is plenty of political unrest.'

At that moment, Lana leaned forward to get a better look at the data on her viewing screen. 'I seem to be getting some kind of signal from the far north of this region, Jon. At our present altitude, our horizon is too limited, but it does look suspicious. Shall I take the ship up to a higher altitude for a better reading?'

'By all means,' Jon conceded. 'The far north of our present location has been a hotbed of political unrest for some time now, and the country's leaders have persisted their innocence regarding their ability to produce any kind of nuclear weapons. Well, we can but take a look.'

With Lana at the helm and Jon checking the monitors continuously as they approached the suspicious area, the most northerly of the Arab countries, the signals on the screens strengthened until they were hovering a mere twenty miles above what would prove to be a potential target at a later date. 'Take me down much closer, Lana,' Jon requested, 'about one mile. The signal is quite definitely emissions from fissionable material, either a bomb ready for launch, or in the making, either way, a covert weapon to be taken out.'

The appearance of their craft, a flying saucer, above the concealed weapons silo must have set the alarm bells ringing in the complex below, as it became obvious a number of ground-to-air missiles had been targeted at them and were rising rapidly through the clear cloudless sky. At an altitude of only one mile, it only took a matter of a few seconds for the rockets to come into contact with their force field. 'More fireworks,' commented Jon calmly. As they continued to watch, further salvos of missiles were launched in their direction, but with the same result. 'I think on this occasion they are not likely to desist simply by us being polite, so we'll retire gracefully, but not before taking out that missile in the bunker below. It is definitely a nuclear device, but in the hands of people like these, it could start a serious conflict in this part of the world.'

Lana had been watching the continuing barrage of rockets hitting the force screens. 'They are certainly determined to destroy us, aren't they, Jon,' she remarked.

'Determined and fanatical,' he agreed. 'So this is one instance when I will destroy their missile and the fissionable material with it, and then let them try to deny that they ever had such a bomb. This may well be the first atomic explosion in decades, but it may serve as a warning to other regimes elsewhere in the world.' With a final look at the monitor screen, Jon said quietly, 'Take us up out of the blast range, Lana. Thirty miles should suffice to begin with, and then we can leave the area immediately.' As the spacecraft swiftly gained altitude, Jon fixed his sights on the complex below, waiting for the right moment. There was an instant blinding flash as the bomb and the complex and all within vaporized in an instant, leaving Jon with a feeling of satisfaction that there was now one less threat to the planet Earth and its inhabitants. If Jon were to be described as an angel, it would surely be an avenging angel.

Having fulfilled their objective, they left the scene of destruction below, and then continued further north, scanning the mountains and desert plains for any further signs of nuclear installations of a warlike nature, but they drew a blank. 'It must have been a one of missile site,' Jon concluded. By this time, they had dropped down to an altitude of ten miles, high enough not to attract too much attention. To an observer on the ground, they would appear to be a bright speck in the sky, easily mistaken for a high-flying commercial aircraft perhaps, and as they were flying at a low speed while carrying out their surveillance, there was apparently nothing unusual in their appearance, unless an observer could see their distinctive shape through a high-powered telescope or binoculars.

It wasn't long before they saw what appeared to be a large city on the horizon, and as they drew nearer, they were able to appreciate

Chapter Nine

its size. Having little to fear from any attack and knowing that their presence would have been broadcast hours ago, Jon requested Lana to bring the craft down to a lower level, until they could see the faces of the people below. There was obviously panic in the streets as the population must have thought they were under threat of a nuclear attack. No doubt the local radio and television stations had already informed them of the destruction of the weapons complex further south, but omitted to inform them it was as a result of one of their own bombs being destroyed, a bomb that their own government denied existed.

As they hovered above the centre of the city, they could still see several hundreds of people. *Fearless citizens, patriots or religious fanatics?* Jon thought. They were gathered in a central square, and on a whim, he said to Lana, 'We haven't been out of the ship for several weeks now, and this could be a good opportunity to make personal contact with the people. Let them know who we are and what our purpose is for being here. Would you like to accompany me? We can teleport down together and leave the ship on auto control.'

As ever, Lana smiled as she replied, 'Thank you, but no, Jon, I'm used to spending many months at a time on board our ship, so I'm quite happy to remain here. Besides, outside I will be affected by Earth's gravity, which no doubt I would find tiring, but if you feel that it would serve a purpose for you to communicate with those people down there,' she gestured out of the now open viewport, 'then I will remain here, ready to assist you if you should encounter any violence. Which reminds me, do wear your protective force field belt.'

'Yes, ma'am,' Jon grinned.

Chapter Ten

A few minutes later, suitably dressed and equipped with the belt, he gave Lana a gentle touch on the shoulder as a gesture of affection, and immediately teleported the short distance to the ground below while a humorous thought passed through his mind. *What a way to travel.* The moment he was on the ground, he adjusted his force field to a distance of twenty feet as a precaution against being mobbed, which is exactly what happened. 'Fear will make people react in different ways,' Jon mused. 'They will either run away or attack.'

He endured the hostile attack of the mob for some minutes without making any sign of retaliation; he just stood silently, surrounded by hundreds of people intent on destroying him by whatever means at their disposal. By far the most common form of aggression was stones being thrown, and without the protection of his personal force field, Jon had to concede he would have died a 'biblical death.' There were also a number of uniformed personnel in the crowd in possession of small arms, pistols, and the occasional submachine gun, and they showed no hesitancy in using them.

Eventually, the concerted attack of the mob had no effect against the lone figure in the square, and one by one, the guns stopped firing, and the rabble gave up throwing stones, leaving the square looking like a building site. The tall, silver-haired man smiling serenely at his erstwhile attackers. Some of the people tried to approach him, possibly with the intention of trying to seize him, but Jon forestalled such a possibility by calmly adjusting his force field to a distance of

Chapter Ten

some thirty feet around him, just by the touch of a button on his belt.

When the press of people came up against the invisible barrier of the force field, those in front found themselves being crushed by the weight of those at the rear and made their objections known rancorously, shouting for their fellows to go back. Eventually, not knowing which way to turn, they compromised and stood still, for the moment speechless in wonder and amazement. It didn't take long before some of the crowd, perhaps more genuinely religious than others, began to question the identity of this stranger in their midst. Who is he? Surely not a mortal man. Is he a prophet, a messenger of God? Look at him; he is like no other. He is fearless! His face and hair have surely been touched by the hand of Allah.

As the noise of the crowd subsided, Jon decided that now would be the time to address them, and raising his hands high as though to command silence, he began to speak in Arabic, a language he was sure would be the common tongue among these people. As they realised that he was speaking as one of their own, they were astonished that an infidel could have such a natural command of their language, as though he was, indeed, an Arab himself.

Jon talked to them for about ten minutes, assuring them that his mission was one of peace, with the welfare of all men of all nations his principal concern, that it was time for all men to live together as brothers. He pointed out that only today, a few hundred miles to the south, a holocaust in the form of an atomic bomb had been unleashed. Hopefully, it was an isolated incident and one which could not be permitted to happen again, and that he would persuade all governments of all countries to reject nuclear weapons in the first step to a world without conflict. Having listened to him with rapt attention, when Jon announced his intention to return to his ship, those who initially had been hostile now pleaded that he should remain as their protector, a son of Allah. To make his departure somewhat easier, he informed them that he still had much to do in

Chapter Ten

his quest for peace, and there were many parts of the world he had yet to visit. 'But my thoughts will be with you all.' Thinking that this was something of a theatrical exit, he immediately teleported back to the ship and to Lana, who had been anxiously watching all the events happening below—the stoning, the mob violence, and gunfire at the hands of the militia.

'I'm glad I didn't accompany you, Jon,' she remarked. That was a threatening situation, even with your force field protection. Do you think it might be advisable to carry some other weapons in the future?'

With a reproving look, Jon smiled grimly as he asked, 'Why would a Teacher need offensive weapons in any situation where he cannot be harmed?' And he said no more. But inwardly, he reminded himself that he had not yet tried his untested 'unworldly' strength and power of telekinesis, but no doubt a time would come.

By mutual consent, without the need to discuss their intentions, they set about taking the ship up to their normal cruising altitude where it was possible to overview the countryside below. The surveillance instruments searched for any further suspicious signs of fissionable materials or military activity. There was no great urgency. They had no particular schedule to adhere to, it was possible to observe and enjoy the view from their high altitude, and when some particular area looked interesting, Lana adjusted the viewing screens to increase the magnification with the effect that it was as though they were only a few hundred feet above the land or sea.

As they passed over the eastern Mediterranean countries, the skies were generally clear of clouds for the most part, although they found that in the heat of the day at sea level, a heat haze prevailed, making it difficult to make direct visual contact, but by enhancing the images on the surveillance instruments, it was possible to obtain a clearer picture. Lana was fascinated by the beauty of the Greek islands in particular. 'They remind me so much of my home,'

Chapter Ten

she said wistfully. 'I seem to have been away for so long, several years in fact.'

Jon could feel her sense of longing, for her home or possibly her parents and family. That was something neither of them had ever discussed. Lana had pursued a single-minded dedication to the space service and her career, although Jon sensed that there was something distracting her recently. As for himself, the memory of his former lifestyle was too recent, his new job as an air traffic controller at an international airport, Manchester, the camaraderie of the people he worked with, and the satisfaction of doing an interesting job. Then, of course, the abrupt termination of his career after the tragedy of losing his wife and children in the road traffic accident; his life would have probably been so different, but for that encounter with Captain Jara and Mort on that fateful evening on a lonely road in the Highlands of Scotland.

'I wonder what happened when my car was found apparently abandoned, miles from anywhere. Was there some kind of enquiry regarding my whereabouts or a search for a body even?' That was all idle speculation of course, something to while the time away. 'Whatever the outcome of the abandoned car saga, it will have been long forgotten by now,' he mused.

As the hours passed, they travelled continually westward and still at high altitude, high enough to be aware of the curvature of the earth and the glorious views of the Iberian Peninsula as they came to the end of the Mediterranean Sea, with the Balearic Islands sitting like emerald jewels in a sapphire setting. 'Does that remind you of home, as well, Lana?' Jon enquired with a smile.

As Lana adjusted the speed of the craft in order to allow more time to study the scene below, she too smiled with pleasure at the sight before commenting. 'The islands, yes, but from what I can see off the mainland, no. Around the coastline and in the north, the country looks fertile and green, but elsewhere it looks mountainous and barren.'

Chapter Ten

'It's a big country, Lana,' Jon remarked. 'I've visited it many times in the past, and while it's true that it looks dry and arid at the moment, during the winter months, if we were to come back, we would see these same mountains covered in snow—even those in the south—for it is a land of contrasts.'

It had been many hours since there had been any indication of their instruments recording suspected nuclear readings. 'Looks like we've left the troublemakers behind,' Lana commented. 'What do you intend to do now, Jon, set course for America and renew your acquaintance with the president?'

Jon didn't reply immediately, but sat down in front of the control console, and without saying a word, he reached out, passing his hand over the navigation system, activating a change of course telepathically, and resuming their normal high altitude cruising speed.

'No Lana,' he finally answered once the ship was set on the course that he'd determined, 'I'm taking you to my own country, the place of my birth. It too is a land of contrasts where we have mountains and meadows, forests, rivers, and lakes, a land of temperate climate, and many millions of people, more people in one large city than there is on the whole of Zel.'

Lana frowned at the mention of Earth's population. 'Why do you allow your people to multiply in such numbers, to me it is already obvious that all the countries we have visited are grossly overcrowded. Zel is only half the size of Earth, but our people are counted in millions, whereas here on Earth.' She raised her hands as though in bewilderment.

Jon nodded gravely in acknowledgement of Lana's question. 'By your own estimate, the population of Earth will be seven billion by the middle of this century and still growing, an unsustainable number for any society.' Smiling ruefully, he exclaimed, 'Here I am, attempting to sustain life and peace, but the other matter of population control

Chapter Ten

is something that must be dealt with in the years ahead. Mort told me that I am quite likely to live for another five hundred years, Lana, but I think I will need every day of that time to bring about and resolve the many problems of humanity.'

Within a short space of time, about fifteen minutes at cruising speed, they passed over the English Channel with the White Cliffs of Dover clearly defined against the green backdrop of the rolling countryside of England, a sight that brought back memories of other occasions when returning from holiday in Spain with his wife and children, memories that he reluctantly put to the back of his mind. *That is a different life now,* he persuaded himself. *I have a mission to complete, one that I didn't ask for, but nevertheless, one that is likely to require my entire dedication, and possibly the rest of my life, all five hundred years of it.*

Lana's voice interrupted his reverie. 'Do you want to reduce speed and altitude, Jon, now that we are over England?'

'If you remain at the same altitude,' he concurred, 'at about fifty miles, then allow the ship to hover in that position. As it is now near nightfall, I would like you to see the lights of the cityof London. It was at one time the biggest city in the world, but no longer; it has been outgrown by many others elsewhere, but at night, it is still one of the brightest.'

Lana smiled in agreement. 'Yes, Captain Jara pointed it out to me when we passed over this country before—when we were searching for you, remember?'

'Yes,' Jon replied, 'and now you will be able to see it all close up, a little later than this, because, for the moment, I suggest that we both deserve a little rest and sleep. It has been a long journey around the world, and this surveillance is exhausting, don't you think?'

Chapter Eleven

When Jon and Lana woke up after a few hours of refreshing sleep, they opened the viewport to gaze down on the city of London, still glowing with lights from the countless buildings and streetlights, which stretched for miles into the surrounding countryside still shrouded in darkness. The contrast made the lights of the city appear even brighter. Although at ground level it was still nighttime, at an altitude of fifty miles, the sun was already appearing over the horizon, and before long, the lights below appeared to dim gradually and different features of the city and surrounding landscape became visible.

***

It also transpired that at that time, a certain professor of astronomy at Jodrell Bank was delighted to inform the air ministry— in the person of a certain air marshal of his acquaintance that— 'Your friends in the flying saucer are back.' He enjoyed the sound of indignation that his report provoked, adding with a malicious sense of humour, 'And they are hovering right over London.'

It appeared that the search for nuclear weapons sites was over, having identified several hundred in America alone, even more in Russia and China, and countless previously unidentified missiles in other parts of the world. Britain appeared to be 'clean,' although Jon was aware that several nuclear submarines were continuously deployed around her shores and in various oceans in strategic positions to deter a possible aggressor, and no doubt some of the superpowers had similar vessels lurking in the depths. But that was

Chapter Eleven

a problem for the future; all that was required was a little patience when the time came.

They maintained their position over London for several hours, unseen by the population below, and although the military was aware of their presence by now, it had to be conceded that the spacecraft was untouchable at that altitude, so they were diplomatically ignored. As the inactivity began to pall on Jon and Lana, they mutually agreed, telepathically, of course, that they should move on, with the intention of seeing London and the surrounding areas from a closer viewpoint. As the whole world was by now aware of the visitation of a flying saucer, there was little point in trying to remain out of sight, so long as they didn't cause any panic in the civilian population or trigger-happy military types.

In due course, Lana brought the craft down to a point where they were only about two thousand feet above the city, but kept them moving at a very slow speed, still heading inexorably to the west, since their final destination was still the United States. Eventually, they cleared the vast Greater London area and could see that they were passing over a rural landscape with the occasional small town or village. Not wishing to cause alarm to the many animals they could see in the fields below, Jon suggested that a higher altitude might be more suitable, and accordingly, Lana took the craft several thousand feet higher, but they were still capable of retaining eye contact with the ground rather than being dependent on their instruments.

Out of idle curiosity, they followed the general direction of one of the motorways leading to the southwest, the M3, and observed the congested traffic below. Jon remembered the many times in the past when he had himself been in a similar situation, trying to get to work at Manchester airport and the chaos on the motorways in the north, which was nothing but frustration and delays. Lana read Jon's thoughts, which were quite vivid, and remarked, 'Even at this

Chapter Eleven

slow speed, we will cover a greater distance in a shorter time than those unfortunate motorists down there.'

'Yes,' Jon replied in a dry tone of voice, 'but they are probably travelling for their own pleasure.' Then he laughed openly. 'Not that I would want to change places with them; if you want to travel a long distance, then fly, preferably in a craft like this, for this is what I call a pleasure.'

Although their speed was comparatively slow after leaving the London area, they nevertheless reached the point, according to a strategically positioned road sign visible on their scanner, where they were approaching the city of Winchester. From their elevated position in the sky, it was possible to see that the traffic ahead had come to a complete standstill on the southbound carriageway, but they were unable to determine why.

Still maintaining their altitude so as not to cause any further distraction, Lana brought the craft to hover directly above the leading vehicles on the motorway below and was greeted by a scene of chaos and carnage. It appeared that an accident had only just occurred. A number of lorries and several cars had been involved, but fortunately, a police car was already on the scene. The sight of the accident immediately brought memories flooding back to Jon's mind, giving Lana an insight into his memory of that past event, something he hadn't talked about or discussed with her, but now graphically explained in every detail.

'I must go down there, Lana, and help in any way I can. There appears to be only one police crew available, and they will need all the assistance they can muster until the other emergency services arrive. Looking at the congestion and tailbacks down there that may be some time.'

'Of course, Jon,' Lana replied, 'you must do what you can; you are better equipped to help in that situation down there than any

Chapter Eleven

dozen men, but don't forget your force field belt. It may prove useful.'

Having selected a point on the road to materialise without causing any further problems, Jon immediately teleported. He arrived in the space between a number of vehicles, lorries, and cars strewn all over the motorway, where dozens of people were running around in panic, while the two police officers tried to bring some kind of order to the scene.

From his own experience as a driver, Jon concluded that what appeared to be a petrol tanker had jack-knifed for whatever reason, had skidded, and blocked all three lanes of the motorway. One of the following cars had run into the back of the lorry and was now firmly wedged beneath it, and to make matters worse, yet another lorry had impacted the rear of the car, ramming it even more tightly beneath the tanker. Jon's first thought was, *The people in the car, have they survived?* Comparing the similarity to the accident in which his wife had died, he moved forward to investigate, and in doing so, he noted that the road was awash with petrol, which was a potential fire hazard, and there were no fire services in sight.

As he made his way forward through the crowd toward the petrol tanker, his intention must have been obvious as the two policemen rushed towards him. 'You can't go near those vehicles, sir; the whole lot could blow up at any moment. It will only take a single spark and everything will go sky high.' As Jon persisted in his advance, the officers attempted to restrain him by taking him by either arm; the fact that he was an exceptionally well-built man of striking appearance was not going to deter them from doing their duty.

Jon, however, was equally determined to get to close quarters to ascertain if the people in the car had survived, but he could not do so with a policeman hanging on to each arm. 'Gentlemen,' he exclaimed, 'it is my intention to see if there are any survivors in that

Chapter Eleven

car, and I would suggest that you release me and organise the removal of that lorry at the rear as your first priority.'

The two officers, the senior being a traffic sergeant, were flabbergasted to be addressed by a mere civilian is such an authoritative manner—and so calmly at that—so much so that they clung onto Jon even more tightly. 'Sorry, sir, we can't let you do that; it's far too dangerous.'

By way of reply, Jon grabbed each man by the neck of each uniform jacket, and using his as yet untested unworldly strength, he hoisted them off their feet and placed them on the bonnet of their own patrol car. 'Please do as I say,' he remarked calmly, 'every minute we delay makes it more likely that the situation will only get worse.'

After such a physical confrontation, the officers realised that they were no match for this extraordinary man, so with a nod of agreement, the sergeant motioned his fellow officer toward the lorry in question, the one at the rear. 'I'll get the driver back into his cab if you'll organise a crowd of men to push the vehicle back out of the way. We can't start the engine in case of fire.'

As the junior officer set about mustering a group of men to get the lorry out of the way, Jon made his way in close to the crushed car, firmly and ominously wedged under the rear of the tanker, where petrol dripped down over its windscreen. As he peered into the interior, he could make out the form of the driver, a female who was apparently unconscious or dead. When he then turned his attention to the passengers in the rear, he could see two young children. At least one of them was alive, but moving feebly. The parallel between this incident and the accident that had claimed the life of his own wife and children was so blindingly similar that he resolved to ensure the survival of this particular family as though in atonement for his inability to save his own.

By this time, it had taken some twenty men to roll the lorry several yards clear of the car, and as yet no emergency services

Chapter Eleven

vehicle with lifting gear had made an appearance. The clock was still ticking and the possibility of fire breaking out was imminent. Calling the two police officers to his side, who now seemed to accept Jon's authority without question, he outlined his plan. It was a simple one, but one which caused them to gasp with disbelief.

'I'm going to lift the tail end of the tanker a few feet in the air and hold it there while you and some of these men,' he said, indicating the other onlookers, 'pull that car out into the clear, then I'll let it down gently. When I've done that then we can see about getting the driver and passengers out to safety.'

'You must be barmy, mate,' the sergeant blurted out. 'That tanker must weigh all of twenty tonnes fully laden, and you're going to lift it up, on your own, without any tackle or lifting gear, just like that?'

'I can understand your scepticism, sergeant,' Jon said in assurance, 'but it's something we have to try.'

The sergeant turned to his colleague. 'We can only humour him, but try to drag the car out just the same. My missus will never believe this story I know.' As the officers organised the volunteers into position around the crushed car and tanker, Jon stood back a few yards in anticipation of a successful lift. He had every faith in Mort's programming technique on board the spacecraft; now he only required faith in himself.

As he closed his eyes in concentration, he felt his mind connect with Lana, who encouraged him in his mental effort to perform this feat of telekinesis, to lift a huge, twenty tonne tanker. Still with his eyes closed, he raised his arms above his head and visualised the scene, willing the vehicle to rise just a few feet above the crushed remains of the car. After what seemed like a lifetime, he was rewarded by hearing the gasps of astonishment of all the people around him, not least the sergeant, all of whom were watching the tanker lift above the other vehicle. It was the work of only a minute or so to drag the wrecked car completely free and for the sergeant to say loudly, 'You can drop it now, mate. I don't know how you did that; it must be some kind of miracle, but you deserve a medal.'

'Come to think of it, sarge,' the younger constable remarked, 'this guy looks like a miracle worker, doesn't he, with that long white hair and that face; he looks a bit like a biblical prophet, especially when he had his hands raised in the air.'

Jon was smiling in amusement at the remarks made by the police officers, echoed by many of the people who had witnessed the 'miracle.' By now, he was getting used to the references to his physical appearance as a Teacher.

'And now the most important thing is to get the people out of that car,' Jon said. 'There's a woman in the driver's seat and two children in the rear; I would suggest that you take the children out first, sergeant, the driver may not have survived.'

'Right away, sir.' the sergeant said enthusiastically, moving toward the car that had now been pulled well clear of the petrol-soaked area. 'We'll have them out in a jiffy.' But as he pulled at the rear door handle, it became obvious that the crash impact had distorted the body shell, a result of which, he was unable to open the door. 'No good, sir,' he exclaimed, 'it's well and truly stuck. We'll need cutting gear to get the kids out, and we don't know how long it will take the fire service to get here.'

While the danger of fire had temporarily been averted, now that they were clear of the spillage area, Jon was not prepared to allow the children to remain trapped the car. *What would I have done if it had been my family?* he thought. 'If you stand back for a moment, sergeant,' he said quietly but firmly, 'let me see what I can do.' Taking a firm grip on the door handle, he pulled, and such was his strength that the handle partly came away in his hand, leaving the door slightly open, but still jammed. Stepping back, he allowed the two officers the opportunity to prise the door fully open, so it would then be their rescue. But try as they might, all their efforts were to

Chapter Eleven

no avail. Sensing their exasperation, he again asked them to step aside. 'It is badly distorted,' he said by way of consolation. 'Let me try again.'

As he gripped the edge of the door with both hands, he was aware of Lana's voice advising him that one of the emergency services vehicles was not far away, but was having difficulty getting through the crush of vehicles on the motorway. *Thank you, Lana,* he thought, *this will only take a moment, and then I'll be back with you as soon as possible. I've come to the conclusion that I don't like crowds.* This he thought with a laugh of relief. Again, to the amazement of the onlookers, Jon had to exert all his physical strength to pull the door open, peeling it back like the lid on a sardine can, and again he stood back to allow the police officers to remove the children, both of whom were now showing signs of recovery. During these last ten minutes of high drama, the rescuers had been so engrossed with their mission that they had not been aware of the dozens of cameras taking photos of their actions, Jon, in particular, had been the target of most of the lenses, a photogenic hero to most of them. In among the crowd, there were a number of professional photographers who were already transmitting their sensational images back to their respective editors. 'Looks like you're going to have your pictures in the papers tomorrow,' said the sergeant, 'which reminds me, I have to make out a report on all this before I go off duty, so what do I call you, sir? I have to have a name.'

Jon calmly turned to the police officer and said, 'My name is Jon, but before you can make out your report, we've still got the driver of the car to attend to, so let's get her out now.' Fortunately, the front door of the vehicle was less difficult to open, and there was no shortage of volunteers to remove the driver, who had sadly died as a result of massive head injuries, again reminding Jon of that other fatal accident only a few months ago. *Yes,* he thought, *only a few months ago, but how my life has changed in that time. I can't relive the past, and I don't know what my future will hold. I do know that*

Chapter Eleven

since my encounter with Jara, Mort and Lana, I am a different man, mentally and physically. My outlook on life is quite different to the Jon Bradburn of old, and even my appearance has changed in those months. How many acquaintances will recognise me when they see all these photographs published? None, I would think.

By this time the fire service vehicles had arrived on the scene, and a senior officer took charge and organised what was left of the clean-up operation. An ambulance and doctor arrived belatedly, and Jon passed the two surviving children into their care. Only then did Jon turn his attention to the police officers. 'What information do you require for your report, sergeant,' he asked.

With a smile of satisfaction, *at last—cooperation,* the officer thought as he pulled out his proverbial little black notebook. 'Well, if we can start with your full name and address, sir,' but got no further because Jon found it impossible to contain his laughter.

'In this situation?' Still smiling with amusement, he laid a hand gently on the officer's shoulder in a friendly gesture. 'Sergeant, my only name is Jon, and that is all I will be known as. My address is in a spacecraft about two thousand feet above your head at this moment, but can be anywhere in this country in minutes if I so choose, or indeed, anywhere in the world within hours.'

Shaking his head in disbelief, the sergeant put his book back in his pocket. 'I said my missus would never believe what has happened to me today; good job it will all be reported in the newspapers, otherwise my superiors won't believe it either.' Then he added as an afterthought, 'Just as well I'm retiring in a couple of years.'

'And now it is time for me to say good-bye, sergeant, constable. Make sure someone takes good care of those children; they may have a lucky father somewhere.' Even as they watched, he suddenly disappeared as he teleported to rejoin Lana, who was aware of everything that happened, as though she was one with Jon.

Chapter Twelve

'Well, did you enjoy yourself down there?' Lana enquired on his return. 'From my point of view, it all looked very chaotic, but I must say that your performance was very impressive.'

'I do feel that I achieved something worthwhile,' Jon replied. 'It gave me the opportunity to try out my newfound powers. My language ability has already been proven to be useful, and no doubt any future contacts will benefit from the personal touch achieved by direct communication rather than by interpreters.'

'That I can believe,' Lana remarked. 'The manner in which you dealt with the hostile crowd in that Arab country, and your command of their language was a decisive factor in dealing with that situation. Although, it has to be said that your command of Mandarin Chinese didn't defuse the Korean incident, but they were at least aware of your presence.'

As Jon sat down in front of the control panel, he took one final look at the viewing screen, noting that the chaos on the motorway below was being dealt with efficiently, and there was now a limited amount of traffic movement. It prompted him to think, *Time for us to be on our way, next stop Washington. Only one other decision, do we make it a fast trip, which means flying outside Earth's atmosphere, or a comparatively slow one, near sea level, which means we have to limit our speed to about two thousand mph because of atmospheric friction.*

Knowing that Lana was aware of his thoughts, he was quite prepared to keep an open mind for her, literally. He asked, 'Are you

Chapter Twelve

in a hurry to get to Washington, Lana, or would you like to make a detour on the way, do something of a sightseeing tour over the Caribbean islands and then up the East Coast of America?'

Lana hesitated before answering. 'Since we haven't been informed of any progress in arranging a meeting with the President of the United States, or for that matter, the UN Assembly, there's no hurry, is there?'

'No,' Jon replied with his usual quiet smile, knowing already what the answer was going to be. 'In which case, you would like to see a little more of this planet before we get engaged in any other serious business, yes?'

'I would definitely opt for the slow flight at low altitude and a view of the islands. I can see from the pictures in your mind that the Caribbean is very much like my own world. Do you think it possible that we could both teleport down to one of the islands, Jon?' As Jon nodded affirmatively, she continued, 'Although I visited Earth on a number of occasions with Captain Jara, it was never considered convenient to land, but having seen the similarity between the Greek islands, and the vision in your mind of the Caribbean islands with my own planet, I have a certain longing to walk freely on your Earth.'

Jon smiled sympathetically, understanding her need to leave the confines of the spaceship, for a young woman to be restricted to such a small craft for—what was it—some two years? She deserved a 'run ashore.'

'Very well, Lana,' he said, leaning over the control console. 'I'll set course for one of the smaller islands where we won't attract unwelcome attention, and then you shall have your wish to walk freely on the beaches of a tropical paradise. You'll be able to feel the sand between your toes and the sun on your face, and to enjoy the taste of freedom for a time, hours, days, possibly even weeks, so long as Earth's gravity doesn't prove too much for you.'

Chapter Twelve

'I am looking forward to my first walk on this island you describe, Jon; it sounds so similar to my own country on Zel.'

'Then here we go,' Jon said with a laugh and adjusted the navigation controls of the ship. 'We will be leaving the shores of England behind in a few minutes, and we will reach the Caribbean islands in about two hours at most, then we will forget all about the problems that have beset this planet, for a short time at least. It will be our private time together.'

Again, Lana experienced that union of minds that caused an inner glow of contentment, something that had never occurred before in her young life.

Once the course had been set on automatic control, there was nothing further for either of them to do. At a speed of two thousand mph and at low altitude, the sea below them was just a blur of grey water. If there had been ships in the area, they were passed unseen. With a final visual check of the instruments and scanner screens to affirm that all was well, they both settled down for the short journey, comfortable in each other's company, but Jon's mind still dwelled on the events relating to the accident on the motorway.

Of course, that raised questions in Lana's mind as well. 'From what I've seen of your special abilities so far, Jon,' she remarked, 'being able to teleport and use your powers of telekinesis, Mort would be gratified to know that your training program has proved to be so successful. You don't appear to have any difficulties teleporting a short distance; it was about two thousand feet to ground level at the motorway, but it remains to be seen how far you can travel in the extreme.'

Noting Jon's questioning look, she added, 'Although it is an ability that all our people have, I've had only the occasional need to use it and then only for short distances, whereas people like Jara and Mort can travel for hundreds of miles so long as they are aware of the coordinates of their destination.'

Chapter Twelve

'I'll have to practice as and when the opportunity arises,' Jon said with a laugh, but with his own curiosity aroused. 'How far can a human teleport compared with the Zellians? Will that ability also be enhanced? I must try.'

Lana continued with her observations of his performance at the scene of the motorway crash. 'When I realised your intention to lift that huge vehicle by means of telekinesis, I must confess that I was every bit as sceptical as the police sergeant. It was a feat even Mort would have found difficult, and that was your first attempt in using your power,' She touched his hand to emphasise her feelings as she said, 'But I was so proud that you were able to perform what appeared to be a miracle before your own people.' The she added 'To what extent can your powers be developed?'

That, of course, was a question that would have to remain unanswered, only time and circumstances would provide the opportunity to demonstrate his enhanced abilities.

When Jon estimated they were approaching the vicinity of the Caribbean islands, he suggested to Lana they climb to a higher altitude to broaden their horizons. Twenty-five miles would suffice, from which height it would be possible to pick out one of the smaller, preferably uninhabited islands, making their choice less prone to unwelcome attention. Whilst scanning the panoramic view below, Lana reduced the speed of the craft and opened the viewport, the better to get direct eye contact with the beauty of so many islands, some large, spreading for miles into the distance, some small, but with signs of habitation, and yet others which from the air appeared no more than a speck on the ocean. It was toward one of these that Jon suggested they make their way, with Lana duly complying since she was now at the helm.

As had been their practice on similar occasions, she brought the craft into position some two thousand feet above ground level and put the craft into 'hover' mode, a position which could be maintained indefinitely. *Just like parking a car,* Jon thought with satisfaction. As

Chapter Twelve

they carefully scanned the small island below for signs of habitation, and tourists or fishermen were always a possibility, they thankfully came to the conclusion that here was an island they could claim as their own. *A Robinson Crusoe retreat,* thought Jon with a smile, but a mind picture lost as far as Lana was concerned. On further scrutiny, they could see beautiful palm-fringed beaches with dazzling white sands meeting the aquamarine blue of the sea, and the changing colours of the waters denoting shallow sandy bottoms or weed beds and rocky outcrops, and further out, in deep water, a darker shade of blue, though with the sun reflecting off the surface, it sparkled like so many liquid diamonds.

'Oh, but this is so beautiful,' Lana exclaimed. 'I can't wait to feel the sand between my toes; that's how you described it, wasn't it, Jon?'

'It was,' he acknowledged, 'and from what we can see off the island, I believe we'll be safe to land and both enjoy a little shore leave. There won't be any need to teleport down on this occasion.' As the craft was now hovering over a clearing on the ground below, Jon pointed out this convenient 'parking space,' and subsequently, Lana lowered the craft gently to make contact with the ground.

'Its first landfall in two years,' she said quietly as she turned off all power.

After a few moments of silence, of one accord, they rose from their seats and made their way to the exit hatch. Jon activated the control to open the door, allowing Lana to take the first steps out onto the flattened scrub-like area, to experience the warmth of the sun on her face, and the smell of the subtropical vegetation. As he joined her, he said, 'If you want to feel the sand between your toes, Lana, we'll have to go down onto the beach, but I rather think we are overdressed for the occasion. These uniforms we're wearing may be perfectly suitable on board the ship, but out here, I feel stifled.'

Chapter Twelve

To his surprise, not only did Lana agree, but without further comment, she began to peel off her garments. Within minutes, she was standing naked, tall, and proud without any sign of self-consciousness or modesty, for the first time revealing the perfection of her body, slim by earthly standards, but 'perfectly formed' Jon observed appreciatively.

Following Lana's example, but aware that she was watching his every movement, he quickly stripped off his clothing, dropping it on the ground where he stood, conscious of the fact that his tall, muscular physique was a source of pleasure to her. She made no attempt to conceal her thoughts on that score as was evident by the flush on her face. For a moment, they simply stood looking at each other. There was no need for any vocal expression; telepathy eliminated the need for words, and like two magnets, they were drawn together. Just as their minds were bonded together, their bodies were as one.

They spent several hours together on the beach, still in a state of nakedness, a man of Earth and a maiden of another world, yet perfectly suited to each other—two minds, two bodies—in perfect harmony. What their future would hold was something unknown, but as far as Jon and Lana were concerned, they would be together either here on Earth, or somewhere else. The universe was a big place.

Eventually, as the sun began to set in the west and its warmth abated, they both conceded that it was time to get dressed again, and as they did so, Lana commented on the fact that their stock of clean clothing was nearly exhausted. This was not a problem when they were in contact with the mother ship, but now there was a need to replenish their supplies, but where? They would require new uniforms, and if they were to spend any further time outdoors in this subtropical climate, lightweight clothing would be a necessity.

For Jon, the answer to the dilemma was obvious. 'We'll buy some more clothing,' but on reflection, he realised that doing so

Chapter Twelve

raised other problems. 'First of all,' he remarked, 'we have to go into a community with the right type of shops, and I don't think we are going to find an M & S on every street corner or preferably a good tailor. Then secondly, he had a question he put to Lana. 'What do we do for money to buy our clothes?'

'Money? What is money?' she enquired.

Another dilemma, Jon thought. *How do I explain the concept of 'buying' to someone who has lived in a society where everything is provided free of charge, merely for the asking.* 'On Earth, Lana, we still have a fairly primitive system of bartering where if you want a particular commodity, you exchange something of equal value, so that you get what you want, and the other person is also satisfied with what you have given him. You pay him something of value, money, or sometimes valuable minerals such as, gold, silver, or even diamonds. They are all acceptable in all countries the world over.'

Lana smiled in amusement. 'I have seen this kind of behaviour on some of the television broadcasts that we picked up in recent years, but I thought it was only some kind of peculiar game or entertainment that Earth people enjoyed.' As Jon made no immediate reply, she added, 'If we have to buy new clothing, as you suggest, how much money do we need? Or more practically, since we have no money, how much gold, silver or diamonds?'

'That,' Jon replied, equally amused, 'depends on the perceived value of the commodity you wish to buy, and equally the perceived value of whatever you are exchanging.' *This is getting complicated,* he thought, *but here goes.* 'Gold is considered valuable, but it is heavy and bulky to carry around. So is silver, whereas diamonds are the easiest to transport and are considered desirable in all earthly societies, particularly by women,' he added with a laugh.

Lana persisted with her questioning. 'How many diamonds would you need to "buy" the new uniforms or other clothing that we need?'

Chapter Twelve

As it was a serious question, Jon answered gravely, 'One single diamond of good quality and size would normally cover the costs of everything you could carry out of a shop, Lana, and with two or three, you could probably buy the shop as well in this part of the world.'

Now it was Lana's turn to laugh. 'I don't have any gold or silver, but before I left my home, my father gave me a present, some pretty little trinkets that originated on this planet, which he said might be useful if I ever visited here one day. They are diamonds, quite a lot of them too. Would you like me to show them to you?'

Not knowing what to expect, Jon murmured, 'Yes, Lana, let me see these "pretty little trinkets,"' and as she went off to their private quarters. He added under his breath, 'You have no idea what they may be worth, in earthly terms, you could be a millionaire if you have enough of them.' Within minutes, Lana returned, carrying a box of a fair size and obviously quite heavy, which she placed on the control console in front of him, inviting him to open it and look at the contents.

For a few moments, he was speechless, his mind numbed with shock, so much so that Lana was unable to read his mind at that moment. 'Have they any value, Jon, will they be sufficient to exchange for our new clothes?'

As he looked up, he smiled and said, 'These trinkets could buy all the clothes in any shop, even the shop itself, and indeed, any of these islands, lock, stock, and barrel. While I'm no expert, I would say that these stones would fetch billions of dollars on the open market. In earthly terms, Lana, you are one very wealthy lady.'

Not understanding the concept of material wealth, but happy with her union with this man of her choice, her partner, she smiled as she said, 'Our minds and bodies are now as one; if these trinkets will make a difference as to how we can eventually live on this planet, then it is my wish that you take one of them and use it to

Chapter Twelve

"buy" whatever is necessary.' She added with a genuine laugh of amusement, 'Starting with some nice clothes for us both.'

This remark made Jon comment inwardly, *Typical woman.*

There being little point in making protest at the distribution of wealth, *We are both as one now,* Jon reminded himself, he simply pointed out that when the time came, he would only carry one of the diamonds, one of suitable size and quality, to get it valued and exchanged for cash, and that would only be when they arrived at one of the larger islands with a thriving commercial centre. Probably Kingston in Jamaica, rich but corrupt by reputation, but not something he couldn't deal with.

'Very well, Lana, our future financial situation is resolved, so I propose that we close the hatch and take off from our little piece of paradise, a place we will never forget.' This thought was earnestly shared by Lana, of course. 'We will climb to an altitude of twenty miles, out of harm's way, and remain there until we feel the necessity to go shopping.' With that, he assumed control of the craft, and within a few minutes, they were hovering in their chosen position twenty miles above 'their island.' As soon as they were 'on station,' Jon rose from his seat and took Lana firmly by the hand, saying with a gentle smile, 'And now, we have some unfinished business to attend to my dearest.' There was no need to explain. *Telepathy is a wonderful ability,* he thought.

Chapter Thirteen

When he awoke after several hours of refreshing sleep, Jon didn't immediately get out of bed as he would normally have done. For the first time, he and Lana had slept together, and now looking into the face of his still slumbering lover, he noticed her lips were slightly parted, as though about to smile, and her hair was spread out over the pillow, a picture of beauty and serenity. After contemplating whether to wake her or not he decided, *No, let her sleep a little longer, we may have a busy day ahead. I wonder when Lana last went shopping? Never, I suspect. How can anyone go shopping in a society where there is no need to buy anything?* Not wishing to disturb her, he eased himself slowly out of bed and quietly made his way through to the main control room, and after a cursory glance around, he went over to the control console and activated the view window. 'I want to see the sunrise,' he murmured to himself, 'from this altitude, it should be quite a spectacle.'

When he first looked down at the island below, it was barely discernible in the deep blue shadows, contrasting sharply with the sun visible on the eastern horizon and already shining in his face. As he continued to gaze at this daily spectacle of nature, he marvelled at the speed of the rising sun in these latitudes and how the shadows receded to reveal the landscape below, slightly obscured by a dense morning haze. But even as he watched, the air became clearer, and his view improved to the point where the shoreline of the island was clearly defined with a calm sea lapping on the shore. He could see the crystalline white sands where he and Lana had spent those

Chapter Thirteen

wonderful hours together, where they had experienced a merging of minds and bodies, where they had become as one.

Even as he recalled the events of yesterday, he felt the welcome intrusion of Lana's mind as she shared the memory and was aware of her arms encircling his body and her gentle kiss on his shoulder. 'We could spend another day on the beach if you wish, Jon,' she murmured as she turned him toward her, 'I rather liked the feeling of the sand between my toes,' she added with a giggle, 'and everything else.'

'That's a very tempting proposition, Lana, but we have much to do,' he replied. 'Don't forget we have to go shopping; I think it will have to be Kingston, since it's the biggest town in Jamaica. We should be able to buy whatever we need in the way of clothes,' and he added with a grin, 'and anything else that may take your fancy.'

Feeling slightly disappointed that it was to be business before pleasure, Lana pouted in a very earthly woman way. *But very becoming,* Jon thought.

While she said, 'Well, after we have dressed in our old clothes and have had breakfast, you'll have to look at the diamonds again. Select one that you think will cover the cost of our shopping expedition and then make our way to Jamaica. It won't take long to reach that island, will it? We can already see it on the horizon,' she said, pointing out of the viewport.

'Only a few minutes, Lana, but we will remain at our present altitude of twenty miles. That's well above the ceiling height of any commercial jetliners, their maximum is about forty thousand feet, whereas we will remain at almost one hundred six thousand feet, well into the stratosphere and unlikely to be visible to observers on the ground, not even a speck in the sky.'

'But first we must get dressed and have breakfast,' Lana said being practical. 'Then I'll bring our box of trinkets through for you to make your selection before assuming our position above Kingston.'

Chapter Thirteen

It was several hours before they were ready to make the short flight. Breakfast was a simple business, routine, but getting dressed was another matter. Lana took great delight in helping Jon with his tight-fitting uniform, pulling and stretching the garments until they were a snug fit over his muscular frame, and she insisted on brushing his hair, which was still a source of wonder to her. 'It's so bright and shiny; it glows as though the sun was permanently reflecting from it,' she said. Of course, Jon felt compelled to assist Lana with her dressing difficulties.

Eventually, with the large box of diamonds again resting on the control console, Jon opened it, and as before, he gazed in wonder at the display of unimaginable wealth before him, *earthly wealth,* he reminded himself. When he asked Lana how her father had amassed this huge collection of stones, all beautifully cut and polished, she was unable to give him any answer, other than that they had originated here on Earth, but from what time was another question. 'My father was a commander of a mother ship and as such travelled many different galaxies using the timeline technology. I believe Captain Jara explained that to you—where the time and space lines are drawn together, contracting not only time, but distance—and in so doing, passing through space faster than the speed of light. It's a necessity when you consider that it takes light years, centuries, to travel between the stars, and even with our prolonged life, space travel would not be possible.'

'Our people have been in possession of this technology for millions of Earth years,' she continued, 'and have been able to monitor the progression of the human race from his earliest beginnings.'

'Since we came down out of the trees,' Jon interrupted with a laugh.

'Yes,' Lana agreed, also laughing. 'And we introduced Teachers to help them progress and quite a bit of genetic engineering as we told you before. Eventually, modern man evolved into his present

Chapter Thirteen

form, but even so we have provided Teachers, trained by us to help the human race achieve its destiny, and again, Jon, we have provided a Saviour to prevent your people from destroying themselves and the planet and also, you.'

'In which case,' Jon replied, still with a smile on his face, 'I will do whatever I can to bring order out of the chaos the world finds itself in, but first things first.' He pulled one of the diamonds out of the box, not a particularly big one, since there were far bigger ones to choose from, but one that caught his eye as its many facets reflected the light of the sun probing into the interior of their craft. He held it delicately between finger and thumb and raised it to eye level, the better to appraise its beauty. 'Well, if its sparkle is anything to go by, this stone will cause a bit of excitement for one of Kingston's diamond merchants, if we can find the right one.'

At this point, Lana expressed her anxiety at the prospect of not only landing on the planet for the purpose of the shopping trip, but the means of getting there, to teleport. 'Although it's only twenty miles, that's more than I've ever done before. On previous occasions, it was always at ground level, and then only for the fun of it, but this is for real, and I'm scared, Jon.'

Perhaps it was due to his training and indoctrination programming, but to Jon, teleporting short or long distances was not significantly different, although he was still curious as to how far he personally could travel.

'So long as we check the coordinates of our intended destination, either visually or with our instruments beforehand, in order to ascertain that we are not likely to materialise with another object in the way, there should be no problem.' He paused while he gave Lana a sympathetic hug. Fear of the unknown was a very human trait and for the very young of the Zellian people, apparently.

'I have a plan in mind, Lana, that could give you more confidence when we teleport down to Earth level for the first time,' Jon said.

Chapter Thirteen

She looked dubious as she replied, 'What can give me confidence to do something I'm afraid of?'

Jon answered reassuringly, 'When we are over Kingston, I will scan the area below to ensure that we don't frighten the life out of any of the locals by suddenly appearing out of the blue. I remember what happened when I did that in the president's office.' He smiled briefly at the recollection.

'It's not the locals I'm concerned for,' Lana retorted. 'It's my own fear of teleporting from this height.' To emphasise the point, she went over to the open viewpoint. 'Looking down there, I can't even see the ground.' As Jon joined her to appreciate her prospective, the heat of the day had increased the haze over the small island below, rendering it invisible to normal eye contact, but not, of course, to the ship's instruments.

Again encircling her with his arms to allay her fears, he said, 'My plan, my dear, is that we will teleport together, as one.' By way of demonstration, he held her a little more firmly. 'Like this, I'm sure that my power alone will be sufficient to transport us both.'

In protest, Lana reminded Jon of the occasion when he had been 'found' on the lonely road in Scotland. 'On that occasion, the combined powers of Jara and Mort couldn't teleport you to the ship; I had to land the craft to bring you aboard.' Then smiling, she continued, 'But I have every confidence in your enhanced abilities, and I look forward to being as one again.' This she said in a provocative manner, and Jon was very much aware that she was not referring to the manner of teleporting. Having decided to act 'on the plan,' Jon sat at the instrument console to scan the area below while Lana piloted the craft for the few minutes' flight to bring them directly above the city of Kingston, which, as expected, was slightly obscured by the heat haze at sea level and some cloud over the mountains. Looking down at the tropical forests and imagining the rivers running their courses down to the sea, Jon commented, 'And this is Jamaica, the Jewel of the Caribbean.'

Chapter Thirteen

While Lana maintained their 'anonymous' altitude, Jon continued to do an instrument scan for a suitable coordinate for their proposed landing, not too far from the main commercial centre, but not a position likely to pose a problem for themselves. 'I've never been to this part of the world before, Lana,' he confided, 'so you are as wise as I am as to what to expect down there,' he said while inclining his head to the scanner screen. 'What I'm looking for is an open space, a plaza or small parkland with not too many people about, then having fixed the coordinate in my mind, we will be ready to go.'

'And what about getting back?' Lana asked anxiously. 'Do we need to find the same spot to teleport back to the ship?'

'No,' Jon hastened to assure her. 'In an emergency situation, we can return immediately, whatever our location at the time, but we don't want people to be aware that we can do a disappearing act whenever we want; we must keep some tricks up our sleeves.'

'Is that another of your funny metaphors, Jon? English is a peculiar language.'

In his mind, Jon could only agree.

After some ten minutes of careful scrutiny, a suitable location for their arrival in Kingston was decided on, and as Jon indicated the chosen position, Lana reminded him, 'Wrap the diamond in something suitable for safety and wear your force field belt, and I'll do the same.'

With a final check around the bridge of the ship, which would remain in its position above the city for years if they chose not to return, Jon smiled as he again wrapped his arms around Lana. 'Are you ready?' he asked gently. As she nodded affirmatively, he said, 'Together as one,' and before Lana had time to reply, she found herself looking around a small plaza, their arrival as yet unnoticed by several people in the area.

Chapter Thirteen

'You can let go now, Lana,' Jon exclaimed with a laugh. 'We're here in downtown Kingston, although I've no idea where to go exactly never having visited Jamaica before.'

Having recovered from the sudden transfer from ship to shore, 'Which wasn't so bad,' she decided, Lana still held onto Jon's hand for reassurance. 'Then finding our way around and all the new places will be an enjoyable experience,' she said contentedly.

Chapter Fourteen

Their sudden arrival in the plaza had gone unnoticed, but their presence was something different. In a town of predominantly black people, a man of Jon's stature and appearance was enough to cause people to turn and stare, some out of curiosity, and others downright wonder. His above-average height was in itself not all that unusual in Jamaica, as there were plenty in the local population who exceeded six feet in height, but not of his physique, accentuated by his tight-fitting uniform, and of course, his hair. As Lana had commented earlier, it glowed a bright silver normally, but now with the sun beating down on his bare head, it was like a beacon, attracting all eyes in his direction. Those who chose to look at his face had cause to wonder at the expression of calm and serenity and the hint of a smile playing about his lips as he found himself scanning and reading their minds. *No, I'm not some kind of angel. I'm here for a purpose.*

Lana too was the subject of many admiring glances, both from the males and many envious women. Her tall slender figure, quite unattainable to the majority of her counterparts on Earth, and the unique beauty of her features, both lent an air of mystique to everyone who gazed at her. Where had they seen such a beautiful woman before?

Aware that they were causing quite a stir in this quiet area, Jon grasped Lana's hand a little more firmly, as though in protection. 'Let's go into the busier commercial area where we might blend in a little more easily.'

Chapter Fourteen

Mentally, Lana laughed. *Do you think that is possible, Jon? We are both of an appearance that could only be described as 'different.' If you were to suggest to these people that we belonged to an alien culture, they would readily believe you; just read their minds.*

As they continued through the throngs of people, they came to what appeared to be the older part of town, a blend of smart shops and cafes and bars, but still crowded with many locals and others who undoubtedly were tourists. 'I believe that this old part of town was the original Port of Kingston,' Jon told Lana. 'And it was destroyed by an earthquake more than one hundred years ago, but has since been rebuilt as you can see.'

'Obviously that has long since been forgotten by these people,' Lana replied with a smile of understanding. 'They appear to be a very happy and contented people, even though they do stare,' she added.

'I rather think that is something we will have to accept, Lana,' Jon remarked. 'What would people on your own planet think if you were to take a black man home with you?'

Having pondered the question for a moment, she smiled as she answered, 'What would they think if I take home a man with hair that glows like the sun and the face of an angel?'

Jon laughed at that reply. 'Point taken. But now let us be like any other tourists while we look around. Look for a jeweller or possibly a diamond broker's shop; there is bound to be one here about, I'm sure.'

They continued to stroll around, hand in hand, just like many of the other tourists. They even stopped when Jon asked for and was given freely, two very large ice creams. After explaining to Lana that it was a special type of food to be consumed in hot weather, and after a demonstration of licking, complete with ice cream on his nose, Lana found that it was indeed 'special,' but it didn't last very long.

Chapter Fourteen

Although they found many distractions on their tour of the commercial district, it wasn't long before Jon spotted a small shop with the name Jacob Bernstein blazoned across its frontage with the added information that said Jacob sold precious metals and gems. 'That looks a likely place, Lana,' Jon declared, 'not too pretentious, and if the name is anything to go by, run by an honest, though sharp, businessman.'

Not having had any dealings with the human race, other than Jon himself, Lana queried his judgement. 'Can you tell from a man's name alone that he is an honest man?'

Not wishing to enter into any discourse on the ethics of humankind generally, Jon simply smiled as he replied, 'No, Lana, but his name implies that he is a Jew, of a certain religious cult, a race of people who benefited from one of your Teachers two thousand years ago, and who, for many hundreds of years, have been renowned for their business acumen. Reputedly, they founded the modern system of banking. It is because of the reputation of his people that I would prefer to do business with him, an honest Jew can be trusted completely.'

'And if he isn't honest, what then?' Lana asked.

'With two of us reading his mind, we will soon know if he is trustworthy, equally, if he is in any way devious or dishonest, we can just politely walk away and find another jewel merchant.' As they were about to enter the premises, Jon quickly scanned the area around them to ensure there were no 'undesirables' in their vicinity. He then gently ushered Lana into the coolness of the interior display area of the shop, with its cabinets of precious jewellery for all to see.

Their attention, however, immediately became focused on the figure of a large elderly man, of portly build and completely bald, or with a shaven head, which was not unusual in these islands, but more importantly, with a smile of welcome on his face. He was appraising these visitors to his premises. *What have we here,* he thought, *two people of distinctive appearance, but so different from each other. They have only one thing in common, a beautiful woman, and yes, a beautiful man.*

Well, this seems a genuine welcome, Jon, Lana thought telepathically. *So far, so good, but let's see how he reacts when you provide the diamond for valuation.*

'Welcome to my humble premises. I am Jacob Bernstein, owner and proprietor in charge of sales, valuations, and everything else.' He then burst out laughing. 'In fact, as you can see, I'm entirely on my own. But what can I do for you? Do you want to buy an engagement ring?' He had already noticed the absence of any ring on the second finger of Lana's left hand. 'Or perhaps a special piece of jewellery to match the beauty of madam?'

His compliments are every bit as genuine as his welcome, Lana. I feel that here we have a man we can trust, thought Jon, *so here goes.* 'Sorry, Mr Bernstein, but we are not buying.' Noting the expression of disappointment on the good Jacob's face, he continued, 'We would like you to give us a valuation on a diamond we wish to sell and ask if you would consider buying it?'

Buying or selling, it's all business, was the thought that went through the merchant's mind, unknowingly shared with his prospective clients. 'Let me have a look at it then; buying or selling, it is always a pleasure to do business.'

I believe you, Jacob, thought Jon as he carefully withdrew the small package from the inside pocket of his tunic. 'This is it.' He spread the cloth out on top of the counter to display the jewel.

At first, there was no reaction from the merchant other than a sharp intake of breath as he realised that this was possibly an exceptional gem. For a few moments, he stood with his hands wide apart, as though he was preparing to scoop the cloth and jewel up in his embrace, such was his obvious pleasure at this first sight of the diamond.

Chapter Fourteen

Suddenly, he breathed out again, visibly relaxing as he reached for his ever-present eyeglass, which he screwed into his eye socket. For a few further seconds, only his heavy breathing could be heard, and Jon and Lana were aware of a mounting excitement in the man. 'Ah moie, ah moie!' they heard him exclaim. Then purring like a big cat, he said 'Beautiful, beautiful.'

'I take it that you approve of our diamond, Mr Bernstein,' Jon eventually asked, knowing that the man was ecstatic, but wanting verbal confirmation.

Lana was also aware of the merchant's enthusiasm for the diamond. Although having a very large box of similar stones in her possession for a number of years had never excited her; they were 'trinkets' as her father had called them.

Jacob used a pair of tweezers to hold the gem up to the light, turning it this way and that to inspect its purity, and he eventually laid it reluctantly down on the counter, back on its cloth. 'I've never seen a diamond of such purity and the manner in which this has been cut. The lapidary responsible must have been a superb craftsmen, none finer.' Then in answer to Jon's question, he said, 'Yes, sir, I more than approve, I congratulate you on your possession of such a valuable piece of merchandise. I'm afraid I have some good news and some bad news for you regarding its value. In my estimation, it is worth at the very least one million on the open market, and if anyone were to offer you less, they would be trying to rip you off.'

'That is indeed good news, Mr Bernstein,' Jon declared. He had never expected such a valuation on a single diamond. 'Who would be prepared to buy it?'

Sadly, Jacob shook his head. 'And that is the bad news, my friend. Look around at my shop; it is small and generates a comfortable living for me and my family. While it would be a dream come true for me to possess such a gem, I could not raise that kind of money at short notice; maybe in a week or two perhaps, but I take it you are tourists in need of the money very quickly?'

'Something like that,' Jon agreed. 'We had hoped to make the sale and do some shopping in Kingston before moving on to our next destination, possibly the States.' Then still feeling disappointed, he asked, 'Do you know of any other merchant who might be able to afford to buy this stone and pay cash up front?'

Jacob pondered only for a moment. 'Yes, Turner. He is a big-time importer of precious jewels, gold, and silver, and he deals with the richest tourists and people on the island, but he . . . ." Jacob continued with a note of caution in his voice, 'is a hard man by reputation and has been known to use dubious tactics to get whatever he wants.'

Both Lana and Jon could see from the Jew's mind what he meant by 'dubious tactics.' 'You mean he can be dishonest and violent,' Jon said bluntly.

'You catch on quickly, my friend,' Jacob replied, 'but he is also the only one in Kingston who could pay $1 million over the counter without batting an eyelid, but he'll need to be handled very carefully.'

Forewarned is forearmed, Jon thought, and a picture went through his mind of the possible danger facing them if they had to deal with this Turner person.

Lana, as ever, was in tune with his mind and thought in reply, *I'm sure we can both 'handle' this violent man quite easily, Jon. Being a telepath makes his intentions as easy to anticipate as reading a book; besides, if we want to go shopping, we need the money.* This she added with a mental laugh.

'Very well, Mr Bernstein, we will heed your advice and approach this Mr Turner with caution,' Jon said gravely, 'and with your personal valuation of the diamond in mind. We'll see what he has to offer, but Turner will find that he is bargaining with a man who knows his opponent's mind, like in a game of poker,' he said by

Chapter Fourteen

way of clarification. He did not wish to tell the whole truth about the telepathy.

'You know, you have the advantage of me,' the elderly merchant said. 'My name is above the shop, but you never introduced yourselves, and I always like to know the people I'm dealing with, even when I'm not in a position to buy,' he added with a genial laugh.

Nodding with approval, Lana answered for them both. 'This is Jon,' she said, touching his arm gently. 'You will undoubtedly hear more of him in the years to come, and I am Lana, who will always be with him.' She almost added, *for the next five hundred years*, but thought, *That you wouldn't believe.*

As Jacob escorted them to the door, he made a suggestion or proposal that had suddenly come to mind. 'If you don't have any success with Mr Turner or if he tries to rip you off, come back to me again, and I'll try to raise an advance of two hundred thousand dollars on that beautiful diamond.'

As he said it in all sincerity, Lana and Jon smiled and assured him that if their negotiations with the other jeweller proved negative, they would indeed return. The sum mentioned as an advance would be sufficient for their shopping expedition.

Having been informed of the whereabouts of the Turner emporium, only two blocks away, they made their exit from the shop and out into the heat of the afternoon sunshine. Holding hands, they strolled casually for the ten minutes it took to come in sight of Mr Turner's premises, a far larger and prosperous-looking building than Jacob Bernstein's place. As they pushed their way through the door, they were greeted by a large assistant, who looked more like a nightclub bouncer. He was almost as tall as Jon, but not as muscular, and was very fat and abrupt in manner. 'What yo folks wantin',' he said. 'If it's business, I'll get the boss.'

Chapter Fourteen

'It's business,' Jon calmly assured him. 'We were advised to ask for Mr Turner personally.'

Apparently satisfied with that explanation, although curious about the nature of their business, the man turned away without further question since it wasn't part of his duties to be nosy. 'I'll get him,' he said, and walked toward a door that was partly concealed in a corner of the shop.

As they waited for Mr Turner, Lana took hold of Jon's arm. 'I didn't like what was going through that man's mind; he is of low intelligence, a brute.'

'Yes, I could see his thoughts regarding us, but you in particular, Lana,' Jon replied. 'If he were to step out of line in any way . . .' He didn't finish what he was about to say, but Lana could read his mind also and nodded approvingly.

It was several minutes before the owner made his appearance, keeping them waiting intentionally, it appeared, which was probably something he always did with potential clients or customers. As Turner came toward them with a hand outstretched in a pseudo-friendly greeting, he was unaware of the mental scrutiny of this beautiful woman and her companion who looked into his mind. They knew why he made this delayed appearance; he had remained hidden from view behind a screen while appraising his new clients, or 'victims.'

'Sorry to keep you waiting,' he said with a smile. 'But now that I'm here, what can I do for you?' While he was talking, he continued to look them over, wondering what the nature of their business would be. They didn't look particularly prosperous and were wearing what appeared to be some kind of uniform. *But then,* he thought, *you can never tell from outward appearances; it all depends on if they are buying or selling and how much profit is in it for me.*

Jon then explained that they were in possession of a particularly expensive diamond that they wished to sell, omitting the fact it had

Chapter Fourteen

already been valued by another jeweller, an honest one, and would Mr Turner care to have a look at it, and if interested, would he be prepared to buy the gem for a fair price? He also emphasised that the stone was unique in quality, something not offered for sale every day in Kingston.

Thinking to humour them, *I buy and sell merchandise of quality every day,* he thought. 'If you would care to show me this "unique" diamond, I will let you know if I'm interested. and if it's worth buying.' As he had done so recently in Jacob's shop, Jon took the small package out of his tunic pocket and laid it out on the table. Turner was already sitting down with his eyeglass ready to examine the gem. *I won't be wasting my time on some nondescript piece of junk,* he thought. While Jon and Lana didn't betray their thoughts on the matter, they were both curious to learn if Turner would prove to be an honest dealer or a crook.

The process of examining the stone was quite unlike that of Jacob Bernstein. There were no exclamations of wonder or delight at the quality of the gem, although there was a noticeable stiffening of the shoulders after a time, when he realised that what he was looking at was truly unique, the quality, purity, and its potential value. As Jon and Lana exchanged their thoughts silently, they agreed that Mr Turner was more than impressed; he wanted the diamond for himself, but was already planning to acquire it at the cheapest possible price.

Eventually, he looked up with a smile on his face for the benefit of his clients, pretending a slight indifference to the purchase, but, of course, not fooling the Teacher who could read his mind like an open book. 'I'm prepared to take this off your hands for three hundred fifty thousand dollars. It's a nice stone, but it needs a little more polishing to realise its full potential,' he said, as though doing them a favour.

Jon and Lana had the same thoughts at that moment. *The man is definitely a crook; he knows that the diamond is worth far more, and*

Chapter Fourteen

that it is also the most perfect stone he has ever handled. They then exchanged glances, as if considering the offer, then both shook their heads slowly in refusal. At the same time, Jon picked up the diamond and casually wrapped it in the cloth and made to turn away as though genuinely disappointed with such a low offer.

'Hold on a moment,' Turner exclaimed. 'Perhaps I could stretch the amount by another fifty thousand, but I'll have to check that I've got that amount of money in the safe.' He made a signal to someone on the other side of the screen, the same one where he himself had inspected his clients. He must have made some prearrangement with some of his 'staff,' as a few seconds later, four of his thugs came bursting into the room with guns in their hands. Judging by the looks on their faces, they were eager to use them, an intimidating sight to most people. But Jon and Lana were not most people. They were telepaths, who had foreseen what Turner intended to do, and as a consequence, they were already prepared to take whatever action might be necessary, but waited for Turner to make his intentions known.

With a confident smile on his face, Turner leaned back in his chair, the master of the situation, he thought. 'I'm a reasonable man, and I've made you a good offer for the merchandise.' He held out his hand and continued, 'So, if you hand over the diamond without any fuss, I might even let you out of here with your money.' But his laugh was not very reassuring, and what was going through his mind was thoughts of murder.

Lana, Jon thought telepathically, *adjust your force field belt to maximum as I do so, now.* Within the confines of the shop, the sudden expansion of their force fields threw Taylor and his henchmen violently back and into the walls with a crushing force, along with all the furniture and the display cabinets. It was all over in a few seconds, and by all appearances, Taylor and his staff were all dead. Killed by something they couldn't even see, a force field, and not a shot had been fired.

Chapter Fourteen

Standing silently in the centre of the room, they surveyed the scene of carnage and destruction. All the furniture and display cabinets were reduced to so much matchwood, and the bodies of Taylor and his henchmen were still held against the walls by the force fields. Jon said calmly, 'We can switch off the force fields now, Lana; they won't be a threat to us or anyone else now.'

They watched with a morbid fascination as the bodies were released from the force fields and slid down to the floor. All life had been driven from them by the impact with the walls and the crushing effect of the force fields. 'That,' Lana exclaimed, 'is the first time that a defence mechanism has been used in aggression and very effective it was, too.'

Jon smiled grimly as he nodded in agreement. 'It is something to consider if we should have a similar situation sometime in the future, but . . . .' He again looked at the bodies now lying amid the mangled wreckage of the shop. 'It won't be long before someone comes on the scene and the police are called, so I would suggest that we avoid any confrontation with the law and make our exit.'

'And what do you think the police will conclude when they inspect the bodies and the extent of the damage to the shop? It's not a typical crime scene that I've watched on your terrestrial television, Jon, is it?'

'At first glance, they will probably think that a bomb was responsible for all this damage,' he replied, 'but a reasonably efficient forensic team will soon conclude that no explosives were used. The epicentre of the blast is where we are now standing, but they will never guess what kind of force was responsible for all this damage.'

'And presumably Mr Turner was a well-known businessman in Kingston, and as Jacob Bernstein implied, he had a reputation for what you call shady dealings.'

Jon had to smile at Lana's knowledge of the criminal underworld. 'What kind of TV programmes have you been watching, Lana?' Then

Chapter Fourteen

he added, 'We had better get out of here, or we will be held as witnesses at a crime scene, and that could prove awkward to say the least.'

Making sure they would not bump into any bystanders on the way out, they casually left the premises, closing the door carefully behind them, then, without a further glance, they turned in the direction of Jacob's jewellery shop, reminding each other that they could possibly collect a large sum of money to fund their shopping expedition.

With all thoughts of their encounter with Mr Turner temporarily forgotten, they made their way back through the busy commercial area, stopping from time to time to enter some of the more upmarket premises. It seemed that Lana had a natural eye for quality goods, *Like a child in Wonderland,* Jon thought with a smile, forgetting that Lana was aware of his every thought.

'What is Wonderland, have we been there before?' she asked.

'No, Lana,' he replied, still smiling. 'But when we get the money from Jacob, that's where we will be heading for, shopping to buy whatever you find attractive, anything you like.'

Eventually, they found themselves back at Jacob's premises, and on entering, they found the proprietor standing behind the counter, as though he hadn't moved since they last saw him. But as they entered the shop, he came forward to meet them with a quizzical expression, or was it a hopeful one on his face. 'Did your meeting with Mr Turner prove successful, Jon?' And on receiving a negative shake of the head, he continued, 'I couldn't imagine that man making a realistic offer for the diamond; it wouldn't be in his nature. Some people are born honest, and others?' He gave an expressive shrug of his shoulders, but made no further comment.

Jon and Lana communicated telepathically for a moment. *Shall we tell him what happened? He is an honest man. Can we take him into our confidence as to who we are and our purpose for being here?*

Chapter Fourteen

He will find out eventually, especially after the meeting with the UN Assembly in New York. Having decided that that would be the best course of action for them, Jon faced their newfound friend and said, 'Jacob, you will soon find out that our meeting with Mr Turner proved to be something of a disaster, for him.' Jon hesitated while he searched Jacob's mind for his reaction to that statement, but found only curiosity. 'He tried to cheat us, offering only a fraction of the value of the gem, and when we were about to walk out, he made an increased offer, thinking to detain us, but signalled for some of his bully boys to come to his assistance, thinking to rob us at gunpoint.'

So far, Jacob had listened impassively, but now he felt compelled to ask. 'And this, I take it, was when the disaster occurred, but how and in what way? I take it that Mr Taylor called on several of his men to rob you; that would be his way, but . . . .' He spread his hands wide in a gesture of questioning, 'You are here now, safe and well.'

It was Lana who now decided to inform the merchant of their identity. Their long-term objectives could wait until he had had time to grasp who and what they represented. 'Jacob, when we first entered your shop, you decided that we were somehow different in some way, did you not?'

'Yes, but in the nicest possible way,' he honestly replied. 'I thought you were a most beautiful woman, but with a certain air of mystique about you, and Jon, he is a man of exceptional physique and . . . .' he hesitated and smiled. 'Yes, a man of angelic appearance, the hair, his face, his air of calm composure, together they generate a feeling of trust in the minds of most people you will meet. Pity it didn't work on Mr Taylor,' he added dryly.

'All that may be so, Jacob,' Lana continued, 'but your observations may make it easier for you to believe what I am about to tell you; I am an alien, a being from a different planet.' It was at this point that Lana could read a thought in Jacob's mind that she found difficult to comprehend, *Pull the other one.*

Chapter Fourteen

As she looked at Jon in question, he answered, 'He finds that hard to believe, Lana, understandably.'

'Nevertheless, it is true Jacob,' she smiled in understanding, before adding, 'at this moment, some twenty miles above Kingston, our ship is waiting for our return. Jon is a human being selected by my people to fulfil a certain role, which I won't explain at this moment. But he is endowed with several abilities unique among men. His appearance is a sign of the training he has undergone, but his destiny is linked to the welfare of humanity. Put your trust in him.'

Since Jacob found all this too much to take in, he sat down heavily in a chair. 'How can I believe that you are an alien with your spacecraft, is it a flying saucer somewhere above, and what are these unique abilities that you say Jon is endowed with? His appearance is the only thing I can believe to be true.'

'If I were to give you a demonstration of just one of my abilities, Jacob,' Jon said quietly, 'would that help you to accept what Lana has already told you?' With an affirmative nod of the head, Jacob waited for the proof he required. 'Hold on very tight to your chair,' Jon instructed. He asked Lana to step aside, then remembering the occasion when he had lifted the twenty tonne tanker, he concentrated on Jacob clinging onto his chair, who had no idea what was about to happen.

After a few seconds of mental concentration, the chair, and Jacob, who weighed a 'mere' twenty stone, began to rise slowly but inexorably from the floor until he was about six feet or shoulder high.

When Jacob realised that he was airborne, he let out a yell of alarm. 'Put me down, put me down!'

'Not yet, my friend,' Jon murmured quietly. 'You wanted a demonstration of what I can do, so now you shall have one; besides, I'm quite enjoying this.' Lana too was smiling at the discomfiture of

Chapter Fourteen

the jeweller, but conceded that he had to be convinced of at least one of Jon's abilities, in this case, telekinesis.

'Hold on tight, Jacob, you could be going for a ride,' she called out loudly to make herself heard above the noise he was making.

Jon continued to concentrate on keeping the chair aloft, but then began to make it circle around the room, ever higher, but quite slowly, as he didn't want Jacob to fall from his lofty perch. He persisted with this demonstration for only two or three minutes before relenting, then he gently lowered the chair and its 'passenger' down to the floor again.

This was to the relief of one very heavy Jewish gentleman, who was wailing piteously, 'I believe, I believe.'

After giving Jacob a few minutes to regain his composure, Lana said to him, 'That was just one of Jon's unique abilities that he shares with my people, although his skills exceed all but the most powerful in order to carry out his mission on Earth, but more of that another time perhaps.'

'Yes,' Jon agreed, 'another time. In the meanwhile, you should be aware of what has happened to Mr Turner as a result of his treachery. When he and his gunmen were about to attack us, acting in self-defence and using another of our 'abilities,' we repelled them in a violent, but necessary manner, in the process of which they and the premises were destroyed completely.'

'You shot them,' gasped Jacob in disbelief.

'No,' replied Jon. 'When the police eventually check out Taylor's shop, they will find four dead men who have, in effect, been crushed to death, but not a bullet was fired. I won't try to explain the circumstances.'

'No need,' Jacob said. 'I believe you entirely, self-defence you say, besides,' he added, 'you have probably done this neighbourhood a favour; a lot of people will be able to sleep at night now.'

Chapter Fourteen

'In which case,' Lana politely reminded them, 'we have some business to discuss regarding the sale of a certain diamond, after which, you, Jon, are going to take me shopping.' Even after the shocks of the recent events, even Jacob had to laugh at this matter-of-fact statement.

'That being so,' he remarked, 'I have the two hundred thousand dollars I said would be available for the down payment, if that is a satisfactory price?'

'That will be entirely satisfactory, Jacob, and may I say, it is a pleasure to do business with an honest man.'

This was a compliment which the jeweller knew to be not only complimentary to him, but given in all sincerity. 'In a moment, I will return with the money. I keep it in the safe in the back of the shop,' he said, and he disappeared for a short time, leaving Lana and Jon to themselves.

'Well, it looks as though we will be spending a few hours in the tourist area of the city now,' Jon remarked. 'That's probably where all the best shops are, Lana. This will be your first shopping trip ever, and you will be able to buy anything you want.' Then he added with a smile, 'Just remember, we do have to carry it when we teleport back to the ship.'

Jacob reappeared within a few minutes, carrying a neatly wrapped bundle. 'Not too conspicuous,' he explained, 'but nevertheless, I would suggest that you are discreet when paying for any purchases, as there are many thieves in Kingston, and they are not all shopkeepers,' he said with a laugh.

As Jon handed over his 'small package,' the diamond, he assured Jacob that they would be careful and would not publicly flaunt so much money. In fact, before they left the shop, he thought it would be best if they stowed the cash away on their persons, in the concealed pockets of their tunics.

Chapter Fourteen

As they were making their final preparations for departure, Jacob had one more pertinent question to ask. 'How and where do I contact you to make the final payment on our transaction? I can't phone you or drop a letter in the post, can I?'

'Don't worry about it, Jacob,' Jon said reassuringly. 'It's only eight hundred thousand dollars.' Then with a laugh, he added, 'I'll call you in two weeks' time to come and collect the balance, but in the meanwhile, I must take my lady shopping.' With that, he opened the door to allow Lana to precede him out onto the street, with the friendly farewells of Jacob ringing in their ears, and in their heads as well. He was sincere to the last.

Chapter Fifteen

Having spent more than two hours touring around the downtown shopping area, wandering in and out of the different fashion shops, neither Lana or Jon had made any purchases, and as it became obvious that what was on offer was of no particular interest to them, they conceded that they already had everything that they could possibly need. Jewellery? They already had more wealth tied up in their cache of diamonds on board the ship than they could ever spend. Buy a car? What on earth for? They had the ability to teleport from one location to another, if they wished to do, and as far as the luxury items that would appeal to the normal woman, Lana dismissed them as irrelevant.

The only interest they shared became apparent when they stopped to look into a fashion store, particularly a display of casual wear for men and women. 'As we agreed, Jon,' Lana remarked, 'we do need to replace our uniforms before we go back to the States, especially as you will have to address the UN Assembly, and those garments,' she said, pointing at some display models in the store windows, 'look very similar to our present uniforms, although I doubt they will fit either of us.'

'Not a problem, Lana,' Jon replied. 'I daresay that we can find a tailor or seamstress to make us some outfits. It may take a few days, of course, but if the people here can recommend someone suitable to make several outfits for us, waiting for a few days will give us some time to relax. We could even go back to "our island" while we wait and possibly make contact with the President to find out if a

Chapter Fifteen

meeting has yet been arranged.' He paused before continuing, 'No doubt he has already connected our presence to several incidents that have occurred in the world recently, in particular, the nuclear explosion in the Middle East country that denied having any nuclear capability. I would be interested to hear his comments on that one.'

'Well, all that can wait, Jon,' Lana smilingly replied. 'First we will arrange for our new outfits to be made, and I would suggest that we have them modelled on our present uniforms, since they are practical and comfortable to wear, although a change of colour would not go amiss. I rather like the idea of something more striking for formal occasions, silver or white, such as my father used to wear for the ceremonial functions he had to attend when he was commander of a mother ship.' Noting the look of doubt on Jon's face and the reservations in his mind, she added, 'You will look even more impressive when dressed in something other than our normal everyday uniform; in fact, I will design a new uniform for us both.'

When they approached a supervisory member of the staff regarding their requirements, they were informed that the store employed a seamstress, who was prepared to accept a commission to make the required garments at a price. When Lana implied that the cost was not a relevant factor, they were ushered through to a small, but well-lit workroom to meet the person in question, a small, black lady of a friendly disposition. 'My, but you are big people,' she exclaimed as she eyed them. "It will take a lot of material to cover you two.'

For the next hour, Lana explained exactly what they required as she selected the materials and colours, dress uniforms in white and silver and everyday clothing in a pale grey. With Jon's approval, she also made some sketches of what she envisaged the garments would look like, all of which the seamstress approved with some appreciative murmurs.

The only drawback to the whole transaction was not the price, although Jon privately thought, *these are more like Bond Street,*

Chapter Fifteen

London prices, but time. To complete the order would require some two weeks; after all, they wanted three complete outfits each. Even by commandeering extra help, the seamstress would be hard-pressed to deliver their new uniforms any earlier. The only compromise she could suggest was, 'Why don't I just do one set of the dress uniforms for each of you and one set of your everyday clothes? Those I could have ready within three days, and the remainder of the order will be complete in two weeks' time.'

Jon smiled at this compromise situation and he nodded his agreement to the 'little lady's' suggestion. For Lana's benefit, he thought, *Two days on our island to relax together, to get the sand between your toes, and maybe get in touch with the President again, then in two weeks' time, we can return to Kingston to collect our new uniforms, and also the matter of collecting $800,000 to consider.*

Lana was in complete agreement with every suggestion made by the seamstress, but the 'sand between the toes' and two days of isolation on the island, 'our island' she reminded herself, swayed her decision. 'That will do perfectly,' she said for the benefit of the little lady. The fee required for making the clothes having been agreed, $6000 was paid as a deposit, the balance on collection of the first uniforms in two days' time, a further $4000.

Then came the measuring for the outfits. The seamstress was very efficient, deft and accurate when taking Lana's measurements, jotting down the figures neatly and accurately. But with Jon, *Daft and far from accurate would be a fair description,* thought Lana. Jon agreed in amusement. It seemed that every measurement had to be double checked, giving the little lady the opportunity to run her hands over Jon's fine physique again. *I think this is her 'sand between the toes' moment,* Lana thought, but she was not altogether amused.

Eventually, they were able to leave the shop behind them and continued to walk, hand in hand, until they had reached a secluded spot, clear of other pedestrians and traffic. 'This is where we teleport back to the ship, Lana,' Jon said softly. 'Do you feel confident enough

Chapter Fifteen

to try on your own, or would you rather have my arms around you, we are as one style?'

'I would always prefer you to be holding me,' Lana replied sincerely, but with a contented smile on her face. 'Let us wait until we are back over our island again and at a much lower altitude, then I will teleport solo.'

As Jon readily engulfed her in his arms, holding her firmly to quell any nervousness, he said cheerfully, 'Here goes,' and a moment later, they were back on the familiar control deck or bridge of the spacecraft. The first action on Jon's part was to open the viewport and look down at Kingston twenty miles below, where the first lights were appearing in the streets and homes with the onset of dusk, although at their present altitude, the sun was still well above the horizon. 'Looks peaceful down there now, Lana, doesn't it? I wonder what the police made of the mess in Mr Turner's shop?'

After a moment's reflection, he concluded, 'They probably made the easy decision, gang warfare, and left it at that.'

Lana joined him at the window and contentedly put her arms around him. 'It has been an interesting day. First we met that nice man, Jacob Bernstein, who has proved to be quite a friend, then Mr Taylor, who got his just desserts after his attempt to rob us, then that friendly little seamstress who was determined to ensure that your clothes are going to be a perfect fit.'

Jon grinned as he could see what was going through Lana's mind. It wasn't concern that his uniforms would fit, perfectly or otherwise. Turning away from the viewport, he said teasingly, 'How would you like to measure me up? I'm sure we will fit perfectly together.'

Chapter Sixteen

For the next two days, they alternated their time between the spacecraft and the silver sands of the beach below, with Lana teleporting from an altitude of only one thousand feet for her first attempt. Then as time went by, she increased the distance so that by the time their 'holiday' was over, she was confident enough to teleport from twenty miles, the same distance as would be required when they docked above Kingston on their return trip. Fortunately, they would not be heavily burdened by excessive clothing, but how would their new uniforms look and fit?

On the third day after the 'measuring' appointment with the seamstress, they decided to return to the shop to collect their new uniforms, one for formal occasions and one for daily use. As Lana had commented, the on board cleaning and laundry facilities were somewhat limited compared with those on a mother Ship, adequate for the normal short trips that their type of craft would normally undertake, but as she and Jon were both fastidious about their personal hygiene and appearance, their new clothes would be a welcome addition to their wardrobes.

As they were preparing to make their departure from the ship, Jon made a final check of the communications system for any information regarding world events, much of which was recorded and edited by the computer systems. As yet there had been no contact with the president. 'Presumably it must take time to convene a large-scale meeting of the representatives of the United Nations,' Jon commented, 'but there is no great urgency at the moment.

Chapter Sixteen

Besides, I haven't decided what to say to the delegates. No doubt that will depend on what is happening elsewhere in the world, or what has happened in the recent past.'

Lana too was doing some final preparations, closing the viewport and checking the coordinates for their landing in Kingston. They still had to ensure that they didn't materialise in the middle of a crowd of people. *That would cause some kind of sensation,* she thought with a smile. 'Everything is clear for us to go Jon,' she said confidently. The prospect of teleporting the twenty miles down to ground level was no longer an issue.

There being no need for further delay, Jon took Lana gently by the hand, giving a smile of encouragement. 'Together then, Lana, now.'

Their arrival in Kingston didn't go entirely unnoticed. There was a group of elderly 'townies' sitting nearby, enjoying their favourite pastime, sitting under the trees in the shade, chatting, some still half asleep with their eyes closed. The few who did notice the sudden appearance of the two unusual-looking people were not quite sure if they were still dreaming, and one old gent, probably of some kind of religious inclination, took one sleepy-eyed look at Jon and crossed himself in the belief that he was seeing an angel.'

'Well, that was an enthusiastic reception,' Jon said with a grin. 'I don't know what that old boy would have done if I'd been dressed in my new ceremonial white uniform.'

'In keeping with the quaint religious customs of your people, Jon,' Lana replied in amusement, 'he might have organised an impromptu prayer group, if he could have persuaded his companions to wake up.'

Apart from making a mental note to question Lana about her people's beliefs—did they have a religion, or was that something they had outgrown as an ancient race? Jon merely smiled. Taking Lana again by the hand, they began to walk unhurriedly toward the

Chapter Sixteen

downtown shopping area, stopping occasionally to browse around a shop where the goods on display were of some interest to one or either of them. They generally just enjoyed being together in the midst of the crowds, although they were continually aware of the scrutiny of the passers-by. Lana was head and shoulders taller than most of the women, and Jon, of course, with his silver locks glowing like a beacon in the early morning sun, and his exceptional height and physique, attracted many admiring glances, from the women in particular. *I wonder if the women on my own world would be equally attracted to him,* Lana thought. *But of course they would; perhaps, it is just as well that as a Teacher, Jon must remain here on Earth. Otherwise, I would have a great deal of competition for his affections.*

'Oh, no you wouldn't, Lana.' Jon had unintentionally read her thoughts. 'You will be the only woman for me for the rest of my life, even if I do live to be five hundred years old as Mort forecast.' Lana was quite unabashed that her mind was an open book, and in answer, she squeezed Jon's hand affectionately and did something that no woman on Zel would have done, she kissed Jon gently on the cheek, in public.

As they continued their stroll in the direction of the outfitter's shop, there was one thought uppermost in their minds. Assuming that their uniforms were ready for collection, would they then return immediately to their ship or spend a little more time in Kingston, where there was still plenty for them to see as tourists? They were also feeling the need for a little privacy, to be continually stared at as though they were some kind of celebrities might be considered flattering, by a celebrity, but for them, the novelty of such attention was wearing thin.

There was no difficulty in making the decision; they were two minds with but with one single thought, go back to the ship, and enjoy a little more time together. 'It may be,' Jon said verbally, 'that once we do go back to the White House, there may not be many opportunities for us to be alone. We may be expected to do a little

Chapter Sixteen

socialising with members of government and their families, not to mention delegates of other countries.'

'In which case,' Lana replied, also verbally—normal speech was good practice—'I want you to myself for whatever time may be left before the demands on your presence become too great.'

Jon agreed with a smile. 'First of all, we will collect our new uniforms and make sure they are a good fit, although I think they will be perfect judging by the care the seamstress took in measuring us.'

'Measuring you, you mean,' Lana reminded him. 'It will be interesting to see if she is satisfied with her handiwork.'

A few minutes later, they entered the outfitter's shop, and were instantly recognised as 'the big spenders,' and were ushered into the privacy of the fitting rooms where the seamstress was waiting with a smile of anticipation on her face and two additional assistants. *Or are they spectators,* Jon wondered? Having been greeted enthusiastically, the new garments were produced and laid out on a table for their inspection. Lana checked to ensure that her design changes had been incorporated into the making of the garments, and being satisfied with the end product, the seamstress invited them to try on the uniforms for comfort and fit.

Modesty demanded that initially they enter private cubicles to try on the lower part of the uniforms, which, in effect, were like fairly tight-fitting trousers, of a clinging nature. These were the same design for the everyday uniforms as the ceremonial ones as well, apart from the colour. On being assured that the fit was perfect,—surprise, surprise—the seamstress beamed with satisfaction, but not before pulling and stretching the fabric a little at Jon's waistband. 'Just to make sure there are no puckers or wrinkles,' she said.

Then it was the turn of the tunic part of the ensemble. The neckline of the everyday uniform was modelled on their original

Chapter Sixteen

tunics, of the open square-cut variety, whereas the tunic to be worn for more formal occasions had a collar similar to a military-type uniform. 'Just like my father and other mother ship commanders wear,' Lana assured Jon.

As expected, the quality and fit of their new uniforms was superb, and the staff were congratulated on being capable of completing the first part of the order on time, and that they, Jon and Lana, were confident that their extra uniforms would be ready for delivery as promised. As they stood in the fitting room, with the seamstress and her assistants still fussing around them, pulling and smoothing 'imaginary' wrinkles, Jon thought, *They're giving Lana the full treatment as well.*

Eventually, when there was no further excuse for the hands-on approach, Jon thanked the little woman with a smile, which melted her heart, so she assured other people in the shop later on. He handed over the remainder of the money to complete the transaction and promised that they would return in two weeks' time to collect the other outfits. Being curious as to where Jon and Lana lived, local or at one of the other Caribbean islands, the seamstress enquired if they had a forwarding address. 'In case of any problems,' she said.

Amused to learn from reading her mind that the little lady was slightly infatuated by this 'beautiful man,' Lana was quite sympathetic. 'I'm afraid we will be travelling around quite a bit during the next week or so. We are not likely to be attainable by normal means, so you will have to wait until our next visit to the shop.'

Jon was also amused by what was said, unattainable by normal means. 'Very good, Lana, you are going to be quite a diplomat.'

As they left the premises, carrying the shopping bags provided for their purchases, they happened to pass a newspaper stall with a headline that displayed, 'THE MAFIA IN TOWN.' 'So that is the conclusion the police came up with,' Jon remarked to Lana, briefly

Chapter Sixteen

explaining for her benefit that the Mafia was a worldwide criminal organisation.

'Oh, yes,' Lana blandly replied. 'I've seen them many times on television. Why do you tolerate them?' But Jon didn't even attempt to answer that one.

As on their previous visit to Kingston, they waited until they were no longer observed by any onlookers, then Jon enquired if Lana was ready to teleport back to the ship, complete with their packages. 'No problem now, Jon,' she declared confidently. 'When you're ready.' At that moment, had there been anyone watching, they vanished into thin air, only to materialise twenty miles above in their spaceship, home.

Chapter Seventeen

As the days slipped by, Jon and Lana established a daily routine while waiting for word regarding the meeting in New York at the United Nations building, as promised by the president. 'He may be the most powerful man on Earth,' commented Jon after the first week had passed, 'but he can't command the other nations to do his bidding, not while so many of them possess their own nuclear weapons,' he added grimly. 'And while that situation remains, I doubt that they will listen to anything I have to say, either.'

Having taken part in the reconnaissance of Earth's nuclear installations recently, and being aware of the reason for doing so, Lana enquired, 'When will you begin to decommission their warheads, Jon?'

'I've given the matter some thought over the weeks,' he replied, 'and I've reached the decision to do nothing until I've had the opportunity to address the delegates of all the nations, but . . . .' He smiled sadly. 'I know even now that they will never agree to dispose of their weapons. The nuclear deterrent is seen as the reason that no major power has declared war on a minor nation. The major powers have literally hundreds of warheads each, but how many bombs will it take to commit suicide?'

'So, you will act after your meeting at the UN,' Lana insisted.

Jon pondered the question for only a moment before replying. 'Immediately after the UN meeting, which will end without resolution, believe me, we will simply disappear for as long as it takes to revisit every nuclear site that has already been mapped out

Chapter Seventeen

by the computers. As there will be no need for stealth, we will cover all the designated areas very quickly. It will only take seconds to neutralise the uranium in each bomb, rendering it nothing more than a very expensive firework, and they won't even be aware of it until the time of launching the missile. It will explode within seconds of being fired, causing more damage to the aggressor then the intended victim.' He paused for a moment before continuing, 'At most, I would estimate that we will complete our decommissioning task within two weeks, and only then will I inform all the nations that their precious weapons are useless, and the consequences of attempting to use them will result in danger to themselves.'

'But surely they won't believe your statement, Jon,' Lana exclaimed. 'And what will you do if there are still a few missiles as yet undetected? You could then find yourself in a position of having to defend those who have been stripped of their deterrent.'

'That is true, Lana,' Jon agreed, 'and while we can't be everywhere at the same time, I have an idea where and what countries are most likely to be troublesome.'

'So, what do you intend to do to counteract the military of those countries should they seek to be aggressive?' Lana persisted.

Again Jon smiled as he reminded her, 'Part of my training programme with Mort dealt with the weapons systems on board this craft, weapons of defence and aggression. One of those weapons is a laser-type beam, which we will use to destroy the uranium in the missiles as they lie dormant in their silos, but if any do succeed in being launched, the same beam, but of a higher intensity, will cause them to destruct within the first fifty miles after take-off.'

Lana nodded her understanding, the technology of the spacecraft's weapons systems had been part of her basic training as a cadet, but this could possibly be the first time that she would be involved in the practical application of a destructive weapon. The

Chapter Seventeen

Zellians always tried diplomacy first, and used force only as a last resort, and this was Jon's intention as well.

Having explained his intentions as to how to deal with events after the expected negative outcome of the UN meeting—he was quite sure of his prognosis—he said, 'But enough of the doom and gloom, Lana. We are still on holiday. We should just be relaxing and enjoying our time together, so until we can contact the President again, we will just forget all about the troubles in the world for the time being. In fact, I suggest we go down to the beach for a few hours, get the sand between your toes again, have a swim and top off your tan.' Then he added with a laugh, 'With your dark hair and skin colour, having spent so much time in the sun this week, everyone we meet will think you are of Mediterranean origin, not from the planet Zel.'

Laughingly, she replied, 'And with your silver hair and golden tan, where will they think you are from, Zel or from this very planet?'

It was a question worth considering because Jon had long since determined to play his role as a Teacher, so his country of origin had to be concealed and his true identity kept secret. His masquerade as a citizen of Zel had to continue. *After all,* he thought, *will the heads of governments the world over respect the advice of a mere air traffic controller from Manchester, or will they be more prepared to listen to someone they believe is an extraterrestrial, a member of an ancient and wiser race of beings?* One other aspect to consider regarding his country of origin, while they had been in contact with English-speaking people, that was the chosen language of conversation, and he had no regional Manchester dialect, which had been eliminated during the training programme. The same applied to the other ten languages he had assimilated. He spoke all of them perfectly and without a trace of any foreign accent of any kind, so much so that, if he were in conversation with a Russian diplomat, it could easily be assumed that he had been born and bred in Moscow. So, no one

Chapter Seventeen

would guess his true country of origin, and he had no intention of enlightening them otherwise.

Lana had been following his thoughts telepathically, and she agreed with his decision of concealment, but Jon's suggestion of the day on the beach was now uppermost in her mind. 'I'm ready to go when you are, Jon.' She promptly disappeared, leaving him to teleport immediately after her. 'I quite enjoy these trips to the beach,' she said. 'I love the peace and tranquillity, the sea air, the feeling of the sun on our bodies, and the freedom of not having to wear our uniforms.'

They wandered around the island like a latter day Adam and Eve. 'Of course, it gives you a nice, all-over tan as nature intended,' Jon remarked as he reached out to embrace her.

Lana was, as always, only too willing to experience that 'sand between the toes' feeling, as she now referred to those moments of physical contact, and so their time on the beach passed quickly. They were oblivious to the heat of the sun, the sound of the sea lapping the shore, and the breeze against their naked bodies as their minds fused together in ecstatic embrace, the cares and responsibilities of the Teacher forgotten for the moment.

Chapter Eighteen

It was now almost two weeks since their last visit to Kingston, and there had as yet been no contact with President Cooper or his Secretary of State George Lane. This being so, Jon suggested they return to the outfitter's shop to collect the rest of their uniforms from 'the little lady.' They didn't know her name, and while they were in Kingston, they would also pay a return visit to Jacob Bernstein, a social visit and to collect the outstanding $800,000 from the sale of the diamond. 'Will we be doing any more shopping while we are there, Jon, or just do a little sightseeing?' Lana enquired. She wasn't particularly interested in buying anything; after all, what good would clothing, shoes and handbags be on a spaceship, but she did enjoy mixing with the local people, the vibrant holiday atmosphere, and the colour of Kingston. *And I rather think I would like another ice cream*, she thought.

'And so you shall.' Jon had again picked up her thought wish. 'You can have the biggest ice cream the vendors can provide, so long as I can have the same. One word of caution, though, it won't be advisable to wander around the town with a great deal of money on our persons. We will take enough to fulfil our immediate requirements, but as our clothing is already paid for, we will do our tour of Kingston, probably go down to the harbour area where there is a bit more going on, and have some refreshment.'

'And my ice cream!' Lana interrupted.

Chapter Eighteen

'And your ice cream,' Jon agreed with a laugh. 'Then we will collect our uniforms from the shop, and last of all, give Jacob a visit and hope that he has the cash ready for us.'

'That sounds as though we are going to have a busy day,' Lana remarked, 'but I'm quite looking forward to it.' Having agreed on how they would spend the day, and there being nothing to delay their departure, Lana took over the control of the craft for the few minutes' flight over to Jamaica and their docking station at fifty thousand feet above Kingston. As they had no need to arrive at their destination at any specific time, Lana decided to linger awhile, opening the viewport to get direct eye contact with the scene below, the deep blue of the sea, and the hazy blue of the sky mingling so that it was difficult to know where the horizon was. 'So much like my own world,' she breathed.

Jon had joined her at the window, and knowing how she must feel at being so far from home, he placed a hand gently on her shoulder. 'When the time eventually comes for us to choose where we will settle down to live, that is, when the immediate threat of wars has subsided, we will find a place like this where it will remind you of your home, sunshine, sea, and sand,' he added with a laugh. 'I won't expect you to live in England for long; you would soon lose that gorgeous tan.'

After a time, feeling content with life, but aware that time was going by, they mutually agreed that they should begin the schedule for the day, and as always, when they arrived above Kingston, Jon did a scan of the ground below to determine where they should land or materialise. Lana was by now quite relaxed about teleporting the twenty miles down to the surface, while Jon still had to contain his curiosity as to what distance he could travel. He had heard that Mort and Jara could teleport for hundreds of miles. *My time may come,* he thought, *so long as I know the coordinates beforehand, I would like to try, but I will be patient.*

Chapter Eighteen

Lana moved away from the viewport and into the middle of the flight deck to sit at her control console, and within a few minutes, she had set the coordinates for the short flight to bring them into their docking position above Kingston, Jamaica. In preparation for them both to teleport down to ground level, they stood hand in hand in readiness. 'Shall we go now, Jon?' Lana remarked calmly. He nodded in compliance, and they both focused on their intended point of landing. Moments later, they materialised in a quiet area as they had done before, but this time, there was no group of old townies; just a stray dog that gave a yelp of alarm and ran off with his tail between his legs. They both laughed as the dog retreated. 'I suppose we have that effect on people or dogs,' Jon quipped.

As on their last visit to Kingston, they gradually made their way down to the old part of the town, the harbour area, thronged as usual by locals and tourists alike. Europeans, Americans, and visitors from many of the other islands as well, but in general, they all had something in common, happy smiling faces, a love of life, a sense of well-being. *Wouldn't it be perfect if everyone in the world could live a peaceful existence like this,* Jon thought, *without the Jamaican Mafia,* he added.

Among the colourfully dressed local people, Lana and Jon weren't too conspicuous, especially now that they were so deeply tanned themselves, only the fact that they were so tall attracted attention as they pushed their way through the crowds, and of course, Jon's mane of silver hair gleaming in the sunshine. *I rather think that if I intended to stay in this tropical paradise,* he thought, *I would have to wear a hat.*

'I like you just the way you are.' Lana was quite emphatic. 'No hat.'

'Yes ma'am,' Jon replied, pretending to be submissive, which caused them to burst into laughter and attracted curious stares from the people around them.

Chapter Eighteen

When they arrived at the quayside, they stopped to admire a different kind of ship, a giant cruise liner, which had earlier disgorged many of the passengers, many of whom no doubt were even now mingling with the townspeople. 'That's about the same size as the mother ship that took Jara and Mort away, isn't it, Lana? Even though I actually saw it happen, it's still hard to believe that anything that size could become airborne and fly into space.'

'We have some even bigger interstellar ships than the one you saw that spend many years in space. Some of their voyages last twenty or thirty years at a time. My father did one tour of duty like that during his career.'

Jon was suitably impressed, but didn't envy anyone being cooped up in a ship for such a long time, for years, no matter how big it was. 'Time for that ice cream, Lana,' he said as he spotted a vendor. A few minutes later, they were both walking around with the largest ice cream imaginable. 'I like this kind of food,' Lana exclaimed with a laugh. 'Pity it doesn't last very long.'

'It's the heat of the sun,' Jon said gravely, 'and nothing to do with licking so vigorously!'

Having spent a pleasant hour wandering around the harbour area and older shops, they then made their way back into the more modern shopping area and the outfitters with the intention of collecting the remainder of their order, the two sets of everyday uniforms and another set of dress uniforms each. Everything was ready for them, but the 'little lady' in charge insisted that they try on each garment to ensure a perfect fit.

'It's more than my reputation is worth to let you just walk out without a proper fitting,' she said. So for the next hour, they put on and took off the various garments until the 'Boss Lady' was assured that her customers were fully satisfied. It was only then that she reluctantly escorted them to the door, assuring them that should they pass through Kingston again, she would be only too willing to be of service to them once more. Lana, at least, felt glad to have completed that part of the shopping.

Fortunately, it was only a short distance to the jeweller's shop, and despite being laden with the bulky packages in the heat of the day, they arrived at the premises of Jacob Bernstein in reasonable condition. 'We must have acclimatised,' remarked Jon with a sense of humour when Jacob enquired after their welfare.

'Yes, you have the look of residents of the island about you,' agreed their host as he ushered them into the coolness of the shop.

He invited them to take a seat. 'Make yourselves comfortable while I go and fetch a pitcher of fruit juice to refresh you,' Jacob said with a smile. 'And I'll also bring your money from the safe where it has been for a number of days now.' As he was about to go through the door into the rear of the premises, he turned half round and said, 'I will be glad to have that amount of cash off the premises; it would be quite a haul if I was broken into by the criminal element.' He then disappeared only to return ten minutes later carrying a small briefcase, which he placed carefully on a table in front of them. 'There we are, my dears, the balance of the transaction as agreed, eight hundred thousand dollars—a lot of money for you to carry around, especially in Kingston.' He excused himself once more. 'I will now get your refreshment while you count the money; the briefcase is also yours.'

He tactfully remained in the backroom to give his clients time to check the large sum of money, and so was surprised on his return to find the briefcase still lying on the table where he had left it, and Jon and Lana wandering around the shop, admiring the many pieces of jewellery in the show cabinets. 'Pretty, aren't they,' he said to Lana in particular. 'But you will no doubt be surprised that I have already sold 'your' diamond to a very wealthy lady, a well-known film star, and even now, I'm still working on it, mounting it in a ring as a solitary diamond. Even if I say so myself, when finished, it will be the envy of every woman who sees it, it will be exquisite, and I

Chapter Eighteen

dread to think how much it will cost to insure. But Madame can afford it.'

Jon was surprised that Jacob had managed to find a customer for the diamond so quickly and been commissioned to produce such a valuable piece of jewellery. His shop was not the most pretentious on the island, but presumably, his reputation for honesty was well known.

'I'm curious, Jacob, would you mind showing us your handiwork? It would be nice to see what our diamond looks like in a proper setting.'

Jacob look pleased at the interest shown in his handiwork, the exhibition of his craft, and had no hesitancy in agreeing to show the ring to these valued clients. 'As I said,' he explained, 'it is not yet completely finished, but it is still breathtakingly beautiful, and if you don't mind me telling you, Jon, I've made a handsome profit on the sale. Mr Turner, God rest his soul, will be turning in his grave.' The pious remark was made with a mocking laugh, appreciated by Jon, but the irony of it was lost on Lana.

Once again, Jacob went through into the backroom where he kept his safe, and a few minutes later, he returned with a small presentation box nestled in his hands. Almost reverently, he placed it in front of Lana, knowing that this was something any woman, even a alien woman, would appreciate and invited her to open the box, which she did.

For a moment, there was complete silence, then turning to Jon, Lana gasped and said, 'This is so beautiful. I never imagined that a diamond could look so gorgeous in a ring. The women of my people never wear such decorations, but if they could see this,' and she held the ring above her head to see the light reflecting off the perfect facets of the stone. 'All the women would want one.'

Jon didn't have to probe far into Lana's mind to see that at last, here was something that she really admired, something that she

Chapter Eighteen

desired. A box full of trinkets hadn't appealed to her, but a beautiful stone in an appropriate setting had fired her imagination. She could see herself with such a ring on her finger.

'Would you like such a ring, Lana?' Jon asked gently, already knowing the answer. Her mind was in turmoil with excitement, unusual for Lana, he knew.

'Yes, Jon, I would very much like a ring like this, a ring I would always wear. Yes, yes, yes, I want such a ring!'

With a laugh of genuine merriment, Jon looked at Jacob as he asked, 'Would you make such a ring for Lana, Jacob, my friend?'

'But where would you get such another stone?' he asked. 'This is the first time in my life that I've seen and handled a stone of such perfection. How long will it take to acquire another diamond equal to this?'

Again, Jon was smiling, first of all at the thoughts in Lana's head, and secondly, at the concern Jacob showed about the acquisition of another gem of equal perfection.

'If I were to say to you that I can produce another diamond within the hour,' Jon said casually, 'and that it would be even bigger and better than this one,' he said as he held up Jacob's masterpiece, 'would you agree to making a ring for Lana? You can name your own price for the commission.'

After a moment's stunned silence, Jacob said hoarsely, 'Within the hour, you say; unbelievable. Whenever you can bring me the diamond, I will assess its value and determine the cost for making the ring, but . . .' Shaking his head in amazement, he queried, 'Where can you go in Kingston to bring back a diamond of such value within the hour?'

Jon smiled at Jacob's understandable doubt. 'Did I say in Kingston, Jacob? No, I meant from above, twenty miles above, from our spaceship.'

Chapter Eighteen

Lana could now see what was in Jon's mind and what he intended to do, to teleport back to the ship, select a diamond, a large one, one of even greater beauty and value, and return to Jacob's jewellery shop, all well within the hour, and this he intended to do alone. 'If you prefer to go back to the ship on your own, Jon, may I suggest that you carry all these packages with you,' she said, indicating the results of their shopping expedition. 'I would feel happier if I were empty-handed when I go back, and I will be quite happy to remain here with Jacob and look at some other designs and settings for my own ring, but please, be back within the hour. We've never been parted for so long,' she pleaded wistfully.

'How are you going to get up there?' said Jacob, indicating with a pointed finger at the ceiling. 'Twenty miles is a long distance!'

'Are you ready for another surprise?' Jon said with an amused smile, noting the look of confusion on his friend's face. Lana helped to gather up the bags of clothing, then embracing her with his free arm, Jon said softly, 'I'll be back well within the hour.' Then he was gone, leaving Lana to continue perusing the jewels on display, and Jacob to recover from the shock of seeing a man disappear into thin air.

On his return to the ship, Jon carefully stowed their new uniforms away in their personal lockers, then retrieved the box of diamonds from their stowage space in what had been Lana's quarters, quarters that they now shared. Taking the box through to the bridge or control room, he activated the viewport window; he wanted natural light to determine the purity of whichever stone he selected. Knowing that the quality of every gem in the box was beyond compare, he selected one of the largest stones for the intended ring, one in particular that had caught his eye. As the sunlight passed through it, the many facets of the diamond reflected the light with a prismatic effect, causing the many colours of the spectrum to dance off the surrounding walls, in effect, lighting up the control room with their brilliance.

Chapter Eighteen

'This is the one,' he decided. 'Jacob will be astounded when he sees this one; I'm no expert, but apart from being bigger than the original stone, this one also outshines it in every way, literally.' Having made his selection, he carefully searched for a much smaller stone, one with an equal lustre and purity. When he found a suitable gem, he wrapped the two stones carefully in a cloth for security, placed them in an inside pocket of his tunic, then returned the full box of diamonds to their sleeping quarters. The 'trinkets' were indeed proving useful.

Well, that hasn't taken long, he thought. *I'll be back well within the hour, and I'm looking forward to my reception.* After his customary look around the bridge, he closed the viewport window, made sure he had the correct coordinates in his head for Jacob's premises, and teleported down to ground level.

As Jon materialised in the jewellery shop, Jacob again gasped with surprise, while Lana greeted him with an enthusiastic embrace, despite the fact that he was back well within the hour, only half an hour to be precise. 'That didn't take long, Jacob, did it? Twenty miles up and twenty miles down again, it's called teleporting, and any time in the future, now that we've established your coordinates, we can come straight into your premises at will; no need to even open the door,' he added with a laugh.

'However you decide to come,' Jacob replied shakily, 'you will always be welcome, my dears.'

Trying to contain her impatience, Lana said, 'Did you bring a suitable diamond to make me a beautiful ring, Jon? I've been looking at the first one, and if mine can be as beautiful as that, I'll . . . I'll,' and she didn't know what to say in her excitement.

Smiling in anticipation of the reaction he expected from both Lana and Jacob, Jon carefully withdrew the small bundle from his inside pocket, and cautiously unrolled it only partly to reveal the

Chapter Eighteen

first stone he had selected, the 'rainbow stone' he had privately named it, and was rewarded to hear Jacob gasp in wonder.

'But this is amazing that I should be so privileged to see not one, but two such beautiful diamonds in my lifetime. Ah moie, ah moie.' He then picked the stone up delicately with his tweezers, and with his eyeglass firmly in position, he sat for several minutes scrutinising the gem, giving an occasional sigh of appreciation.

Eventually, he sat back in his chair. 'This stone must be without parallel anywhere in the world, I know many who would commit murder to possess it, excluding Mr Turner, of course,' he added dryly. 'As to valuation,' he hesitated for a long moment, 'priceless, I would be tempted to say, but in the market, everything has a price, and this stone would bring you many millions of dollars at auction. I've never seen anything like it.'

'And can you make a ring with this diamond, with a setting to complement the stone,' Jon enquired softly, but knowing what Jacob was already thinking.

'It would be my privilege to accept such a commission from you, Jon, to work with such a diamond would be a dream come true, but alas, I hesitate to name a price for such a work of art, as this will become.'

This being the expected answer, Jon calmly unrolled the remainder of the bundle on the table to reveal the second, but smaller diamond he had selected, and as Jacob stared at the equally brilliant stone in wonder, Jon again spoke softly. 'Would this be enough to cover the cost of your commission, Jacob? I believe you would appreciate a diamond like this rather than dollars.'

Jacob stuttered in confusion, 'But this is worth far more than my work would entail; it's worth more than I would earn in a year, probably several years.'

'I offer you this as your fee,' Jon continued, 'not only for your skill as a jeweller and craftsman, but for your past honesty and friendship. Tell me, have we got a deal?'

'A deal, how could I refuse?' Jacob said emotionally. 'Lana's ring will be a masterpiece, the envy of the ladies of high society; even royalty will covet such an exquisite stone.' Shaking his head to convince himself that what was happening was real, he continued, 'The other ring will take several more days to complete and be ready for collection by madam, and then I will begin work on this wonderful gem and its equally wonderful setting. I can visualise it already.'

Jon got the impression that Jacob was prepared to enthuse on the perfection of the ring with the rainbow diamond, but he was now intent on their departure and their return to the ship. 'Tell me, Jacob,' he said, 'as we won't be readily available for some time, as we will be travelling the world, when would you suggest that I call on you to collect the ring? There's no hurry, since perfection is not achieved in haste.'

'True, very true,' Jacob agreed. 'I would suggest two months' I can guarantee my work will be completed by then.'

'That would be most satisfactory,' Jon declared. 'I only hope Lana will be patient,' he said, giving her a 'mental' nudge.

'Oh yes.' she agreed. 'It's hardly a lifetime to wait, is it Jon?' Jacob, of course, could not be aware of the implication of that statement from a citizen of the planet Zel.

'In which case, Jacob,' Jon added, 'we will take our leave of you and return to our ship, and may you have many happy hours with your work and good health to enjoy it.'

As Jacob was about to make some reply, he realised that his guests, his friends, were gone.

Chapter Nineteen

It had been several weeks since the departure of Jon on his reconnaissance mission, and the president of the United States and his secretary of state were debating the events unfolding around the world as a result of his various appearances and intervention on at least two occasions. 'Our representative of the alien Zellian people has covered a lot of territory since we last saw him,' said the president, 'and he is making his presence felt in some quarters.'

As secretary of state, George K. Lane was in a position to be aware of any incidents that occurred worldwide on a daily basis, and his reports were duly filed and appeared in the Oval Office as soon as the relevant information could be printed, usually within hours of the event taking place. Such was the case when reports were received regarding the first incident in the Middle East, the attempted assault and stoning of a strange white man who had appeared, 'from who knows where.' After surviving the hostile attack of a large mob, bullets and rocks thrown by the crowd had apparently left him untouched, and he had changed the mood of the people from hostility to one of adoration.

'Sounds as though he simply talked to them awhile, Mr President, as a result of which they were begging him to stay.'

'Yes, George, when I read the report it sounded more like a religious gathering,' Davis Cooper replied. 'Our friend Jon seems to be regarded as some kind of prophet or holy man in that part of the world, no doubt from his ability to appear at will, even in the middle of a crowd, and the fact that he was impervious to a sustained attack

Chapter Nineteen

convinced the mob that he was a figure of divinity.' 'I suppose his appearance, his stature, his hair and his calmness under duress,' George agreed, 'would all support that impression.'

'Well, sir, as secretary of state, I also had a report on an "accidental" explosion in one of the northern Arabic countries, which, for diplomatic reasons, shall remain nameless. But the explosion was violent enough to be recorded by our listening apparatus here in the States, thousands of miles away, some 4.5 on the Richter scale; now that's some accident.'

'Yes, George,' the president replied. 'It was pretty obvious that it was caused by the detonation of a nuclear device, but we can't comment officially as that same country has denied being in possession of any nuclear capability for years. They have always insisted they've only pursued nuclear research for the purpose of energy requirements.'

'Apparently, our roving representative of the planet Zel was in that area at the time of the accident. We've kept track of him by satellite, and I wouldn't be surprised if he were somehow involved. Perhaps the General, as chief of staff, might be better informed, if that were possible.'

In reply, the president inclined his head, 'You mean if Jon could be directly responsible for the detonation from his spaceship?' He paused briefly and then continued. 'If we had access to that kind of technology, it would solve many of our problems.'

'General Clintock would probably say that it was unlikely that Jon was responsible,' commented the secretary of state. 'He would probably blame the incompetence of the scientists for the explosions—you know what he can be like, the military man versus the "Boffins"—give him a few thousand well-equipped men, and he will beat any enemy into submission. The fact that a potentially hostile nation can't control its own weaponry can only be greeted with derision.'

Chapter Nineteen

'Well, you know our favourite general can be difficult at times,' laughed the president, 'but in this case, my bet is that Jon will be able to enlighten us on what actually happened in that area of the Middle East when we see him. Which brings me to the point, George, our request for a meeting of the United Nations was submitted to the General Secretary of the UN several weeks ago; have you any information forthcoming on when that meeting will be convened?'

'Not yet, Mr President,' the secretary of state replied. 'I talked to the people concerned dealing with the proposed assembly, and I am reliably informed that all the relevant nations have been invited to attend a meeting on . . . .' He referred to some notes from his briefcase. 'Oh. Yes, here we are, ten days from today, in fact, but so far not all the representatives have as yet confirmed their attendance.'

President Davis Cooper smiled soberly. 'I have no doubt they will as the various governments become aware of such events as the accidental explosion in the Middle East. Wasn't there something else, an incident over Korea where a UFO was fired upon?'

George confirmed that such an incident had occurred, but that the UFO hadn't retaliated. It had simply allowed the Koreans to expend millions of dollars' worth of missiles to no effect, then had simply flown off. 'The spaceship showed no signs of aggression, so we can assume that it was Jon again on his reconnaissance,' he reported.

'So,' the president continued, 'from these various incidents, which have happened in different parts of the world, and the continuous sightings of the spacecraft,' he smiled as he commented, 'there is no denying the existence of flying saucers now, George, is there?'

'Hardly,' was the reply. 'The craft has been seen by millions of people worldwide, and the military, our own included, have been keeping track of its movements for weeks now. Its movements appear to be haphazard, but it travels at approximately two thousand mph, making frequent stops. When I discussed this with General Clintock, he thought Jon's reconnaissance was a mapping exercise.'

'He could be right,' Davis Cooper conceded, 'but for what purpose?' With a thoughtful expression on his face, he enquired, 'I take it that you are aware of Jon's whereabouts at the present, George, assuming that there our satellites are still tracking him? It might be advantageous to attempt to communicate with him, a radio or television broadcast may establish a link. What do you think?'

'We know exactly where he is, Mr President,' the secretary of state replied. 'He is above a small island in the vicinity of Jamaica; in fact, he has been there for some time now.' He smiled as he commented, 'There's always the possibility that he is awaiting word from us and is having a holiday in the meanwhile.' Then he laughed. 'Many a true word has been spoken in jest.' Unknowingly, he was right.

As a result of the meeting between the president and the secretary of state, it was decided to send out a televised broadcast, repeated daily, for Jon to contact the White House, at his convenience, for a discussion, but they gave no details. As a result, the computers on the spaceship alerted Lana, who was nominally in charge of communications, to the effect that the message had been received and recorded.

'Looks like our holiday could be over for the time being, Lana,' Jon commented. 'Duty calls, but as it doesn't sound as though there is any great urgency, we will have just one more day on our island where no one can distract us from being as one.'

Chapter Twenty

When they returned to Washington, they docked the ship at their usual altitude of twenty miles, well above the level of commercial flights, but intentionally not concealed from military surveillance. Their presence was noted and reported to the president within minutes of their arrival, and his only comment was, 'They got the message.'

Not expecting an immediate visit from the representative of the Zellian people, Davis Cooper summoned his Secretary of State George K. Lane, and his senior General Robert E. Clintock to the Oval Office for a discussion on how to handle the debriefing after the round-the-world surveillance expedition of the spacecraft and its crew. For them, this would be a unique experience, the world's only superpower meeting the representatives, Lana was to be included, of a super race whose intentions were fortunately benign.

No doubt the first item to be discussed would be the result of the surveillance flight. Jon and Lana would have covered all of those areas of the world where nuclear arsenals were known to exist, and other countries suspected of covert activity, as had been proven by the 'accident' in the Middle East. The report from the agency responsible for tracking the spacecraft showed in detail its every movement since it had left the White House on its previous visit, height, speed, direction, all variations and duration of stoppages. They could only marvel at the area covered in a comparatively short time. A similar survey by conventional aircraft would probably have taken months to complete. 'And at great expense to the American

Chapter Twenty

taxpayer,' commented the secretary of state dryly. 'I'm glad we're not paying the fuel bill for this operation. How many thousands of miles has that craft travelled in the last few weeks, and come to think of it, when does it refuel and where?'

Both the president and his general had considered this particular question themselves, but it wasGeneral Clintock who came up with the most feasible answer. 'The spacecraft must be like our own nuclear submarines in some respects; they don't have to return to base in order to refuel every month or so. In fact, all of our most advanced subs can stay at sea for a year at a time, as well as being capable of remaining submerged almost indefinitely. There are certain parallels to be drawn between the spaceship and our subs, don't you think, Mr President?'

Davis Cooper had listened with interest to the comments and views of his two most senior advisers, both of whom he regarded as personal friends and political allies. 'Yes, General, but whereas we know everything there is to know about our subs, we know absolutely nothing about the spaceship other than it can fly faster and further than anything we have on the planet. Regarding its weapons, we know nothing, although we did have a demonstration of its invulnerability when it first appeared over Washington.'

'You mean when that pilot got too close and flew into some kind of force field?' queried the general.

'Exactly,' the president agreed.

'What do you make of this "representative," this Jon,' the president enquired from his secretary of state. 'You're a pretty good judge of character; what do you make of him?'

'Well, Mr President,' George replied, 'he must be a pretty complex person, and his intelligence must be extraordinary. We have yet to learn what he knows about our way of life, but from what I can gather, our radio and TV broadcasts have been picked up by his people for years, some of which have no doubt been educational to

Chapter Twenty

them, but the rest—I dread to think—so much garbage. If I were in his place, I don't think I'd be much impressed by the human race, and yet he does seem genuinely concerned for our welfare.' Turning to the general, he asked, 'How about you, Robert, how would you sum him up?'

Robert E. Clintock was not a politician to mince words, but rather a forceful minded man who had risen to the highest rank in the services by sheer ability and a shrewd mind, who was respected by his peers and all the men in his command, and he was ready to give his judgement. 'I trust him,' he said and left it at that.

'So gentlemen,' the president said quietly, 'when our "friend" decides to contact us, which hopefully won't be too long, he may satisfy our curiosity regarding the events that have taken place in the parts of the world he has visited. He may even enlighten us as to his intentions for the future and this meeting of the United Nations Assembly, which, incidentally, you said George was only about ten days away, right?'

The secretary of state confirmed with a nod of the head, and added, 'That's when the meeting will be, Mr President, but apart from what Jon may want to say, I have no idea what will be on the agenda or who will be attending as yet.'

General Clintock gave a growl. 'I'm glad I won't have to sit and listen to all the bickering and clap trap that that bunch of politicians are likely to come up with. I daresay "our man" will be the only one to have anything of interest to say, even though it is only a weather report for the Middle East,' he added caustically.

The president smiled at his chief of staff's comment. 'Sounds like you've welcomed Jon as a brother-in-arms, Robert, can it be that you not only trust him, but that you like him also?'

'I haven't known him long enough to say I like him, Mr President,' the general replied, but now smiling broadly he added, 'but as I said earlier, I trust him.'

Chapter Twenty

The conversation was all set to go on between the three men when the telephone on the president's desk rang. 'Dammit, I said we were not to be disturbed,' he exploded impatiently, but picked up the phone with a brusque yes.

The telephonist on the switchboard immediately apologised for the interruption. 'Mr President, there is a man called "Jon," he wouldn't give me any other name, he is now on the line, and he assured me that you were waiting for his call. Shall I put him through?'

Davis Cooper put his hand over the phone and turning to his friends, he gasped, 'It's Jon; how the dickens has he got through to my office on my personal line?'

General Clintock grinned in amusement. 'Well, Mr President, as George here said, Jon is a man of extraordinary intelligence and with all the technology at his disposal, so to "hack" our computer systems would be like taking candy off a child.'

The president simply nodded in reply, but took his hand away from the phone to speak, determined to be as natural and calm as possible. 'Jon, I've been waiting to hear from you. We've been following your progress around the world over the last two weeks, and I trust you and your companion are both well?'

There then followed a few minutes of polite small talk culminating in Jon asking, 'When would it be convenient for me to "drop in" and see you?' He laughed at his own pun.

Without any hesitancy, Davis Cooper replied, 'Would ten a.m. tomorrow morning be convenient, Jon?' There was no need to consult with the general or his secretary of state when the president spoke.

Jon immediately accepted, saying, 'That will be fine, Mr President, and I'll be bringing my companion, Lana, with me. She is curious to meet you and your staff, but please, on this occasion, make sure that your security people are not in the room. I don't want any repetition

Chapter Twenty

of my first visit.' He then added, 'I shall arrive precisely at ten a.m.' Then without any further word, he cut off abruptly, leaving the president looking vacantly at the phone.

'Well, that seems to be that,' he said, 'tomorrow morning, all will be revealed,' and he put the phone down. 'I think, my friends, we had better decide what we want to put to Jon regarding his intentions, to ask what an alien culture's interest is in our planet, and not least, to inform him of the meeting of the UN Assembly in New York in ten days' time. So, let's get down to some details, since tomorrow may prove to be an interesting day for us all.'

Chapter Twenty-One

By 9.30 a.m. the following morning, President Davis Cooper, Secretary of State George K. Lane, and General Robert E. Clintock, accompanied by several senior members of the Senate, were assembled in the Oval Office amid an air of expectancy. Rumour had it that a visit from a man from another planet was expected, and they were all aware that such a man existed, since TV reports from the Middle East had shown him being stoned and fired upon, and his miraculous survival, unscathed and apparently unperturbed by the ordeal. Other snippets of information, like the motorway incident in England, were largely put down to hearsay. Anything for a newspaper story was the general opinion.

'Gentlemen.' As the president spoke, the hubbub of conversation in the room died away. 'Gentlemen, you have been summoned to my office this morning to witness a meeting between a representative of an alien culture, whom I am sure you are already aware of from the various media reports.'

There was a muted whisper of comments from the small assembly. 'So, it is all true; this man is for real.'

Expecting some disbelief initially, the president continued unhurried. 'This man will be known only as "Jon." He insists that is how he wishes to be addressed, so apart from being the representative of the people of the planet Zel, he has no distinguishing title, like ambassador for instance.' Davis Cooper carefully scrutinised the faces of the small assembly. Everyone had been known to him personally for a number of years, and they were

Chapter Twenty-One

all good men regardless of their political affiliations, men who could keep a confidence if required to do so. *Although there won't be any secrets where this meeting is concerned,* he thought.

'Jon is scheduled to arrive at precisely at ten a.m., but I called you to my office to brief you as to how he will arrive; it will be unorthodox to say the least.' He again looked around, noting the quizzical expressions on some of the faces. He will teleport into the room as is his normal method of arrival, one of the many abilities possessed by our Zellian representative." Then continue. Any questions, gentlemen?'

One elderly senator sitting at the front of the group raised a hand. 'You mean to tell us that this alien being can gain access to this office, bypass all security at will, and that we can't prevent it?'

'Quite so, Senator,' the president calmly replied. 'From what Jon told us before, being able to teleport is a natural ability among the Zellian people; although some can do it better than others apparently.'

Yet another senator, known for his wit and sense of humour, stood up briefly. 'Being able to jump from place to place by teleporting must save them a lot of money in gas,' and he sat down amid the general laughter of the other people in the room, even General Robert E. Clintock.

The atmosphere in the room was a little more relaxed in readiness for the arrival of 'the representative,' so the president decided to add a little more detail about their visitors. 'One thing in particular. gentlemen,' he began. 'The word alien may conjure up in your minds a picture of the mythical little green men of science fiction, but when you see Jon for the first time, you will realise that he is in every way a perfect specimen, if that is the word to use, of a man. Physically, he is well over six feet tall with a physique like the best of our athletes. The only outstanding difference is he has one thing many of you don't possess . . . .' He smiled gently as he waved a

Chapter Twenty-One

hand in the direction of some of the senators. 'Is an exceptional head of hair, silver in colour, but it appears to shine like a halo. It has to be seen to be appreciated. If he were to be put on TV for the next presidential elections, I'd be out of a job, as all the women in the country would vote for him on his looks alone; he is one handsome guy.' Most of the small audience joined in the general laughter this statement provoked, although some did smile in disbelief, since seeing is believing.

When all was quiet again, the president continued. 'On this occasion, Jon will be accompanied by a female companion, a crew member possibly, a lady whom we have not yet had sight of, so I can't make any comment on her appearance, but if she is anything like Jon, if she does eventually go public, the media will go frantic.' With yet another look at his watch, Davis Cooper gently reminded the assembly that it was now almost 10:00 a.m., time for the visitors to make their appearance, and time for the fainthearted to brace themselves. While they waited for the seconds to tick inexorably away, a hush of expectancy fell on the room. As predicted, one moment they were gazing at the centre of the room, the only clear space, at 'nothing,' and then, precisely on time, Jon and Lana appeared, to a gasp of astonishment from the assembled senators. *Pity this is not being recorded,* some of them mused inwardly. Although it had not been mentioned, everything was indeed being monitored and recorded by several covertly concealed cameras. This was an historic event to be preserved for posterity.

Trying to remain calm and composed to impress the visitors and the senators present, not to mention the hidden cameras, the president welcomed the guests quite simply. 'May I, on behalf of all the people present, my Secretary of State, the senior military General, both of whom you have met before, and these,' he said, indicating the senators, 'the representatives of the people of the United States.' Turning to his audience, he then introduced Jon and Lana, equally simply. 'Gentlemen, this is Jon, the representative of

Chapter Twenty-One

the Zellian people of the planet of the same name, and his companion, Lana, whom none of us have met before, but, observing her obvious beauty enhanced by her Caribbean suntan, will, I am sure, delight everyone she meets in future.'

Old smoothie, the general thought.

Yes, he is. Jon had caught his thoughts, but as he knew that the compliment was well meant and sincere, he simply smiled in acceptance of the welcoming words.

'Thank you, Mr President,' Jon began, 'for receiving us at such short notice. I'm sure that affairs of state must keep you very busy, and the same applies to the senators who have given their time to be present. I hope our discussions will be fruitful.'

More than one of the senators thought, *For an alien, this guy speaks better English than we do, and no accent at all!*

'Not so busy as you appear to have been, Jon,' the president replied with a laugh. 'Ever since your departure from the White House on your last visit,' and he emphasised this for the benefit of the senators. 'We've followed your progress with our tracking satellites and observed exactly where you've visited and the duration of every stop you've made.' As Jon didn't volunteer any information at this point, Davis Cooper continued pleasantly. 'Having circumnavigated the globe with hundreds of stops on the way, some longer than others, and some reported incidents of interest to us, which we hope you will divulge, it appears that you remained in the Caribbean area for the last two weeks before making contact with us again.'

It was no surprise to Jon and Lana to be informed that their every movement and that of the spacecraft had been monitored. It was no more than expected, but the reference to the 'incidents' of interest to the US government was something different. They were not aware that, during the first incident, the stoning and assault on Jon had been televised for all to see on the Arab networks and

Chapter Twenty-One

subsequently relayed to the American agencies. As for the probe into the Korean country, Jon didn't think that was anything to comment on. They had just sat there like the proverbial sitting duck while the military had bombarded them with missiles, which was an expensive and futile exercise and unlikely to have been filmed or televised, especially not by such a secretive government.

'You know from our movements that we have visited all the countries of the world that you suspect of being in possession of nuclear weapons, Mr President,' Jon said.

'We guessed as much,' Davis Cooper affirmed, 'but you seem to have covered a lot of ground in your search. I thought we were aware of all the potential assailants, although the accidental explosion in that one Middle East country was something of a surprise. We thought they were still trying to develop a bomb, not that they had succeeded.' He laughed gently, as did a number of the senators. 'At least they won't try to deny our accusations in future, especially to the UN Assembly.'

'They were in a state of readiness to launch the missile,' Jon informed them. 'We didn't know the intended target, and we didn't wait to see.' He smiled without humour. 'We were responsible for the destruction of their bomb and the manufacturing complex with it.'

With a grave expression on his face, one of the elder statesmen stood up to ask, 'Can it be that you can "take out" a missile before it even leaves its silo, Jon?' On being assured that it was entirely possible to do so, or even after the launch, the senator then asked, 'But what would happen if a dozen missiles were launched simultaneously, which could happen in a real war scenario, what then?'

Jon had to admit that in such an event, many of the missiles would reach their targets, and no doubt the aggressor would have to face retaliation; that was a certainty. And with the number of warheads available, there would be few survivors of a nuclear

Chapter Twenty-One

holocaust. It was then that he informed the president that, as a result of the survey he and Lana had completed, there were many more unsuspected countries in possession of nuclear missiles, probably obtained illegally. 'Is there some kind of black market to purchase these weapons?'

It was the general who growled, 'Bombs or bullets, makes little difference, some countries will starve their own populations in order to buy munitions of whatever kind, just so they can be top dog.'

'And this, Mr President,' Jon declared, 'is why I wish to address the UN Assembly. Every government in the world already knows that the path to self-destruction is assured by the proliferation of atomic weapons, but they won't relinquish their own deterrent for fear of attack, so every country must disarm. That is the message I will bring. Not to do so means living under a continual threat, and one day, some petty dictator will be tempted to unleash the bomb, regardless of the consequences, and so the ultimate war will begin.' As his audience sat in stony silence, most acknowledged in their own minds that everything Jon had said was true, but the questions were, how could every country be persuaded to destroy whatever arsenal they maintained, how long would it take, and the biggest question, how could it be guaranteed that all would comply?

Both Jon and Lana read these questions going through the minds of the various individuals, and the confusion among so few people would be replicated many times over when this same dilemma was presented to the delegates at the UN. *Shall I tell them that I've seen the remains of several planets devastated by nuclear war,* Lana transmitted to Jon telepathically.

No, Lana, he replied sadly. *These poor people and the delegates at the UN meeting will never be able to agree to the unanimous destruction of their weapons, and I doubt that they would believe or even envisage the scale of destruction that a nuclear war can leave. No. I will still attend this meeting and talk to the representatives of the different governments, with little hope of reaching any settlement,*

Chapter Twenty-One

and then we will quietly slip away again on the pretext of doing a little sightseeing, and carry out the neutralising process as we discussed.

But in that case, Lana persisted, *'is it a waste of time to talk to the assembly if you are sure that they won't listen?*

Jon smiled inwardly, but still communicating telepathically, he thought, *Yes, I agree it will be a waste of time talking to them, but the result is that we will be able to render all their weapons useless before they become aware of it, when it is a fait accompli. They will have to accept that the difficult decisions have been made for them, and there's little point in any continued aggression.*

Meanwhile, the president and his advisers were exchanging their personal views on how any negotiations should proceed when the assembly convened in nine days' time. The senators were at a loss as to how to forecast the outcome of such a meeting, to save the world from the destructive actions of humankind. But then, just like a volume of water finding its way to the sea, they opted for the easy option, to take the path of least resistance, to wait and see. The debate and the vote at the UN would determine their future actions, so there was no conclusion or no plan of action proposed, and this from the top men of the most powerful nation on Earth. As Jon stated, *It will be up to us, Lana, one "modified" Earth man and an alien from the planet Zel.*

When it became obvious that there was little point in continuing the meeting with the president and his men, Jon and Lana began to take their leave. The general noted that there was no attempt to shake hands with anyone present, just the hand on heart gesture. *Okay by me*, he thought as he returned this old-world salute, and watched the various senators attempt the same gesture. Some were a little sheepish despite the fact that their own president saluted that way on many public occasions.

Chapter Twenty-One

Having said their farewells to everyone present and assured that they were welcome to 'drop in' any time, Lana and Jon once again stood in the centre of the room. *A handsome couple,* thought George K. Lane. *I must make some social arrangements before the UN meeting.* By this time, they were gone, twenty miles above the White House.

As there was little for them to do while waiting for the UN meeting, and knowing that the trip to New York could be done quite quickly, a leisurely one-hour flight, Jon's mind turned to a question he had thought of sometime before, and a remark Lana had made regarding the peculiar religious beliefs of humankind. They were standing, as they frequently did out of habit now, gazing at the clouds several miles down below, with the landscape around Washington clearly visible, which was a picturesque sight.

'Lana,' he began softly. 'The Zellians are an ancient people. Your history goes back many millions of years, long before humans evolved on Earth. But presumably, your evolutionary path was similar to ours, yes?'

'No,' Lana contradicted, 'the only part you are accurate about is that we, the Zellians, are an ancient race, and that we appear to have evolved to our present level, again, millions of years ago, at least on the physical level. Since then, it is our mental powers that have changed and our way of life. As I said to you some time ago, there is no war in our whole galaxy, we only have a small population due to the fact that the reproduction of our species is intentionally limited to the size of the planet and its natural resources, and there is plenty of food for all, unlike Earth. Here there is starvation, disease, and death in many of the poorer countries, most of which can be contributed to overpopulation.'

As he listened, Jon was forced to concede that she was right. There were simply too many mouths to feed, and insufficient resources to satisfy the needs of the ever-expanding populations, a situation that was destined to be exacerbated, since go forth and multiply was something the human race excelled at.

'And what other evolutionary patterns are different between man and the Zel? I know you did say that when your people first visited this planet, my ancestors were still up in the trees. How long ago was that, and how did we manage to evolve to look so much like your own people, the Zel?'

Lana smiled and tightened her arm around his waist. 'I'm glad your people did evolve to look like us; otherwise, I wouldn't be here like this,' she said, giving him a gentle kiss on the cheek. She then continued her narrative. 'When my ancestors came to this planet some millions of years ago, the most intelligent form of life was a small monkey-like creature, though one in constant danger of extinction because of its size and inability to protect itself from other creatures.' She paused for a moment to convey the picture in her mind of this early species. 'It's possible that the Zellians shared a similar beginning, but extending many millions of years back in time, so far back that we have never found any traces of fossil remains as you have done on Earth. However, the early Zellian visitors to your planet only noted the flora and fauna, but then moved on to visit other planets, only returning at intervals of about every thousand years.

'By coincidence, this was only about once in a lifetime for a Zellian. Apparently, they did this on a number of occasions, but didn't find any sign of the species developing or evolving in any way, so they decided to lend nature a hand. They left a team of biologists, volunteers every one, for a number of years to carry out a series of genetic experiments on the native species, a people who bred and multiplied rapidly, making it easy to note the changes in them and to allow them to establish themselves naturally. After about one hundred years, our scientists withdrew, leaving nature to take its course.'

Chapter Twenty-One

'And that was it?' Jon exclaimed. 'Man then evolved to his present form?'

'Far from it,' Lana replied. 'Initially, the experiment did prove moderately successful, but on subsequent visits, again about one thousand years apart, the scientists carried out further genetic experiments. I believe they transplanted certain Zellian genes into the native species in the belief that this would improve and accelerate their physical size and mental development.'

Again Jon exclaimed, 'And?'

'Sadly no,' Lana continued. 'The creatures hardly changed in size or intellect, so yet another group of scientists persevered with the experiments. For some of them, it was almost a lifetime of commitment, but they began to see an improvement in the species over many generations. Their life spans were short, apparently no more than twenty to twenty-five years, which was again an advantage to the scientific observations being carried out.'

While Jon was tempted to question the progress of 'the species,' his ancestors, he waited for Lana to tell the story in her own time, seeing it as a picture in her mind.

She continued, 'And so the millennia passed, and the visits of the Zellians continued, although their activities had to be restricted to an equatorial region where these creatures were most prolific, but their perseverance was rewarded. It seemed that for a period of a few thousands of years there was no apparent change, then suddenly there was a notable difference in their stature. It was a definite step in their evolution, and many of them began to walk upright for the first time. It was then decided to withdraw from the planet to continue our research elsewhere. There are many other planets similar to Earth, some more advanced than your people are now, Jon, though many others are just emerging from the primordial slime where all life seems to begin.'

'But that's not the end of the story, Lana, I can see that you have much more to tell,' said Jon. 'Humankind had to make much more progress to satisfy those early scientists.'

'Yes,' agreed Lana, 'they still wanted to see early man make progress, since they were now in this stage of "assisted evolution." They were increasing in size and brainpower, so it was decided to embark on a radical form of research.'

'Go on,' said Jon. 'I used to wonder if Darwin's theories had some truth to them, although man's evolution didn't quite fit the pattern.'

Lana paused to scan Jon's mind. 'Darwin's theories? Oh yes. He was one of your latter-day biologists, wasn't he?' Without waiting for confirmation of the statement, she explained the radical research programme. 'The point was reached when, having been involved with humankind's evolution for nearly two million years, man's physique and stature had improved, and he was living longer, so our people set about teaching these early human creatures to make crude tools for hunting, which eventually enabled them to become the top predators on the planet. They taught them how to make clothes to protect themselves from the weather, since the climate was changing very gradually but noticeably, and finally, how to make fire. All these educational elements were introduced under a form of hypnosis, by controlling the mind and inducing the knowledge without these early humans being aware of any influence. When this had the desired effect, it was decided that there was only one more step to take. Over the next two or three hundred years, teams of our biologists began a programme of artificial insemination. They rounded up many of the females in the process, selecting only the healthiest and fittest for their purpose.'

Jon had the feeling that he already knew the answer to his next question. 'Whose sperm did they use for this experiment?'

Chapter Twenty-One

'Their own, of course,' Lana replied. 'That way they could insure that it was pure and uncontaminated and fresh.'

'And was it successful?'

'To a point,' Lana replied. 'As on previous occasions, the initial trials were carried out over a period of time, several generations of the man creatures, and a significant improvement was observed in every aspect of their development. But again, it was decided to leave nature to take its course, so the scientists withdrew. The climatic change by this time was quite noticeable, and the area where they had conducted the experiments was becoming more arid, causing the wildlife to migrate to the north. However, it was decided to wait another million years before returning to Earth to check on the evolution of man, and to observe if the breeding programme had been successful and if the migration had continued.'

'But that would be about the time the last ice age engulfed the planet, so the man creatures were contained within a limited area,' Jon said.

'Yes,' Lana confirmed, 'that was the case, and it also meant that much of the breeding programme had suffered a setback due to inbreeding of the species between the originals and the descendants of the Zellian scientists, so again drastic action was taken.'

'What more could they do?' Jon enquired. 'Further insemination programmes?'

'That was the ultimate solution,' Lana replied. 'But to avoid the possibility of further inbreeding, they selected a fairly small number of the creatures who showed the most advanced physical development and separated them from the main population and moved them to the far north, almost to the fringes of the ice barrier. It was there that the artificial insemination of the females continued. None of the males were allowed to breed.'

'That must have been difficult and frustrating for the males,' Jon commented with a smile.

Chapter Twenty-One

'Yes,' Lana agreed, 'you will have to imagine how that was achieved, but I think the only feasible answer was to sterilise all the adult males for the next few hundreds of years to allow the new stock to develop.'

'And could that be when Cro-Magnon man appeared on the scene, apparently a different species with little in common with his predecessors?'

'Exactly,' Lana agreed with a smile. 'And it was from that moment on that natural evolution was allowed to take its course, with two separate species existing on the planet at the same time—those who were descended from the Zellians, who continued to flourish and multiply, and the humans who could not adapt to a changing world and perished as a result.'

'Well, it is certainly a very interesting story,' Jon concluded. 'I wonder what our ancestors would have become without the intervention of the Zellians. Would we still be swinging from the trees? Would speech and communication have developed?'

'Well, I'm glad that you have developed into the ultimate man,' Lana said, giving Jon an affectionate squeeze, 'even although it has taken five million years and a little more intervention by Jara and Mort to achieve the end result.'

'There is one other question I'd like to ask about the Zellian people.' Jon hesitated, wondering if the question was inappropriate. 'Your people are such an ancient race . . . you made a remark some time ago about our quaint religions . . . do you believe in a divine being, a God, or is that a taboo subject?'

Lana turned to face him, smiled, and said, 'In the millions of years of the history of the Zel people, there has never been any evidence of some kind of controlling force like your people believe, evil or benign, only nature. We believe that everyone has a capacity to live a good life or a wicked one, although much depends on their environment and upbringing. Many of the concepts of your religions

Chapter Twenty-One

are in agreement with our beliefs; it's a pity that humans choose to ignore them.'

She smiled and continued. 'My remark about your quaint religions stems from the fact that humans have existed for some five million years, and in that time, he has worshipped everything from the moon, the sun, to mother nature herself, and it has only been over the last five thousand years, a moment in time, that your modern religions have evolved. Various cultures have had different prophets and messiahs. They have given their gods different names, but from the information given by our Teachers, who visited those cultures as recently as five thousand years ago, the religious beliefs have not necessarily benefited humankind.'

'So, in other words,' Jon said somewhat sadly, 'your people don't believe in or worship any god.'

Sensing his uncertainty, Lana remarked, 'No, we have no such illusions, and our people live happy lives. We have flourished for millions of years and helped to establish civilisations on other worlds and hope to continue our good works long into the future, without relying on imaginary gods, whereas your people, despite having so many gods, are spiralling out of control and heading for destruction. If you can prevent that happening, Jon, will that make you a god in the eyes of your people?'

Although their conversation was of a serious nature, Jon still had to laugh as he replied, 'I don't think so, Lana. On the contrary, there will be many people, politicians and military personnel, in particular, who will try to stop me from destroying their bombs. They represent power, and power makes them feel like gods.' Gazing out of the viewport window, observing the apparent scene of peace and tranquillity below, Jon held Lana a little more tightly to him, murmuring quietly, 'It won't be long; my work will begin soon.'

Chapter Twenty-Two

There were still several days to go before the meeting of the United Nations when Lana intercepted some interesting news on one of the television channels broadcast from Washington, directly below them. She called Jon to listen. 'This sounds as though there is more trouble in the Middle East. Do you think it may cause some political disruption between several countries and affect the forthcoming UN meeting?'

Jon watched the broadcast on the monitor screen and listened to the debate between a presenter and a prominent politician, as it happened, one of the senators whom he had met in the Oval Office. After listening for some ten minutes, he decided that the only coherent facts he was likely to obtain would be from Davis Cooper himself or alternately, the Secretary of State George K. Lane.

'Yes, Lana,' he commented as he turned off the computer monitor. 'This sounds like a situation that could have serious consequences for the political stability in that region. The leaders of that country have denied all knowledge of the existence of a nuclear bomb. Until the "accident" proved otherwise, and now they say they know nothing about the disappearance of one of the top scientists from another country in that region, a nuclear scientist as it happens. A kidnapping was carried out in broad daylight and witnessed by dozens of people.'

Lana had, of course, watched the broadcast herself and commented. 'The fact that the kidnappers were in military uniform speaks for itself, doesn't it?'

Chapter Twenty-Two

Jon agreed, adding, 'But as yet, there is no indication as to where the prisoner has been taken, and the only way of getting to know will be if there are any Secret Service personnel operating in that region.'

'Presumably you would like to get in contact with the president as soon as possible to discuss the matter, Jon?'

'Yes,' he replied. 'If you can break into his private switchboard, as you did before, I'll speak directly to him, and if he is not available, then the secretary of state should have any information relevant to the situation.'

After a few minutes at the communications computer, Lana heard a surprised voice at the end of the line. 'Who's calling and how did you get this restricted number?'

Calmly she replied, 'The President and his number is always available to this caller. His name is Jon, and he requests that he be put in immediate contact with the President wherever he might be, as the call may be of national importance.' Lana could hear a confused murmur of voices as the operator conferred with a colleague, then after a few clicks on the line, she heard the voice of Davis Cooper. She then indicated to Jon that he was through, 'The president, Jon.'

Without any preamble, he said quietly, 'I heard a broadcast on television a short time ago giving details that a scientist has been kidnapped. As he was a nuclear scientist and bearing in mind the country where he has been 'snatched,' is this situation likely to derail any part of the UN meeting?'

Davis Cooper replied, and his tone of voice implied the seriousness of the incident. 'The scientist concerned was the top man in his field, nuclear physics, and if he could be coerced or persuaded to work for this particular government, his knowledge and expertise would be invaluable to them. Tensions in that part of the world are already volatile, and this kidnapping is seen as a

Chapter Twenty-Two

further threat to stability in the region, so we must do everything possible to get him back, short of declaring war.'

'Is there any certainty as to who is responsible for this act?' Jon asked, 'and if so, where the scientist is being held?'

'Yes,' the president replied. 'We are aware of the perpetrators and where they are holding their prisoner. We have already made a demand for his release, but as expected, they deny any involvement in the kidnapping, despite the fact that the people involved are in the uniform of that country. As for the prisoner, their embassy just says, "prisoner what prisoner?"'

'Well, Mr President,' Jon calmly replied, 'they also denied the existence of a nuclear bomb until it exploded "accidentally," so can you believe them on this occasion?'

Davis Cooper could be heard spluttering on the other end of the line. 'I wouldn't believe them if they swore on a stack of Bibles, or copies of the Koran. They are not a regime to be trusted in any way. Our agents in the country in question have infiltrated their Secret Service, and I've no doubt we'll have all the details at our fingertips within hours. The only problem is wherever the scientist is being held, probably a secure house, so getting him out of there will be difficult, even using our special forces, but getting him out of the country may prove to be impossible.'

As he listened, Jon was already formulating a plan, but before he could carry it out, he would need far more information. 'Mr President,' he said, 'spying and espionage are not my speciality, but when you have all the details as to the location of the safe house where the prisoner is being held, it's just possible that I might be able to help, but alone. Sending in a unit of the special forces would be translated as an act of war, further escalating the troubles in that region, am I right?'

'Yes,' the president reluctantly agreed, 'but if we don't get him out now, and they extract any relevant information to help them

Chapter Twenty-Two

build another bomb, we could be in even more trouble in the near future. I appreciate your offer to help, Jon, and I will gladly accept. We must talk as soon as I have all the information you mentioned. Our agents are very reliable and should be contacting us soon. Might I suggest that you call back in about, say, four hours? That should be enough.'

'Very well, Mr President, four hours.' As he broke the connection, Jon turned to Lana. 'Well, you heard the conversation, and you can read me, so you know my intentions already, Lana, so what do you think?'

She looked at him quizzically as she replied with a smile, 'I don't fear for your safety, Jon, but I do fear for the people you will come up against. If they knew what you are capable of, they would hand the prisoner over quietly and run.'

'Let's wait and see, wait and see,' he replied with a grin.

Promptly on time, four hours later, Jon was greeted by the president in a despondent tone of voice. 'Sorry, Jon, but the situation is far more difficult than we imagined. We have located the prisoner and the good news is he is safe and well. The bad news is, and it is very bad news for us, is that instead of being held in one of the usual safe houses, because of the importance of the prisoner, he is being held in a cell at the centre of a military barracks. Not only is it manned by some of their elite guards, but the place is also heavily fortified. I think mission impossible sums it up.'

'It does make it appear a difficult assignment,' Jon replied, 'but I am still prepared to accept the challenge of getting your man out of there. I assure you that whereas a regiment of your best troops would probably fail, a lone operator stands more of a chance, since stealth may achieve more than force.'

'I've heard that before, Jon,' Davis Cooper replied sceptically. 'But the cell in question is in the middle of the jail block, in the centre of the barracks with guards inside and out, just to make it more interesting. Anyway, I couldn't possibly ask you to risk your life by sending you on such a mission, one man against hundreds possibly. No, the odds are too great for success.'

After a moment's hesitation, Jon put a question to the president. 'I take it that your agent has given you full details of this militarily barracks, location, size, defences etc.?' He was assured that all the information had been made available, so he then asked, 'And have you also managed to obtain a detailed plan of the layout of the barracks itself?' Again Jon was assured that not only was that available, but at that very moment, he and General Clintock, with the assistance of George K. Lane, had the map in front of them and after scrutinising it from every angle, their consensus was still the same. In the unlikely event that a task force could get in, they could never get the prisoner out alive.

Not to be deterred by this pessimistic view, after a few moments of deliberation, Jon said, 'If it is convenient for you, Mr President, I would like to see these plans of the barracks and make my own assessment of the situation. Four heads are definitely better than one when it comes to planning an operation like this. If you have no objection, I can be with you in a moment.'

He could hear a voice faintly in the background, presumably the general, saying, 'If this guy can get in and out of the White House without a "by your leave," I can't see why he couldn't get into some crummy barracks.'

Then the president's voice answered. 'But how does he get out with the prisoner?' Then Davis Cooper spoke directly to him on the phone again. 'We are standing by for your arrival, Jon, any time now.'

'They seem to be in some kind of dilemma,' Jon said as he turned to Lana. 'So, if you remain here, I'll drop in again and persuade the President that this rescue mission is possible, but only if I go alone. Do you agree?'

Chapter Twenty-Two

Lana smiled as she replied, 'I can just picture the General sending in dozens of men with guns blazing, but still failing on such a mission, whereas on your own, Jon, you will succeed, of that I am confident.'

Taking her in his arms for a moment, he kissed her gently. 'Now I must go and boost the confidence of the President and his men.' He then stood back from Lana, smiled briefly, and then teleported.

His arrival in the Oval Office was, as always, an event that startled the occupants, even though they had been expecting him. 'Will we ever get used to this?' the president exclaimed with a smile, whereas the general gave his military salute as a greeting.

The secretary of state grinned with pleasure at seeing the big man again, but remained at the table where a number of papers were already on display. 'We have everything ready for you, Jon,' he said as he arranged them in order. Let's hope you can see a way of carrying out this mission successfully.'

Within minutes, all four of them were grouped around the table, and General Clintock, being the military strategist, explained the layout of the site and the location of the prisoner. 'Our man is here. He is isolated from other political prisoners in this small room, the door is permanently open, and he is accompanied at all times by his personal guard. I guess they want to make sure he doesn't try to bump himself off. That is one thing in our favour, since it implies that he is being held against his will, and if you can get as far as the prisoner, at least he should be willing to escape with you given the chance, which is much easier than if you had to drag him along biting and screaming, eh!'

'Will you be able to teleport directly into that room, Jon, or will it be somewhere nearby?' asked George K. Lane. 'We know you can "drop" in here without any trouble, so we assume that you possibly can do the same with the barracks.'

Chapter Twenty-Two

Jon frowned slightly before answering. 'The only drawback in attempting to materialise in such a small room is the possibility of there being more than the prisoner and his guard there at the time. There is a distinct chance that he might be undergoing an interrogation or such, and for me to add to "the party" at short notice is fraught with danger. I believe one of your scientists said something to the effect that, "two material bodies cannot occupy the same space at the same time," Einstein, wasn't it?'

'Probably,' the general grunted.

'So, how many other guards are there likely to be in and around this main central block?' Jon asked. 'And which area would you think suitable for me to teleport into, bearing in mind it would have to be about the same size as this office.'

General Clintock stabbed a position on the diagram with a stubby finger. 'Here. But it's a fair distance from the holding cell, and there's bound to be a strong guard presence, soldiers of the elite guard are just like any others, though. Thinking themselves in a secure environment, I think they could be caught off their guard. That's one point in your favour.'

'And how many others are around the building,' Jon persisted. 'If they think there's trouble inside the building, they'll come rushing in with reinforcements.'

'You sure make it sound tough, Jon,' the general commented. 'That is why we,' he said, indicating his two senior colleagues, 'said that we regarded this as one mission too many. It is too dangerous for a normal task force and certainly too risky for the representative of the Zel.'

In the meanwhile, Jon continued to study the various diagrams and thought of a scenario whereby he would have to deal with a large number of hostile troops. He remembered Lana's comment: 'if they knew what you are capable of, they would run.'

Chapter Twenty-Two

'Tell me, Mr. President, have you anywhere in this country, any installations similar to this?' he said, indicating the foreign barracks. 'Heavily fortified, with hundreds of troops around, and considered impregnable to everything other than a nuclear attack, possibly somewhere that only a madman would dream of trying to break into? If you have, I would suggest that we do an exercise, a dummy run if you like, where I can teleport in, make my way through corridors, simulating conditions that I will probably encounter on my mission. Then finally, I will remove a volunteer prisoner from a room in the complex and teleport out.'

The general drew a deep breath before he spoke. 'Jon,' he said, 'you make it all sound so matter of fact, teleport in, okay. We know you can do that, but from that moment onward, even simulating your progress to the prisoner's room, you are likely to be intercepted by, at the very least, a dozen very angry soldiers spitting "fire and brimstone," or more likely firing automatic weapons at you at close quarters. Then secondly, assuming that you can reach the prisoner, he may be in such a state of panic that you might have to subdue him, almost kidnap him yourself, before you can then teleport out of there.'

Jon smiled in quiet amusement at the general's protestations, natural, of course, for a soldier trained in normal warfare, but this was going to be different. Turning to the president again, he said, 'If I may return to my first question, Mr President, is there a suitable location for this exercise?'

As one, the three other men looked at each other and chorused, 'Fort Knox.' The president added, 'It is the most heavily guarded establishment in the world, much more so than this other barracks that you propose to enter.'

'And you, General,' Jon asked, 'you have some doubt as to my ability to protect myself from the onslaught of the elite guards at close quarters, yes?'

Chapter Twenty-Two

'I certainly do,' the general protested, 'this won't be like going to the movies; this will be the real thing, with bullets coming at you thick and fast and smoke everywhere.'

'Then,' Jon said, again turning to the president for confirmation, 'no doubt you have your security people outside the door?' After a nod of confirmation from him, Jon then said to the general, 'Would you ask three or four of your men to step inside, General, complete with their weapons?'

Robert E. Clintock looked enquiringly at the president who again nodded his head. He was guessed what was about to happen— a demonstration. The general left the room for a few minutes, returning with several uniformed personnel, his own men, who lined up as though on parade.

Jon then walked slowly over to a wall, well out of line with the president and his advisers, and then he turned to the general with an unworried expression on his face. In fact, he was smiling, knowing that the man in question was wondering what was going to happen next. 'And now, General, you asked how I was going to protect myself from the fire of the elite guard. Now for a demonstration, but as we don't want to damage the interior of this lovely room,' he said and gestured with both arms, 'I want your men to aim very carefully at me and fire, once will suffice to prove my point.' *And I may add, by the looks on their faces, and what is in their minds,* he thought, *you may have to be very forceful with your command.* 'It may help if you absolve them of all responsibility in the presence of the President.'

The general shook his head in disbelief, but he was a soldier accustomed to taking orders, *even orders that sound crazy*, he thought. He said to his men, 'You heard what Jon said, aim accurately, try to hit him on the body, since we don't want any shots going wide. Think of the decor,' he said sarcastically. There were four soldiers, hardened veterans of many other conflicts, but this was the strangest order they had ever received, but orders were orders.

Chapter Twenty-Two

Unhurriedly, they all raised their weapons, heavy service weapons, aimed very carefully at the body of this tall giant of a man—how could they miss—and as one, fired.

As the smoke cleared, they were shocked to see their target still standing, seemingly unharmed and quite unperturbed, but were soon brought back to their senses as the general barked an order. 'Right, men, that will be all, dismissed.'

All was quiet in the room while the men filed out through the door, then Robert E. Clintock enquired in an awestruck voice, 'How the hell did you pull that trick, Jon?' Then without waiting for a reply, he raised his hands as though in surrender. 'Okay, okay, I'm convinced you can protect yourself, but how are you going to deal with one very frightened scientist if he struggles to get away? Fear can lend a man extra strength in dangerous circumstances.'

Again Jon smiled, but then in answer enquired, 'How heavy are you, General?'

Clintock looked at the president and the secretary of state in turn, puzzled as to the relevance of the question, but he answered with a grin and perhaps personal satisfaction since he was a big man himself. 'Two hundred and twenty pounds,' he replied.

Jon walked over slowly and deliberately toward the general, took a firm grip on his uniform jacket, and said, while still smiling, 'Now, do you think I'm strong enough to restrain the prisoner?' And with one hand, he raised General E. Clintock at arm's length and well clear of the floor, holding him there effortlessly, and asked again, 'Well, General?'

Not accustomed to being handled like a rag doll, the general spluttered, 'Put me down, dammit, put me down.' But he was visibly shocked at this display of phenomenal strength by the representative of the Zellian people. 'Okay, okay, I believe you,' he said as he straightened his jacket and regained his composure. Then he put his last question, 'And presumably, you intend to teleport out of the

Chapter Twenty-Two

barracks with the scientist in your arms?' He said it a little sarcastically, still smarting from the indignity of being handled like a child.

'You guessed it exactly,' Jon exclaimed with a laugh, 'but that needs to be practised; want to volunteer, General?'

Before General Clintock had time to reply, Jon continued with a smile of inducement, 'Not only will I get you out of Fort Knox, but I will bring you back here to Washington much quicker than in the presidential plane. Now, would you like to volunteer for this key role in the mission?' Noting the look of doubt on the general's face and guessing the reason why, he laughed as he added, 'Don't worry, General, I don't have to pick you up and carry you when we teleport, only embrace you as brothers-in-arms would do.'

'That puts a different perspective on it,' Clintock replied in obvious relief. 'It will be good for the morale of the men to see their leader actively involved in this exercise.'

Jon smiled as he read the general's thoughts. 'Nothing to do with the opportunity of inspecting the inside of an alien spaceship?' Jon then continued, 'One other aspect of this rehearsal for the release of the scientist, General, is that again, I would suggest that we make it as realistic as possible, with live ammunition and smoke, if need be, to deliberately create confusion as may be the case in the real event.'

Robert E. Clintock looked troubled at the thought of how the interior of Fort Knox was going to look after this escapade. 'it may take a little patching up of the decor,' he replied in an attempt at humour. 'The smoke contamination and bullet holes will show where the action has taken place. Which reminds me, will you be armed in any way, and will you return fire on my men?'

'Don't worry, General,' Jon replied. 'I have no need of firearms, you just had a demonstration of my invulnerability in this type of situation, and you can also be assured that I won't intentionally injure any of your men. But I may have to inflict some damage if I

Chapter Twenty-Two

find doors locked that impede my progress; in that case, they will be destroyed.' As Clintock raised an eyebrow in question, Jon continued. 'I won't demonstrate that particular ability in this room, save the decor,' he added with a smile. 'But during the exercise, I won't hesitate to break down a few doors to gain my objective, you.'

'I'm beginning to believe you're a one-man task force, Jon,' exclaimed Clintock. 'In fact, I believe you might just pull off this mission. What do you say, Mr President?'

Davis Cooper smiled as he looked down at the paperwork on his desk, then looked up again as he said, 'The more I see of you and what you are capable of, Jon, the more I believe in this mission. Although I would like to be present when you whisk the general off to your spaceship!'

With the atmosphere of the meeting now decidedly cordial, the secretary of state reminded all of them that they would not have much time before the meeting of the UN. 'This rehearsal will have to be set up for the day after tomorrow, and assuming that all goes well, when will you attempt, no, that is the wrong word, when do you intend to complete your mission, Jon?'

Chapter Twenty-Three

'Within twenty-four hours of returning from Fort Knox,' Jon said gravely, 'the method and purpose of this exercise will have been fully clarified. It isn't so much as to what I can do, for that I already know, but I have never been in a situation where I have been in conflict with so many armed men.' And yet, he smiled before adding, 'I want to see how they will react to a lone intruder in their midst, an intruder against whom they have no defence. Will they continue their aggression or blow the place apart or simply panic.' Turning to the general, he said, 'While you're sitting in your room waiting for me, no doubt you will hear the noise of conflict, gunfire and you will know that I'm getting near, whereas the scientist in question will only have the behaviour of his guards to alert him to any danger.'

'Will it be okay to let the soldiers "guarding" me in that little room know that this is only an exercise?' the general enquired. 'Not for real, otherwise you could be forced to kill them as they try to defend me.'

Jon deliberated only for a moment. 'Yes, General, I have no wish to injure any soldier, and the fact that I have actually reached you, my objective, means that the mission is a success. From that moment on, it will only take a few seconds for us to teleport out of there, but how you explain that to any subsequent enquiry I leave to you.'

George Lane had been listening intently to all the talk of the impending kidnap/rescue mission, and now he asked Jon the question weighing heavily on his mind. 'Do you think you have enough time to complete this visit to Fort Knox and return to

Chapter Twenty-Three

Washington, then fly halfway around the world, release this prisoner, and fly all the way back again, and still be prepared to address the UN Assembly, Jon?'

At the mention of that particular engagement, Jon's thoughts turned to the question of how to arrive at the New York venue. 'Yes, George,' he replied quietly. 'Whereas if this mission were to be carried out using conventional military transportation, it would take a day just fly into the target area, and if it were possible, you would then have to rely on helicopters to get your troops on the ground, which is quite a logistics challenge. The alternative would be an airborne assault.' He smiled as he reminded the secretary, 'But in my case, it will only take about five or six hours to arrive at the rendezvous point, a few minutes to verify what is happening in the barracks below, and then teleport into the building. Only then will I know how many of the enemy I will have to contend with. As to how long it will then take to reach the prisoner, well, our rehearsal at Fort Knox will clarify that question.'

After observing the dubious expressions on their faces and reading their minds, Jon could see that they were confident about the mission itself, but less optimistic about the timing of the campaign and his return to Washington. 'Mr President, gentlemen, let me assure you that I have every confidence that I shall complete the mission and return the prisoner to this very office in plenty of time to address the UN Assembly in New York.' He laughed as he saw the relief on their faces. 'My only question has nothing to do with the recovery mission, but is something much simpler.' Then turning to the president, he asked, 'Not wishing to cause alarm to the delegates or reveal my ability to teleport into any secure area of my choosing, but would you mind if I accompany you and your entourage when you travel to New York? I will have Lana by my side, of course. It will be quite an experience for her to travel in a car, her first time.' He didn't mention his own experience of the past.

Chapter Twenty-Three

However, George Lane also wondered if or when Jon had last been in a car.

'It will be our pleasure to have you accompany us, Jon,' the president replied. 'We will fly up to New York and then travel by car to the UN building, although you will find the journey somewhat tedious. How long would it take if you went in your own craft?'

Jon grinned at the thought of the time comparison. 'No more than twenty minutes, Mr President, and that would be quite a leisurely trip.'

As ever, the general was interested in the potential of any military equipment, in this case, the spaceship, and took the opportunity to enquire, 'And what speed does your ship attain on such a short trip, and what is its maximum speed?'

Knowing that his previous flight on the reconnaissance flight had been tracked from start to finish, and also that the flight from Earth to the moon after he had been picked up in Scotland would likewise have been observed, Jon had no hesitancy to answer the question candidly. 'When we fly in Earth's atmosphere, up to forty thousand feet, we limit our speed to about two thousand mph because of friction concerns, although we could fly much faster if we wished. But if we did so, we would appear to be a shooting star, trailing red hot sparks, or perhaps a comet entering Earth's atmosphere.'

Suitably impressed, General Clintock eagerly asked the next question. 'And outside Earth's atmosphere, what would your maximum speed be?'

Again, Jon was aware that when he and Lana had approached Earth on their own, their instruments had recorded that they were being tracked by various radio telescopes from different points of the globe. Knowing that he would only be confirming what must already be known, he answered, 'Our type of craft is only designed

Chapter Twenty-Three

for interplanetary flight, what you would probably refer to as a short haul.'

He was interrupted by the general. 'Such a flight, even to our nearest planet, would take years to complete, so I wouldn't describe that as a short haul.'

Smiling in agreement, Jon continued, 'Yes, if we were forced to attempt the same journey in my craft, it would take us several months to complete. Our maximum speed would then be in excess of fifty thousand mph, but that would be considered far too slow for trips between the stars. Therefore, the Zellians use a different kind of ship, but for the moment, I won't even attempt to explain the technology involved; it's very complicated, even for me.'

As there were no further questions forthcoming from the other three men, Jon reminded Davis Cooper that he and Lana would join the presidential party the day following the Fort Knox rehearsal, meeting here in the Oval Office. 'What time will be suitable for you, Mr President?'

'No need to start at dawn,' was the reply. 'Nine thirty in the morning will be fine. That gives us plenty of time for the trip. In fact, we'll probably stop off for lunch before we go on to the UN building. Can you arrange that, George?'

'Well, one of my staff will,' George replied with a smile.

'When Lana knows that not only will she be making her first car journey,' Jon said, 'but that we will be having lunch in your company, gentlemen, she is going to be as excited as you are General at the prospect of travelling in a flying saucer.'

'A first for both of us then,' retorted General Clintock with a hearty laugh.

'Well, I will now take my leave of you,' Jon said quietly, 'until I join you at Fort Knox, the day after tomorrow. What time would you like the exercise to begin, General, morning or afternoon?'

Chapter Twenty-Three

'We will be ready for you whenever you appear, Jon,' Clintock replied. 'The element of surprise works better in keeping the men alert, and I shall be the only one waiting to be rescued,' he added. Giving his pseudo-Roman style salute, in finality Jon promptly disappeared from view as he teleported back to the ship and Lana.

Chapter Twenty-Four

As he gazed at the scene twenty miles below, Jon adjusted the viewing screen to enhance and enlarge the image on the ground. 'Well, there we are, Lana. Fort Knox, the most heavily fortified military establishment in the world.'

Lana scrutinised the layout of the sprawling system of roads and buildings, noting the airstrip and several parked planes and helicopters nearby. 'Looks like the presidential plane is already here,' she commented, 'so General Clintock is probably in position in his cell, waiting to be rescued.'

Jon gave his usual smile as he remarked, 'He did say that he would be ready whatever the time of day, and that the garrison would always be on alert. I chose this particular time of day on purpose as this will also be the time when I carry out the real rescue bid on the scientist, just as day breaks when the senses of most people, and that includes the military, are at their lowest ebb.'

'And how about your own senses, Jon?' Lana enquired as she gave him a gentle kiss.

'All my senses are alert, and well you know it,' he replied with a grin. At least their minds were as one at this time, so he then returned the kiss and said, 'No time like the present, so I will be on my way; this shouldn't take long.' With a final touch on her face, he stood back, and was gone, arriving at the predetermined area within the main building of Fort Knox a moment later.

Chapter Twenty-Four

As luck would have it, there were no military personnel in the immediate area, so after a quick look around to confirm his bearings, he set off down a wide corridor in the direction of the rendezvous. He hadn't gone very far before he came to the first door to block his path. It was obviously electronically controlled, but as he wasn't in possession of the requisite pass or code number, this was his first serious obstacle. As he contemplated the problem of how to open the door, he thought. *I can't realistically use my personal force field in this instance, since its power would be dissipated by the length of this corridor; it's much more effective in a confined space.*

As he considered the alternatives, he heard the sound of running feet coming from behind him and a voice yelled, 'Who the hell are you, and how did you get past the checkpoint?'

As he turned round, he became aware of several armed men approaching at a run, with weapons already drawn, brandishing them with the obvious intention of using them. Jon was aware that the guards were likely to fire on any unauthorised intruder if their initial challenge was ignored. As he had already discounted the use of his personal force field for anything other than his own protection, which he had set it to a radius of three feet around him, he realised that once again he would have to use his power of telekinesis. *If I can lift a twenty tonne lorry,* he thought, recollecting his previous incident, *then I'm sure that I can stop these men.*

No sooner than the thought went through his mind, he raised both hands in front of them as though to physically bar their rapid approach, at the same time he concentrated urgently, drawing on the inner power of his mind. As he watched, all the men came to an abrupt halt, dropped their weapons with a clatter, bounced off the telekinetic force field, and ended up sprawled over the floor of the corridor, stunned by the impact and effectively out of action, all in the space of a few seconds. Jon noted with a satisfied smile that at least none of the men had suffered any serious injury. *The general will be pleased,* he thought.

Chapter Twenty-Four

With the immediate threat from the guards removed, he then turned his attention to the door that barred his way to the rendezvous point. Apart from being electronically controlled, it appeared to be of substantial construction, probably armoured steel. Under normal circumstances, to make a forced entry would require a charge of dynamite or some other explosives, *But these are not normal circumstances,* he reminded himself with a wry grin, *and I have no other recourse than to use my telekinesis power again.* Knowing that this would require more power to blow the door than he had used to stop the soldiers, he again raised his hands as before, and to help his concentration, Jon closed his eyes and summoned all his mental power to imagine the door being destroyed. He heard the crash as the door gave way, and with it, the wall on either side also. When he opened his eyes again, the scene before him was obscured by the dust from the disintegrating wall. The steel door hung crazily from the remnants of the wall, while the torn electrical cables spit sparks and arced furiously. Without waiting for the dust to settle, he strode purposefully forward through the debris littering the corridor. *So much for the decor, General,* he thought with a smile. As he gained the continuation of the corridor, it was as though all hell had broken loose.

First, a Klaxon horn sounded the alarm, and the noise bounced off the walls and ceiling in the confined space. Then, as the air became less polluted, he saw a group of soldiers running toward him. There were no warning shouts to surrender, just guns blazing at this seemingly hostile figure emerging from the dust. Jon had fully expected a show of defensive strength immediately after the first door was blown and had accordingly adjusted his personal force field to counteract the hail of bullets directed at him.

No doubt the enemy was shocked to see the tall figure of this silver-haired man advancing on them, and they continued to fire without respite, desperately loading and reloading their automatic weapons to no avail. Secure from their firepower, but impatient to

Chapter Twenty-Four

reach the rendezvous, which he knew lay just beyond one more door, Jon strode forward. He raised one hand, mindful not to use too much force against these men, and again exerted his telekinesis power. As before, the troops never knew what had hit them as they went down in a heap like inert rag dolls, but at least they were still alive.

As he approached the final door, which was also electronically controlled and armoured, Jon didn't even break his stride, but from a distance of about fifteen yards, he raised both hands for a greater effect. He again closed his eyes momentarily as he walked forward and exerted his mind force. Even above the sound of the Klaxon horn, which was still blaring, the noise of the door being ripped out of the wall was ear shattering, but as Jon opened his eyes again to observe how effective his mind control exercise had been, he almost complimented himself. *Not quite so much damage this time, General, at least the wall is still standing.*

Once he had negotiated the blast area and was clear of the rubble-strewn floor, he walked quickly along a short stretch of corridor, at the end of which he could see the open door of the room where he expected General Clintock to be waiting, no doubt alerted by the destructive approach of Jon, the representative of the Zellian people.

Still on the alert, but confident of his invulnerability, Jon approached the entrance of the room with caution. There was always a possibility that one of the guards might be nervous or trigger-happy, and his sudden appearance could provoke a typical military reaction of fire on sight. As it happened, the first person he saw was the general, perched on the edge of a table, swinging his legs nonchalantly as though he didn't have a care in the world. *Wait until your department gets the repair bill, General,* Jon thought.

'Well, Jon,' Clintock exclaimed. 'I reckon you only took about ten minutes to negotiate the corridors, blow two reinforced doors, immobilise a dozen men, and here you are. A bit dusty, it would

Chapter Twenty-Four

appear, but otherwise unharmed.' Then turning to his guards, he said, 'Stand down, men, this is Jon, a man you will undoubtedly be hearing a great deal of in the near future.'

The men had been made aware that this was only a 'mock' rescue mission, but after the noise of gunfire and the sounds of the security doors being destroyed, they both had had one single thought, *Sounds pretty realistic to me.* The general was highly delighted with the outcome of the exercise, although he did enquire after the welfare of his men.

'Shaken and probably a few bruises, General,' Jon assured him, 'but apart from that, no fatalities.'

'And now for the next part,' Clintock said dubiously, thinking there was going to be a lot of explaining to do regarding his own part in the rescue.

Jon took the general to one side and said quietly, 'I think it would be advisable to order your men to go out into the corridor and carry out an assessment of the damage and casualties, then we can carry out the next part. It may avoid awkward questions later, don't you think?'

'Sure thing,' Clintock agreed, then turning to his keepers, he gave the necessary order. 'You men go out and do a damage assessment. I want a report first thing in the morning. Expect the doors to be destroyed and the surrounding areas to be wrecked, and also compile a list of casualties.' And as an afterthought, he added, 'And make a note of the extent of all injuries sustained by the guards, and when you've finished, give the report to the senior officer in charge of cleaning up, then forward it to me in Washington. Go to it, men.'

Left on their own, Jon regarded the general who was displaying signs of anxiety at the prospect of teleporting to the spacecraft, which was still in position above Fort Knox. 'Don't worry, General, this is one ride that you won't have time to enjoy or otherwise. It

Chapter Twenty-Four

will be over before you can say George Washington.' With that, he stepped forward saying, 'Do as I do,' and embraced Robert E. Clintock as a brother-in-arms. When they were locked together, Jon said, 'Here goes, General,' and a moment later, they materialised on the flight deck of the Zellian spacecraft where they were greeted with a warm smile from Lana.

'Welcome aboard, General,' she said. 'You are the first American to step foot in our craft.' She then turned to Jon and continued, 'I take it that all went according to plan, Jon, and the mission was a success?'

'Apart from messing up the decor a little more than was necessary, yes,' he replied. 'But it was good practice for me in controlling my telekinetic power.' He then added, 'And on the real mission, whatever obstacles may be in the way can simply be destroyed without regard to the damage I may cause, although I will still avoid any unnecessary bloodshed, since this will be a rescue mission, not a conquest of the enemy.'

In the meanwhile, the general was gazing around at the spacious interior of the spacecraft, overawed at the display of control panels and computer equipment. *More like Cape Canaveral than a flying machine,* he thought. *By comparison, our spacecraft are like toys.* Then he turned to Jon. 'How long has it taken your people to develop this kind of technology, Jon?'

'The Zellians,' Jon replied, avoiding the reference to his people, 'are an ancient race and have been travelling between the stars for millions of years in ships much larger than this one. In fact, our craft,' he said as he gestured around them, 'is only considered a short-range vessel, although it could be used as an interplanetary ship if necessary, but that would only be considered in an emergency, otherwise one of the star ships would be used.'

General Clintock had it in mind to go further in his questioning. Both Jon and Lana could read the chaotic thoughts in his head and

Chapter Twenty-Four

decided against answering any further enquiries regarding the capabilities of this or any other Zellian spacecraft.

'So, we just say, General,' Jon concluded, 'that if progress is maintained at its present rate, humankind may be ready to reach for the stars in two or three thousand years, if they don't destroy themselves in the meanwhile. And that is why I am here on Earth, to divert your military and scientific people into the path of lasting peace and stability.'

Knowing that he was unlikely to gain any further information regarding the spaceship's military application, Clintock asked if he might be allowed to look around. The flight deck fascinated him, although he couldn't begin to even guess the purpose of the hundreds of controls and display panels that he could see. His curiosity knew bounds, and as he was given a tour of the living, sleeping, recreation and sleeping quarters, he was amazed at the spaciousness of the craft as a whole. Finally, he had one more question to put to Jon. 'If this is considered a short-range craft, how big are the star ships you mentioned, the ones that are used for long-distance travel between star systems, the intergalactic flights I believe you called them?'

'Tell him, Lana,' Jon said with a smile. 'He may find it difficult to believe me.' Jon remembered that one and only occasion that he had himself actually seen a star ship, which was a sight he'd never forget.

'Do you regard this ship as being very big, General?' Lana asked, already knowing what was in his mind.

'Well,' Clintock answered with a frown of recollection, 'it must be at least one hundred feet in diameter, and yes, I would regard that as being big for any flying machine, and it must require an enormous amount of power to keep it airborne.'

'A star ship can accommodate several craft of this size quite easily in the on-board hangars,' Lana remarked. 'The ship itself is approximately two miles in length and has at least twenty separate

Chapter Twenty-Four

deck levels.' Noting the look of disbelief on the general's face and the rejection of this information in his mind, she continued. 'Yes, General, they are so large that they never actually touchdown on a planet, which is why this smaller type of craft is utilised for the transfer of supplies or personnel, what you would refer to as a shuttle.'

For the moment, Clintock was silent as he thought of the enormity of the star ships. 'So, if these vessels never land on a planet, how do they get up there in the first place?' he said, pointing upward.

Lana couldn't help but smile at this silly question. 'Because they are built in space in the same way your own present-day space stations are being built, only our ships are many years in the process of construction, with anything up to one hundred years considered normal.'

'That's quite a project,' Robert E. Clintock conceded. 'And I take it that would require thousands of technicians a lifetime to complete the building of one ship?'

'Well, not quite,' Lana mused momentarily, thinking of the longevity of the Zellians. 'But certainly a fair proportion of their lifetime.'

Having been back on board for some time now and knowing that the presidential plane must have long since departed on the flight back to Washington, Jon asked the general, 'Did you have any breakfast this morning?'

'I was too excited at the prospect of some frontline action for a change,' was the reply, 'but I could sure eat something now.'

'Well, General, our on-board catering facilities are somewhat more advanced than what you are accustomed to, all artificially simulated food, but indistinguishable from the real thing and just as nutritional and tasty, believe me. I'll show you how to order whatever you wish, although the simpler the order, the quicker it

Chapter Twenty-Four

will be delivered, since anything more complicated takes a little longer.' It was no great surprise to Jon that despite the huge choice of dishes available, the general chose burgers and fries, with plenty of coffee to wash it down.

Finishing his breakfast, the general declared, 'Best burger I've ever tasted.'

Jon opened the viewport and invited their guest to look out at the clouds far below and the occasional glimpse of the countryside.

'What's our altitude now, Jon and what speed are we travelling at?' the general enquired. Since he was a soldier, his experience of air travel was limited to being a passenger, not a combat role.

Jon replied, 'We have come down to the normal cruising speed and height of your civilian aircraft in this region, altitude thirty thousand feet and speed five hundred mph, and although we are taking our time so you can enjoy the scenery, General, we should be back over Washington in time to rendezvous with the President in the Oval Office. Then we will teleport down to join him and presumably George K. Lane as well.'

'Won't I have a story to tell,' the general said, rubbing his hands in boyish glee.

'I take it you have enjoyed your frontline experience,' Jon said. 'To be held a prisoner and then released as you were this morning can only be described as different, wouldn't you say?'

Clintock smiled as he recollected the events of the day, from the moment the sounds of gunfire and explosions had alerted the garrison of Fort Knox to the presence of an intruder, to the moment of arriving here in this spaceship. 'Yes,' he replied, 'it's been quite a day.'

After the leisurely flight back to Washington, as they hovered above the White House, high enough not to be a distraction the people in the city, Lana made a call through to the president's

Chapter Twenty-Four

private phone number only to be informed that he was at that moment still on his way back from the airport. Air Force One had landed only a short time ago, but the president was expected in his office within the hour.

'So, despite having time out for breakfast and a slow flight home,' the general growled, 'we still beat them; what a way to travel.' He also added with a smile of satisfaction, 'Ya know, I've never experienced such a smooth, quiet ride in any aircraft. There was no vibration or even the sensation of speed; it was as stable as sitting in the comfort of my own home.'

'I take it then that overall you've had a good day, General,' Lana stated with a laugh of amusement. *This big man is so easy to read, and his emotions are so vivid,* she thought.

After a time, Jon invited Robert E.Clintock to come and sit down in front of one of the viewing screens, which he adjusted for clarity and magnification, so that it was possible to see individual people in the streets in the vicinity of the White House. They were tourists, no doubt, as well as local office workers and residents. 'If you wait awhile, General, you'll see the presidential car and its escort arrive, and after that, we can give Davis Cooper ten minutes to get back into his office, before we join him.'

General Clintock smiled, relishing the prospect of appearing in the Oval Office unannounced, and in the company of the hero of the moment, Jon, the representative of the Zellians.

"In due course,' Jon said with a grin, 'come along, Brother-in-Arms; it's time to go. Do you wish to accompany us, Lana?'

'Yes,' she replied. 'I'm interested to hear what the President has to say about the whole operation, so if you look after the General, I'll follow you.'

The brothers-in-arms embraced and a moment later materialised in the Oval Office, as always to the consternation of the onlookers, the president and his Chief of Staff George K. Lane.

Chapter Twenty-Four

Greetings were exchanged all round and congratulations on the success of the mission. 'If all goes so well on the real operation, Jon, we will look forward to the return of the scientist in question. I'm sure he will be relieved to be released from captivity, but undoubtedly confused by the manner of your rescue and subsequent escape. Talking of which,' he directed his attention to General Clintock, 'what was it like to be on the frontline again, and more to the point, the escape?'

'Took me back thirty years to my operational days,' Clintock replied. 'The only thing missing was the bullets flying around me, although there were plenty flying around in the corridor outside,' he added with a laugh. 'Now the boys at Fort Knox will have a problem with the decor. Jon told me that two of the security doors were completely blown out and most of the walls with them. You will have to decide which department will be responsible for the costs involved. On the plus side,' he continued, 'there were no serious injuries sustained, although if the garrison learns that the enemy was a single combatant, one man, their pride will be severely dented.'

The president smiled sympathetically. 'Not if they knew the calibre of that combatant and what he is capable of.' He chuckled as he added, 'Our secret weapon.'

Lana had been listening to what was being said and was aware of Jon's thoughts on the rescue mission, but all she had to say was, 'And tomorrow, we will have to do it all over again, for real.'

'Yes,' Jon agreed, 'and bearing in mind the time differential, if we are going to be in position before dawn, we will have to leave here shortly. It will take about eight hours to fly that distance, plus the fact that we are racing the rising sun, but we can get rest on the way as the ship will be on autopilot until we reach our destination. Then the fun will start again in earnest.'

As ever, it was George K. Lane who had a thought about their ally, Jon. *How does he speak such perfect English? All the colloquial*

Chapter Twenty-Four

expressions as well, far better than we do. Where did he learn the language? He would be further confused by events in the near future when other people of different nationalities would ask the same questions relating to their own language also.

'So, we will now take our leave, Mr President, gentlemen,' Jon interrupted, 'and we will return with your guest' in due course.' He added with a laugh, 'We will ensure that it is a reasonable time of day for the handover.' Taking Lana by the hand, they disappeared, back to their ship. 'Gee. I wish I could do that,' exclaimed the general. 'It would get me out of some dumb meetings.'

'No need, Robert,' the president said dryly. 'You're excused now.'

Chapter Twenty-Five

When the spacecraft arrived in position for docking twenty miles above the barracks that Jon intended to enter, it was still pitch dark at ground level, although at the altitude they maintained, it was possible to see the first hint of light on the eastern horizon. Dawn was not be far away for the occupants of the prison below, the sleepy headed soldiers, Jon hoped.

Jon carefully calculated the coordinates of the most suitable area to materialise, which was almost the same layout as in Fort Knox, same type of area, same corridors, although they appeared narrower than the plans the secret agents had provided, and instead of only two doors to open or destroy, there were four. *A small matter,* Jon thought grimly, *no need for finesse, just blow them away and get to the prisoner as quickly as possible.* His telekinesis force would be his only weapon of aggression, and his personal force field a guarantee of survival.

As these thoughts were going through his mind, Lana approached him, placed her arms around his body and gave him a gentle hug. 'Remember, Jon, that while it is not the way of the Zellians to kill unnecessarily, it may be essential for you to do that on Earth, not only for your own survival, but so that you can get the prisoner out alive. Don't hesitate if in doubt; kill the enemy!'

'I will,' he assured her grimly.

He waited until the first light of day made it possible to make out the shape of the buildings down below. 'Wish me luck, Lana, and hope it goes as well as the rehearsal.' After giving her a gentle kiss,

Chapter Twenty-Five

he stood back and was gone in an instant, materialising in the middle of the complex below.

Unlike Fort Knox, however, there were several military personnel in evidence, but as he had hopefully anticipated, they were slumped or crouched down, fast asleep against the walls. Having again confirmed his whereabouts, he walked over to the nearest door leading into the corridor where the prisoner's cell was located; it was nothing technical. In fact, it was nothing more than a stout wooden door, which, when he tried it by moving the handle, proved to be unlocked. Giving a gentle push, it opened inward with a loud creaking noise. *Enough noise to awaken the dead*, he thought, *but not enough to awaken the soldiers nearby, who are probably so used to the sound of the door opening that subconsciously they ignore it.*

Passing through the door without incident, he closed it behind him, rear-guard action, he reminded himself, and proceeded to the second door. Just as he came within a few yards, the door opened and a sleepy eyed soldier came through it. *If I hit him full on with kinetic force, he'll go crashing backwards into the corridor and possibly raise the alarm,* Jon thought. Instead, he lifted the man upward so violently that the man hit the ceiling with his head, rendering him unconscious or possibly breaking his neck. After a few moments, during which the soldier remained motionless, Jon allowed him to sink slowly to the ground, and on closer inspection, he noted the grotesque angle of his neck and head, concluding he definitely had a broken neck.

Stepping over the corpse, he continued along the corridor, alert for the appearance of any more guards and thought, *Where are they all? We were assured by the secret agents that the place would be swarming with military personnel. Is it too early for them, or are they simply too complacent in their belief that no one would be mad enough to effect a rescue from such a secure compound?*

Chapter Twenty-Five

He was just murmuring 'two more to go' when the door ahead burst open and a group of heavily armed soldiers appeared and attempted to run toward him, but they were impeded by their own numbers and got jammed in the narrow corridor. Nevertheless, they managed to fire a few shots. In such a confined space, only the leading attackers had an open line of fire, so Jon didn't feel particularly threatened, but decided to quell the enthusiasm of the soldiers immediately. Once again, directing his kinetic energy at full power, he raised both hands in front of his body, felt the force directed at the enemy, and had the satisfaction of seeing them bowled over, as though struck by a hurricane-force wind.

It all took place in a few brief seconds. What had potentially been a hazardous situation was now clear. 'And only one more door to go,' he reminded himself. As he approached the final obstacle, he noticed that this was of a type similar to the ones installed in the secure complex at Fort Knox, a robust steel construction set into a concrete wall. In view of his recent—was it only yesterday—experience in opening doors, he didn't hesitate, but summoned his mental powers for this final assault. He again raised both hands as before and blasted the door and the wall out of his way to reveal, through the smoke and dust clouds, another group of guards cowering down against the wall outside a small room. *A small room with a permanently open door, my target area,* he thought.

He continued to stride toward the men, showing no fear or hesitancy, when to Jon's surprise, they all turned tail and ran. To them, this apparition of a giant with silver, glowing hair was no mere mortal, and therefore, they couldn't be expected to guard their prisoner. So, with the exception of one guard still inside the small room, they all beat a hasty retreat, leaving the scientist to whatever fate decreed. The remaining guard was obviously terrified, crouching with his head to the floor, calling for Allah's intervention. Whereas the other man, while equally frightened, knew that here was a

Chapter Twenty-Five

possible saviour, someone come to free him from this miserable cell, but how?

To reassure the man, Jon first of all spoke in English on the assumption that the prisoner would recognise that his rescuer was from a Western country, but he received no response. So he then spoke in Arabic, the scientist's own language, and this did provoke a response. 'Allah be praised! Deliverance!'

With no time to waste, still talking in Arabic, Jon told him that, in a moment, he would be a free man, but that he had to do exactly what he was told. He didn't elaborate, just said, 'Embrace me,' which was something the man wanted to do anyway. Jon, in turn, wrapped his arms securely around the much smaller man and teleported them out of the cell, leaving the guard still cowering with his head down on the floor, and with the problem of explaining how the prisoner had vanished without a trace.

A moment later, Jon and his guest materialised on the flight deck of the spaceship and were greeted by Lana. 'That didn't take as long as I thought it might. I hope you didn't frighten the soldiers down there too much.'

In reply Jon said, 'Sadly, there was one definite fatality, then a number of guards were rendered unconscious at the third door, and after I destroyed the final obstruction, the remaining soldiers appeared to take fright and bolted.'

'After seeing you coming toward them and aware of your power, they were very wise to run away,' Lana said with a smile.

The rescued scientist had, until that moment, been silent. He was awestruck by his surroundings and didn't fully comprehend where he was or how he had gotten there. 'I know I have been rescued from the military,' he said, 'how I don't know. It seems like some kind of miracle, for which Allah be praised. Or should I say,' he said, turning to Jon, 'you should be praised. I don't as yet know your name, or this young lady, either, but if I may introduce myself, I am

Chapter Twenty-Five

Professor Mahmoud, a physicist recently in the employ of a certain Arab country that shall remain nameless. But I was abducted by a rival government, for the obvious reason of working to produce a nuclear device, which is an offer I have repeatedly declined.'

So far, the scientist had carried on the conversation in Arabic, which Lana didn't understand, so Jon decided to communicate in English again. After all, the man was going to America and would possibly seek asylum there; a knowledge of the English language would become essential.

'First of all, professor,' Jon said in English, 'my name is Jon, and this young lady is Lana. We are the crewmembers of this vessel.' Seeing the questioning look on the little man's face, he explained, 'You are on board our spacecraft.'

The first reaction to Jon's words was, 'I apologise for not speaking English before. Your command of Arabic is so impeccable that I did not think it necessary to use any other language, but I am very grateful for the rescue mission and your government's intervention.' He paused for a moment as he scrutinised the crewmembers for any clue to their nationality. 'May I enquire which government you represent?'

'Your own command of English, professor, is impeccable also, and at this moment, you are on your way to meet the President of the United States and members of his government. As for me,' Jon continued, 'I am a representative of the planet Zel, and Lana is a citizen of that same planet.'

The scientist gave a smile of relief; in the first place, relief that he wasn't being 'snatched' by a hostile regime, and second, happy to be going to a country where, if he was lucky, he would remain a free man and still be employed in the type of work in which he was an acknowledged expert. 'Well,' the professor exclaimed in shocked disbelief, 'I've never even heard of such a planet or met any of its people, but nevertheless, I am overjoyed to have been rescued by

Chapter Twenty-Five

you and am very happy to be going back to the States. I have spent some time there in the past.'

'And I'm sure you will be made very welcome on this occasion, professor. As far as not having heard of Zel, that's no surprise, since it is in a galaxy many hundreds of light-years away.' Seeing the inevitable question forming in the scientist's mind, he added, 'Maybe we can enlarge on that subject at a later time.'

'Just one question more,' Professor Mahmoud said, 'as all Earth people are similar in appearance, apart from colour, is it the same on your planet? You, Jon, have this exceptionally coloured hair while Lana's hair is so dark, and you are both so big . . . and if I may say so, so beautiful.'

Compliments again, Jon, Lana thought, *but sincere. Just don't let him know you are a man of Earth; don't spoil the illusion.*

Jon kept his reply simple as he explained, 'Most people on Zel are tall because of the lower gravity of the planet, although it has to be said that the colour of my hair is considered unique.'

Again, Lana projected her thoughts. *All very true, Jon, but let's change the subject while I set the course for Washington.*

'Now that you know you are on our ship,' Jon said, 'and that you will be in America in a few hours, you can settle down and relax, professor. If you will excuse us, we will set course and speed for Washington. Again he saw the question forming in the scientist's mind. 'We will be travelling in excess of two thousand miles per hour at an altitude of fifty miles, and it will take approximately six hours.'

'That's incredible,' the professor gasped. 'Nearly halfway round the world in only six hours, incredible.' Then he lapsed into silence, leaving the crewmembers to their duties.

Within the estimated time, they arrived over Washington. Whereas they had departed the country in the Middle East midmorning in that time zone, travelling from east to west meant

Chapter Twenty-Five

that the sun was chasing them. As a result, it was just after daybreak when Jon said to Professor Mahmoud, 'Here we are, professor, Washington. You are now in the land of the free.' He laughed. 'We'll give the President time to have his breakfast before we interrupt his day, although I've no doubt he will be expecting to hear from us pretty soon.' He then explained that only two day's previously, a rehearsal of the rescue mission had been carried out to ascertain the feasibility of such a mission. Everyone concerned was aware of how long it would take to break and enter the military barracks, retrieve the prisoner and make the escape. 'Fortunately,' Jon declared, 'everything went according to plan, well, almost; no doubt the place will require a complete makeover after our visit, and the guards will have some explaining to do regarding the loss of a valuable scientist.'

In the meanwhile, Lana had opened the viewport, and gesturing to Mahmoud, said, 'Come and have a look, professor. That is the White House you can see below.' Although at their present altitude, it was barely discernible. 'If you want a clearer view, though, you can use one of the viewing screens, which will enhance everything down there.' She led him over to the control console and demonstrated its use.

The professor was silent as he adjusted the instrument, amazed at the clarity of the images and the details he could pick out. At one point, he blurted out, 'I can even read the headlines on a street vendor's newspaper stall, amazing.'

Lana and Jon exchanged their thoughts silently. *Leave him alone to play with his new toy; it will keep him occupied until we're ready to call on Davis Cooper.* In due course, Lana put a call through to the White House switchboard and asked to be put through to the president's office, if he was available. The operator must have been briefed to expect a call from Jon at about this time because, without any delay, the connection was made.

Chapter Twenty-Five

A moment later, Davis Cooper's cheerful voice could be heard. 'Jon, is it good news? I take it the mission was a success?' He then continued, 'We've been picking up signals from a certain foreign government to the effect that they've suffered a hostile attack involving an elite commando task force. There was substantial damage to the facility, many casualties, and a prominent scientist has been abducted.' He laughed as he continued once more. 'The General will be pleased that his one-man-commando task force has been so successful.'

Jon's reply was to the point. 'That "certain government" has exaggerated the scale of the raid to save face. There was only one fatality that I would confirm, and the rest of the garrison was either stunned by the explosions of the doors being destroyed or,' recalling the last obstacle, 'were frightened out of their wits and ran for it. However,' he continued, 'we've got your man with us right now. His name is Mahmoud, Professor Mahmoud, and he is ready to join you whenever convenient.'

'Ready and waiting,' was the breezy reply. 'Unfortunately, General Clintock isn't with us this morning, but the secretary of state, George K. Lane, is and he is eager to listen to the debriefing and to renew the acquaintance of the professor. Apparently, they met some years ago at some scientific seminar.'

'In which case, Mr President,' Jon said, 'I'll ask Lana to descend to a lower altitude before we teleport. Not that it makes any difference, but the prof will be able to accept a distance of one mile more readily than our customary twenty miles for a docking station. I'll be with you in a few minutes.' He then turned to Lana. 'As you heard me say, Lana, take us down to about five thousand feet, which is a comfortable distance for our guest to teleport. Are you ready to make this trip?' he asked the professor. On being given a very shaky affirmative, he added, 'And you, Lana, are you coming on this occasion?'

Chapter Twenty-Five

'No,' she replied. 'I would have little to contribute to the debriefing session, and as I know from your mind exactly how the mission went, it would be like going over the same story again. Interesting though it was, I'll give it a miss this time round.'

Jon smiled his understanding. His thoughts were received by Lana, who simply embraced him gently and said, 'Take care of the professor and then find out what arrangements are being made for our car journey to New York; now that is something I'm looking forward to.'

Having returned the embrace, Jon turned to the little scientist, held his arms wide again, and with a smile said, 'Your turn now, professor.' He promptly wrapped his arms protectively around his passenger, before he had time to make any protest, and they were gone. A moment later, they materialised in the Oval Office to find Davis Cooper and George K. Lane waiting patiently for their expected appearance.

'You'll have to take me on one of these, trips Jon,' the president laughed. 'The General has told half of his staff of his experience already, and if I don't miss my guess, he's telling the other half right now.'

'I'll keep it in mind, Mr President,' Jon replied with a smile, 'but for the moment, let me introduce you to Professor Mahmoud.' Then turning to George K. Lane, he said, 'I believe you have already met Mr Secretary?'

For the next hour, Jon was plied with questions regarding the rescue mission, everything from his time of arrival at the military barracks to the number of men guarding the establishment and their state of alertness. Finally, Jon was asked to recount his progress through the doors and corridors until he achieved his target, the room with a permanently open door and with only one soldier inside to guard the prisoner.

•

Chapter Twenty-Five

The professor listened to the account just as attentively as the other two men, realising that, apart from the unfortunate death of only one guard, Jon had achieved the rescue mission with far less casualties than a conventional hit squad or elite commando task force, as the president remarked with a smile.

After the debriefing session, George K. Lane brought up the subject of the trip to New York, now only two days away. 'If you can arrange to meet us here in the Oval Office, Jon, with Lana, of course, we will then be driven in the presidential car to the airport, not to JFK, but another military base. From there, will be Lana's treat of the day, the cavalcade to a restaurant for lunch and finally the arrival at the UN building where you are going to deliver your speech.'

'That sounds like an interesting itinerary,' Jon remarked with his usual smile. 'I hope Lana will not be too alarmed by the traffic on the roads in New York, although while we're waiting for that event, I intend to return to the Caribbean for a time. On the trip down there, we can fly over the city, and Lana can get a first-hand view of the chaotic road conditions of one of America's biggest cities.' Then giving a reassuring grin, he said, 'Don't worry, Mr President, we will be at such an altitude that the citizens of New York won't even be aware of our presence. And we won't hang about for long, as I want to spend as much time as possible on a certain little island, after we have done a little shopping.'

The president stood up and was about to shake hands with Jon, who suddenly remembered that that was not done. Instead, he gave the presidential hand-on-heart salute, which Jon returned with a smile, bypassing another difficult moment. Davis Cooper remarked, 'Well, enjoy the next couple of days, Jon, and your shopping trip. In the meanwhile,' he said, indicating the patiently waiting professor, 'we have to arrange for our guest's long-term stay in the United States. That's for you to sort out, George,' he said, gesturing at his secretary of state.'

Chapter Twenty-Five

'Gentlemen,' Jon concluded, 'I will now take my leave, and I'll see you in two days' time.' A moment later, there was only an empty space in the middle of the Oval Office where he had been.

Chapter Twenty-Six

On his return to the spaceship, he was greeted affectionately by Lana as always, who was already setting up the course to take them on to their next trip to Jamaica. 'Kingston the first stop, Jon, or our island?'

'We'd better call on Jacob Bernstein first of all,' he replied, knowing from her ill-concealed thoughts what the attraction was in Kingston, the ring. 'Assuming your trinket is ready for collection, we can then fly over to our retreat for a short time before returning to Washington. Perhaps I should have arranged to meet at the UN building; we could then have spent an extra day on the island.'

'Oh, no,' Lana protested. 'I am looking forward to travelling with the President in his old-fashioned means of transport; both the plane and car journey will be such a novelty for me.' Then she added, 'In your previous life, Jon, that is, before Captain Jara and Mort picked you up, did you use those methods of transport yourself?'

With a smile, he assured her that, although he didn't have cause to fly very often, he had used a car as everyday transport; therefore, being in the presidential car would no doubt be very comfortable, but hardly a novelty.

As there was little point in remaining above Washington any longer, Lana activated the power and navigation systems, passing her hand gracefully above the control panel, and within seconds, the craft was heading south for the blue Caribbean, Kingston first of all, then the remaining time on their paradise island.

Chapter Twenty-Six

A few hours later, they were in their customary docking position twenty miles above the city. As it was still late afternoon, a time for the commercial sector to still be active, Jon suggested that rather than teleport directly into the jeweller's premises, they should do as they had done on previous occasions and find a quiet area to materialise then walk the remaining distance. Utilising the enhancing viewfinder, they surveyed the area below, and as luck would have it, they spotted an area clear of pedestrians, who were their main concern. 'That's the same place we saw those old men last time, isn't it?' Lana remarked.

'Yes,' he replied, 'and it will only take ten minutes to walk to Jacob's shop from there.' Taking hold of Lana's hand, he said, 'Let's go while it's clear.' A moment later, they found themselves looking around warily, but no one had sighted them as they had materialised. After a leisurely stroll through the busy shopping area, they came to the door of Jacob Bernstein's premises, only to find the door locked and the shutters drawn. Their thoughts merged. *Is Jacob away or possibly working in his workshop? Only one way to find out—teleport!*

As soon as they had materialised inside the shop, Jon called out loudly, 'Jacob, are you here? It's Jon and Lana; we're back again!'

Within seconds, the flustered face of Jacob appeared as he burst into the room, a look of relief spreading over his countenance at recognising his visitors. 'Ah moie, Ah moie. Who else but you could enter my premises so easily or so silently? But welcome, my friends, it is so good to see you again.' He then went on to explain. 'I was busy in my workshop, putting the finishing touches to a certain piece of jewellery, your ring, Lana. A few more hours and it will be ready to grace your finger, a lovely jewel for a lovely lady.'

As they laughed at his flattery, Jon passed the thought to Lana, *He means every word of it with sincerity, and I wholeheartedly agree; you are a lovely lady, and no jewel will outshine your lustre.*

Chapter Twenty-Six

Lana smiled with pleasure at the comments of Jacob, and the mental thoughts of Jon. 'I'm impatient to see what you have done with my diamond, Jacob. If it's anything like the first ring you made, I will be delighted,' she said.

Jacob laughed at the recollection of Lana's pleasure at seeing the smaller diamond, which he had mounted into that first ring. Indeed, it was a beautiful gem, and he also had the personal gift of yet another diamond as his commission. Then referring to his latest masterpiece, he said, 'Not only have I mounted the stone in a platinum ring, I've made some additions. It would be impossible to improve on the cut and beauty of this stone, but to enhance it, I've surrounded the diamond with a number of blood-red rubies, and although, as I've said, it is not quite finished, it is now worthy of being worn by a queen.' He added with a laugh, 'If she could afford it. In my opinion, it is priceless beyond compare, which is why I keep my shop secure and locked unless both rings are locked in the safe.'

'We can hardly wait to see your masterpiece, Jacob,' Jon said with a smile on his face. 'But what of the other, smaller diamond we presented you with? When we last saw it, it was a beautiful example of the jeweller's craft, which was why Lana was so eager to have one just like it.'

Jacob rocked back and forth with pleasure at what he was about to say. 'As you know, Kingston attracts many international and wealthy tourists, and it was only yesterday that another lady, a very rich lady, came into my shop, and like Lana, she was smitten by the beauty of the ring and bought it.'

'Just like that,' Jon exclaimed, thinking of the value of the first diamond ring.

'Just like that,' Jacob agreed. 'No haggling or bargaining, she said she just had to have it whatever the price.'

Chapter Twenty-Six

'And would I be indiscreet if I were to enquire how much?' Jon asked out of curiosity.

'Not at all,' Jacob replied. 'It will then give you some idea of how much Lana's ring would fetch on the open market.' He paused for a moment to add effect to the statement he was about to make. 'One and a half million American dollars.'

'Then I can understand why you keep your doors locked, Jacob,' Jon remarked. 'If any of the criminal elements in Kingston got wind of your possession of such valuable merchandise on your premises, you would probably have some unwelcome visitors.' He inclined his head in question. 'And when is this lady going to collect her acquisition? Not until it has been paid for, I trust.'

Jacob shook his head in denial. 'She paid me an instalment by cheque, of course, in the sum of a quarter of a million dollars to secure the purchase, and the balance her husband will pay, again, no doubt by a bank cash transfer. Only then will I hand over the goods.' He gave a broad grin. 'Old Jewish custom: money first and then immediate delivery of the goods.'

'Very wise, Jacob,' Jon commented.

Lana, who had listened to the conversation between the two men, said, 'To the Zellian people, the process of buying and selling is unknown. If we want or need anything, we just ask or possibly exchange different items; we have complete trust in each other.'

'That level of trust may take a few thousands of years to attain on Earth, Lana, so in the meanwhile, business is conducted very much as Jacob's ancestors have done for centuries,' Jon explained. 'Fortunately, we don't have any issues of trust regarding your ring. Jacob has already been rewarded by selling the diamond that we gave him, which was a very profitable transaction, if I may say so,' he said. Turning to the jeweller with a smile, he added, 'One that your ancestors would be proud of.'

Chapter Twenty-Six

Jacob bobbed his head in acknowledgement. 'Yes, thanks to you, I shall be a very rich man in the near future, and I shall be able to expand my business, buying and selling in precious stones.' He added with a laugh of satisfaction, 'The name of Jacob Bernstein will become known far beyond the Caribbean.'

'But now, Jacob,' Lana asked, 'are you going to show me your masterpiece, this diamond and ruby ring that only a queen could afford?'

'Most certainly,' he said, 'but I suggest that we go through into my backroom, away from prying eyes,' he said, gesturing toward the windows of the shop. 'It is still in the safe, and as I said, it only requires the finishing touches, and then you will be the proud possessor of the most remarkable ring in the world, priceless perfection.'

As Jacob led the way through into his inner sanctum or workshop, Lana exchanged her thoughts with Jon. *I'm so very excited. If the ring is as beautiful as Jacob implies, I will want to wear it always.*

And so you shall, Jon silently replied. Then mentally laughing, he said aloud, 'But you will have to contain your excitement a little longer.'

They followed Jacob through into the small backroom, and as he indicated that they should sit down, he went over to a curtain concealing part of the wall to reveal an old-fashioned but sturdy safe. It took a little time to dial a lengthy combination code number, but eventually, he swung the door open, reached in, and drew out a large jewellery box. He then turned around and placed it, almost reverently, on the table between Lana and Jon, who both then leaned forward expectantly.

With what could only be described as a flourish, Jacob raised the lid of the box to reveal his masterpiece, the huge diamond surrounded by blood-red rubies. It was a sight that drew a cry of

Chapter Twenty-Six

delight from Lana and a sharp intake of breath from Jon. Jacob, in the meanwhile, stood back proudly, noting the reaction of his friends to this vision of perfection, a ring of immeasurable value fit to be worn by a queen. *If she could afford it,* he reminded himself.

It was several long moments before Lana could bring herself to speak. 'It's so beautiful,' she breathed. 'Can I touch it, Jacob?'

'But of course,' he replied, knowing that yet another lady was smitten by the sight of a perfect diamond, in this case, one enhanced by the blood-red rubies, the most perfect of their kind that can be obtained. 'Try it on,' he encouraged Lana. 'It is now yours to wear, or it will be very soon,' he added with a satisfied chuckle.

As Lana placed the ring on her finger, the second finger of her left hand, Jon nodded with approval. She waved her hand gently in front of her face, and even in the subdued light of the workshop, the many facets of the diamond reflected the light with a kaleidoscopic effect, causing Lana to cry out with delight. 'I can hardly wait to wear this ring permanently, Jacob. It is so much more beautiful than my other diamonds, and of course, the rubies are such a contrast; this ring will bring me great joy.'

'You have other diamonds?' Jacob queried as he turned to Jon. 'How many?' He added excitedly, 'Are they as perfect as these first two gems that you brought to me?'

Not wishing to reveal even to this new friend how many stones they possessed, Jon answered cautiously. 'Quite a few, Jacob, and yes, they are all perfectly cut and polished; several are even larger than Lana's and much too big to wear as a ring. You would probably say that it would be impossible to put a value on them, but as we have no need for more money, we won't ask you to sell them for us at the moment. But who knows, we could ask you to perform that service for us sometime in the future.'

Jacob tried to subdue his excitement, since the prospect of handling diamonds of such immense value made his senses reel. He replied soberly, 'Then I look forward to that time in the future when I can be of further service to you.' Having allowed Lana time to enjoy the beauty of her new acquisition, the ring, Jon reminded her gently that if they were to leave Jacob to complete his work, they could return in two hours' time, and she could then wear the ring permanently.

With that promise in mind, she reluctantly removed the ring from her finger, and with a sigh, she returned it to Jacob's safekeeping. 'But only for two hours,' she said forcefully, but with a smile.

'We will now go spend the next two hours wandering around like normal tourists,' Jon said. 'When we come back, there is no need to open the door for us, Jacob. We will teleport inside as we did earlier and that way you will be secure in your own premises.'

'And I will spend my time completing my work on your ring, Lana,' Jacob replied. He added a knowing smile as he remembering upon which finger she had placed the ring. 'I shall have pleasure of witnessing Jon placing the ring on your finger permanently.'

At that moment, Jon resolved to inform Lana of the significance of the ring being placed on the second finger of the left hand, but he felt it could wait until a more appropriate time.

'If you would like to see us off the premises,' Jon remarked, 'we will return promptly in two hours' time to collect the ring. Afterwards, we will teleport back to our ship immediately as we intend to spend another day or so on a certain little island where it will be all peace and tranquillity, until we have to return to Washington.'

It was exactly two hours later when Jacob became aware of Jon and Lana entering his workroom with a subdued hello. They didn't want to startle him, and as he returned their greeting, he held the jewel box out to Lana. 'Here it is, all completed and ready to wear.'

Chapter Twenty-Six

As she accepted the box, she turned to Jon. 'I want you to place it on my finger.' While they had been wandering around like normal tourists, with their minds as one, Jon had explained the ritual of giving and receiving rings. 'How quaint, but nice,' she had acknowledged. Now holding out her hand, she was smiling in delight as she participated in this quaint custom, encouraged by Jacob, who clapped his hands enthusiastically.

'All we need is a rabbi now,' he declared.

I will explain that remark later, Lana, Jon thought. They had stated their intention earlier, to return to their ship immediately after collecting the ring. After a few minutes of conversation regarding Jacob's plan for extending his business, now that he was going to be rich, Jon and Lana stood together, holding hands, and with a last gesture of farewell, they teleported to the docking station twenty miles above, both content with the events of the day. They looked forward to revisiting their island the next day.

They waited until dawn of the following morning before completing the ten-minute journey from Kingston to the island where they intended to remain for the next day or so. It gave them time to relax a little, to get sand between their toes, to be as one in complete privacy, away from the stresses and demands of Jon's mission as a Teacher before their return to Washington to rejoin the presidential team.

As he reflected on his life since he had left the Manchester Airport, it became difficult for Jon to relate to his role as the representative of Zel to his former life as an air traffic controller. He had been a happily married man with two children, who had been tragically taken from him in a road accident. Subsequently, he'd had his meeting with Captain Jara and Mort, who had persuaded him to become a Teacher.

So far, he thought, *I haven't done much teaching of the variety expected of me. I've taught a few difficult lessons to criminals and*

Chapter Twenty-Six

rogue governments, perhaps, but my true mission will hopefully begin after I've addressed the United Nations Assembly. Then what shall we see? But now that we are here, above our island, the past is forgotten, and the future happens come what may, but the present is for us to enjoy and to be as one.

Chapter Twenty-Seven

'Good morning, Mr President, we have returned from our visit to the Caribbean and are now ready to join you and your party on the visit to New York.' These were the first words spoken by Jon as Davis Cooper answered the phone.

'Good to hear from you again, Jon,' the president replied. He was reassured that the principal speaker at the United Nations Assembly would be in attendance. 'I take it you have enjoyed your few days of relaxation?'

After confirming that he and Lana had benefited from their holiday and shopping trip in Jamaica, although he didn't mention anything about their activities on their secluded island, Jon repeated that they were now ready to teleport down to the Oval Office as soon as it was convenient to the president.

'Any time, Jon, any time,' Davis Cooper exclaimed with a laugh. 'The General has already gone, but we will rendezvous with him at the airport, so there will only be George and yourself, and Lana, of course, in the car with me. Since all of the roads are comparatively quiet at this time of day, our escort will see to it that we get through fairly quickly.' He chuckled in amusement as he added, 'At least we know the plane can't take off without us.'

It was Jon's turn to laugh as he retorted, 'As soon as Lana has decided what she intends to wear for this trip, we'll be with you. As you'll gather, Mr President, the women of the planet Zel have much in common with Earth women, and knowing what to wear can be a big decision, true?'

Chapter Twenty-Seven

'Very true,' Davis Cooper replied, still in a jovial mood. 'Although, in the case of my wife's wardrobe, she is advised what to wear to suit the occasion, but it has to be an outfit that she approves of herself.' He nearly added, do you and Lana always dress in those uniform tunics, but thought better of it. Still smiling, he continued, 'Whenever you're ready, just drop in,' and he again laughed at the spontaneous pun.

It was less than five minutes later that Lana and Jon teleported into the Oval Office, resplendent in their new tailor-made uniforms, a style slightly different to their everyday tunics, and in dazzling white.

Well, the president thought in admiration, *with their stature and good looks, dressed like that, they will stand out in any crowd. When they take to the podium at the assembly of the United Nations, all eyes will be riveted on them, but whether the delegates will be listening, though, is another matter,* he thought cynically.

Jon and Lana silently agreed with him, but diplomatically let the comment pass. But they mentally noted Davis Cooper's observations regarding their new uniforms and personal appearance. *It would appear that we meet with the President's approval,* Jon, Lana thought with a smile, *and I must say that I feel very confident to be dressed in something so different from our usual uniforms.* Thought transference being so much quicker than verbal exchanges, they were able to complete their telepathic conversation before walking forward to greet the president and his Secretary of State George K. Lane.

It was then that Davis Cooper made his comments aloud with regard to their new outfits, expressing his admiration for the styling changes from their previous uniforms. 'I think you could possibly start a new fashion trend when you are seen by the public,' he said warmly, 'and your time in the Caribbean sunshine has given you both a complimentary golden glow; it goes well with the white uniforms.'

Chapter Twenty-Seven

Not to be outdone, George commented on Lana's appearance, the style of uniform, the elegant picture she presented, and one other item the president had not noticed, the magnificent ring worn on her left hand. 'Lana,' he said with a smile, 'does that ring have any significance, or is it just for decoration?'

As she held her hand out to display the ring to the secretary, she laughed with delight to see the expression of wonder on his face and to read the thoughts going through his mind, *That must be worth millions.*

'No, Mr. Secretary, until we have exchanged rings, this one,' she said, holding her hand forward again, 'is only for decoration, but I intend to, as you say, "buy" a ring for Jon to wear so that your people will know we are observing your custom of declaring your love for another by exchanging rings.'

His attention having been drawn to Lana's ring, Davis Cooper asked if he could have a closer look, which Lana was more than happy to allow, as she held her left hand out for closer inspection. Over the years, the president had mingled with women from every walk of life, the famous, the rich, film stars, and even royalty, but he had never seen such a wonderful example of the jeweller's art before. And he had the same thought in mind as George K. Lane, *How much did it cost to buy?* He had to ask in amazement, 'Where on Earth did you get that diamond? It's so huge, and the rubies set it off to perfection.'

Lana smiled as she replied, 'It was a gift from my father who visited Earth many years ago. As to where it originated, I have no idea, but he thought it was a trinket that might give me pleasure. Displaying the ring again for all to see, she continued, 'Jon had a jeweller in Jamaica make the ring for me; it is beautiful, isn't it.'

Davis Cooper raised an eyebrow at Lana's reference to the trinket. 'I think you will need your own security guard if you're

Chapter Twenty-Seven

going to wear that ring in public, or will you only wear it on special occasions like today's visit to New York or to public receptions?'

Lana had no hesitancy as she replied, 'I will always wear it, wherever I go. It is a constant reminder of the two men I love, Jon and my father. As far as requiring a guard for my protection, that won't be necessary,' she said and gave an intriguing smile. 'Jon and I have already experienced a situation involving some very "bad" men who wanted to deprive us of our possessions . . . .' She paused for a moment, thinking how best to phrase her next sentence. 'But we deterred them quite forcefully.'

George K. Lane thought, *What you're telling us, Lana, is that some crooks tried to rob you and you slapped them down, but I for one appreciate your delicate choice of language.* Aloud he said, 'Well, while you're in our company, there is little likelihood of any bad men trying to rob you. There are always a number of bodyguards present when the President is out and about, although they keep their presence very discreet.'

With a disarming smile, Jon intervened. 'It is just as likely, Mr Secretary, George, that we may have to protect you and the president at some time in the future. Even with bodyguards, I believe that several of your presidents have been assassinated in the past.'

'That's true,' George acknowledged, 'so it will be reassuring to have you around, Jon, although it has to be said that Davis Cooper here,' he touched the president's shoulder, 'is one of the most popular leaders of the American people in modern times.'

'And what of people of other races or cultures?' Jon enquired. 'Are they likely to share such benevolent feelings? I have experienced some hostility toward me, violence, in fact, by people who had no reason to doubt my popularity, since they didn't even know me.' He smiled again before continuing, 'But that is a situation I hope to address when we go to New York. No doubt there will be many

Chapter Twenty-Seven

representatives of governments from all over the world in attendance.'

'Within hours of your introduction to the delegates, Jon, your face, name and the fact that you are the representative of an alien race and culture will be widely known throughout the world,' Davis Cooper confirmed. Then he wryly admitted, 'But that doesn't mean you will be universally popular; in fact, you could yourself become a target for assassination.'

Jon conceded that that was always a possibility, but he added, 'If you remember, Mr President, I invited several of your security people to shoot me in this very office, and they couldn't succeed even at such close range. If necessary, I could include you within my protective shield or,' he laughed in anticipation of Davis Cooper's reaction, 'I could teleport you out of harm's way in seconds.'

As expected, the president was not altogether enthusiastic about being teleported anywhere, despite General Clintock having described the experience as amazing. 'Let's just hope that won't be necessary, Jon,' he said with a dubious smile.

As they all exchanged pleasantries and compliments, George K. Lane reminded the president that it was time to go. 'The General will be getting anxious if you're late, and Air Force One will be waiting on the tarmac for us.'

'Very well, we mustn't keep anyone waiting,' was the cheerful reply. 'Punctuality is the politeness of kings and presidents,' he added with a laugh, as he ushered Lana and Jon toward the door, followed by his secretary of state. Ten minutes later, they were all settled into the presidential limousine, and accompanied by the usual entourage of officials and security personnel, were whisked quickly to the military airfield outside the city, where General Robert E. Clintock was waiting, surprisingly patiently, for their arrival,

After formally saluting the president and secretary of state, he then turned his attention to Lana and Jon, shouting to make himself

Chapter Twenty-Seven

heard above the noise of their waiting aircraft. 'This is going to be a new experience for you both, to fly at such a slow speed and in a normal aeroplane. It may take the best part of three hours to reach New York, but at least you will have every comfort on board and no security concerns.'

Jon smiled inwardly at the mention of the new experience, for Lana, yes, it was. Her first flight in an earthly flying machine would be something different, albeit in a jumbo aircraft fitted with every luxury to make any journey as comfortable as sitting in a luxury hotel, apart from the noise. As for himself, he had spent years controlling the flights of craft such as this, and he had travelled extensively all over the world, until he was married and had settled down to raise a family. *So, this is nothing new for me, General,* he thought.

However, to keep in character as a representative of Zel, and therefore one accustomed to travelling in spaceships and flying saucers, he pretended to be very interested in this antiquated method of transport. While inwardly, he communicated with Lana. *This is how the rich and famous, not to mention the most powerful, people travel.*

For her part, Lana was fascinated by the interior of Air Force One. 'It's like a luxury home in miniature,' she said aloud, which brought appreciative smiles to the faces of the president and his men, the secretary and the general.

Turning to Jon, she added, 'While it is much smaller than the flight deck of our own ship, I must concede that it is much more comfortable than our own living accommodations, although our sleeping quarters are much the same in terms of luxury.'

Once they were all comfortably seated, it was General Clintock who reminded them that for their own safety they should observe the usual regulations and fasten their seat belts, although he didn't think to explain why.

Chapter Twenty-Seven

Jon communicated with Lana, briefly but telepathically. *These aircraft have to gain flying speed by running along the ground for some distance before they can lift off or overcome gravity. And while aircraft such as this are considered extremely safe, there have been occasions in the past when accidents have occurred on take-off, such as engine failure, which consequently brings the craft to an abrupt halt.* He didn't use the term 'crash' as he didn't want to alarm Lana unnecessarily. *Let her enjoy this unique experience of winged flight,* he thought.

They all relaxed as Air Force One taxied to the end of the runway, and Jon reached out to take Lana's hand to reassure her. Reading her mind, he could sense her alarm at this new experience. All her previous flights had involved vertical take-off until an altitude of several miles was reached before directional speed was called for, plus the Zellian spacecraft had antigravity and anti-inertia systems which eliminated all feeling of motion to the occupants, and of course, were completely silent in flight.

Lana became even more tense when Air Force One paused momentarily at the end of the runway while the pilot built up the engine power to propel the aircraft forward and to build up to take off speed. As the plane surged forward, the g-force was noticeable to any passenger, but not alarming to the average traveller. However, for Lana, this was unlike any previous flight in her lifetime, and when the point was reached when the aircraft became airborne, it seemed as though the g-force was pinning her back in her seat. Moments later, the pilot boosted the power to a maximum, pointed skyward, and the plane climbed and climbed until the plane felt as though it was standing on its tail. They were well above the ground far below, and only then was the rate of climb reduced. It would take a further ten minutes to reach their estimated cruising altitude, normally about thirty-five thousand feet.

Chapter Twenty-Seven

Feeling concerned for Lana's emotional well-being, Jon asked aloud, 'Was that what you expected of a twenty-first-century aircraft, Lana?'

To which she replied somewhat shakily, 'I was very frightened and scared, and at the same time, excited by the experience.' Relieved that she hadn't been overwhelmed by the fear aspect of the take-off, Jon hastened to assure her that she had coped extremely well with the experience. He added telepathically, *I felt the same on my first ride on the Big Dipper at Blackpool.* He then went on to describe that event in some detail, while the other members of the presidential team thought Jon and Lana were merely being silent as they absorbed the new experience.

Eventually, having attained the required altitude and cruising speed, the pilot was able to throttle back the power of the engines and subsequently reduce the noise in the passenger compartment. It was then that Davis Cooper left his seat, and standing over Lana enquired, 'I take it that you found Air Force One somewhat different from your own craft. The General never tires of telling me how impressed he was with the flight back from Fort Knox; he'll never forget it.' Then laughing, he added, 'And I won't be allowed to forget either.'

Trying to portray a calmness she did not feel, and not wishing to appear ungrateful for the hospitality of the president, Lana answered, 'I had no idea what to expect of your aircraft and its performance, but I found it interesting and very different from our own, and yes, quite exciting.'

As he listened to Lana's statement, Jon thought, for her benefit only, *You are very definitely a diplomat in the making, Lana, but having said that, you will probably be expected to fly back to Washington on the return journey if the President thinks you are enjoying this flight.*

Chapter Twenty-Seven

Still on a telepathic level, she answered, *A new experience should be savoured, but not necessarily repeated. We will talk about it later.*

Now that they were safely airborne, one of the cabin stewards came in to enquire who would like breakfast and produced a menu, which, whilst not extensive, would have done credit to many first-class hotels. Lana was curious to know how the food was prepared, and their steward explained that there was a small galley or kitchen on board. All the meals were precooked and only required a few minutes in a microwave oven to heat them up and ready them for consumption. Lana turned to Jon and said, 'That's quite similar to our own arrangement, except that we have a far greater choice, and we only need to press a few buttons to select whatever we require.' Then she laughed as she added, 'But we don't have a steward to serve us, except on the mother ship.'

Jon noted that apart from the president, who only ordered a coffee, most of the presidential team intended to fortify themselves against the rigours of the day by ordering a typical American-style breakfast. 'Too much for me at this time of the day,' he said as he eyed General Clintock's tray. 'I'll wait until lunchtime before I attempt to eat such a substantial meal.'

Lana was also somewhat surprised at the quantity of food being served to the other members of the party, the general in particular, and when she mentally commented on her observation to Jon, he replied, *Now you know why he weighs two hundred twenty pounds; he's a big man with a big appetite!*

More out of curiosity than anything else, since she had never tasted food prepared by anyone other than her own crewmembers, Lana asked for a very small American breakfast. When it arrived, it caused her to comment, 'I couldn't possibly eat all that, Jon. Will it cause offence if I leave most of it?'

Laughing sympathetically at her dismay, he said, 'I haven't ordered anything other than a coffee, so we will share your breakfast between us, although there's more than enough for two people on that plate.' He added, *If we were to eat like the General, we would have to have new uniforms every week.*

Once the meal was out of the way, the stewards cleared and tidied up the cabin, leaving the passengers to relax and enjoy the flight. However, Lana again privately communicated her thoughts to Jon. *The cabin itself is very comfortable, and our travelling companions entertaining and sociable, but I don't like the noise and constant feeling of motion, not to mention the vibration in the aircraft.*

Jon visibly smiled at Lana. He held her hand in sympathy and thought, *Never mind, Lana, we will have to think of returning to Washington in a different manner to this. Just give me time to consider the alternatives.* He then added, *Here on Earth, the science and engineering of flight has only been in existence for about one hundred years, but even so, it has progressed tremendously in that time.* Lana conceded that the people of Earth had been under surveillance constantly during that time, and it had been noticed that their first flying machines were flimsy contraptions. But with the advent of two world wars, the progress of which caused the Zellians some concern, aircraft improved rapidly, to the point that they could transport hundreds of people over long distances in a degree of comfort unheard of at the beginning of the twentieth century. However, their war machines had also improved their efficiency to deal in death and destruction.

Jon ruefully agreed with everything that Lana was saying telepathically, but pointed out that their mission on Earth was to bring about peace between the warring nations. *If we can achieve that, Lana, and it is a lasting peace, something like two hundred years without conflict on the planet, then we may consider advancing humanity's knowledge even further, which is what the Teachers before me have done.*

Chapter Twenty-Seven

While they had been communicating on a telepathic level, George K. Lane had been quietly observing them. This had been the longest time he had spent in their company, and he had noted from time to time the apparent lapses in conversation between Lana and Jon, but a degree of understanding between the two of them not consistent with their conversation. He shrewdly considered the possibility that they were telepathic, but how could he prove it? If asked outright, would they confirm that they were, and if that was the case, could they also read the minds of those around them?

Now that is an ability I wish I had, he thought. *It would make my negotiations with the representatives of other governments so much easier. Half of them are lying through their teeth when they try to convince us of their sincerity.* Having considered the question for a time, he resolved that while Davis Cooper and the general were involved in some discussion at that moment, he would the take the bull by the horns, the direct approach, for he was convinced that in answer to a direct question, Jon would not lie. *Just like George Washington,* he thought with a smile.

He waited a few minutes longer. Jon and Lana were making no obvious attempt at conversation, but varying emotions showed on their faces, which suggested to George that there was some communication taking place between them. He quietly walked through the cabin and sat down on one of the comfortable armchairs opposite the couple, who looked up with interest.

Jon was the first to speak. 'Yes, George, we do know what you are going to ask. You cannot keep your thoughts from us, no matter how hard you try, and the same applies to any man, woman, or child who is near us, unless we choose not to "read" them.'

'I thought as much.' George exclaimed. 'Presumably, you are both telepaths, but I believe I may be the first member of the White House to recognise your ability; you amaze me, Jon.' With a hint of amusement in his voice, he recounted the day in the Oval Office when General Clintock had been effortlessly hoisted into the air,

Chapter Twenty-Seven

demonstrating Jon's remarkable physical strength. 'You also have other powers you used when you rescued Professor Mahmoud. I believe telekinesis is one of them, and you also mentioned that you have a protective energy shield around you. Does Lana share these same abilities?'

Taking the opportunity to answer for herself, Lana spoke just loud enough for George K. Lane to hear above the now subdued roar of the jet engines, but soft enough not to include the other personnel in the cabin. 'All my people share the ability to communicate by telepathy and to read other people's minds, but as individuals, we can block any unwelcome intrusions into our thoughts. This is something you and the other people of Earth cannot do, so we know what you are thinking, even on a subconscious level. We are aware of what you are about to say, but as Jon said a moment ago, only if we choose to read you.'

Lana stopped talking, giving Jon the opportunity to come back into the conversation. 'All the people of the planet Zel have an inherited ability to be telepathic,' he declared, 'and some, like Lana, can teleport from an early age, but only for short distances. It is an ability that is normally developed over a period of many years, but Lana also has another valued gift, superintelligence.' He smiled as he continued. 'She is the product of a civilisation that is many millions of years older than any on Earth, and although she is considered by her own people to be a very young woman, she already has more knowledge regarding spaceflight, navigation, and engineering than all the technicians at NASA put together.'

Although he was secretary of state for the most powerful democracy on Earth, George K. Lane felt slightly overawed in the presence of these two super-beings. Addressing yet another question to Jon directly, he asked, 'We assume that your people have learned about our languages by listening to our radio and television broadcasts. Apart from your command of English, which you both speak perfectly, better than us Americans,' he added with

Chapter Twenty-Seven

a laugh, 'we know from Professor Mahmoud's account of his rescue that you also speak perfect Arabic, like a native he assured us. So, do you speak any other languages, Jon?'

After a moment's hesitation while he reflected on the consequences of giving further information regarding his abilities, Jon decided that an occasion was quite likely to arise when he would have to communicate in other languages with other foreign nationals; therefore, it would do no harm to enlighten George a little more. With a smile on his face, he answered, 'Apart from English and Arabic, which you already know about, I also speak eight other widely spoken Earth languages, including Russian and Mandarin Chinese. So I may prove useful to you personally, George, if you have to get into a debate with one of the inscrutable Asians. To read their minds, it is essential to also speak their language.'

After the initial shock of this further revelation of this amazing man's abilities, George was able to say, 'I'll certainly bear your offer in mind.' Then laughing, he continued, 'It would be the first time ever that we would have the edge on them at the negotiating table; just don't get too far away from me.'

Having assured the secretary of state that he would make himself available should the need arise, Jon then informed his listener that while Lana also had a protective energy shield that she could activate when necessary, she had no powers of telekinesis and only limited language skills. But she was a very good pilot and navigator. Reaching out to touch her hand fondly, he said, 'And she is a wonderful companion while we are here on Earth.' Then he added thoughtfully, 'Which is likely to be for the rest of our lives; we have much to achieve in that time.'

Now that much of his curiosity was satisfied, although there were still a few questions he would have liked to ask, George thought, *How much time is required to travel the immense distance from another galaxy? How can one so young as Lana acquire so much*

Chapter Twenty-Seven

knowledge of astral navigation, physics, and engineering, since she only appears to be in her early twenties?

Jon was typical of the male population of the planet Zel. He replied, 'It never occurred to me that it could be otherwise.'

However, at that moment, the pilot announced they were commencing the descent and their approach to their destination, the military airfield outside New York City. From there, they would complete their journey, first to the hotel where they would have lunch, and thence to the United Nations building in the city. The secretary of state made his excuses to Jon and Lana, 'I've got to remind the president of our schedule for the next few hours.' He added with a smile, 'Since he's been talking with the General for the last hour or so, his mind will no doubt be on other things, like flying in your craft or war talk. Maybe even discussing what our representative of the Zellian people intends to say at the assembly meeting this afternoon.' With that, he rose from his seat, leaving Jon and Lana to themselves while he rejoined Davis Cooper and General Clintock, a satisfied smile on his face. He now knew a little more about their guests from another planet. *Think good thoughts, George,* he reminded himself.

The descent of Air Force One was uneventful, apart from Lana experiencing the change of air pressure in the cabin as they lost altitude, but Jon assured her that this was quite normal. He asked the steward to provide her with a sweet to suck on. 'Keep swallowing, Lana, and it will take the pressure from your ears.'

Even so, the discomfort caused Lana to comment, 'I don't like flying on this kind of aircraft. Have you thought of any other alternative as to how we can do the return journey, Jon?'

'Yes,' he replied sympathetically, 'but we will discuss that a little later today, after the UN Assembly meeting. In the meanwhile, it will only be a few more minutes before we land and your ordeal will be over.'

Chapter Twenty-Seven

Once the aircraft had landed, it was guided to its parking area adjacent to the administration block where the presidential cavalcade was waiting for them. Without any delay, they were all ushered into their respective vehicles, officials and security people in the leading cars, the president after them, with the other vehicles to follow behind. As George K. Lane commented to Jon and Lana, 'They,' he said, indicating all the security personnel, 'are our only means of defending the President.'

Jon made no comment, but remembered a previous presidential cavalcade where the popular president had been assassinated. The security guards had been powerless to stop the bullet, which had hit him in the head. *Will Davis Cooper fare better in the future? I can protect him only if I am near enough in the event of an assassination attempt.*

In due course, the cavalcade arrived at the designated hotel, near the UN building and on the waterfront. 'We can walk from here after lunch, George,' the president confided. 'It will do us all good after sitting about for so many hours; besides, it will give our guests an insight into the life in the big cities on Earth.'

'So long as you don't give them a tour of Brooklyn or the Bronx, Mr. President,' was the cryptic reply. 'I don't think they would be favourably impressed, but this area near the river is altogether different and not so congested as the downtown area.'

On entering the hotel, their arrival was, of course, expected and senior members of the staff were lined up to greet them. *An old-fashioned welcome,* Jon thought, catching Lana's attention. *You have to be someone rich or famous to get this kind of attention.* They were led into the dining room by the head of the security team and two of the guards. Even in this supposedly safe environment, their hands were never far from their guns, and once seated, the president, secretary of state, General Clintock, and the two guests of honour, Jon and Lana, were left on their own whilst the rest of the entourage filed into an adjacent room.

Chapter Twenty-Seven

'Well, this is all rather splendid, George,' Davis Cooper remarked. 'You did well to choose this place and location. What do you think, Jon? As hotels go, this is one of the better ones, not palatial by any means, but beautifully presented in every way. Pleasant surroundings, well-trained staff and hopefully . . . .'

At this point he was interrupted by the general, whose only comment was, 'A really good chef.'

That raised a laugh from the others, setting the tone for a relaxing meal and some enjoyable conversation. 'Presumably, even with your advanced civilisation on your home planet, Jon,' the president remarked, 'you socialise in much the same manner, with a few friends who meet for dinner on the odd occasion, polite conversation, and all that, yes?'

Knowing little or nothing of the social niceties observed on the planet Zel, but unable to admit it, Jon laughingly passed the question onto Lana. 'Lana is not only a good pilot and navigator, but an excellent hostess and one day,' he said, giving her a meaningful look, 'we will buy a residence somewhere on Earth similar to her home on Zel. Then you will all be invited to our new home to sample our hospitality, and you will not be disappointed.'

Lana took it on herself to add wistfully, 'No doubt once I have attended several of your social gatherings, we will find that, as with all civilised societies, how we behave on Zel is in no way different to how people on Earth conduct themselves, with two noticeable exceptions. We have never smoked since tobacco doesn't grow on our planet, and while we do drink a type of wine, no one ever drinks to excess. I've never seen any person drunk, except on some of *your* television programmes.'

General Robert E. Clintock gave a loud laugh as he enquired, 'Hell, Lana, what do you do for kicks?'

She had a puzzled expression as she said, 'Kicks?'

'Yes,' he said, 'enjoyment.'

Chapter Twenty-Seven

'Oh!' she pointedly replied as she looked around the table. 'This would be considered one means of enjoyment, to meet with friends and discuss any points of interest that affect our daily lives or educational interests. When any of our mother ships return from the stars, the crews have much to tell us about their travels and what they have experienced.'

'But don't you do anything else by way of entertainment?' the general insisted. 'You must have seen our games of baseball on television, surely?'

With understanding dawning on her face, Lana answered, 'With our people, we do participate in games, but rarely as mass spectators.' Giving a slight frown of disdain, she added, 'I would find it very boring to sit and watch someone else enjoying themselves; it's far better to be a participant. Many of our people enjoy physical challenges so long as it doesn't cause injury to others.' Noting the curious expressions on their faces and the questions in their minds, she added for clarification, 'When our planet was young, it was very similar to Earth in many ways. Its development followed a similar path, albeit millions of years earlier, and we too had a race of people who enjoyed sports such as you play nowadays. We have watched with approval your television programmes of what you call the Olympic games, athletes competing against small groups or individuals, which to us has some meaning, and that is today a means of providing sport, healthy activity, and entertainment.'

'Can't argue against that,' the general commented. 'I sometimes wish that I was a little fitter,' he said as he patted his waistline. He added, 'But it's a bit late for me to start training for the Olympics.'

As they all laughed at the thought of the general trying to be an athlete, George K. Lane put out a question of his own, purely out of curiosity. 'If your people developed in a similar way to us, Lana, the people of Earth, did they ever hunt wild animals? Indeed, did wild animals ever exist on Zel?'

Chapter Twenty-Seven

'Oh, yes!' she exclaimed, 'but the last of those were hunted to extinction millions of years ago. And this will surely happen on Earth unless all the species are conserved rather than destroyed, but we still have hunting parties of a kind, purely for entertainment and to preserve some of the ancient hunting skills. We use primitive weapons; otherwise, there would be no challenge if we were to use modern weapons to kill.'

'But you said you didn't have any wild animals left on your planet,' George K. Lane stated. 'So what do you hunt?'

'Artificial life forms,' Lana replied. 'Our technology allowed our scientists to develop animals that are an exact replica of their ancestors of millions of years ago, and while they look and act like a real animal, they are expendable and can even be repaired if they are badly damaged by the hunters. Also, they are programmed to be menacing, as they would have been originally, but to stop short of actually killing a living person. Although, having said that, injuries do occur when the hunters become too complacent. The ALFs are not necessarily aware of the fine line between aggression or killing, but it all adds realism to the hunt.'

'Sounds as though that would provide enough excitement for me,' the general exclaimed. 'I don't know about the primitive weapons, though. What would that entail, Lana, spears or bows and arrows or would you classify guns such as we use as primitive weapons?'

Lana laughed with amusement. 'Your guns are much the same as we were using one million years ago, but even so, the ALFs wouldn't have had much of a chance of survival if they had been real animals. It would still have been classified as a slaughter, and not very sporting.' Still smiling, she continued, 'Yes, General, you guessed correctly. Our very early ancestors used bows and arrows, spears when hunting bigger game, and harpoons when fishing. All the weapons that we introduced to your ancestors before and since

Chapter Twenty-Seven

your last Ice Age, but Jon may tell you more about that. He is, after all, the Teacher.'

Davies Cooper remarked, 'Sounds like Jon is going to have a busy time bringing us up to date on the past activities of the Zellian people, and in particular, the role of a Teacher. I'm slightly confused, though. I gather that you, Jon, intend to remain on Earth for as long as it takes to bring this planet to order, but how long is that likely to take? We've already been fighting each other on a really large scale for at least one hundred years and so-called minor skirmishes for centuries before that.'

It was at this point that their conversation was interrupted by members of the hotel staff bringing in their light lunch, which had been preordered by George K. Lane. He was the man responsible for ensuring that everything was organised for a trouble-free day for the president and his party. The meal was served efficiently, and suited the palates of all present. The only comment came from the general who, despite the huge breakfast on Air Force One, said, 'The portions are a bit puny.' Otherwise, everyone else was more than satisfied. On conclusion of the meal, there still was plenty of time before their estimated time of arrival at the UN building. They continued to linger at the table and added to their conversation, in particular, Jon's length of stay on Earth and how much he could hope to achieve in his lifetime, bearing in mind the fact that humankind had always been at war with each other, fighting over territory, possessions, food, and religion.

'You name it, and we've fought over it,' declared the general. 'Seems we're never happy unless we are trying to impose our will on other people.'

'So, what do you hope to achieve in your lifetime on Earth, Jon?' Davis Cooper asked. 'I'd say you were in your early thirties now, am I right?' Jon merely smiled and nodded in confirmation, knowing which way the conversation was going. 'So, that would probably leave another thirty years absolute maximum,' the president

Chapter Twenty-Seven

continued, 'by which time, the toll of politics will have aged you far more than an ordinary job would have done; just look at all the world leaders.' He then laughed as he commented, 'It makes me glad that here in the States, the presidency is only for two terms in office.'

Jon knew that what he was about to divulge was going to be a shock to the president, and to the other two men also, but it was something they had to be made aware of if they were to have confidence in his credibility as a long-term Teacher. He decided to inform them of his estimated longevity, but to make it more believable, he directed their intention, first of all, to Lana.

He started with a direct question to George K. Lane. 'George, when we had our conversation on the plane coming down from Washington, you made a remark questioning how a young woman like Lana could be such an accomplished astrophysicist and navigator, not to mention an engineering specialist, didn't you?' On receiving a nod from the secretary of state, he continued with yet another question. 'Look closely at her now, George, very closely, and tell me candidly, how old do you think she is?'

Pursing his lips as he pondered the question, the secretary thought he could estimate any person's age reasonably accurately, and in this case, it was a pleasure to run his expert eye over Lana's exquisite features. He noted the subdued golden tan acquired during her time in the Caribbean and her long elegant figure, a figure that many so-called supermodels would die for. He took note of her air of general confidence in her ability to perform the tasks in running her ship, and of course, coping with the social niceties in what to her was an alien environment.

Eventually, he came to a decision in his mind and replied slowly, 'I would say no more than twenty-four or twenty-five years of age, and I say that in view of the fact that she is so highly qualified, but if you tell me she is younger than that, I'd quite happily accept that I was wrong.'

Chapter Twenty-Seven

During the time that she had been under scrutiny, Lana had been reading the mind of the secretary of state, observing the changing estimates of her age with some amusement, but like Jon, she knew that it was unlikely any human being would relate her age to her appearance. *By their standards, I'm only a young girl.*

Jon waited for a few moments before answering.

George, waiting in suspense, thought, *How accurate was my estimate?* But he was totally shocked when he received the answer.

'Hold on to your chair, George,' Jon said with a grin, anticipating the shock that not only George K. Lane was going to have, but Davis Cooper and the general as well. They had been listening to the conversation intently and trying to estimate Lana's age in their own minds. 'You will be surprised to learn, George, that you are way out on your reckoning.' Then Jon turned to the other men, knowing that they also had been trying to come up with the right answer. 'And you General, how old would you think this young lady is?'

General Clintock hesitated before replying. 'Well, if George's estimate of twenty-four to twenty-five years old is way out, although it goes against the grain for a gentleman to say so, then I take it that Lana must be a little older, perhaps twenty-eight to thirty years old, but she's remarkably youthful for her age.'

Before confirming or denying the guesses of the other men, Jon exchanged a mental question with Lana. *Do you think now is the time to tell them?*

'George, General, I didn't really expect either of you to give an accurate assessment of Lana's age. She is a native of the planet Zel where it is considered normal to live far beyond the normal lifespan of people on Earth. In Earth years, she is eighty years old.' As he noted the look of shock, or was it incredulity on their faces, he waited expectantly for their reaction.

'You're kidding!' General Clintock exclaimed. Disbelief was written all over his face. 'Even when I said she looked up to thirty years of age, I thought I was being a bit over the top, but eighty, geez!'

Recalling their earlier conversation, it was Davis Cooper's turn to ask a question. 'Jon, I put your age, judging by your appearance, to be in the early thirties. If Lana looks as though she is in her mid-twenties, but is in fact eighty, then pro rata, that should put you well over one hundred years old.' Shaking his head again in disbelief, he added, 'What, then, is a normal lifespan on Zel?'

Accepting that he would have to go along with the deception of being a native of the planet Zel, and therefore, by the president's calculation of being over one hundred years old, Jon could only smile as he answered the question. 'Illnesses are rare, and as long as no injuries are sustained or accidents, it would be quite normal to exceed a thousand years, and in some cases, well past that age.'

Again, still looking bemused by the information he had received, the president continued. 'Then, that would mean that you could possibly live for another thousand years; that's incredible.' He added with a smile, 'That should give you time to sort out the problems of the nations of Earth.'

Not wishing to cause further confusion by informing Davis Cooper that his own longevity was estimated to be 'only' five hundred years, and Lana's of a similar period if she stayed permanently on Earth, Jon let the matter pass. After all, so much could happen during that period of time, and who would know the difference?

There being no further revelations for the moment, since Jon and Lana's ability to teleport had already been demonstrated, and the lunch was concluded to the satisfaction of all concerned. The general had consumed several of the puny portions, so their thoughts turned to the final stage of the day's journey, the short walk to the UN building about two blocks away, according to George K. Lane. At that moment, the senior security official came into the dining room and approaching Davis Cooper, held a furtive conversation with

Chapter Twenty-Seven

him, which culminated in a nod of understanding, after which the security man withdrew silently.

'Well, folks,' the president remarked. 'There's been a slight change of plan. I've just been advised that because of the nature of today's meeting, there will be so many dignitaries attending that we won't be safe to travel on foot with the crowds, so we will be driven the remaining distance, but we will arrive on time nevertheless.'

As they all pushed back their chairs and made their way out of the dining room and into the foyer, Jon communicated telepathically with Lana. *It seems as though you will see New York at its busiest, not an experience to enjoy, Lana. I much prefer a quiet lifestyle and our island.*

Turning her head, she smiled as she mentally phrased the question, *Can we go back there for just a few more days after the meeting, please, Jon, please?*

Of course, my darling, of course. Just let us find out what the delegates intend to do about my proposals, not a lot, presumably. After that, we'll have a few days on our island before we begin our work of rendering all the world's nuclear missiles useless.

As before, they were ushered into the waiting vehicles, and with lights flashing and motorcycle riders clearing the traffic for them, they drove the short distance to the United Nations building on the edge of the river, where they were greeted by even more officials and security personnel. Within minutes, they were conducted into the debating chamber, already filled to capacity by the representatives of most of the nations, large and small, of Earth. *But how united are they?* Jon asked himself.

Chapter Twenty-Eight

After a brief but courteous introduction to the assembly of the United Nations by the secretary-general, accompanied by Lana, Jon was led to the rostrum from where he would deliver his address. As they took up their positions, the eyes of the hundreds of delegates, and on this unique occasion, the eyes of the world's media, television cameras and press reporters were focused on the representatives of the planet Zel, guests of the United Nations.

While the people present in the assembly could plainly see Jon and Lana, the various reporters were describing the 'aliens' in every detail, despite the fact that the television audiences could probably see the visitors more clearly and in close-up. Lana, of course, attracted the attention of all the reporters, and her beauty was rightly described as 'out of this world.' 'She has the grace and bearing of a princess,' one reporter was heard to say, while another suggested that with her looks and figure, the moguls from Hollywood would be trying to entice her with lucrative contracts.

The seating arrangements in the assembly were such that every representative had a clear view of the principal speaker, Jon. As he stood there silently waiting for the hubbub of excited conversation to die away, mainly from the media reporters, he tried to shut out the conflicting thoughts of the people he was about to address. He had given some thought to the content of his speech. It was not too long, since this was not to be a lecture on the failings of the different governments, but more about the Zellians and their hopes for Earth, but first, he had his own introduction.

Chapter Twenty-Eight

During the time he waited for a suitable moment to begin talking, he himself was subjected to the same scrutiny that Lana had undergone. Without exception, every reporter began his description of Jon by commenting first of all on his mass of glowing silver hair. A leonine style was the observation of one lady, causing Jon to reflect that, since he had forsaken his old lifestyle in England, it hadn't occurred to him to have his hair cut. *Must do it soon,* he thought.

The matching uniforms in brilliant white were likewise commented on; the tailors in Jamaica had excelled themselves in designing, producing, and fitting the garments to perfection. Lana's feminine figure was shown perfectly, while Jon's muscular physique was enhanced to such a degree that, in any crowd, he would be the envy of most other men. He caused the ladies to think, *Are all the men on planet Zel such perfect specimens?*

It seemed to take a long time before Jon decided to begin his speech, but when all was quiet, there was an electrifying air of expectancy in the auditorium, and then he formally introduced himself, keeping it brief and simple. 'Ladies and gentlemen of the United Nations of planet Earth, my name is Jon and my companion, the lady you have all been admiring . . . He said this with a smile, knowing it to be true, 'is Lana. We have no other names, but we are representatives of the people of the planet Zel, which I'm sure none of you have ever heard of before, not surprisingly, as it is in another galaxy many light-years in distance from your Earth.' He waited for a moment before continuing, giving the audience time to take in this statement. 'The purpose of us being here is to continue the work of our own ancestors in helping your people to develop and mature, so that one day you can become citizens of the stars and join your own universe to the other galaxies beyond here.

'The people of the planet Zel were already an ancient race before your own ancestors became men. In fact, we were responsible for the development of certain primitive creatures into the kind of modern men that you recognise today.' Knowing that revelations or

Chapter Twenty-Eight

references to the early ape-like creatures of the distant past might not be welcomed by the delegates, Jon decided not to dwell on that aspect of history. 'I will be quite happy to give further information on that subject to your anthropologists and historians at a more appropriate time.

'Suffice it to say, we have kept the planet Earth and its people under surveillance for millions of years, doing what we could to help the progress of civilisations and to educate the early races. We taught them various skills to make their lives more productive, enabling them to cope with the harsh environment of the African continent at one point in history, and then the recent Ice Age of some ten to twelve thousand years ago, a time when much of this planet was uninhabitable to early man.' Despite the fact that many of the delegates were probably aware of some of the prehistory mentioned, they continued to listen attentively, waiting for something new to emerge, so Jon continued.

'Zellian scientists have visited Earth regularly, normally at five-hundred-year intervals and when it was deemed necessary, a Teacher, such as myself, was left behind on the planet to live and work beside your people, sometimes for two or three years, sometimes much longer.' He smiled disarmingly as he remarked, 'As you will gather, our early Teachers integrated with humans very successfully.

'During the course of your history, our teachers were largely responsible for the rise of various cultures and dynasties. The earliest civilisations were not in Europe or America as many imagine, but in Asia, China and India, in particular, and of course, Egypt, Greece, and the Roman Empire, all of which rose to the pinnacle of success and then crashed disastrously, leaving behind only a memory of their greatness. The Egyptians left behind their pyramids, the largest structures on the planet for thousands of years, and the Romans and the people of Greece, well, their legacy to the world was the beauty of their architecture. If it had been

Chapter Twenty-Eight

possible for them to visit Zel, that is where your people would have found their inspiration for such structures, motivated by the teachers from Zel.'

Still holding the attention of his audience, Jon continued, 'But what legacy will you leave for future generations?' he asked. 'If you continue as you are doing, raping the planet and destroying your own environment? There is one issue in particular to address, which is why we are here on the planet at this time, the threat of self-destruction by nuclear activity.' Again, he paused as he noted the guilty looks between certain members of those known to possess the so-called nuclear deterrent, and some who denied its very existence. 'Our awareness of the use of such weapons was made some sixty-five years ago, which brought to an end yet another of your major conflicts, but if you depend on such weapons, their use could possibly escalate to the point where the planet could be destroyed, rendering it uninhabitable. Then what will happen to humankind?'

Assuming a slightly less abrasive tone of voice, Jon went on to point out that war, on whatever scale, rarely achieved a lasting solution to any problems; whereas, in its wake, it left death, disease, starvation and misery for millions. 'Far better that you eliminate conflicts and the results that wars inevitably bring,' he exhorted his listeners. 'For many years, the Zellians have listened to broadcasts on your radio and television programmes, and we've heard a phrase used repeatedly, "ban the bomb." That would be a sensible thing to do, but instead, the proliferation of nuclear weapons is now commonplace. Recently, one country, which has strenuously denied having such a weapon, had an "accident," revealing the existence of such a missile. Other accidents could happen, enough to trigger a nuclear war, possibly.'

Jon dissuaded the various governments to stop manufacturing weapons of mass destruction and instead to concentrate their resources on conserving all that was good for the planet and its people. As a reminder, he again pointed out that if Earth became uninhabitable, where would the survivors go? 'As with all Teachers in the past, with the help of Lana, I will give you the technology to take you to the stars, if the people of Earth can lead a life of peace for a period of one hundred years.' He added with a wry smile, 'It will probably take your scientists all that time to reach the planets of this solar system, and if or when you get there, your astronauts will find their journey will have been futile, since none of the other planets in the solar system can sustain life as you know it. Believe me, the Zellians have been there in the past.'

Although no one had interrupted his speech or raised any questions thus far, he had a strong mental thought from a delegate sitting at the front of the audience, and sure enough, the man in question stood up to ask the question. 'You suggest that you and Lana will provide us with the technology to improve our future and to reach the stars, in one hundred years from now. We accept that everyone sitting here at the moment will have been dead for years by that time, so how will you be around to help us, Jon?' There was a slight ripple of laughter from many of the delegates at this moment of perceived amusement. One hundred years?

Understanding the natural scepticism of everybody present, with the exception of Davis Cooper and the general, Jon replied gravely, 'The average age of men and women on Earth nowadays is around eighty years, is it not?' The question was directed at the same man who had asked the original question.

'Yes,' he replied reluctantly, not knowing what was to follow.

'But when the Zellians first took an interest in man's early ancestors,' Jon continued, 'it was unusual for an adult to exceed twenty-five years of age. This was partly due to the environment in which they lived, but also because of genetic restrictions, which the Zellians improved in the course of time. Can you accept that as being true?'

Chapter Twenty-Eight

Slightly embarrassed to be singled out for questioning, the man replied, 'Unfortunately, I'm neither a historian nor a biologist, but I accept that life in those far-off times was very short compared to our life expectancy in the twenty-first century. I suppose it is a comparison in lifestyle and environment.'

'It is indeed,' Jon smiled as he agreed, then he continued. 'From the environmental point of view, Zel is much smaller than Earth, so gravity has less of an ageing effect or stress level on its population, with the result that they can expect to live to a far greater age than the people of Earth. I won't tell you how old, as you would find it difficult to believe.'

Somewhere in the background, the general nodded in agreement.

Jon continued. 'But I can assure you that, assuming we are allowed to live without accidents, both Lana and I will be on Earth for several hundreds of years into the future, which is time enough to fulfil our pledge to benefit humankind.'

Encouraged by the response to the first question, yet another delegate stood up, eager to put his own question. 'It's all very well to talk of technological advances in one hundred years' time, but what of the immediate future? How can we improve the environment of the planet and secure its future? Greenhouse gases and emissions are contributing to global warming and the destructive forces of nature, aren't they?'

'Yes,' Jon conceded, 'man is responsible in part for accelerating what is normally a natural cycle of weather patterns, and it would slow down global warming if humankind used different power sources. We are prepared to advise you on this, in return for the immediate destruction of every nuclear weapon on Earth, which would then herald a new beginning for clean energy on Earth.'

Disbelief showed on his face as the delegate sat down without pursuing his question further. Then Jon decided to suggest the means by which a clean environment could be obtained, but again, stating it was dependent on a commitment to abandon nuclear weapons. 'A number of nations represented here today have already harnessed the power of nuclear energy for peaceful purposes, to generate power, and they should be encouraged. The fear of the consequences of accidents would be eliminated if the technology was safeguarded. That is where the science of the Zellians could be applied, because nuclear energy has been the main source of power on Zel and for many other advanced civilisations for millions of years without mishap. Other applications of nuclear power can be utilised, too. You already have nuclear submarines, and although the technology is in its infancy, how many accidents have occurred to date? Not many, I believe, but even that could be improved beyond measure.'

Warming to his subject of the possibilities for the future, Jon then went on to the subject of fossil fuels. 'Think how many vehicles on the planet are running around burning oil, churning out carbon monoxide and other gases into the atmosphere; the amount of pollution will undoubtedly have a detrimental effect on the flora and fauna of the entire planet in time. But how much time do you have? Aircraft, there are thousands of aircraft in use at any given time, and they too cause massive pollution. Envisage a future where all ships, aircraft and motor cars use a nuclear fuel cell as a means of propulsion, then you will have an environmentally healthy planet. All this can be yours, but again, the first step toward this goal is to destroy all nuclear weapons immediately.' By this time, Jon thought, *I've given them enough to debate on for the next few days or weeks or months. Now I'll leave them to it whatever the outcome.* He then turned to smile at Lana and thought, *We're going to have those few days on our island, my darling, but after that, it will be back to work.* As he gazed out over the assembly, he said in conclusion, 'Ladies and gentlemen, members of the various governments of Earth, I am a Teacher, a representative of Zel. I cannot make you do what I suggest, destroy your nuclear weapons, but if you comply, I can hold out hope for a much improved future for you and every living

Chapter Twenty-Eight

creature on this planet, with health and prosperity for all, but if you fail to comply, you may not have a future at all.'

With that bleak warning, he thanked the delegates for their attention, promising that he would always be available to answer any queries or concerns they might have. To a rapturous applause, he was escorted to his seat beside the president of the United States, with Lana clasping his hand by way of encouragement.

She questioned him in her mind. *Do you think the governments represented here today will comply with your requests, Jon?*

On the contrary, was his telepathic reply, *they listened politely, but I could read the minds of many more of the powerful politicians in the assembly, and they simply don't trust each other to disarm unilaterally. As usual, they will prevaricate indefinitely, and nothing will be done. In which case, we will have those few days on our island as promised, and then we will begin our tour of the world, during which we will neutralise every nuclear missile that we have already identified.*

Chapter Twenty-Nine

On conclusion of Jon's speech to the assembly, he and Lana, in company with Davis Cooper and his entourage, were escorted out of the chamber with the intention of returning to the hotel, leaving the delegates to begin their discussions regarding the proposed destruction of all nuclear missiles. A matter that, as Jon had predicted, would occupy them for some time to come.

As the presidential car pulled away from the UN building, General Clintock leaned forward in his seat to lend emphasis to his words. 'That was a good speech, Jon,' he said, 'not too long and plain talking. I think the delegates were all interested in everything you were saying, except for the message you were trying to get across, to get rid of the nuclear arsenals.' He frowned. 'I'm no politician, but I suspect Congress will reject that idea every bit as much as the military. They will argue that the cost of our deterrent can't simply be ignored by scrapping every missile in our own defence armament, and no doubt, they will query the cost of doing that as well.'

'Shall we wait and see what the outcome of the United Nations debate is likely to be before we make any kind of decisions ourselves?' Davis Cooper remarked with a smile.

'In which case, I don't think there will be any urgency for Congress to vote on the issue.' With a snort of derision, General Robert E. Clintock stated his opinion of all politicians, 'Present company excepted,' he added with a grin. 'If there was a fire, they would argue how many buckets of water were needed to put it out or just piss on it.'

Chapter Twenty-Nine

Lana communicated telepathically with Jon. *If our top General has such a low opinion of the politicians of this and every other country in the world, even the president doesn't deny his assertions, then it's just as well that we don't intend to wait for a mandate from the United Nations before deactivating all the nuclear weapons. But that, of course, will be after our holiday on our island, Jon, won't it?*

He gently assured her. *Yes, we will spend a few days away from the political scene here in New York.* He added with a smile of affection, *And I have given the other matter, the flight back to Washington, some thought. I know how much you disliked travelling in Air Force One, so I have given it some consideration.* At that moment, the car drew up at the entrance to the hotel, so Jon said hastily, *I will let you know what I propose to do when we get back to our room.*

After getting out of the car, preceded by the security staff, the presidential party made its way into the foyer of the hotel and was greeted by the senior staff only on this occasion. Then the group had to be divided to take the lift to the upper floors. The president was accompanied by only one agent whilst the remaining security agents crammed into the remaining lifts. Their faces were as dark as their suits; to be separated from their charge in this way was not on their agenda, but it was not something that could be avoided under the circumstances. On gaining the required level, the door of the lift opened, and the security agent stepped out, who gave a quick nod of assurance to the president that all was clear. He then walked slowly along the wide corridor in the direction of the allocated rooms for the party, followed by Davis Cooper and Jon, who walked side by side, with General Clintock, George K. Lane and Lana bringing up the rear. As yet, the lift carrying the remainder of the security agents had not arrived on that particular floor, but as everything appeared to be quite normal in the otherwise deserted corridor, the group followed the single agent, who was by now some ten paces ahead of them.

Chapter Twenty-Nine

Jon stopped abruptly, putting his arm across the chest of the president, effectively stopping him in his tracks. 'Wait.' he exclaimed. He had caught a menacing thought from someone hidden from sight, an assassin with murder on his mind.

Davis Cooper had just time to say, 'What the...?' when a solitary man dressed in black clothing jumped out of a side room. He had waited for the security man to pass before emerging to ensure a clear line of fire at his intended targets, the Alien first then the President followed by his entourage as well. Then he made his first mistake; thinking to ensure his own safety, he turned his gun, a machine pistol, on the guard, cutting him down with a deadly accurate hail of bullets before turning to face his other intended victims. He was one man armed with an automatic weapon against five unarmed people, but he had no knowledge of what he was really up against.

As the guard was killed, Jon quickly concluded that he couldn't prevent that from happening, but he could protect Lana, and of course, the president, the secretary of state, and the general, all in that order, he afterwards privately recalled. He had several options, but the quickest and easiest was simple; he stepped forward toward the gunman, concentrating his mind force, his telekinesis on the man. Recalling the method he had used when rescuing Professor Mahmoud, he expanded his personal energy field to fill the corridor and block any stray bullets, and to stop the gunman was but the work of a moment. He lifted the assassin abruptly from the floor with such force that his head and shoulders went completely through the ceiling, leaving his torso and legs dangling lifeless; there was not even a twitch from his limbs.

The echoes of the gunfire had barely died away, and a thick pall of smoke still hung in the air, when the first of the backup security squad could be heard as they emerged from the lift. They no doubt feared, from the noise of the gunfire, that they would find the corridor strewn with corpses, and as their cries died away, there was an

Chapter Twenty-Nine

unnatural silence as they viewed the scene. They saw the shocked president, the secretary of state and the senior army general, still wide-eyed in amazement, and the white clad figures of Lana and Jon calmly standing together, looking up at a body hanging from the ceiling.

'Thank God you're okay, Mr President,' the senior security officer said with obvious relief. 'From the sound of the gunfire, we were convinced that you'd run into an ambush party.' Then he glanced at what could be seen of the would-be assassin. 'How did he get like that?'

Having recovered his composure, Davis Cooper was able to reply drily, 'Well, while God may have had something to do with saving us,' he turned and clapped his hand on Jon's shoulder, 'it was this man, the representative from Zel, who saved the day and your president's life.'

While they were talking, the remaining security staff hurriedly went further along the corridor, opening and checking every room for any other possible assassins. Finding it to be all clear, they ushered Davis Cooper, George K. Lane, and the general into a suite of rooms on their own, while Lana and Jon were located slightly further down the corridor, strategically positioned to be on hand should they be required.

Once their charges were safely into their respective rooms, the senior security officer went back to the point where the body was still hanging from the ceiling, and repeated his earlier question to anyone listening. 'How did he get like that? How does a man stick his head through the ceiling with enough force to break his neck?' As no one volunteered an answer, he continued, 'Looks like we'll just have to get him out of there, but don't make too much of a mess when you do it, and watch the carpets! The management aren't going to be happy when they see this lot.'

Chapter Twenty-Nine

Two of the men allocated to the task of extricating the corpse from its unusual location did so unceremoniously, by bringing all their weight to bear, pulling with all their strength on the legs, and then jumping back out of the way as the body was released, bringing a large area of the ceiling down with it. Looking at the scene in mock horror, one of the men quipped, 'That's another fine mess you've got me into.' He was obviously a fan of Laurel and Hardy.

'And it's a fine mess that's got to be cleaned up,' remarked the officer in charge. 'Get the hotel manager up here to organise the operation, and make sure no reporters are allowed until I say so.' As he surveyed the scene, he continued, 'I'll call the morgue to remove the body, and in the meantime, there will be no interviews to the press or media. Any reports will have to be cleared by the president himself.'

In due course, the corridor was restored to some semblance of order, and despite the curiosity of the hotel staff when they saw the damage to the ceiling and the corpse being wheeled out, the confidentiality of the incident was maintained. When it was reported to Davis Cooper that all had returned to normal, he commented, 'Jon is a useful man to have around; he deserves some kind of recognition for his services today,' which was a sentiment agreed to by the general and the secretary of state.

In the meanwhile, Jon and Lana were looking around their suite with interest. 'A far cry from the hotels I used to stay in during my previous life,' Jon admitted, while Lana was equally impressed by the luxurious surroundings.

'Will we be able to live in a house comparable to this, Jon?' she asked. 'That is, when we eventually decide where to live on Earth?'

Jon took her in his arms and laughingly replied, 'If we wanted to, Lana, we could buy this complete hotel as it stands, so long as the ceiling is repaired. But I'm sure that when the time comes, the choice will not be a difficult one. A small private island in the

Chapter Twenty-Nine

Caribbean and a fairly large, villa-style residence where we will undoubtedly be called upon to entertain the world leaders in our capacity as representatives of Zel. And of course, whatever friends we make in the ensuing months or years ahead, but we have much to do before any of that can happen.'

Lana was thoughtful for a moment. 'When we have neutralised all the nuclear weapons, Jon, that will be a big step in your work toward bringing peace to your planet. I was thinking that it would be more appropriate if you were to regularise your position on Earth by being appointed Ambassador of Zel rather than merely a representative.' Noting the look of doubt on Jon's face, she continued, 'As an ambassador, you would be politically on a level footing with all the world leaders and probably their heads of state as well.'

'Possibly, Lana,' he agreed, 'but how can I be accredited as ambassador to the Earth when we are light-years away from Zel? Wouldn't such an appointment have to be conferred by your own government or high council?'

'Normally that would be the case,' she replied, 'but as you are aware, we are a long way from my home planet.' She hesitated before continuing with a smile, 'But we know that there is a mother ship in the region of the solar system, and every commander of such a vessel is automatically a member of the High Council. Because of the importance of your mission, he would be empowered to appoint you as an official ambassador and bestow all the privileges of that rank.'

'That could well make a difference when the time comes to enter into any negotiations with the leaders of some countries,' Jon remarked. 'And yes, ambassador does sound better than representative; it's not too pompous though, do you think?'

'It's a title you will deserve for your continued service to humankind, Jon, for the next, say, five hundred years?' Lana smiled as she continued. 'You will never be mistaken as a native of Zel, at

Chapter Twenty-Nine

least not by any other member of our people. You are too big and too muscular, and with your hair,' she affectionately ran her fingers through his silvery thatch, 'no other man of Zel ever had your physical attributes, and of course, with your enhanced abilities, courtesy of your transformation by Mort, you are capable of so much more than any other person on this or any other planet!'

Jon smiled with pleasure at the thoughts going through Lana's mind, some relating to his future status as ambassador, but others concerning his physical attributes, especially his physical prowess in their more intimate moments. But putting aside those thoughts for the time being, thinking about Lana's remarks regarding his enhanced abilities in other matters had sidetracked him for the moment, what about the trip back to Washington?

'I take it that you are not looking forward to the return journey in Air Force One tomorrow, are you, Lana?' he asked.

'No,' she replied with a grimace. 'If that was the only means of travelling on Earth, I'd rather walk.'

With a pleasant laugh, Jon remarked, 'I believe you, but seriously, we will be asked to join the president on the trip home, and we don't want to cause offence by refusing, do we?'

'There's something going on in your mind, Jon, but I can't understand what it is. Your thoughts are very scrambled.'

'That's because I haven't fully made up my mind about what I intend to do,' he replied. Pausing for a moment, he took Lana by surprise with his next question. 'How long do you think we will have before dinner, two hours, perhaps?' Not waiting for a reply, and not expecting any prediction, he continued. 'I intend to teleport back to the ship and bring it back here to New York before dinner, then tomorrow, instead of you having to endure the discomfort of flying in an old-fashioned aircraft, we will return in our own ship and . . . .' With a grin of delight at Lana's look of astonishment, he said, 'Go off on our own to our island for a few days as promised.'

Chapter Twenty-Nine

Once the initial pleasure of Jon's proposal had sunk in, then the doubts crept in. 'But to teleport from New York to Washington is a distance of hundreds of miles; it took two hours or more for the President's plane to make the journey,' Lana said. With a moment of panic, she added, 'And you've never teleported more than twenty miles before. Can you achieve such a feat?'

'Mort and Jara assured me that they could teleport such distances with ease,' Jon replied. 'With my enhanced powers, I should be able to do the same. All I have to do is concentrate on the coordinates of the intended destination, in this case, the ship, which is something I am very familiar with, so twenty miles or one thousand miles will make little difference.'

Still not fully convinced, Lana clung tightly to Jon as she asked, 'But can you go back to the ship and return here before dinner? If anyone were to hear you say that, they would think you can perform miracles.' Then relenting, she added, 'But I know you are capable of the most extraordinary feats, so when are you going?'

'No time like the present,' he said confidently. His mind was already processing the necessary coordinates of the ship. Then with a final embrace and gentle kiss, Jon stepped back from Lana and was gone.

For a few moments, Lana stood looking at the empty space where Jon had stood a moment before, trying to visualise how he would be transported through space purely by the power of his mind. To teleport such a distance was impossible to all but most of the adepts of Zel. Then she reminded herself that Jon was by far the most powerful of all of them, with his Zellian abilities and his earthly physical strengths; he was going to be a truly great ambassador.

Chapter Thirty

As Jon materialised on the flight deck of the spacecraft, he gave a smile of satisfaction. To teleport twenty miles or one thousand miles was indeed of little consequence to him, but what, he wondered, would be his limit. Could he traverse even greater distances and even cross oceans, perhaps? As he looked around the familiar control room, he wondered, Given the right coordinates in my mind, *will I be able to dispense with this craft and teleport to any part of the world?* He gave a rueful smile. *Now is not the time to speculate on my potential travelling arrangements, for in the future, wherever I go, I want Lana to be with me, and as she has a limited ability to teleport, we will have to keep this craft until such time as the commander of the mother ship demands its return.*

Normally, Lana would have set the navigational coordinates and taken over as pilot for whatever journey was to be undertaken, but Jon was equal to this task, since he was fully conversant with every system in the ship, everything from navigation, the weapons systems and the engineering propulsion systems. Mort had ensured that his four weeks of his indoctrination period had been as comprehensive as Jon's brain would allow, so it was with every confidence that he sat down at the control console. By passing his hands over the necessary instruments, *Not as gracefully as Lana would do,* he thought with a touch of humour, he set the course and speed to put the ship into position above New York, altitude twenty miles, with an estimated flight time of thirty minutes. *That will leave me ample time to collect a change of clothing for both of us, get back to the hotel, and be ready*

Chapter Thirty

for dinner this evening. The round-trip will have taken less than one hour; Lana will be pleased.

Comfortably within the estimated time, Jon arrived over New York just as dusk was falling, revealing the glow of the city. Even at an altitude of twenty miles, the myriad lights of Broadway could be seen, a build-up of traffic and headlights only slightly dimmed by the neon advertising displays. *So, this is New York by night,* he mused. *It's the city that never sleeps; well, we will experience the sumptuous comfort of our hotel suite tonight, but tomorrow we will be on our way to our island.*

He had already gathered up the necessary change of garments for the evening's dinner in the hotel. *Luckily, our wardrobes don't leave much to the imagination,* he reminded himself. *Now it's time to rejoin Lana.* A moment later, he materialised once more in the hotel bedroom. He quickly looked around; Lana was not in sight, but he could hear the sound of water running in the en suite shower room. Thinking to surprise her by his early return, he entered the bathroom to find it full of steam and Lana's figure showing through the opaque glass of the shower enclosure, where she was emitting little moans of pleasure as she revelled in the sensuous feeling of the hot water running over her body, something she hadn't enjoyed since she had left her own planet.

But of course, Jon reminded himself. *We don't have water-cleansing systems on board the ship. Even with recycling facilities, that would be a waste.* To get the equivalent of a shower meant being subjected to a sonic bombardment; it was still in a cubicle like a shower, but with little or no sensation of the pleasure that Lana was enjoying at the moment. So, with a smile and a gentle telepathic message, *I'm back again, my darling,* he withdrew, leaving Lana to enjoy her first real shower in several years, with real water!

Knowing that they had plenty of time before they would be called to join the president, an arrangement previously made by George K. Lane, Lana was in no great hurry to forego her time

Chapter Thirty

luxuriating under the steaming hot water of the shower. Her body was covered in lather from the fragrant soap, but she was nevertheless still in contact mentally with Jon. *When we have our own house, Jon, we must ensure that we have a shower in every bathroom, big ones, so that we can be together even when taking a shower. I believe that would give us both a great deal of pleasure.*

At that moment, with a smile of anticipation on his face, Jon walked into the bathroom. He had already undressed when Lana's reference to showering together had been received. So he opened the cubicle and stepped in beside her, commenting, 'It's a tight squeeze in here, but it will give us even more pleasure; pass the soap, Lana.' For the next half hour, there were many more little animal sounds to be heard from both of them.

In due course, they returned to the main bedroom to dress and prepare for dinner, expecting the phone to ring at any time with the invitation to join Davis Cooper in his suite, no doubt for an aperitif before dinner. And sure enough, the call came through. With their faces still flushed from their exertions of the previous half-hour, they made their way along to the presidential suite where George K. Lane opened the door. 'Welcome, come right on in,' he enthused. 'My, but you are looking lovelier than ever, Lana. The excitement of being in New York must be stimulating for you.'

Mentally suppressing a laugh, Jon thought, *It was the excitement of being in the shower that was stimulating, George.* Lana blushed a little more at the recollection of their togetherness, but they returned the secretary of state's greeting, politely allowing themselves to be ushered into the palatial surroundings of what was, for the moment, the presidential suite.

'Good evening, Lana, Jon. I hope you're both recovered from the incident out there in the corridor earlier on,' Davis Cooper remarked. 'Now we can all have a few drinks, and a nice dinner, which incidentally, we will have served here in my suite. I'm told the dining room of the hotel could be a security risk, but not to

Chapter Thirty

worry, with just the five of us, it will be a much cosier feeling, away from the public gaze and those security guards hovering over our shoulders all the time.' With a gesture, he invited them to take a seat. 'Make yourselves comfortable,' he said. 'General, would you do the honours and give our guests a drink?'

General Clintock was slightly nonplussed when Lana reminded him that in common with the vast majority of the citizens of Zel, they only drank wine, nothing stronger, and included Jon in that category. 'Are you sure, Jon?' he queried. 'Would you like to try something a little stronger,' he asked, adding, 'I remember the first time I had to be persuaded to try liquor, but once I got the taste for it, there was no stopping me after that.'

Jon smiled at the picture of the event in the general's mind. He had been absolutely 'stoned' by his first introduction to the demon drink, but had learned his lesson while still very young and now only drank in moderation, *as befits a general,* he would insist.

'No thank you, General, as Lana says, the Zellians never use strong liquor, not even on social occasions, and I have never wished to experience the loss of my mental faculties, which alcohol can induce. But go ahead yourself; I would imagine that you enjoy a drink, in moderation of course. We will, however, join you with a glass of wine, if we may.' Once they were all provided with their preferred tipple, they settled down for a chat about the day's events so far.

'Your speech went down very well at the UN today, Jon,' Davis Cooper began. 'All the delegates seemed to be mesmerised by your presence, although,' he added with a smile, 'I think Lana standing beside you may have concentrated their attention somewhat.'

With an inclination of his head, Jon replied, 'I only hope they were taking heed of what I was saying and that their respective governments will take the necessary steps to destroy all nuclear weapons. But I rather think it will take a lot of persuasion for your

Chapter Thirty

own country, and Russia also. Between you, you have enough destructive power to blow the world out of existence.'

At that suggestion, the president's mind went into denial, in effect rejecting the possibility of the United States starting a nuclear conflict. But he conceded, *Yes, we do possess enough missiles to cause worldwide destruction, but we would only use them in retaliation if attacked.* Outwardly, however, he said with a disarming smile, 'Let's hope that war on a nuclear scale never develops, and that all the delegates at the meeting of the UN convey your message to their respective governments. But it remains to be seen as to how long it will take before any decisions can be made.' He added with a note of caution, 'In a democracy like ours, any future actions will depend on the Senate and the House of Representatives, though we, that is the Secretary of State, the General, and myself can only make recommendations, so it could take some time before all the nukes are decommissioned.'

'And in the meanwhile,' Jon remarked, 'if some rogue state were to unleash just one nuclear missile, that could be enough to trigger a wholesale onslaught by any state that feels threatened.'

'That's a frightening scenario, Jon,' the president admitted, 'but we would try to show restraint before retaliating to a limited attack. Although the General here, I'm sure, would take some holding back.'

'I'm not the only one, Mr President,' General Clintock said grimly. 'We have enough "hawks' in Congress to make retaliation a certainty; although, the final decision would be yours, sir.'

Davis Cooper was becoming uncomfortable with the way the conversation was going, so trying to change the subject, he said, 'Well, I think we will just have to wait and see how the politicians handle the situation and await the outcome of their deliberations. But for the moment, let's enjoy ourselves with a little light conversation about what we ourselves intend to do in the future, with no more gloom and doom.'

Chapter Thirty

Jon and Lana were both thinking on a telepathic level. *Don't worry, Mr President, what happens over the next few weeks will be beyond the control of all the politicians. We will ensure that all nuclear missiles are decommissioned in their bunkers, and no one will be aware of it, until they try to launch them for an attack.*

It was George K. Lane who opened the light conversation by enquiring, 'And how do you like your accommodation in this hotel, Lana? It must be very different from your living quarters on your spaceship, although the General tells me that he was surprised that the flight deck was so big in comparison to some of the other compartments and living quarters on board the ship.'

With a smile, Lana replied, 'Perhaps he may get the opportunity to have a proper tour of our ship. Indeed, you are all welcome to do so at any time or to join us for a short flight, perhaps back to Washington.' As she made the suggestion, she mentally asked for Jon's approval, which he willingly gave.

'That would be an experience that I, for one, would look forward to,' Davis Cooper exclaimed. Then the thought occurred to him. 'Back to Washington? But we're in New York at the moment.'

The general added, 'And you left your ship hovering above Washington this morning, am I right?'

Jon and Lana enjoyed the moment, as they were aware of the confusion in the minds of their friends. 'Shall we tell them, Jon?' Lana asked aloud.

With a nod, Jon explained. 'Yes, General, we did leave the ship above Washington this morning, but since then, we decided that we would prefer to travel in our own craft rather than in Air Force One.' Diplomatically, he decided not to mention Lana's aversion to old-fashioned aircraft. 'So, I have brought the flying saucer, as you call it, down here to New York. At this very moment, it is hovering twenty miles above the city, ready to transport us wherever we wish.'

Chapter Thirty

Visibly impressed, General Clintock enquired, 'How long did that trip take? From New York, back to Washington and the return trip, and all before dinner? Now here you are, all showered, changed and relaxed. It was no more than a walk in the park for you, Jon, was it?'

Lana then recounted Jon's activity since the incident in the corridor, but kept it brief, and again, she avoided mentioning her own dislike of travelling in Air Force One. 'We decided that it might be more convenient to have our own ship available to travel onward after the UN meeting, back to Washington or wherever. We have time to spare as no decisions are likely in the near future regarding the question of nuclear disarmament, so Jon teleported back to the ship, collected a few items of clothing, and flew back in plenty of time to shower and change, all ready for dinner.'

'Just like that,' Davis Cooper gasped in astonishment. 'You teleported about one thousand miles. That's incredible in itself, but then you flew back in your ship to New York, and now you are sitting here calmly having a drink, after another walk along the corridor. How can you do so much in such a short time?'

Knowing that such an accomplishment would seem remarkable to his listeners, Jon explained. 'Whatever distance we teleport takes place in a moment of time, whether it is twenty miles, such as when we return to the ship, or like when I went back to our craft above Washington.'

Out of curiosity, the general asked the next question. 'And how far can you do this teleportation stunt, Jon? Is there a limit?'

'I don't know what my limits are,' Jon replied truthfully. 'But theoretically, any distance is possible as long as I can concentrate on a set of coordinates; otherwise, it would be like navigating in the dark.'

Turning to Lana, the general put the same question to her, which she answered candidly. 'Even among the Zellian people, Jon's

Chapter Thirty

teleporting ability is exceptional. Not only can he cover immense distances, but he can carry another person with him, as he did when he carried you out of Fort Knox, General, and then two days later, when he rescued Professor Mahmoud.' She then added, in answer to the general's question, 'As for me, my teleporting ability is considered average among my own people, and I doubt that I could carry anybody or a heavy object with me.'

At that moment, one of the security agents came into the room to announce that several of the hotel staff were outside in the corridor with the meal prepared and ready to be served; they asked permission to enter with their trolleys. With a grin, General Clintock exclaimed, 'Wheel 'em in, boys; we're ready for 'em.' In due course, the meal was served by the staff, but always under the watchful supervision of the president's security men. It was only when dinner was completed to the satisfaction of the diners and the table cleared that the guards ushered the staff out of the room, leaving the president and his guests to resume their conversation in private.

Once they were on their own again, Davis Cooper took up the conversation where they had left off before dinner. During the meal, they had indulged in small talk about families, holidays, anything other than politics. There were too many ears listening to their every word, and confidentiality had to be maintained.

'Were you serious, Jon, when you said that you could take us with you when we go back to Washington?' Davis Cooper asked. 'Is that possible, all three of us together? Can you accommodate extra passengers?'

Lana took it on herself to answer the question on Jon's behalf. 'Our ship would normally have a crew of four, who would live on board for weeks or months at a time, but there is ample space in the ship for double that number, if necessary, so it would be no problem to have three passengers for such a short journey.' She smiled in satisfaction as she added, 'It will only take about half an hour to deliver you back to the Oval Office.'

Chapter Thirty

'And could you stretch to an additional passenger?' Davis Cooper enquired with a quizzical look on his face. 'Spencer, my chief of security, if he were to lose sight of me, he would be calling out the FBI and the National Guard as well. The thought of the President of the United States of America taking off in a flying saucer would give him a heart attack.' He adding with a laugh, 'Now, you wouldn't want that to happen, would you?'

They all joined in the laughter at the prospect of Spencer, a rather dour individual, having any kind of attack. Jon remarked, 'I will have to transport you one by one to the ship, starting with Spencer, then you, Mr President, followed by George and the General. Lana will accompany Spencer and me on the first trip; otherwise, he may panic to find himself alone in a spaceship.'

'And when will we transfer to your ship, Jon?' the general asked. 'I'm looking forward to it already.'

'Not until tomorrow morning, General,' Jon replied with a smile. 'Lana wants to enjoy the luxury of this hotel first of all. I do believe she is acquiring a taste for the high life here on Earth.'

'That's okay by me,' George K. Lane said with a grin, 'but I'd better inform Spencer to be ready for an unusual event in the morning. Then he can also brief his own men, and they can then follow us back to Washington on Air Force One. He couldn't help chortling with amusement. 'But they'll be hours behind us.'

With the decision made regarding the travel arrangements for the return journey to Washington, Davis Cooper asked several in-depth questions about the spacecraft itself. He had already been informed that it normally carried a crew of four, but he wanted to know its maximum speed, whether it was truly a star ship and what kind of defence or attack systems it could employ. The general also questioned them regarding crew comforts.

While Jon made it clear that he wouldn't discuss the craft's weapons systems in detail, he did say, 'Our destructive power is far

Chapter Thirty

beyond anything you can imagine, Mr President.' He did admit that the defensive systems would make them invulnerable to any kind of external attack, since the ship was a formidable weapon of war, if it became necessary. On the subject of the speed of the craft, he was quite happy to give that kind of information in the knowledge that several observatories had already monitored their approach to the earth and their subsequent journey around the planet while mapping the location of the nuclear weapons. 'Our ship is not truly a star ship,' he began, 'but it is quite capable of flights between the planets of the solar system. But that's only if there were an emergency, as we can only travel at speeds of forty thousand miles per hour, which is too slow for our normal interplanetary journeys. However, to make a trip to Earth's moon would only take about six hours, which is acceptable.'

It was George's turn to ask the next question. 'You say you will have us back in the Oval Office in about half an hour, Jon, so what speed will we be doing on that trip?'

Again, Jon answered with a touch of pride in his ship. 'Oh, we will just saunter along at about two thousand miles an hour. We could, of course, fly much faster if we wanted to, but in the atmosphere, friction would make the ship so hot that it would take some time to cool down again; it would be too hot to touch.'

To emphasise his previous experience of flight in the saucer, General Clintock took the opportunity to inform the president and the secretary of state, 'When we take off or land, there is absolutely no sensation of movement, no G-force, and it's incredibly silent; there's no noise whatsoever.'

Without any similar experience, the other two men were a little sceptical about the forthcoming flight. Lana and Jon could read it in their minds, so Lana hastened to add in a gentle tone, 'When you have flown in one of our craft, even Air Force One, which you quite rightly regard as a luxury aircraft, it will seem like a lumbering

Chapter Thirty

mode of transport.' However, she didn't reveal her true opinion of how noisy and unstable it had felt to her.

Surprisingly to Jon, there were no questions forthcoming about the Zellian star ships. *Perhaps it's difficult to take in all the information about our own flying saucer,* he thought. *I don't think they could comprehend the enormity of a star ship or the technology required for interstellar travel.* He was right!

As the evening progressed, both Lana and Jon could read the excitement in the minds of their companions, particularly the general whose curiosity about the spaceship and its capabilities was stronger than that of the president and George K. Lane. 'Once a warrior, always a warrior.' But as Jon mentally confided to Lana, *If I were to explain our weapons systems in detail, General Clintock would no doubt appreciate the destructive power of the ship, but the technology would be beyond his comprehension. I don't think we're likely to be giving any demonstrations in the foreseeable future, do you?*

Still on a telepathic level, Lana replied, *It's just as well he won't be with us on our mission to disable all the nuclear weapons, particularly those belonging to the United States. I think the old warhorse would object most strongly to that happening.*

While they were silently communicating, George was observing their facial expressions. By now, he had a shrewd idea, by their occasional lapses in normal conversation, that they were using their telepathic abilities to exchange their thoughts privately, but to date, he had not confided to the president or the general that their minds were an open book to Jon and Lana. Then he wryly admitted to himself that his present thoughts were possibly being scanned.

As the conversation continued, Davis Cooper reminded George K. Lane that he would have to brief Spencer, the security chief, of their unusual travelling arrangements for the morrow. 'Prepare him for the shock.'

Chapter Thirty

George said with a grin of delight, 'No time like the present, but I'll bet he will think I'm pulling his leg.'

The general laughed as he retorted, 'Wait until Jon wraps his arms around him. He will wonder what's happening to him. Still, it will all be over in seconds; its the fastest transfer he is ever likely to have.' At the thought of the dour Spencer reacting to being embraced brothers-in-arms style, he again gave a bellow of laughter, which was echoed by the president and George. Spencer was respected for his professional expertise, if not for his personality or sense of humour.

It only took a few minutes for the secretary of state to go out into the corridor, inform the security team of the president's intentions for the next morning and re-enter the suite. 'You were right, General. While he accepted that we will all be flying off in a spaceship tomorrow without batting an eyelid, he didn't much like the idea of being embraced by Jon.' He added with another grin, 'Now, if it was Lana taking us up, they would all have been clamouring to go.'

'I take it we will go immediately after breakfast, or whenever you are ready, Mr President?' Jon enquired, still smiling at the remarks made about the preferences of the means of transfer to the ship. He conceded that Lana was by far the more attractive person to be embraced by than himself.

'Yes,' agreed Davis Cooper, 'but if, as you say, it will only be a half-hour journey, there's no need to make an early start.' He couldn't resist saying with a smile, 'Then Lana can enjoy the experience of living in luxury a little longer, and the general can enjoy a leisurely breakfast, right, Robert?' It was only on rare occasions that he used the general's first name, but as the atmosphere of the dinner party was so relaxed, it seemed the natural thing to do.

The arrangement was favoured by all of them, so it wasn't long before, as though by mutual consent, or was it because of a

Chapter Thirty

suggestion implanted in their minds by Jon, that it was decided to break up the party and retire. *To sleep, perchance to dream,* a quotation from his past life that Jon thought for the benefit of Lana. *Pleasant dreams, my darling.*

Chapter Thirty-One

As predicted, there was little sense of urgency the next morning. Lana revelled in the luxury of a steaming hot shower, on her own, which was less fun, but enjoyable nonetheless, while Jon made ready to join their travelling companions. He wondered, *Will Spencer try to struggle as we prepare to teleport? If he does, he will know the true meaning of a bear hug, albeit only for a few seconds.*

While waiting for Lana to complete her preparations and to don the fresh uniform that he had brought from the spaceship for her the previous day, Jon went over to the window, and looking down at the traffic on the streets below, marvelled at the pace of life in New York City. It was not an environment that he personally wished to share, but brought back memories of the times he and Lana had shared on their island.

I must look into the possibility of acquiring an island of our own, to buy it legally, and set up a permanent home for our stay here on Earth, for the next five hundred years. Even now, it's hard to imagine that I may live to be the oldest human on Earth, and everyone that we know now, the president, the general, George K. Lane, and every other prominent ruler and politician in the world will be consigned to the history books, but what kind of legacy will they leave?

While he was mulling over these thoughts, he became aware of Lana's presence as she approached, and smiled with pleasure as she wrapped her arms around his waist, nuzzling the side of his face with her nose. She whispering tantalizingly, 'What would you like for breakfast, Jon?'

Chapter Thirty-One

Before he had time to answer, although the thought had already formed in his mind, they were interrupted by a knock on the door. With a grin he replied, 'I think what I had in mind will have to wait awhile, darling. Duty calls, breakfast with the President and his men, and then back to Washington. But after that, our island for a few days, and possibly a visit to Jacob Bernstein in Jamaica for another business transaction.'

He didn't elaborate as to what that business was to be, but Lana could see in his mind that it involved the sale of a considerable number of their stock of diamonds. But for what purpose, she could only guess.

Within a few minutes, they were greeted by Davis Cooper and invited to join him at the breakfast table, where George and the general were already seated with smiles of anticipation on their faces as they viewed the platters of food laid out for their consumption. *Not so much a breakfast,* Jon thought, *but more like a mediaeval banquet. Who could eat all this food?*

As anticipated, breakfast was indeed a leisurely affair. It was well over an hour before General Clintock pushed his chair back, and with a sigh of satisfaction, declared, 'Well, that should hold me until lunchtime,' which evoked a ripple of laughter around the table. His appetite for good food was well known among his associates, but they agreed with his statement and accordingly prepared to leave the table.

'Might I suggest that we leave in about half an hour?' George K. Lane said to them all, deferring to the president with a slight inclination of his head. 'That will give us time to collect our personal bits and pieces together, and I can get Spencer in here ready for transportation.'

With a nod, Davis Cooper agreed, grinning as he commented, 'I wonder if he slept last night. The thought of not having his men around during our flight to Washington DC will undoubtedly make

Chapter Thirty-One

him feel very vulnerable, or will our dour guardian be affected by excitement as we all are?'

No one made any other comment, just smiled in agreement, so Jon and Lana retreated to their own room for a brief but pleasant interlude. It only took a few minutes to gather up their bits and pieces, so they passed away the time in a gentle physical embrace. 'No sand between the toes this time,' Lana later exclaimed, 'but totally satisfying nonetheless.'

In due course, there was the expected knock on the door, and again they heard the voice of Spencer himself. 'The President is ready for you, sir.' Then the sound of his voice receded as he gave further instructions to his security staff regarding the imminent but invisible departure of the presidential party. Within minutes, they were admitted into the presence of Davis Cooper and his friends. The general could barely contain his excitement at the prospect of his second flight in the saucer, although the others, Spencer included, were visibly nervous of this unknown experience. Was it the flight or being teleported to a height of twenty miles above New York City? Reading Spencer's mind, both Jon and Lana were amused that the security chief's main concern was the manner of transportation, being embraced by Jon.

Better not let the tension build up, Lana, Jon mentally communicated. *Otherwise, he may attempt to struggle unnecessarily and hurt himself.*

With a final look around at the faces of the others in the room, Jon said in a calm and reassuring tone of voice, 'Right, time to go. Lana and I will go first, with Spencer in my care, of course. Then I will be back in less than a minute for each of you gentlemen, starting with you, Mr President. Your care will give Spencer something to occupy his mind while I collect the others.'

With an enquiring look, George said, 'I suppose the general will bring up the rear guard as always.'

Chapter Thirty-One

With a laugh General Clintock retorted, 'Won't make a lot of difference, George; the evacuation will be over in five minutes or so, won't it, Jon?'

'About that,' Jon agreed as he thought, *I'm going to need my concentration for that five-minute period.*

With a smile, he then approached Spencer and said, 'All you have to do is put your arms around me and hang on; pretend you're a drowning man or something, and before you know it, you'll be on board our ship.' With a dubious look on his face, and giving a sheepish grin to hide his embarrassment, Spencer placed his arms around Jon. As he did so, the embrace was returned, very firmly, and they were gone. They teleported to the ship twenty miles above the skyscrapers of New York City and materialised on the flight deck, followed a few seconds later by Lana.

'Well, that wasn't so bad, Spencer, was it?' Jon enquired with a grin.

As the security chief looked around in confusion, he admitted, 'Not quite what I was expecting, but apart from my ribs feeling as though they've been crushed, otherwise I'm okay.'

'In which case,' Jon replied, 'I'll now bring the president aboard, but there will be no ceremony on this occasion.' With yet another smile for Lana and a nod of assurance for Spencer, he again teleported back to the hotel room where Davis Cooper was waiting apprehensively for his turn to be evacuated, as the general had put it.

'Well, how did Spencer react to the reality of being teleported?' the president enquired out of curiosity.

'He stood up to the ordeal with fortitude,' Jon declared with mock solemnity. 'He is now waiting for your arrival, so I suggest we don't delay your departure; let's go, Mr President.' And so the procedure was repeated, not just once more, but twice, with the

Chapter Thirty-One

general bringing up the rear, and they were all safely on board the spaceship.

Lana had already opened the viewports to give their passengers a full panoramic view of the islands and rivers of New York, including the greenery of Central Park, which was easily discernible, even from an altitude of twenty miles, although the haze of the city did tend to blur their vision. 'If you want a perfect view,' Lana remarked, 'you can get that with the on-board computer screens, which will enhance everything you see now and more.' As though to demonstrate, she led Davis Cooper over to her control console, activated the computer screen with a graceful pass of her hand, then altered the range and focus of the images on the screen. She watched the amazement on the faces of not only the president, but also the general and George.

It wasn't until they could read the number plates on the vehicles down below that Lana was satisfied with the demonstration. 'Wow!' General Clintock exclaimed breathlessly. 'That's as good as our space observatory cameras, which have taken years to develop and perfect. And yet you have this similar technology on this ship, which your people seem to regard as a run-around, so what other surprises have you in store for us, Jon?'

'Only the size of the ship, General . On the last trip you made with us, you only saw selected areas, not including the propulsion and weapons systems. That exclusion still applies, since such technology is too far advanced for you to comprehend. The last Teacher, who visited Earth in the last century, attempted to give one of your best scientists an insight into the mathematics required for the development of space travel and the control of matter, but even he had difficulty in fully understanding it. We were informed that when he attempted to share his acquired knowledge with his fellow scientists, they even questioned his sanity.'

'I take it you must be referring to Einstein,' Davis Cooper ventured. 'He was always acclaimed as a genius, although, as you

Chapter Thirty-One

say, no one could understand his work. He was a man before his time, or was it that he had a Teacher from a more advanced civilisation, like the Zel?'

'Yes,' Jon agreed with his usual smile, 'as I have said before, although not in great detail, the Zellians have been observing and assisting humans for millions of years. More recently, within the last ten thousand years, teachers such as myself have been responsible for guiding humanity, teaching the basic skills of reading, writing, building, animal husbandry, and crop cultivation. The Zellians have observed the rise and fall of many empires, some through natural disasters, but most because of man's own folly, and as I explained at the United Nations Assembly, you are heading for yet another disaster of your own making.

'However, for the moment, while I may be a Teacher, now is not the time to be giving you a lecture on the shortcomings of humankind, but let's move on to something much more pleasant, the return journey to Washington.' And giving Lana a prearranged signal, the speed and course was set for the short flight, during which they gave their guests a tour around the ship. They showed how the crew coped with their existence on board, their comparatively spacious living and sleeping accommodations, the sonic showers and the kitchens. They even offered the general a sample of the food they would normally eat, which was an offer he declined with some suspicion on the grounds that he had only had his breakfast in the hotel a short time before.

He imagined the food would be similar to that supplied to the NASA astronauts, whereas he could, if he wished, select a meal similar to any he could order in a top class hotel, courtesy of the Zellian technology.

By the time their conducted tour was over, they were already hovering above their destination of the White House. When Lana informed them that they were home, they were amazed, and General Clintock chortled with glee as he exclaimed, 'I'll bet the rest of the

Chapter Thirty-One

boys won't even have reached the airport in New York. Goddam it, what a way to travel!'

'Probably not,' Jon agreed. Then turning to Davis Cooper, he said gravely, 'Now that we are back over the White House, Mr President, I give you the choice. We can land the ship on the White House lawn with all the attendant publicity that would cause, or I can teleport you one by one directly into the Oval Office; what would your preference be?'

As he waited for an answer, George K. Lane touched the president on the arm as though to give the president pause before answering. 'Might I suggest that we stick to our original intention, which is to go directly into the Oval Office. There will be enough speculation as to how you left New York; in fact, there are those in Congress who might accuse you of a degree of recklessness by travelling in a flying saucer. Some might even suggest that you could have been kidnapped, on top of the attempted assassination attempt in New York.'

With a wry smile, Davis Cooper commented, 'Apart from the fact that Jon saved all our lives yesterday, he has ensured that we have been brought back to Washington under such secure conditions that there was no likelihood of any further attempt on my life, or yours, George. We've been accompanied by our chief of security all the way ; he hasn't left my side for one minute, so if any Senator or politician has any sour grapes to expound, I'll simply put it down to jealousy.'

But then turning to Jon again, he continued, 'I wouldn't want you to mark the lawn with your ship,' he paused and laughing at his own accusation. 'So if you don't mind, Jon, we'll just teleport into the Oval Office as originally planned, although it could be a surprise to any other security personnel who might happen to be around.'

'In which case, Mr President,' Spencer said, venturing his opinion, 'I should go first with Jon and if it so happens that any of

Chapter Thirty-One

my staff are in the office when we suddenly appear, they aren't likely to start shooting as they did on a previous occasion.'

With the memory of that occasion still in his mind, Davis Cooper willingly agreed. 'That will be fine,' he said, 'then myself, George, and you last of all, General, just as before. Will you be joining us as well, Lana?'

'That was not my intention,' she replied. 'There's something else I have to do before we leave Washington, but that will require some discussion with Jon. It's a matter of communicating with the Zellian mother ship, which is somewhere in the solar system, but that can wait until you have all been safely returned to the Oval Office, Mr President.'

With a wide grin on his face, Jon gestured to the chief of security. 'Come along, Spencer, you're the first to go. You'll be back in the Oval Office before you can say stars and stripes.' Taking care not to embrace the man too powerfully, it only took a moment to concentrate his mind for the short teleport down to the White House, and while Spencer was still mentally saying, *stars and*, he didn't have time to complete his sentence, because they had materialised in the Oval Office.

As it happened, none of the security staff were actually in the office, but prompted by curiosity no doubt, Spencer opened the door to observe a number of personnel patrolling the area outside. 'How the heck did you get in there, Chief?' one of them said. 'We've been out here all morning, and I'm sure you couldn't have passed us during that time. Have you got some kind of secret entrance that we don't know about?'

The normally reticent Spencer had difficulty suppressing a laugh as he replied, 'If I were to tell you how I got into the office, you wouldn't believe me, and you might as well know that the President, George K. Lane, and General Clintock will be joining me within the next few minutes.' Noticing the enquiring looks between the

Chapter Thirty-One

members of his staff, he added, 'And you won't see them walking through the door either.' He then turned without further explanation back into the office to find it empty. Jon had returned to the ship to collect his next passenger, the president.

The process of transporting the other three men continued without any delay between each of them, and Davis Cooper gave a satisfied smile as he consulted his watch. 'It has taken little more than an hour to fly New York to Washington, which included a conducted tour of your ship, Jon, and we've transported into the Oval Office, and everyone is completely relaxed.' Turning to General Clintock, he repeated a remark made by him earlier, 'Goddam it, what a way to travel.'

Before taking his leave of them, Jon explained that, since a decision by the governments of the United Nations regarding the destruction of all nuclear weapons was unlikely within the next month or so, he and Lana intended to have a leisurely tour around the world. He had felt like saying never in reference to the governments, but since he had his own course of action in mind, he was content to let that issue remain unchallenged. While they waited, there was so much for them to see of this beautiful planet. But as that would take a considerable amount of time, Lana, who was in charge of communications, would contact the Oval Office every five days, 'Just to keep in touch,' Jon confided.

Other than to thank Jon for his intervention during the assassination attempt the previous evening, Davis Cooper mentioned that he would like to arrange a civil reception for Jon and Lana on their return. It would partly be a gesture of hospitality to the Zellian representatives, but more a recognition of saving the life of the president and his most senior associates, the secretary of state and the army's top general.

'That's very kind of you, Mr President,' Jon remarked. 'Lana and I will look forward to that event. Will it be a formal dress affair such

Chapter Thirty-One

as we have witnessed on your TV transmissions? Should that be the case, we will arrange to have suitable apparel for the occasion.'

'Undoubtedly, it will be a black-tie reception with the ladies wearing all their finery,' Davis Cooper replied. 'Although I doubt that any of them will have a diamond to rival Lana's. What did she call it, a trinket?'

As they all laughed at the recollection of Lana's understatement, Jon once more stepped clear of them. He said, 'Until we meet again.' He was gone, only to materialise a moment later on the flight deck of the spacecraft, with Lana once more.

Chapter Thirty-Two

Once they had relaxed on their own for a time, they both admitted that having people around them was so distracting. Lana remarked, 'It's quite difficult at times to shut out the thoughts of some of these people, their emotions are so raw and uncontrolled that it can be painful to suppress my own reactions to them, don't you find it so, Jon?'

'I did at first,' Jon admitted, 'but now I can be quite selective in tuning in or blocking their thoughts at will. I find that I can also implant some suggestions in their minds, causing them to alter their behaviour or actions, but like every other ability instilled in my mind by Mort during my indoctrination period, I still require time to perfect the technique.' As he was talking, he could see that there was something on Lana's mind, something she was pondering over, but couldn't quite make up her mind about. The commander of the mother ship was all he could read.

'What is it that you have been thinking of, Lana?' he enquired gently. 'Is something troubling you? Why are you thinking about the mother ship?'

'There's something I wish to discuss with you, Jon,' she replied, slightly relieved that the subject she wished to talk about had arisen so naturally

He nodded his head in agreement, but said nothing in reply. He only mentally thought, *And so?*

Chapter Thirty-Two

Lana then continued, 'I would assume it is likely to take a little longer than it originally took us to locate the weapons, and it may be necessary to double-check in certain areas. In other words, we may have to travel for at least a month or more.' Again, she looked at him questioningly.

'That is a possibility,' Jon grudgingly agreed, 'but our mission must be carried out thoroughly and completely; otherwise, if only a few countries retain these weapons, they could be tempted to dominate the rest of the world, in which case, we would have failed.'

'Would you then be prepared to accept a suggestion of mine, Jon dear?' she cooed in a coaxing tone of voice, which was very unlike a woman of the Zel.

'And that is?' Jon smiled suspiciously in reply.

'I have been thinking about how we can complete the mission successfully, but in a much shorter period of time,' she added.

'In which case, I would welcome your suggestion, Lana,' Jon was prompted to reply. 'The quicker we can complete this particular mission, the sooner we can tell the world's leaders that they have lost the capability of waging nuclear war, and then it will be a matter of persuading them to give up other forms of warfare. But that may prove to be another difficulty, since man and aggression go hand in hand.' After having witnessed the war-like behaviour of humankind over a number of years, albeit from the safety of space, Lana could only agree, so she quietly explained her plan of action for the next few weeks.

'We will be spending a little time on our island, a week or so, but before we leave our position over Washington, I propose to contact the commander of the mother ship, which, I believe, is still in the solar system. Radio transmissions are so slow that it may well be at least a week before he is able to respond to my request.'

Jon continued to listen with interest. *What request?*

Chapter Thirty-Two

Lana smiled as she picked up his thoughts. 'That he delegate Captain Jara and Mort to assist us with this mission; it could easily be done,' she added in a matter-of-fact tone of voice. 'We could supply them with the coordinates of at least half of the nuclear sites that we have already pinpointed, and as they have the same type of weaponry at their disposal, they will be able to destroy or deactivate the nuclear missiles in their silos while we do our part also. Twice the number of crew members and half the time to complete the mission.'

'If the commander will give authorisation for Jara and Mort to assist us,' Jon replied, 'I will be very grateful; otherwise taking out the missiles will be a slow and tedious task, and as you say, if we can give them the coordinates required, the job will be completed much earlier.' He paused for a moment before continuing. 'You have something else is on your mind regarding the commander of the mother ship, something relating to a rendezvous. Why so?'

Lana smiled as she prepared to reply. She hoped for a pleasant outcome to the proposal she intended to make. 'I'm aware that Captain Jara could meet us in Earth's orbit and receive all the information he will need, but I have another reason to request an interview with the commander.'

For a moment, she touched Jon's arm. Physical contact with him was something she always enjoyed, but still smiling, she continued, 'My father, as a star ship commander, will readily agree to such a proposal and will confer your honour and new status when we meet him on board his own ship.'

'Many of the Teachers during the last three or four thousand years were from Zel and were gifted in many different ways, but they remained here only for a short time, not long enough to do what was regarded as necessary to change the progress of humankind. That is why the natives of Earth were selected to take over the role, were trained and modified, and instilled with the new knowledge to guide humankind on the path of progress to a better future.' Lana shook her head sadly, 'Unfortunately, there were many instances

Chapter Thirty-Two

where the Teachers were eventually killed by the very people they were trying to help. Some were revered as gods because of their knowledge and compassion, while others were regarded as being possessed by evil spirits. Even today, Jon, there are people on Earth who may regard you in the same way.'

With a wry smile Jon replied, 'I believe you're right, Lana. Even with the title of ambassador, my physical abilities, being able to teleport at will, telekinesis and mental telepathy, I will still be regarded as having the powers of the devil in some societies. Hopefully not here in America, of course.' He laughed as he added, 'They are relatively civilised in this part of the world.'

'You agree with my proposal then, Jon? I will make contact with the commander of the mother ship and arrange a rendezvous on the far side of the moon as before. Then we can transfer to the mother ship so we can petition the commander for your change of status, Ambassador Jon.'

'I'm quite happy to leave the communication aspect to you, Lana,' he replied quietly, 'but while you're doing that, I will set course for our island and then we can have time to be together, completely alone again, at last.' It was only the work of a few minutes to set all the power and navigation systems to automatic mode, and they were on their way to the Caribbean, heading for the seclusion of the remote island where they had so many memories of enjoyment in the recent past.

In the meanwhile, Lana patiently searched the ship's scanning instruments, hoping to target the mother ship by its radio emissions. She hoped that it was still within the solar system, and eventually, she was rewarded when her viewing screen picked up a strong signal and showed the face of a crewmember of the mother ship. It was not a face she was familiar with, which was not surprising since he was only one of some one thousand personnel on board.

Chapter Thirty-Two

Having identified her ship and location, she then requested to be put in touch with the commander, to give a confidential report on their mission. In due course, the image of the captain of the other ship appeared; he stated that his superior was not immediately available, but would return the call as soon as it was convenient. Leaving the communication lines open, Lana turned to Jon and said, 'Well, at least we know that the mother ship is quite near, probably orbiting Mars, judging by the speed of the radio signals. So if the commander is interested in my proposal, he may agree to our rendezvous, even although it may only be out of curiosity to meet you, Jon. No doubt Captain Jara and Mort have given him a complete report on your transformation during the indoctrination period, which was not so long ago,' she mused.

As it happened, their spacecraft had completed the flight and was in docking position in its usual spot twenty miles above their island before they received the return call from the mother ship. As Lana faced the viewing screen, she was greeted with a kindly smile by the commander, a friend of her own father and her own mentor since her early days as a cadet.

'Well, young Lana,' he said in a booming, authoritative voice, 'what is this request you wish to make? It must be important to ask for a meeting with your old commander and to summon me to this corner of the universe; luckily, I wasn't far away at the time.'

Encouraged by his general attitude, Lana gave a brief outline of her request, but stated that she would be more specific if and when he should grant them a formal interview on his ship. To her relief, it was granted. 'I shall be in a static orbit above the moon's surface as before, in twelve hours' time, and I will have Captain Jara and Mort ready to transfer to your ship to discuss the finer details of the mission you have described. Until then, good-bye, Lana.'

'Twelve hours' time,' Jon said incredulously. 'If the mother ship is somewhere in Mar's orbit, it will take at least a year for a normal Earth spaceship to travel that distance.'

Chapter Thirty-Two

Lana smiled as she replied, 'Agreed, but our spacecraft don't depend on speed alone. Although they can attain speeds near that of light, if necessary, they also bend time itself. I'll have to explain that to you in more detail on another occasion, but for the moment, if it's going to take us six hours to travel to the moon, that only leaves us six hours to experience that sand between the toes sensation again, so shall we go?'

In reply, Jon just grinned in anticipation as he pulled Lana close to him. 'Is this okay to begin with?'

Chapter Thirty-Three

After spending several hours lazing on the pristine white sands of the beach with the occasional swim in the clear blue waters of the Caribbean, they gave themselves plenty of time to return to the ship and make ready for their flight to the moon, a trip they could complete in a few hours versus the several days it would take the NASA astronauts. 'Six hours, to be precise,' Jon marvelled.

The flight itself was completely uneventful, but the views of Earth receding as they distanced themselves from the planet were truly awe-inspiring for Jon. A jewel in the universe, Earth was aptly called the blue planet. The light from the sun reflected off the oceans and clouds, wreathing the earth, and making every detail of the landmasses stand out in bold relief. It was a sight he was reluctant to pull himself away from until Lana reminded him that they were approaching the moon. She switched on the scanners to reveal the harsh landscape of Earth's satellite, grey and forbidding, pockmarked by craters caused by millions of years of bombardment by meteorites. Some craters were many miles in circumference, and by contrast, there were mountain ranges that would never be eroded due to climate changes or weather. It was a sterile and unwelcoming environment, with no atmosphere and low gravity, but useful to the Zellian mother ship as a docking station for their rendezvous as it was hidden from observers on Earth.

They had only been in a static orbit for a short time when Lana exclaimed, 'Well, the commander's ETA is pretty accurate, I can see the mother ship approaching now.'

Chapter Thirty-Three

As Jon also looked at the viewing screen, he could see the image of the mother ship and the information relating to its speed, distance, and arrival time. Within minutes, its mass was so huge that it overwhelmed the screen, but they could see that the entry port was already open.

'That indicates that we are expected to fly our craft into the main hanger area,' Lana said with a smile. 'No need to teleport on this occasion, Jon. Nice and simple and very civilised, don't you think?'

Jon simply nodded in reply, overawed by the sheer size of the star ship. It was enormous, about two miles in length and swallowed its crew of ten thousand with ease. It was a small city in space, capable of travelling between the galaxies, spanning the vast distances by bending or warping time itself, which was combined with speeds only dreamt of by Earth's scientists. It was capable of being self-sufficient in every way for many years if necessary.

Reading Jon's mind, Lana was prompted to say, 'The Zellian star ships are the ultimate in technology, and living on board is a way of life. Every one of the crew is trained to fulfil several functions and has the opportunity to switch to another duty if he or she so desires. That way they can keep an interest in life and maintain their mental health. And in many cases with crew members, they will opt out of technical duties and volunteer to spend a year or two working in the hydroponic farm on board, as it's almost a sabbatical for them.' She smiled as she continued, 'If you would like to see that area of the star ship, just ask the commander, and I'm sure he will provide you with access to the farm. It's immense and grows so many different crops, plus it is part of the ecosystem on board and keeps the air purified for all to breath.'

While Jon was interested in the functions and way of life on board the star ship, his mind was more focused on their approach to the entrance to the main hanger. As they finally passed into the interior of the ship, he watched how skilfully Lana docked their own

Chapter Thirty-Three

craft, which was diminutive in size compared to the mother ship. When they were locked into their allocated parking position, he noted that they were only one of a number of other flying saucers in the immense hanger. Again, he wondered at the technology and resources it had taken the Zellians to build such a ship, not to mention how long its construction had taken.

As always, Lana knew what was going through his mind, and as soon as she had completed the intricate docking procedure and shut down the power source for the first time in several months, she then turned to Jon, and said, 'It takes many years to build each star ship and thousands of technicians are involved.' Having Jon's complete attention she continued, 'From start to finish, construction takes place many miles above Zel, outside all the gravitational forces. The finished ship never actually touches down on any planet, since it would collapse under its own immense weight. Even docking close to the moon could be dangerous but for the fact that gravity here is only about one tenth that of Earth. Even so, landing would still be out of the question, which is where our type of craft, the saucers, are used.' As she was concluding her explanation, the communications computer informed her that the commander was waiting to receive her and Jon in his private quarters and that they should now take one of the internal transport vehicles to the designated living area for the senior crew members. Accordingly, she offered an encouraging smile, since she knew Jon was finding his surroundings intimidating due to the sheer size of everything. She took him by the hand and opened the door of their own ship, and they descended to the deck of the parking area with Lana confidently leading the way. They took one of the convenient shuttle vehicles used to convey crewmembers around the immense star ship. Within a few minutes, they arrived in the complex used by the commander and senior captains of the various exploratory ships of the fleet.

Chapter Thirty-Three

When she was a junior cadet, Lana had never been invited into the inner sanctum of the commander; that was a privilege reserved for the lucky few, and usually for some social occasion. So, as they entered the living quarters of the first time, both she and Jon were amazed to find themselves in what could only be described as palatial surroundings. *Rank certainly has its privileges,* Jon thought, and found Lana echoing his sentiments. *But I suppose this is, in effect, some compensation for being away from home for years at a time, away from family as well, no doubt.*

'Not so,' Lana quietly confided. 'The crew of a star ship, from the lowest to the highest rank, are allowed to have their family on board with them, and that includes the children as well.'

As there was as yet no sign of the commander, she continued, 'The ship is so big that the living quarters for ordinary crewmembers, although not so luxurious as this,' she said as she gestured around her, 'would still be considered to be very comfortable, more so than the accommodation on our own craft and very much more spacious. In fact, a typical family unit is similar to what I've seen on terrestrial television, in the better class homes, that is.'

With a smile of amazement, Jon commented, 'Why go back to Zel when everything they could possibly want or need is already here?'

Tightening her grip on Jon's hand, Lana said quietly, 'That's what I would have said until I experienced life on Earth, especially on our island. Now, despite life on board the star ship being a very comfortable one, I can't wait until our mission is complete, and we can retreat to an island of our very own.'

At that moment, they became aware that they were being scrutinised by a tall regal figure, the commander of the star ship, who smiled as he said, 'You want an island of your own, Lana?'

Aware of the telepathic ability of the Zellian people, Jon was still slightly surprised that the commander had picked up what was only

Chapter Thirty-Three

a fleeting thought in Lana's mind, and then reminded himself that someone as old and experienced as a star ship commander would have above-average abilities in most respects, even for a member of the Zellian people.

This was confirmed a moment later. 'Let me introduce myself, I am Commander Decca, and yes, Jon, an ancient like myself has had plenty of time to perfect the skills of the mind. But I must say that Captain Jara and Mort were correct to state that you are an exceptional man in your abilities.' He paused, shrewdly summing up his own thoughts. 'You are having difficulty reading my thoughts, aren't you Jon?' to which Jon had to agree. 'And I'm having equal difficulty in reading yours, most unusual. I would hazard an opinion that, with determination and practice, you will be able to completely block your mind to any telepathic probe, which is very useful at times.'

Turning to Lana, he then continued. 'You gave me an outline of what we should do to enhance Jon's diplomatic position on Earth. Does a change of title make that much difference to the outcome of your mission?'

It was then Lana's opportunity to explain that the social structure on Earth was quite unlike that on Zel. The higher the perceived title of the individual, the easier it would be to negotiate on a political level, which was something that would undoubtedly become necessary after they had completed the first part of Jon's strategy, the destruction of the nuclear missiles. The title of ambassador would be more influential among the leaders of the nations of Earth. She added, 'It could be regarded as a reward for Jon's dedication to his role as a Teacher. After all, he will be committed to that role for several hundreds of years, much longer than any other Teacher before him.'

With a smile of understanding, Commander Decca said, 'I can see in your mind that it is your wish to remain on Earth with Jon, until the completion of his life's work, even though by doing so, you

Chapter Thirty-Three

will shorten your own life. You are aware of the consequences of living on a planet with a higher gravity than Zel. But your determination is obvious, and it's not altogether about the mission, is it? You are in love with Jon, a true love that will endure for the centuries to come.'

Knowing that she couldn't deny what was in her mind, she happily conceded. 'Yes, I am in love, and I wish to remain with Jon for however long we may live, be it five, six or even seven hundred years. To return to Zel without Jon in order to live to be one thousand is not an attractive prospect to me!'

With another nod, Commander Decca thoughtfully replied, 'Having listened to your request, and bearing in mind your own personal sacrifice, Lana, of giving up your home planet and people, as your reward, I will gladly appoint Jon as the official ambassador to Earth. This I now do on behalf of the Grand Council of the Zel.' Rising above them both, he stretched his arms over Jon's head, and said, 'By the power vested in me, I declare you are now appointed ambassador of the planet Zel.'

Taking care to screen his thoughts, Jon smiled inwardly. *That didn't take long; it was simple, but very much to the point.* He then continued out loud. 'Thank you, Commander, I don't feel any different as a result of the title, but I rather think that certain people back on Earth will regard my status rather differently.'

Her face glowing with pleasure, Lana also thanked the commander for the honour bestowed on Jon and the granting of her own request, something that would be of benefit to them both in their future life on planet Earth and the possibility of having to live the life of high society.

After indulging in general conversation for a time, the commander informed them that when they left the mother ship, Captain Jara and Mort would leave in their own ship, also, and they would all be free to return to Earth's orbit where they could then

Chapter Thirty-Three

finalise their plans to begin the destruction of the nuclear weapons. 'Don't delay,' the commander said with a laugh. 'Otherwise, some despot may take it into his hands to start a war.'

Many a true word is spoken in jest, Jon thought. With a courteous farewell, he accompanied Lana out of the living quarters, and in due course, they arrived back at their own ship, to be informed by the maintenance technicians that every aspect of the weapons and defence systems of the craft had been checked.

'Everything is operational and functioning, and the power pack to fly the ship is good for another thousand years.'

'That's good to know,' Jon said. 'But I am only likely to last another five hundred years. What happens to the ship after that? Will another Teacher be required after me?'

With Lana at the controls, they slowly made their way out of the mother ship, closely followed by Captain Jara and Mort in their own craft. Once well clear, they heard the voice of Mort, and turning to the video screen, they observed the smiling face of their friend.

'Thanks for getting us away from a tedious existence,' he said. 'We will rendezvous at the coordinates we have been given, and once in orbit above the Earth, we will come over and have a talk to discuss your mission and how you propose to go about it. In the meantime, good-bye ambassador.' Then he was gone.

With a grin, Jon turned to Lana. 'A star ship travels fast, but news travels faster, it seems.'

'Yes,' Lana replied. 'I was happy to be with the representative of the Zellian people before, and now,' she said proudly, 'I'm even happier to be with Ambassador Zel.'

'Quite a title, isn't it,' Jon remarked. But he was nevertheless pleased that Lana had had her request granted, an honour shared for work to be done together, for a number of normal lifetimes.

Chapter Thirty-Four

The flight back to Earth was uneventful, and once the automatic pilot was set for the rendezvous with Captain Jara and Mort, all they had to do was sit back, relax, and talk about other matters quite divorced from their mission.

As they sat close together, a position of personal contact that neither of them ever tired of, Jon started the conversation with his usual smile. 'Once we have briefed our friends Jara and Mort and supplied them with the coordinates of the weapons silos, we will no doubt go our separate ways until the mission is successfully completed. Even working as a team, I would still expect that to take several weeks to complete, so I had a thought, Lana, in fact, I've had several,' he said with a laugh. 'At some time in the future, we will have to withdraw from the constant glare of publicity. As the ambassador of the Zel, I shall be in the public eye at all times. And being accompanied by the most beautiful of women, albeit a woman of the Zel, but still the most beautiful woman on Earth, we will be in demand to attend civic functions in our official capacity, as well as many private occasions, such as private parties at the homes of other ambassadors and politicians.'

While Lana was listening attentively to every word Jon was saying, she was also probing his mind to gain a further insight of his innermost thoughts, something he was happy to allow, since there would be no secrets between them. 'So, what have you decided to do, Jon? You seem to have some plan of action other than our tour of destruction.'

Chapter Thirty-Four

'Yes,' he replied eagerly. 'Once Jara and Mort have set off on their part of the mission, we will begin preparations for our own private future, to acquire the wealth to buy our own island in the Caribbean. That will necessitate the sale of a number of our best diamonds, with, I would suggest, the help of Jacob Bernstein in Jamaica. No doubt the handling of such a transaction will take time, and if Jacob is suitably rewarded with a good commission of another diamond for his personal use, he will be able to travel further afield to find suitably wealthy buyers.'

'And I take it that while this is happening,' Lana replied knowingly, 'we will be going about our mission.'

Nodding in agreement, Jon continued. 'Yes, but not before we pay another visit to our tailors in Kingston.'

'Our tailors? Whatever for? We already had new uniforms made on our last trip.' Lana looked slightly puzzled at the apparent need for more clothes.

'Yes my darling,' Jon said enthusiastically, 'and while it must be said that you looked a picture of perfection in your uniform, I would point out that when we begin to live in normal society, neither of us will want to be wearing uniforms all the time. On such occasions, we will be expected to dress as civilians.' Noting the look on Lana's face, slightly baffled by the need to wear a different type of clothing, Jon added, 'Don't the ladies on Zel like to dress up on occasion? Surely, they wear something more ornate when socialising. I can't imagine them all wearing uniforms at parties!'

With the help of the pictures in Jon's mind and an understanding of what would be required of her, Lana was quite excited as she replied, 'Our people do tend to dress very much alike for all occasions. Personal vanity is not unknown, but it is not considered necessary to be different to any other citizen, although from what I have already seen of the culture in America and the clothes the women wear, I will be happy to embrace their style of dress.'

Chapter Thirty-Four

'Then, after we have given Jacob Bernstein a visit,' Jon said, 'we will go on a shopping spree in Kingston and see what the fashion houses have to offer. Probably not the same as London or Paris, of course, but I'm sure you will enjoy the experience, and I will have the tailor make me several new suits, some for formal occasions and two or three for casual wear. They already have all my measurements, so all I will have to do is select the different materials.'

'The lady in question, the tailoress, will be disappointed,' Lana remarked, 'when she finds that she will have to forego the pleasure of measuring you all over again, as she did on our first visit to the shop.'

Jon grinned at the recollection of the attentiveness of the staff on that occasion. He let Lana's comment pass, but though he thought with amusement, *They might want to double-check!*

Lana read his thoughts with a big smile on her face. Then, before moving on to other matters, she enquired, 'Do we have enough money to buy all the clothes, or do we need to sell another diamond?'

'Good question, my dear,' Jon replied, 'but no, for the time being, we have more than enough cash to fund our expenses for the foreseeable future. Although, when it comes time to buy our own island, we will require many millions of dollars, hence the need to persuade Jacob to act as our agent. And that reminds me, we should begin the selection of some suitable stones to fund such an expensive project.'

Lana retrieved the box of diamonds from their living quarters. Their earthly value was beyond her comprehension, but she knew they represented the wealth required to provide them with security for their future life together on Earth and a lifestyle becoming an ambassador of the Zel. She placed the box on a low table beside Jon, and together, they began the careful selection of a number of the largest and most beautiful diamonds in the collection.

Chapter Thirty-Four

When they had finally chosen what they considered to be the best stones, Jon commented, 'When we hand these over to Jacob, I'll advise him to engage an armed guard when he goes on his travels, and probably he would be sensible to have the shop guarded as well. I doubt that he has ever seen such a valuable collection in his entire lifetime.'

As they looked down at the diamonds, Jon picked out six and spread them out on a black cloth. The lights of the flight deck instruments and the illumination in the cabin reflected off the many facets of the gems. With the slightest movement of the head, it was like watching a kaleidoscopic effect as the reflections bounced off the walls of the surrounding area. *Fascinating to watch, almost hypnotic,* they both thought.

'When we take our docking position over Kingston,' Jon declared, 'we will teleport directly into Jacob's shop. It may well take him by surprise, but it will be better for him if we arrive unnoticed by any outside observer. There is always the possibility of an opportunistic thief hanging about, and I wouldn't want to draw any unwelcome attention by having to deal with any incident.'

As there was little more to be said about their intentions for their first day or so back on Earth, the diamonds were carefully wrapped up in the same black cloth and placed on top of one of the control consoles, in open view. *But still more secure than any place on Earth,* Jon thought with a whimsical smile.

As they watched the planet Earth looming ever larger in the viewing screens on the flight deck, it wasn't long before Jon remarked casually, 'There they are; Jara and Mort are already in the prearranged orbit. They will have spotted us by now, so if you would, Lana, signal for them to come aboard in about one hour's time. Then we can begin briefing them in the part they will play regarding the missile deactivation program.'

Chapter Thirty-Four

It was the work of only a few minutes to contact the other spacecraft, and as Jara's face appeared on the screen, he acknowledged their invitation with a smile. 'It's been a long time since we last teleported from one ship to another in space, so we will manoeuvre a little closer, if you don't mind.' In an attempt at humour, he added, 'It could be cold out there!'

Jon thought, *If Mort and Jara can teleport from their craft so easily, then I will be able to do the same if it ever becomes necessary at any time in the future.* This was a thought he would recall in another situation in the not-so-distant future.

Chapter Thirty-Five

As arranged, their guests signalled their formal request to come aboard, and within minutes, Captain Jara and Mort appeared on the flight deck, calm and assured, despite their short hop in space. 'I've no idea how far I could teleport in space,' Jara remarked, 'but until some hypothetical situation arises, I'll be content to only try a short distance, such as we have just done. Going adrift in space is not on my agenda.'

As he said it in a light-hearted manner, Jon only smiled in agreement, while Lana laughed openly. 'I can't imagine the intrepid Captain Jara getting lost anywhere,' she said, which provoked further laughter all around.

As the purpose of the mission was something the commander of the mother ship had already briefed them all on, Jon and Lana recounted the story of their own earlier flight around the world, when they identified the location of all the nuclear missiles, both on land and under the seas. Some were invisible to the visual scanners on board, but were detected by the sensitive instruments at their disposal, since the uranium warheads had a radio wavelength that could be picked up quite easily. Tracking and locating the missiles was now a formality, and all that was required was time and patience.

'And how do you intend to dispose of the threat these missiles represent?' Jara enquired. 'Total destruction, which could trigger a few nuclear explosions, or disablement of the weapons?'

Chapter Thirty-Five

Jon grinned. 'We have already had an "accidental" explosion in one of the Middle East countries, which was denied by the government concerned, so it would be advisable to avoid any further accidental destruction. I had thought to simply neutralise the warheads by altering the atomic structure of the fissionable material, which would render the missiles nothing more than giant fireworks.'

'But we have seen the size of these weapons,' Jara argued, 'and even without the nuclear warheads, they could cause widespread destruction with the force of the impact on landing. Any rocket fuel left in them would effectively give them an explosive power of any of the bombs used in the bygone world wars.' He paused reflectively before continuing. 'Might I suggest, Jon, that in addition to locating all the missiles, we systematically alter the atomic structure of fissionable materials and the fuel for the rocket motors at the same time. That way, every country concerned would be left with nothing but a monument to their folly, and they could be warned that any attempt to rebuild their arsenals would meet with the same discouragement.'

After a moment's consideration, Jon replied, 'That we could most certainly do, Jara, but the weapons systems on board my ship will need some slight modifications before it is capable of altering the atomic structure of the fissionable material and the rocket fuel simultaneously, and to do that, I will need some assistance.' Turning to the technical officer, he asked, 'Would you be able to help me in that respect, Mort?'

With an easy smile, Mort replied, 'You'll be pleasantly surprised to learn that the necessary adjustments to your computerised weapons systems can be done within minutes; in fact, if you come with me now, we can complete the changes while Lana and Jara catch up with their own conversation. I'm sure Lana has much to tell about her experiences on Planet Earth.'

Chapter Thirty-Five

Leaving their companions to their own devices, Jon, accompanied by Mort, went through to the weapons control centre, which was a surprisingly compact area. Although Jon had little practical experience in setting or changing the controls, nevertheless, he found that his implanted knowledge was more than adequate to help him understand as Mort explained the necessary changes to the computer that would be utilised for the energy beam to alter the atomic structure of the fissionable material and rocket fuel. *The Teacher being taught,* Mort thought with an inward smile.

As anticipated, it only took a short time to complete their task, and they were able to rejoin Captain Jara on the flight deck. Lana, her face flushed with excitement, then recounted the various events on Earth that she had recently experienced. The observed way of life, the people, good and bad, their island refuge, the outcome of the UN meeting, and the anticipation of a lack of progress in agreement on disarmament. Hence, the need for Jon to take matters into his own hands, with the willing assistance of Mort and Jara, and of course, the attempted assassination of the president and the subsequent return of Davis Cooper to Washington DC in their spacecraft, dubbed the flying saucer by the people of Earth. Jon returned just in time to hear Captain Jara exclaim, 'The people of Earth have the outward appearance of men, but they have much to learn on how to live a civilised existence before they can be accepted by the Federation of the Stars, and in particular, by us, the Zel, who have been tutoring and moulding them in our image for millions of years.' Looking directly at Jon as he approached, he said pointedly, 'It is just as well that the present Teacher is going to be on Earth for several hundreds of years; it may well take all of that time to reach a successful conclusion.'

Nodding in agreement, Jon said, 'I have no illusions about my fellow men; it doesn't take much to alter their personality and for them to revert to a primitive state of mind and behaviour, which is why my first priority is to take away the weapons of their own

Chapter Thirty-Five

destruction. But then they will no doubt resort to using conventional warfare without any hesitancy.' He paused as he grimaced. 'That could well mean a loss of several million lives, but at least the planet will survive intact. With a population of over seven billion, life will presumably go on uninterrupted.' Then he added as an afterthought, 'If that should happen, I may be tempted not to intervene until the warring factions have realised the futility of their actions.'

'Even so,' Jara exclaimed, 'you may have to take drastic action against those aggressive people in order to convince them wars are not always the way to settle disputes, whatever the grievance. A solution can be found by consultation, and if they can't accept that, then a show of force on your part, Teacher, may become necessary to guide them in the path of everlasting peace on Earth. That was how one of your predecessors put it, was it not, Jon, some two thousand years ago, I believe?'

'I know the Teacher you refer to, Jara. In fact, he gave his own life to the cause of peace, but humans continued to live as they have always done, and very little has changed over the centuries except that the means of killing each other has become more efficient. But that is what I intend to put a stop to by removing the nuclear weapons.' Before the departure of Mort and Jara, Jon confirmed that they were in possession of the coordinates of all weapons to be taken out in their designated search area, and he informed Jara that it would be a few days before he himself would be ready to commence the trail of destruction.

'We have some personal business to attend to,' he said with a smile. 'The other matter will be attended to in due course; after all, it may be months, even years if we're lucky, before any government attempts to unleash their weapons of destruction, only to find out that they have been rendered useless, and even then, we can eliminate them as potential weapons of war.'

As Captain Jara and Mort moved into the centre of the flight deck in readiness to teleport back to their own ship, they both

Chapter Thirty-Five

raised their hands in a farewell gesture, and with a smile, they were gone.

'Well, that didn't take long, Lana,' Jon said in amusement. 'I didn't even have the chance to say "see you around the world," did I?'

Taking Jon by the arm and giving a gentle squeeze, Lana murmured, 'And now can I set the course for the island and the blue skies of the Caribbean? I'm looking forward to our few days of relaxation before we begin our mission. I rather think it is going to be a tedious journey, unless we can devise some other entertainment to keep us occupied,' she said with a giggle. With their minds as one, they were both smiling at the possibilities.

'Business before pleasure, Lana,' Jon remarked with a grin. 'Set course for the island, and when we have given Jacob Bernstein a visit, not forgetting the tailors, also, then we will devote a little time to ourselves before the real mission begins.'

The decision made, they both set about the preparations to take up station above the area of Jamaica in the Caribbean. Lana set the course to bring them into a low orbit first of all, and Jon fixed the coordinates for an accurate position for them to teleport down to Jacob Bernstein's shop in Kingston. One hour later found them hovering in their normal position high above Jamaica's premier city. Although, looking out of the viewport from an altitude of twenty miles, their normal parking position, it was impossible to make out any details of the ground below. Looking down, the heat haze created a blue impenetrable mist. There was no horizon, and above them, the blue vault of the heavens created the illusion that they were suspended in a giant sphere. It was only when the tropical night fell that the air would cool and afford them a clear view of Kingston. Alternatively, they could reduce their altitude, but that carried a risk of collision with civil aircraft, which was not a good option.

Chapter Thirty-Five

As Jon used the computer to enhance the visual images of the city below, unaffected by any weather conditions, he remarked to Lana, 'I can see Jacob's shop quite clearly on the screen and it appears to be quiet. No one has gone in for some time, so now could be a good time to make our grand entrance and hope that Jacob is in his workshop at the back of the premises. But we don't want him to have a heart attack when we suddenly appear, do we?'

'I think our Jewish friend is made of sterner stuff than that,' Lana replied with a laugh. 'I will carry the diamonds in my hands during the transition, and if Jacob is startled by our appearance, the sight of them will soon dispel any fear he may experience, of that I am sure.'

'Well, no time like the present,' Jon said as he took Lana by the hand. He knew that she was now confident to teleport the short distance to the ground below, but still preferred the feeling of security that he gave her. With a gentle squeeze and smile of encouragement, he murmured, 'Now Lana.' A moment later, they materialised in the jeweller's premises to find the showroom of the shop deserted, but very obviously, judging from the sound of music emanating from the workshop at the rear, Jacob was happily employed doing what he enjoyed most, creating works of art for the wealthy.

As they walked slowly to the rear of the premises, they noticed that the door into the workshop area was slightly ajar. As Jon pushed the door open gently, Jacob glanced up with a startled look on his face, but upon realisation of who his surprise visitors were, he immediately relaxed and gave them a bright smile. 'Come in, my friends,' he exclaimed. 'You are the only people who can come into my shop unannounced. Since your last visit, I've had all my security arrangements upgraded, so that now even the most determined criminals would have little chance of breaking in.' He laughed slightly. 'And even if they managed to do that, they would have a hard time breaking into my new safe.'

Chapter Thirty-Five

'I'm glad to hear it, Jacob,' Jon remarked. 'You're going to need all the security possible after this visit, and here's the reason why.' Turning to Lana, he said, 'Let him see the diamonds, Lana. Unveil them one at a time so that he has time to appreciate each individual stone. I rather think that collectively they will blow' his mind away.' And so it proved to be the case.

As Lana revealed the six exquisite diamonds one at a time, pausing between each one, Jacob took a deep breath as he continually repeated his phrase of appreciation, 'Ah moie, ah moie!' As a finale, Lana then produced the extra diamond they had selected for Jacob's commission or reward for handling the sale on their behalf, which, while not in the same class as the six special gems, was still more than equal to their previous gift to the jeweller.

As Lana handed over the single diamond, she explained that, as before, they thought it would be the best way to pay his commission. He could either keep it for his own pleasure or sell it and enhance his own personal wealth.

Despite his protestations regarding their generosity, he was obviously delighted. 'I'm already a millionaire as a result of selling your last gift, and although I haven't had time to inspect this latest stone, I would think that it is likely to sell for double the price of the last one.'

Turning his attention to the six diamonds laid out on his workshop table, he took a deep breath before he began his scrutiny of them, still murmuring from time to time, 'Ah, moie, ah moie.' Jon and Lana waited patiently until he had completed his inspection, listening with some amusement to his soft singsong voice, almost as though he was cooing to a baby. Eventually, he put his eyeglass to one side, leaned back in his chair, steepled his fingers in front of his chest, sighed blissfully, and then he spoke quietly.

'Where did you acquire these stones, my friends? During the course of my lifetime, I've been privileged to see some of the finest diamonds in the world. I've even been honoured to have a private viewing of the Koh-I-Noor diamond, one of the most beautiful that mortal man has laid eyes on, and also the fabulous Cullinan diamond, the largest cut diamond in the world, or at least it was until you brought these in.' He gestured toward the six gems spread out in front of him. Even in the subdued light of the workshop, they illuminated the confined space as the polished facets glinted and sparkled, holding the eyes of the unwary with a hypnotic effect. 'Would I be correct to assume that they do not have their origin on Earth?'

Jon couldn't give a direct answer to Jacob's question, since he only knew with any certainty that Lana had received what she had previously referred to as her trinkets from her father, a commander of one of the Zellian star ships. 'What makes you ask such a question, Jacob? These diamonds are not only real, but absolutely perfect in every sense of the word, are they not?' He put his own question quietly, already knowing from what he could see in his friend's mind what the answer was likely to be. Jacob was in awe of the size and quality of the merchandise, but Jon nevertheless waited for the reply.

When Jacob was able to control his emotions, he said, 'Until now, the Cullinan has been the largest cut diamond in the world, weighing some five hundred twenty carats, and as such, it has been impossible to put a price on it. But any one of these,' he said as he again gestured reverentially, 'exceeds the Cullinan by at least eighty carats. If I am to find a buyer for one or all of them, it won't be here in Jamaica. I will have to travel further afield, Hatton Garden in London, perhaps, or even Paris, Amsterdam or New York.' He smiled. 'What we have here I would estimate to be valued well in excess of one billion dollars, possibly more, to the right buyer.'

'And will the other diamond compensate you for the travelling you will have to do to secure such a buyer, Jacob?' Jon asked, even though he knew what the answer would be.

Chapter Thirty-Five

'Yes,' Jacob replied, his face flush with excitement at the prospect of his journeys to other parts of the world. 'But apart from this, and apart from becoming the most famous diamond merchant in the world, I will also be an extremely rich man, thanks to your generosity Jon and Lana. In fact, on completion of this commission, I am already thinking of retiring from the world of commerce.'

'But in the meantime,' Jon interceded, 'I would suggest that you engage a small team of security staff to protect your person, and your interests, and that means as of now.' Then as an afterthought, he added with a smile, 'But don't give up your career as a diamond merchant just yet, Jacob, for I will need your services again sometime in the near future.'

Raising his eyebrows in question, Jacob didn't try to conceal his surprise as he enquired, 'You have even more stones at your disposal?'

It was Lana who answered him, assuring him, 'Yes, there are still a number of diamonds available to be sold, as and when our finances require a boost, such as when we negotiate the purchase of a private island on which to build a permanent home.'

Whatever Jacob thought of that statement was not easy to see as his mind was still churning and chaotic due to his continuing excitement. 'For you, my friends, I will always be available to help with your business transactions, and if you want to buy an island here in the Caribbean, why, I can assist you in that matter as well.' He laughed as he boasted, 'Jacob Bernstein has a finger in many pies.'

This was a statement that raised a question in Lana's private thoughts, one that Jon briefly but mentally explained, *Nothing to do with culinary skills, my dear!*

With security uppermost in his mind, Jacob went over to a curtain draped over one wall, which he drew back to reveal an obviously new safe of the latest design. After opening it, after much manipulation of the electronic controls, he deposited the collection

Chapter Thirty-Five

of diamonds safely, including his own latest acquisition. Then he rejoined Jon and Lana where he gave a sigh. 'It makes me sad, in a way, to lock those jewels away out of sight; their duty should be on display for all to see, but ah moie, who would protect them?'

With that problem yet to be solved, Jon reminded Jacob that now was the time to organise his security team. 'I have the very people available locally, trustworthy and capable of dealing with any of the criminal element. All of them were trained by the special branch and are currently employed by the local government.' He grinned as he continued. 'But when I offer them a handsome bonus to resign and come to work for me, the only question will be when we can start.' Satisfied that there was little more to be done regarding the safekeeping and eventual sale of the merchandise, Jon informed his Jewish friend that for the remainder of the day, he and Lana were going on a shopping expedition before returning to their ship, after which they would be absent from Kingston for about one month. They would then pay a return visit to Jacob's premises to check any possible progress with potential buyers for the diamonds.

'Don't expect results too soon,' Jacob warned them. 'We are talking about a mega-million dollar deal here, and I'm fully expecting to make a hard sell. There will undoubtedly be much competition and fierce bidding, but be assured, I will earn my commission or my name isn't Jacob Bernstein!'

'You may equally be assured, Jacob, that we are in no hurry to complete the sale, not until you have found a suitable island for us, but in the meanwhile, we're aiming to go back into Kingston centre to complete our shopping list. It's time we got out of these uniforms and started dressing like civilians so that we don't attract too much attention.'

Jacob replied with a smile. 'You will always stand out in any crowd; you, Lana because of your exceptional beauty, and as for you, Jon, well, your hair alone is like a beacon that glows in the sunlight, and I daresay the ladies admire your fine physique as well.'

Chapter Thirty-Five

'I can vouch for that,' Lana remarked somewhat tartly. 'The lady in the tailor shop was somewhat enamoured of him on our last visit, not to mention several other female assistants as well.'

Jon gave a sheepish grin at the memory of the attention paid to him on that occasion, but hastened to assure Lana that they would be in and out the tailor shop as quickly as possible; after all, how many more measurements were needed for his new outfits? 'Once I've instructed them regarding the number of suits, casual as well as formal, you can help me by choosing the materials, then we will be off into the main shopping centre, and you can shop until you drop, I promise.'

Slightly mollified at the prospect of spending time inspecting and choosing a wardrobe to meet her future needs, Lana's good humour and sense of fun quickly returned, and with a charming smile, she turned to Jacob. 'We will leave you now, Jacob, and begin our shopping expedition as soon as Jon has concluded his business at the tailor's shop, and one hour there should suffice.' She gave a mischievous smile as she added, 'And the rest of the day will be mine.' At that remark, Jon raised his eyebrows in mock despair, but smiled indulgently at her nevertheless.

As their host ushered them to the door, he simply said, 'I look forward to seeing you in one month's time; I may have some good news for you by then or perhaps not. But if, as you say, there is no desperate need to sell the diamonds, I will have time to negotiate a better price for you, making your island that much more affordable.' They all laughed at that remark. Jon and Lana knew that cost was not part of the equation of buying, since location was everything.

There were dozens of small islands dotted around the Caribbean, for the most part deserted and off the usual tourist trail, so if Jacob could find one to meet their requirements, they would leave him to negotiate with whatever government was involved. *After that, well,* Jon thought, *we have all the time in the world to plan and build our retreat, but in the meanwhile, let's go shopping, Lana!*

Chapter Thirty-Five

As predicted, despite the attentions of the female staff in the tailor's shop, Jon, with Lana's help, chose all the materials for his new wardrobe and ordered a number of casual and dress suits to comply with their future social life. They anticipated a full calendar on that score and were on their way out of the shop within the hour, with the promise that they would return in one month's time. It would coincide with their visit to Jacob, in order to collect all the garments that had been ordered. 'No, you will not be able to deliver them to my home,' Jon had insisted with a smile of amusement. Twenty miles directly above Kingston was definitely out of reach for the so willing ladies in the shop.

Surprisingly, for someone who had never been shopping in the accepted sense, as it was not something the people of Zel ever had to do, Lana showed remarkable constraint in buying her new clothes. Expense was something that she had no need to consider, as Jon reminded her. 'If you see anything you like, have it.' Then he added with a laugh, 'Just remember, we have to carry it back to the ship either today or in one month's time, but money at least is something we have plenty of.'

Whereas Jon's clothing requirements were dealt with in less than one hour, Lana indulged her shopping experience to the full, and just like any woman of Earth, she visited numerous fashion shops, selecting and trying on the various garments of every style and colour. After an exhausting day, she ended up with only a few beautiful dresses, mainly of the varieties suitable for eveningwear. 'If I want to wear anything more casual,' she said, 'I can always acquire that type of clothing after we have concluded our mission. In the meantime, I am content to wear my uniform for normal daily use.'

Jon realised that since his transformation into a Teacher those several months ago, he was now infinitely more patient as a man, particularly a man accompanying a woman on a shopping expedition

Chapter Thirty-Five

such as this one, but even so, he was relieved to hear Lana say, 'Enough!'

Carrying the various boxes and packages between them, all of them belonging to Lana, they walked away from the busy shopping area until they reached a small deserted garden or plaza. Noting that there were no casual observers in the vicinity, Jon said quietly, 'Now would be a good time to teleport back to the ship, Lana.' With a final nod of confirmation, they both disappeared, leaving Kingston to continue its vibrant existence unabated, while they materialised on the familiar flight deck of their ship, their temporary home until they had realised their dream of living on their own island in the sun.

Chapter Thirty-Six

As two or three days were unlikely to make any difference to the outcome of their mission, Jon and Lana took the opportunity to unwind after the tensions of New York and the traumatic journey in Air Force One. 'Never again,' Lana said with a shake of her head. So they spent the days alternating between lazy days on board their ship, and even lazier days on the pristine white sands of what until now they had always described as their island, noting, however, signs of recent occupation by visiting tourists, which was not something to be encouraged in their future location, wherever that might be.

On the morning of the fifth day, with what was to be a temporary farewell, the spacecraft leapt into the skies, heading east over the Atlantic, bound for Europe. The automatic tracking system was set to seek out the hundreds of hidden nuclear missiles, or so the various governments thought, using the all-seeing eyes of their computers and the laser-guided probes that would change the atomic structure of the uranium warheads of the missiles while rendering the rocket propulsion systems useless as the fuel became like so much water. The Zellian technology would be used in a covert manner, and no government would be aware that their ultimate weapons had been rendered useless. America would be the last nation to be disarmed, but the first to be informed of what the Teacher had done to promote world peace.

Unbeknown to Jon and Lana, Mort and Captain Jara had already begun their mission over the Southern hemisphere, where

Chapter Thirty-Six

admittedly, by comparison there were fewer nuclear installations to deal with. By the time the Teacher and his companion were airborne, much of the world below the equator was considered clean, and it was then that the joint efforts of the two individual spacecraft began to quickly cover the Northern hemisphere. Jon and Lana started in Europe and worked toward the east, while Jara and Mort began over the Sea of Japan, with the intention of covering several islands in that region and then working toward the west.

From time to time, contact was made by the radio-video system to check their individual progress, but apart from the length of time it took, usually about five minutes' exposure to the destruction beam for each individual nuclear missile, the operation was straightforward. Since they could operate from an extremely high altitude, apparently, their presence was not considered a threat by the relevant military authorities. At one stage in the proceedings, Jara commented, 'Pity that someone doesn't attempt to let go a missile; I would be curious to note their reaction when their toys are found to be inoperable.'

It was during one of these periods of communication between the two ships and their crews that Jon commented, 'I note from your present position that you are approaching the area where we were fired upon by a hostile nation. It has been observed that they have been following a missile test firing exercise recently, to the consternation of other governments in the region. Even though the weapons were not armed with nuclear warheads, it was still interpreted as a potential threat to the security and peace in that part of the world. They use a regular phrase to describe it, sabre rattling.' With a smile of derision he added, 'If such an event should occur when you fly over that region, may I suggest that you allow them to fire their missile and then blow it out of the skies when it has reached a safe altitude. A practical demonstration of our abilities will have an instant effect, and then it will render all other missiles inoperable as planned.'

Chapter Thirty-Six

It was only a few hours after this exchange of information that Jara and Mort approached the coordinates of the hostile nation in question, and their instruments picked up missile activity. On consulting the computers, they observed that two missiles had already been launched, each on a different trajectory, one apparently headed over the Chinese mainland, and the other in the direction of Japan, countries that were not likely to encourage any form of testing over their territory. With a smile, Mort, as the technical officer on board, said, 'It looks as though we are going to be able to give a demonstration to the potential aggressors by destroying their missiles before they can get anywhere near their intended targets. Should the recipients be aware of the impending strike, false or otherwise, they are going to be relieved to see the incoming missiles disappear from their radar screens.' Turning to Captain Jara, he said, 'May I suggest that we accelerate out of Earth's immediate gravity and atmosphere in order to overtake these missiles? It will also make it easier to deal with their diversifying trajectories; they are already hundreds of miles apart, but from an altitude of two or three hundred miles, they will easily be in sight of our computer-guidance systems.'

With a nod of approval, Jara turned to his control console, and with a wave of his hands, set the controls to alter their speed, altitude, and course to overtake the maverick missiles; something that was completed in only a few minutes. 'There they are, Mort,' he exclaimed as their targets showed clearly on the viewing radar screens. 'They are well away from any civilian habitation, so can be destroyed safely, but no doubt they are still being tracked by the military responsible for firing them. Aren't they going to be disappointed when their toys appear to self-destruct!'

With a satisfied smile, Mort activated the laser-guided destruction beams and watched the disintegration of the missiles, which illuminated the viewing screens in a bright flash. What a moment before had been weapons of potential destruction, even

Chapter Thirty-Six

without their nuclear warheads, were now but fragments of incandescent, white hot metal falling to the earth below like so many shooting stars, harmless, but spectacular to anyone watching from below.

'Well, that was a little excitement to break the monotony,' Mort declared, 'but now we will have to return to our predetermined course and render any other missiles inoperable, starting with our latest adversary, before they attempt to launch any further weapons.' While Mort busied himself in regaining their previous seek and destroy course, Captain Jara radioed Jon to report the action taken against the weapons launched by the rogue state.

Jon commented, 'By the time they have investigated what could possibly have gone wrong with those missiles of theirs, all the rest of their arsenal will have been reduced to so many expensive ornaments, nice to look at, but otherwise quite useless as weapons.'

With a chuckle of amusement, Jon congratulated the other crewmembers. 'But that still leaves us with several thousands of missiles to deactivate, but hopefully, we can complete our mission covertly and without further incident.'

It was several weeks later that the two spacecraft rendezvoused in the Middle East region, over the area where the accidental nuclear explosion had occurred some months ago. At Jon's suggestion and invitation, they all met in the one craft for a council of war. For Jara and Mort to teleport from their own ship was but the work of a few moments, and when they materialised on the flight deck, Jon and Lana welcomed them enthusiastically.

'Well Captain Jara, Mort, we have almost finished our mission to decommission all the nuclear armaments on Earth and to render the likelihood of global warfare by nuclear means more remote.'

Captain Jara raised his voice questioningly. 'Almost finished, Jon, what more must we do?'

Chapter Thirty-Six

'Ironically, the most powerful nation on Earth has been left to the last to be disarmed,' Jon replied with a quiet smile. 'The United States of America has long been considered the Policeman on Earth, and as such, has had to retain its weapons until the last threat of nuclear war has been removed. So when we part this time, Jara, Lana and I will be visiting every installation in the United States and Canada, neutralising every one of their weapons. Now that all other installations throughout the world have effectively been rendered useless, the Western world will no longer be vulnerable to attack by rogue' nations.'

'And I take it that as our part of the mission is complete,' Jara declared, 'and as you and Lana are finishing off the American missiles, we will be free to rejoin the mother ship. What a pity. It has been an interesting few weeks working with, Jon, but I'm sure that you will have much to do after we are gone.'

'Ah. But your work is not yet finished, Jara. It will be at least another week before we have visited all the missile sites in the States, which will conclude the mission on land, but....' He hesitated with a frown. 'There are still a number of nuclear submarines patrolling the seas, some of which may be under the polar ice caps, virtually undetectable even to our surveillance equipment. I would request in my capacity as Ambassador of Zel that you remain in orbit until the position of every submarine is verified, then at the right time, their weapons can also be neutralised.'

It was Jara's turn to smile as he replied, 'That could mean spending several weeks or even months waiting for these submersibles to show themselves, unless the various governments of Earth can be persuaded to recall their ships.'

'That is something that could be arranged with the correct diplomacy,' Jon agreed, 'but however long it may take to clear the seas, you must remain in Earth's orbit.'

'Yes, Ambassador,' Jara retorted with a grin.

Chapter Thirty-Six

Mort had said little during the conversation between his captain and the ambassador, but he now voiced a question. 'Even after having presumably cleared all nuclear weapons of the nations of Earth, is it possible that some governments will manage to have concealed some missiles, and when they think they have the advantage, threaten the rest of the world?'

It was a question that Jon had already considered. Nodding grimly, he replied, 'If such an event were to occur, I would have no hesitancy in destroying the entire area where the missiles were sited and fired from. If need be, the punishment will be of Biblical proportion, utter destruction.'

'I can see that the people of Earth now have a Teacher they must respect, Jon,' Mort said. 'It's just as well that you have wisdom to guide you as well as strength of character, but to rule over them may require you to instil fear into them occasionally, a prophecy perhaps of the consequences of continued war-like behaviour. That would be my advice as a friend.'

Jon visibly relaxed at that moment. 'I don't see my purpose of being on Earth as any kind of ruler, by fear or any other means. My function is to give guidance to the heads of governments in the quest for peace and prosperity for all the people of Earth. You, especially, Mort, are aware of the knowledge instilled in me during the educational program on board this ship, a complete, month-long period of time when my brain was being indoctrinated with the knowledge acquired by the Zellians over a period of millions of years.' He looked around at his companions on the flight deck before continuing. 'Even now, I'm taken unaware in certain situations and find that without conscious thought, I automatically know the answers to certain problems that I've never had to deal with before; mental telepathy and its control are now second nature to me. Putting suggestions into other peoples' minds is also becoming a useful ability, as is being able to teleport at will.' Giving a rueful smile he added, 'I also had another incident occur when I had to call

Chapter Thirty-Six

on my powers of telekinesis as a means of defence to protect the President and his party while in New York. That too is an ability that has become as natural as breathing.'

Mort gave a smile of understanding. 'Jon, during the month that you were unconscious and undergoing the indoctrination process, it was decided by the commander of the mother ship, and therefore the High Council of Zel, that the next Teacher would have to be mentally and physically superior to any who had been sent to Earth before. The situation on your planet is rapidly reaching a critical stage. Although neutralising all nuclear weapons will give you time to bring about many other changes necessary to ensure the survival of the planet, unfortunately, as we have made you aware, your longevity has only been increased to some five hundred years, whereas Lana's life expectancy will be reduced to much the same. But as she has said before, she is content to spend that time with you.'

Out of curiosity, Jon asked, 'What has been the longest time that any of your people have remained on Earth as a Teacher, and how many native Teachers have been appointed and trained?'

Again, it was Mort who answered. 'In the very early days of humankind, when their life expectancy was very short, normally not much more than twenty of your years, a Zellian Teacher remained with them for several generations, then departed, leaving them to fend for themselves with the skills they had been taught. Then, after a period of some two hundred years, another Teacher would arrive to continue their education. That process continued for many thousands of years, but evolution proved to be so slow that our scientists decided to give nature a helping hand by genetically altering the hominid species over a long period of time, the result of which was the development of what your people now refer to as Homo erectus. Some two million years ago, this species spread out from the African continent, and over the millennia, it evolved into a very early type of man, the Neanderthal, who was primitive, but showed signs of increased intelligence. He gradually spread out over southern Asia and Europe.'

'You have certainly observed and nurtured humankind for a very long time," said Jon with a smile.

'Yes, indeed,' Mort replied gravely. 'Throughout the existence and development of humankind, we have been a benign influence, and continued with the genetic experiments until the appearance of your Cro-Magnon species, or modern man. After that, we allowed nature to take its course, and now man is very much cast in our image.'

'And the Zellians have been providing Teachers ever since?' queried Jon.

'Yes,' Mort agreed, 'we have provided some of our own people as Teachers for several thousands of years to teach the natives the rudiments of civilised life, to grow crops, to learn animal husbandry, and to build cities. Even your ancient temples and pyramids were constructed under the guidance of our Teachers, but eventually, we decided that the time had come to allow humankind to determine his own destiny, and that was when we began to train men of Earth to become the Teachers of their own kind.'

He paused for a moment for Jon to accept this information, but they read each other's minds. *No doubt,* he continued, *from the time Egypt emerged as one of the world's most advanced civilisations, we trained many of the wisest scholars of that time; they were regarded as gods by their own people, and they ruled wisely over the masses. But unfortunately, these civilisations eventually collapsed when they were overtaken by others. And so history repeats itself.*

Mort smiled as he recalled the more recent history of Earth, stories told to him by his own grandfather, of a time when a human Teacher had been educated to lead men into a peaceful way of life, cultivating a religious lifestyle that would lead to a peaceful way of life on Earth. 'Unfortunately, that man had the wisdom to be a leader of men, they called him a prophet, the Son of God, but he didn't have the powers that you have, Jon, and against overwhelming odds and the prejudices of his own people, he was killed in a barbaric manner by the very people he was trying to help.' He smiled grimly. 'After that time, we were careful to introduce human Teachers to the society of men purely as teachers of science, sociology, and politics, in particular, and we didn't forget the arts and architecture. No doubt you can recall many great men and their achievements over the last thousand years.'

Jon nodded in agreement. 'Yes, we have had many great men, and as society progressed, many women who also became recognized as artists, sculptors, musicians and composers, and architects, and many notable politicians as well, but their influence on matters of peace and prosperity has been overruled by the malignant behaviour of evil and corrupt governments.' After a moment of quiet reflection he continued. 'Even after the world is rid of the means of self-destruction, the bombs, I can foresee a period of many years, during which time I shall have to be a mediator between the warring factions on Earth, but there will be a difference between me and the prophet of two thousand years ago. I am, in effect, invulnerable to all attacks and threats from hostile peoples, and fortunately, I have at my disposal the means to destroy all who are not prepared to comply with a peaceful way of life.' He added grimly, 'Sodom and Gomorrah could be quite easily repeated.'

Not being familiar with that particular incident in the folklore of Earth, Mort let the moment pass. Instead, he pointed out that there was little more that Jara and he could do. They had enjoyed their brief stay with Jon and Lara, but it was time to return to their own ship and resume their patrol, looking for any trouble on the planet below, any rogue missiles that might have been missed, and of course, to monitor any calls from Jon and Lana.

'I will contact the mother ship,' Captain Jara said, 'and give the commander my report regarding the removal of the nuclear threat

Chapter Thirty-Six

on Earth, and also inform him of your request for our continued presence to monitor the situation for as long as you deem necessary. He will warp the time lines and be in another galaxy before we've made another orbit of the earth.'

With little more to be discussed, Jon suggested that Mort and Jara continue with their surveillance patrol until he deemed it safe for them to return to the mother ship, while he and Lana would resume their flight to take them to the North American continent, the States, where there were many hundreds of missiles yet to be deactivated. With a smile, Jon briefly laid his hands on the shoulders of Mort and Jara in a farewell gesture. 'No doubt we will meet again before you depart from Earth's orbit, or perhaps if all goes according to plan, you may decide to give Lana and me a personal visit on the surface of the planet.'

'If we do,' Jara replied, 'we will have no hesitancy in accepting your invitation, will we Mort?'

With a nod to affirm any future meeting, Mort then said, 'But in the meantime, we will get back to our own ship, and let you depart for your return to America. I know it will only take a few hours to get there, but the sooner you begin your cleansing operations, the safer the world will be.'

Little more was said, and within minutes, Jon and Lana found themselves alone once more. As they watched the observation screens on the flight deck, they could see the other craft rapidly accelerating on its original course to the West, and then veer away to the North and the Polar Regions. 'Well, Lana,' Jon said, 'we will set course for the West Coast of America and Canada and begin our deactivating program. Apart from Russia, the States have the biggest arsenal of nuclear missiles in the world, so we can expect it to take another week or two before this mission is complete.'

Lana embraced Jon warmly and in a coy manner said, 'It's just as well our computer systems are programmed to locate and

Chapter Thirty-Six

deactivate every missile automatically; otherwise, we would find this operation very boring, with days and days with nothing to do to pass the time away.'

In reply, Jon returned her embrace and said huskily, 'I'm sure we will find something pleasant to do.' Then he laughed as he added, 'We have much to discuss with regard to our future plans once we have completed this part of our mission. We have to file our report with the President and that's going to be a shock to his military advisors and the government. Then we will return to Jamaica and Jacob Bernstein to ascertain how he has progressed with the sale of the diamonds.'

Still smiling, Lana said, 'All of that may be several weeks away, so until that time, I think that we should forget all about missions, presidents and worldly affairs, and for the moment, live for ourselves. The world can wait for a few more days without us.' She firmly grasped Jon's arm and pulled him gently in the direction of their living accommodation and sleeping quarters, leaving the computers whirring and flashing on the flight deck. It would be several hours before their presence was required, so there was time for their own pleasure.

Chapter Thirty-Seven

The spacecraft followed its predetermined flight path to reach the western coast of Alaska and then progressed down the Pacific coast, pinpointing the nuclear installations identified on their first circumnavigation of the globe. The computer system alerted them to the presence of uranium radio emissions, while still hundreds of miles from the nearest landfall. 'In this area of the world,' Jon exclaimed, 'this is likely to indicate the presence of a nuclear submarine; whether American or Russian remains to be seen, but if you attend to the scanners, Lana, we'll go down and take a closer look.'

Accordingly, Lana reduced their altitude until they were only about five miles above the source of the emissions. 'Well, well,' Jon exclaimed. 'We are in luck. Two Russian subs that appear to have made a rendezvous at sea, for whatever reason. Mort and Jara either missed them because of their latitude, or possibly because they were still under the polar ice cap.' He focussed the scanners on the vessels below, and after a lengthy inspection, he came to the conclusion that they were indeed Russian. Both submarines were carrying nuclear ballistic missiles. As a point of interest, he confided to Lana, 'The one is a Delta III, and the other is an Akula-II attack submarine, the deadliest of all Russian nuclear-powered craft.' Then with a grimace, he added, 'We will immediately activate the laser-destruct beams on each of them in turn; five minutes will suffice to make them both as harmless as a duck in a bathtub.'

Chapter Thirty-Seven

Fortunately, the commanders of the Russian vessels below were unaware of the presence of the spacecraft above, and remained on the surface for much longer than it took to deactivate their missiles. Out of curiosity, Jon and Lana remained in their position, still at high altitude, but as the two submarines showed no sign of moving off or separating, it was mutually decided to continue on their course for Alaska and North America. 'I wonder what the captains of those vessels would do if they realised they were carrying so much useless but expensive hardware, and more to the point, how would the Kremlin react if they ordered any kind of attack on another nation only to find that their teeth had been drawn.'

While Lana didn't fully understand the terminology used in this conversation, she could follow the pictures in Jon's mind and replied, 'But won't all the nations in the world be in a similar situation very shortly, Jon?'

'By the time we have completed our tour of the United States, and Mort and Jara have eliminated any other stray missiles,' he replied, 'we will have the beginnings of a truce in the arm's race, and peace between the so-called superpowers. Any minor conflicts we will be able to control, with a little persuasion.' The discovery of the Russian submarines and the time it took to deactivate their deadly weapons had only taken a little more than half an hour, so without advertising their presence, Lana set their craft back on its original course for Alaska, but they were still alert for the possibility of further contact with any other enemy-type submarines. There were rumours that the Russians possessed ten similar vessels, mainly deployed in the Northern hemisphere. The only other sea power with a definite nuclear ability was Great Britain, but their vanguard-class subs had been one of the earliest of their targets at the outset of their European surveillance. Now their biggest challenge was to render the American arsenal impotent.

As expected, once the automatic computer-tracking systems were locked on, it was only a matter of observing the mountainous

Chapter Thirty-Seven

terrain below to know when the spacecraft needed to stop. The laser directional equipment did its work of activating the destruction beams and changing the atomic structure of the uranium warheads of the missiles in their hidden silos. Many of them were several hundreds of feet below ground, but still vulnerable to the superior technology of the Zellian spacecraft. At one point, Jon commented, 'Y' know, Lana, but for the widespread devastation we could cause throughout the world, we would have been much quicker to simply detonate every bomb as we found it.' He added with a grimace, 'But unfortunately, there wouldn't have been much of the planet that would survive such a holocaust.'

It was some two weeks later that the computers gave a clean reading of the North American continent, but to be absolutely sure, Jon decided to give a last coast-to-coast sweep across the country. He finally conceded that the once-mighty atomic arsenal of the United States was no more; the States were devoid of all weapons of mass destruction, but no doubt the military still believed that their government was still the most powerful in the world, with the possible exception of Russia. 'When we inform the President that the age of atomic warfare has now safely passed, I can imagine the repercussions with the military, and Congress in particular. We can only hope that the knowledge that every nuclear power has been similarly dealt with will soften the blow.'

Lana gave a smile of derision. 'How long do you think it will be before the military chiefs decide to prove that their weapons are still operative before they try to do a test firing exercise, Jon? Without a live warhead, of course.'

'Not long, Lana,' he replied soberly. 'This is a situation that they can never have visualised, but in a way, the sooner they are convinced that their weaponry is effectively now obsolete, the sooner the threat of global warfare will subside. Although, I've no doubt that there will be some regional warfare to control, but we will wait and see.'

Chapter Thirty-Seven

As they were making their final approach to Washington, they contacted President Davis Cooper to inform him of their impending arrival. However, they didn't mention the success of their mission; that was best left, they decided, for a face-to-face meeting. In turn, they had a communication from Captain Jara and Mort to report the interception with a number of Russian submarines in the northern Baltic regions, apparently on what appeared to be a training exercise. They had taken the opportunity to deactivate their missiles.

'So, it looks as though the two superpowers can now only bark at each other, but can't bite!' Jon remarked.

'Talking of biting,' Lana said with a smile playing about her lips. 'I know one person who is going to bite when we inform the President and his advisers of the loss of their nuclear ability, or deterrent, as they choose to refer to it, and that's General E. Clintock. The old warhorse will be absolutely devastated at the loss of their arsenal.'

Jon nodded his head in agreement. 'Once their initial anger has subsided, they will realise that the status quo is still the same, but I'm sure that it won't take long for them to come to the conclusion that, without superior weaponry, the next important consideration will be manpower.' He grimaced. 'Any general will concede that to win a battle doesn't mean that the war is won. Victory over the enemy entails occupation of the disputed territory, and the ability to be able to hold and control it.'

With a shake of his head, he added, 'We have taken the first step toward world peace by eliminating all nuclear weapons, but I can foresee that the difference in manpower between East and West will still possibly lead to further conflicts. For the Western world, to lose several million personnel would be a crippling blow, from which there would be no recovery, whereas, in a hypothetical situation, if Communist China were to lose double that number, out of a population of one billion, I don't think it would greatly concern their political masters. To them, life is cheap.'

Chapter Thirty-Seven

By this time, they had arrived back in their usual docking position above Washington, and as Lana established the audio-visual link with the president's office, they were greeted cheerfully by Davis Cooper himself. 'Nice to have you back again, Jon, Lana. We have been kept updated by our intelligence people of your whereabouts over the past few weeks, or is it months? You have certainly covered most of the world on your survey or sightseeing tour.' He turned to others out of range of the microphones and cameras and commented, 'We'll be interested to hear all about your travels, won't we, George, and you too, Robert.'

So, we have a reception committee, thought Jon. *So much the better.*

Assuming that the president would wish to have several senior advisors present at their forthcoming meeting, Jon and Lana delayed their arrival to the Oval Office for little more than an hour. It gave them time to prepare for the delivery of the momentous news of the successful conclusion of their mission, but they were aware of the hostility that would be aroused among the majority of the government members. The first cause for concern would undoubtedly be the loss of their deterrent capability, and secondly, the trillions of dollars involved in the costs. How would they explain that to the taxpayers.

General Clintock would probably be accompanied by several other senior members of the armed forces. The president might be regarded as the chief of staff, but as always, he relied on the guidance of his generals and navy personnel in matters of national security. Once the news of the loss of several thousands of missiles had penetrated their collective minds, Jon expected to be on the receiving end of their hostility. Would diplomacy alone defuse the situation, or would further action have to be taken to convince every government that world peace was now in their grasp? That was the relevant question in Jon's mind.

Chapter Thirty-Seven

As soon as they deemed it appropriate, Jon and Lana teleported down to the Oval Office of the White House, but were surprised to find the president alone with his Secretary of State George K. Lane. Smiling at the obvious look of doubt on their faces, the president hastened to assure them that it wasn't lack of interest in their meeting; on the contrary, due to the large number of military and civilian personnel who had expressed an interest in the ambassador's report, a much larger room had been acquisitioned to accommodate them all. After exchanging their usual cordial greetings, Davis Cooper opened the door into an adjoining room and led the way through, to the applause of all present, some of whom were instantly recognisable from previous meetings. Others were complete strangers, but had friendly expressions on their faces nevertheless. *Once I've delivered my report,* Jon thought, *will they still regard me as a friend of the American people, or public enemy number one?*

The president didn't waste time on useless oratory, but simply introduced Jon as the ambassador of Zel and Lana as his partner, and said that both were on Earth to serve in their capacity as Teachers. He then added that for the last month or so, they had undertaken a survey of the planet to assess what measures were necessary to bring stability to the United Nations in general, and to determine how peace for all countries could become a reality. In doing so, they hoped to begin the process of eliminating poverty and hunger in the poorer nations. After inviting Jon to take over the meeting, the president then sat down with the rest of the audience and waited for Jon's report with interest.

Jon felt gratified that he had so many senior government and military figures present. *They will be able to spread the news throughout the country and the media in particular,* he thought. *My first part of this report must be about the elimination of the nuclear threat, which they are going to find difficult to accept.* With Lana standing close beside him, he took a deep breath, and then began to speak. 'Ladies and gentlemen, as you are all aware, a meeting of the

Chapter Thirty-Seven

United Nations was held in New York a few months ago, and among the subjects under discussion was the predominant one on the subject of nuclear disarmament.' He smiled as he recollected the confusion of the delegates and their inability to reach any conclusions on the matter.

'As I expected, in the intervening weeks and months, not one country has made any suggestions as to how this problem can be dealt with.' He paused before adding, 'To be the first military power to give up the nuclear deterrent can be seen as stripping the country of its defensive capability, leaving it open to aggression and intimidation by lesser powers, which is not something easily contemplated. Unilateral disarmament by those holding vast quantities of nuclear missiles will never happen, at least not by mutual consent.' He grimaced visibly as he added, 'Humankind has always been aggressive and had little trust in his fellow creatures, and yet, as I said at the United Nations meeting, the future of humankind in general is very bleak, and the future of the planet is in jeopardy.'

Again, Jon paused as he surveyed the faces of his audience. 'My question to you all is, what would you do if I said to you, as of now, that several thousands of nuclear missiles that are distributed around the globe, on land and under the seas, have been deactivated; they are immobilised and monuments to a past method of warfare, disarmed and fit only to be scrapped?' Jon noted the expressions of shock and disbelief on their faces, first of the military personnel and then the politicians.

Finally, Davis Cooper stood up to ask the question uppermost in the minds of everyone present. 'Are you telling us, Jon, that you have taken it upon yourself to render the United States defenceless against any aggressor by destroying our nuclear missiles?'

As this was the question that Jon had long anticipated since the conclusion of the mission, he calmly answered, 'Mr President, your country is in no danger of attack from any source now, and your conventional weapons and manpower are more than adequate to repel any invader, or indeed, to continue in your role as peacekeeper throughout the world.'

One of the senior Congressmen in the audience rose to his feet, and in a belligerent tone of voice, he demanded, 'And how do we explain to the public that we now have trillions of dollars' worth of obsolete weapons lying around the country?'

Jon smiled wryly. 'Might I suggest that you don't even try to explain that state of affairs, and just allow the era of peace to take place without announcement.'

The next person to put a relevant question to Jon was General Clintock, and in a surprisingly calm manner, he asked, 'Are you assuring us that any future warfare will be on a level playing field, conventional weapons only, but will depend more on manpower?' As Jon nodded briefly in acknowledgement of that question, the general continued, 'And what happens if we have certain countries who persist in war-like aggression on their neighbours or threaten regional unrest that we can't deal with ourselves? Will you help in such a situation?'

'General, I see my role primarily as a Teacher, but I can only begin to pass on my knowledge for the benefit of humankind once a state of peace exists over much of the planet. But I can assure you that, if all persuasive means fail to curb the war-like behaviour of certain regions, yes, I will intervene, even if it necessitates destroying much of the country involved, with destruction on a biblical scale.'

Apparently assured by that assertion, although not sure of how that destruction would come about, General Clintock joined the president and several other military figures to discuss the security situation of the country, as they cast dubious glances in the direction of Jon and Lana; were they friends or foes? Time would tell. Since they were being ignored during the hubbub of conversation in the room, Lana drew Jon to one side and quietly suggested that it might

Chapter Thirty-Seven

be diplomatic to withdraw and return to the ship, and to contact the president a few days later, when he'd had time to discuss the issues of national security with his security advisors. Accordingly, they passed through the door into the empty Oval Office and teleported back to the peace and tranquillity of their ship.

Chapter Thirty-Eight

Twenty-four hours later, standing motionless but in close contact with each other as always, they were gazed down at the city of Washington several miles below. Jon murmured, 'Even from here, there seems to be much more activity going on around the White House than usual, and I don't mean tourist traffic. As we've been watching, there have been at least a score of official and military limousines passing the security people at the gates, and that's not normal at this time of day.'

In reply, Lana said, 'Yes, Jon, but we agreed that our presence might not be welcome for some time, at least until the President and his military advisers have accepted, or rejected the fact that America is no longer a nuclear power in common with Russia, China, and many of the other nations. In fact,' she added 'they may now view with apprehension some of the smaller countries that they have suspected of having the bomb, in case of some covert action on their part.'

'After the thoroughness of our surveillance operation,' Jon replied, 'between Captain Jara, Mort, and ourselves, it is most unlikely that we overlooked one single missile, but in the event we did, I intend to make a broadcast to the world, courtesy of the American and British television networks, to the effect that the deployment of any nuclear weapons will no longer be tolerated. The penalty for the aggressor will be the annihilation of the largest city in that country, a harsh penalty, but one that will strike fear into the military and governments alike. And to make sure that my message

Chapter Thirty-Eight

is understood by the masses, as I broadcast, I will speak at intervals in all the languages of Earth that I have at my command.'

'And in the meanwhile, Jon,' Lana asked, 'all these people going into the White House at this moment, what will they be discussing?' Lana frowned as she added, 'Do you still think it is a possibility that they don't entirely believe that all their missiles have been deactivated, and will still attempt a test-firing exercise during the next few hours? They'll be desperate to prove their invincibility.'

'Strangely enough, Lana,' Jon replied with a smile, 'the sooner they attempt such a test firing, the sooner they will be convinced that nuclear wars are now ended.' He gave a frown as he thought of the next logical step in the military mind. 'People like General Clintock are very quickly going to compare the manpower available to the armies of the East and of the West, and realise that America and her allies can never put enough men with conventional weapons onto the battlefield to contain the Communist countries.'

So, what can we do in that respect, Jon?' Lana asked. 'We want to avoid all wars, not simply to give one side a victory over another.'

'That is something that will require some planning for the future,' he replied soberly, 'but I have a demonstration in mind to convince the President and his advisers that I have the means, or rather, this ship, has the power to equalise armies of any size, regardless of manpower or conventional equipment. However, it is something they will have to see or experience before they will willingly believe it. I can only say that I'm thankful for Mort's educational program all those weeks or months ago; otherwise, I wouldn't be aware of the potential power available in this craft, power for defence or for the purpose of demonstration, but destruction on a scale that they can't even dream of. But for the moment, we do nothing but wait. We must give the generals time to try out their toys, as they surely will, and then, when they are convinced that their missiles are useless, I think they will be more willing to listen to their Teacher.

Chapter Thirty-Nine

President Davis Cooper did consult with the war cabinet as Lana had predicted. Collectively, none of them could believe that their nuclear arsenal had been neutralised, so it was with some urgency that the decision was taken to carry out a test firing of a medium-powered missile. They chose the location of the northern end of the White Sands missile range, a facility rarely used in this modern day and age, but more than adequate for that purpose. Within hours, authorisation had been approved and the order given to fire one missile when the area was cleared. As the war cabinet sat around a table waiting for the expected report, the minutes ticked away, and the suspense began to build. All eyes were either on the clock on the wall or alternately glancing at their wristwatches.

'Goddamn it,' blurted out General Clintock, 'how long does it take them to press a button?'

Still nothing was reported, and after a further five minutes of silence, the president's phone rang out shrilly. He picked it up, said, 'Yes,' and listened intently for several minutes before replacing the receiver without answering.

He sat wordlessly for several long minutes, his face drawn with anxiety. He was the supreme commander of all of America's armed forces, but a commander who had just been informed that his country had been deprived of its most powerful weapons. They had just taken a long step back in history to an age of old-fashioned, conventional warfare, where men on the ground would be a decisive factor in any future conflict. *God help America,* he thought after

Chapter Thirty-Nine

surveying the faces of the generals, admirals, and other senior personnel. *At least,* he thought with a touch of irony, *congress won't have any difficulty raising the finances for other more worthwhile purposes,—other than war.*

Davis Cooper came to the conclusion that only the harsh truth would suffice. 'Gentlemen, the ambassador of Zel and his lady must have had a very busy time while they were away on their world tour. That was the chief technician at the White Sands firing range on the phone, and the news is not good.' He paused while he thought how best to explain to his war cabinet how trillions of dollars' worth of hardware were now mere ornaments, sitting in dozens of locations all over the country. As weapons of defence or aggression, they were obsolete due to the handiwork of Jon, our friend.

'What should have been a coded response from this cabinet, and an immediate firing of the missile proved to be negative. The technician in charge ordered his team to run a trace to find any faults, but there were no obvious electrical or mechanical faults. Their instrument readings indicated that no ignition occurred in the propulsion system. Why? The fuel wasn't volatile enough to light a cigarette lighter, nil octane. On top of that, the nuclear warhead showed no signs of uranium radiation, so effectively, it was a dud. I've put it to you in the simplest possible terms, not being a scientist, but if this scenario has been repeated all over the States and every other country with a nuclear capacity, or should I say that had a nuclear capability, then the war game is due for a drastic change.'

'I can see that we are going to have to come to some far-reaching decisions,' General Clintock added, 'with regard to manpower and whatever aircraft and ships we can muster.' With a thoughtful look on his face, he asked a question of the war cabinet in general, but without looking at anyone in particular. 'This loss of nuclear power, will it only apply to missiles, or will it also affect our subs and aircraft carriers? How about nuclear energy for power stations?' Now looking directly at the president, he asked, 'Don't you

Chapter Thirty-Nine

think this would be a good time to get in touch with the ambassador, Mr President?'

Knowing that the time had passed for evasiveness, David Cooper reluctantly nodded in agreement. 'The sooner the better. No doubt while we've been sitting here talking about the situation, our counterparts in Russia and China have been putting their plans forward. Some people want religious domination of the world, and others just total domination, while our aim in life is peaceful coexistence with all.'

With a doubtful shake of his head, Davis Cooper remarked to his secretary of state, 'Do you think you can get through to the ambassador on the radio, George? We assume he is up there,' he said, pointing figuratively towards the skies. 'I've no doubt he is waiting expectantly for our call.'

While the cabinet members began talking amongst themselves again, George absented himself for a time, returning half an hour later flushed with success. 'I got him, Mr President, and he will be here within the next few minutes by the usual method. He and Lana will teleport directly into the Oval Office and then come through here to join us.' He hesitated for a moment before continuing, with a quizzical expression on his face. 'He did ask me a most peculiar question, however, Mr President.'

Despite the gravity of the situation, Davis Cooper smiled in amusement at his friend's discomfort. 'It couldn't have been all that bad, George surely; what was it?'

Still looking puzzled, the secretary of state replied, 'He asked me how many old tanks and trucks we could collect and assemble in a suitably deserted part of the country within the next week.'

Looking over the table in the direction of General Clintock, David Cooper remarked, 'If that's going to be a serious question, General, you're probably the best man here to supply that information, although from past stories that I've heard, there must

Chapter Thirty-Nine

be hundreds of obsolete tanks littering many army establishments all over the country.'

'Trucks as well, Mr President,' the general replied. 'What the heck will be the point of collecting a lot of scrap vehicles; what does Jon intend doing with them?'

'No doubt he'll get round to telling us when he joins us, which, I think, will be any time soon,' Davis Cooper commented dryly. And sure enough, it was at that moment the ambassador of the Zel and his lady walked into the room, unannounced, but with an easy confidence.

After being invited to sit between the president and the secretary of state, Jon apologised for not having contacted the senators and members of government sooner. 'We deemed it advisable to allow you to come to terms with the changed world in which you now find yourselves in, a world without the constant threat of nuclear warfare and the possible destruction of the planet and everything on it.'

As he ran his eye quickly over the more prominent military figures around the table, he commented, 'By now, I have no doubt you've discovered other reasons to be concerned about the security of the United States and its people. But if I can allay your fears in that respect, I will do so. I'm here to answer any questions you may have. Mr President, would you like to begin the questions?'

As a means of creating a more relaxed atmosphere in the room, Davis Cooper laughingly referred to the request for the pile of old junk tanks and trucks. 'What on Earth do you intend to do with them, Jon, recycle them?'

Without giving a direct answer to that question, Jon concentrated his attention on the senior general in the room, putting a question of his own. 'Now that you no longer have any long-range nuclear missiles for attack or defensive purposes, you will presumably have to rely on old-fashioned means of waging war, but what do you see

Chapter Thirty-Nine

as an advantage for the armies of the Asian and Middle Eastern countries?'

Without any hesitancy, General Clintok barked, 'Manpower. They probably outnumber us at least twenty to one, and in the field, they could sustain casualties that would cause our armies to collapse.' He snorted in anger as he continued. 'We couldn't possibly allow an invading force to gain a foothold in this country; it would be impossible to repel or hold back such numbers, even though we could use all these old tanks and trucks you have asked for, Jon.'

'But in previous wars here on Earth,' Jon replied, 'in the First and Second World Wars, tanks of all descriptions were used with devastating effect on the battlefield, were they not, General?'

Clintock nodded in agreement. 'And trucks were essential to transport army personnel quickly from one part of the country to another. Mobility was the key to success in many instances.'

Jon paused for a long moment while he considered his next question, not just to the army chiefs, but to all the politicians present in the room. 'If I said to you that I could guarantee, in the event that an invading force were to land a huge, well-equipped army here in the United States, with tanks, trucks and thousands of men, that I could destroy all of them without your armies sustaining one single casualty, what would you say?'

Every man in the room, the president, politicians, and the military, as well, were struck speechless by that statement. Dumbfounded as George K. Lane was later to recall.

'I can't believe that,' General Clintock blurted out in his usual forthright manner. 'How do you expect us to believe such a claim?'

'I don't, General,' Jon calmly replied, 'not without a practical demonstration of my ship's capabilities and our superior Zellian technology.' Addressing Davis Cooper, he smiled and added, 'The demonstration in question will require a large number of tanks and trucks, but in this instance, we can do without the human guinea

Chapter Thirty-Nine

pigs. It is essential that the test ground is barren and remote from any human habitation.' Again, he put the question to the assembly, 'Can the test site be prepared within one week? For those who doubt the outcome of our destructive power, I'll invite a limited number of you to witness the annihilation of what might have been an enemy force, from our spacecraft, with the assistance of yet another of our vessels, which is, at present, within Earth's orbit.'

Davis Cooper was surprised to learn of the presence of another Zellian spacecraft in the region, but at least it gave credence to the claim of the destructive demonstration. 'Yes,' he remarked, 'the storage area for all our obsolete military vehicles is in the middle of a desert, nothing but low hills and scrubland where not even a jack rabbit lives. Given a week, we'll have a few hundred vehicles lined up for you. Are you going to burn them, Jon, or just shoot them up?'

Raising an eyebrow, Jon replied quietly, 'As I said, Mr President, they won't only be destroyed; they will be annihilated and will disappear without a trace.'

'This I've got to see,' General Clintock said in disbelief, 'but we have other issues that need to be clarified, Jon. Regarding nuclear power, all our missiles have apparently been neutralised due to the uranium warheads being restructured, something to do with the molecular or atomic structure of the fissionable material. So, will that also affect our nuclear aircraft carriers and submarines as well?'

Jon shook his head. 'No, the uranium in the ship's engines or power plant has not been as refined as in the missiles, and as long as your ships are not used as a means of aggression against other peaceful nations, you may patrol the seas, and continue as a peacekeeping force, the policeman of Earth.'

'And to what extent will that be necessary, if as you say, Jon, you and your craft will be able to destroy invaders of our country and presumably similar situations elsewhere in the world?' one of the

Chapter Thirty-Nine

senators asked. 'If you can demonstrate how effectively you can destroy an army with just two of your flying saucers, then what governments would be mad enough to wage war without missiles?'

'Those governments that believe they can overwhelm a country such as America by sheer weight of numbers,' Jon answered. 'There is no need for me to make accusations; you all know the nations in question.'

The president had listened to the observations of both the general and the senator, and now with a slight frown on his face, he put a question of his own. 'You are prepared to give us a preview of the destructive power of your craft, which to all of us here sounds unbelievable, but even if you do manage to convince us of your superiority in a battlefield situation, how do you intend to let our potential aggressors know what could be in store for them? Are you going to invite some of them along for the show?'

Understanding the scepticism behind the question, Jon answered confidently, 'Mr President, I will take up to ten of your senior military and civilian advisers with me in my craft to give you a first-hand experience of what we intend to demonstrate, and my fellow Zellian captain will take a similar number of witnesses in his craft. After the event, you will, I'm sure, be able to convince your own members of the Senate, and the government, that you will have nothing to fear from invasion by any hostile nation, at least not while I am ambassador to Earth, and that is going to be for many years,' he smiled in assurance.

'While we are flying over the desert region in question, might I suggest that you bring along with you one cameraman for each craft? We will automatically record the event ourselves, but Joe public will probably accept your version of events rather than ours. In addition to which, your newsmen can broadcast scenes of the destruction for the benefit of the outside world. I can assure you that even those potential enemies, who outnumber you by as much as a hundred to one, would deem it unwise to attack your country,

Chapter Thirty-Nine

or any other country, knowing the kind of retaliation they could face. Jon then leaned back in his chair with a calm expression on his face, his silver hair glowing like a beacon of hope, and waited for some reaction from the men around the table.

As expected, General Clintock, being the senior military commander, was the first to voice his opinion. 'If you can do what you say you can do, Jon, it won't be quite so bad to be without nuclear missiles. I never thought that fighting a war in that way was how a soldier should fight; at the very least, you should be able to see the enemy eye to eye.' He paused, adding as an afterthought, 'You said we would be flying over the simulated battlefield; how high above the action will we be? Will we be able to observe this simulated battlefield with the naked eye?'

Jon's answer was brief and to the point. 'Yes, General, we will be just one mile above the desert country and the enemy vehicles. Our two spacecrafts will be side by side and sweep a swathe of destruction through their ranks, and regardless of any defence they might attempt, they will be powerless to avoid their inevitable demise. Within half an hour, there won't be an enemy left in sight.'

'That sounds pretty conclusive, Jon,' Davis Cooper commented, 'so I take it that it's up to us to provide a suitable shooting range to facilitate the demonstration.' Turning to General Clintock, he said, 'Does that storage area in Arizona still exist, General, and will there be enough hardware available to satisfy our needs?' Having been assured on that score, the president persisted, 'And can you arrange for the vehicles to be spread out in simulated battle order and that all personnel, military or civilians, are cleared out of the area within seven days?'

The general grinned as he replied, 'No problem. Our logistics corps are going to have fun towing all the old vehicles around in the desert, with no need to worry about having a few collisions. As regards personnel, how far from this test area would you recommend that we keep clear? Two hundred or more vehicles in battle

Chapter Thirty-Nine

formation will cover at least ten square miles, and it could be even more than that if they get spread out in battle conditions.'

'I would suggest an area of about twenty square miles for safety,' Jon commented. 'Even at that distance, some of the observers on the ground are going to feel what they will think are earth tremors and pretty violent ones at that.'

'You can induce earthquakes using your craft, Jon?' Davis Cooper queried incredulously.

'Yes, more, much more than that,' Jon affirmed, 'but the results of our technology will be controlled, whereas natural earthquakes are unpredictable.'

'But how will this situation affect an armoured division of an invading force?' the general wanted to know.

Jon merely smiled as he retorted, 'Just wait another seven days, General, and all your questions and scepticism will be answered. You will, in effect, get your eye-to-eye encounter with the potential enemy.' Then once more turning his attention to the president, he said, 'We will leave you to select the people that you wish to accompany us to the testing ground in Arizona, although on this occasion, if you could have them all assembled here at the White House, we, that is, Lana and I, will land on your lawn to pick up our passengers. Once we have become airborne, Captain Jara and his crew member will do likewise.' Laughing, he said, 'I can assure that we won't leave any marks for the gardeners to complain about.'

As various senior military and civilian personnel sitting around the table looked questioningly at each other, Jon smiled as he said in confirmation, 'Yes, twenty of you will be travelling to Arizona in a flying saucer, as you call our craft, but unfortunately, the experience won't last long, only about two hours at most.' As there was little more to be discussed, and it was obvious that the war cabinet was eager to talk among themselves, Jon and Lana stood up, after bidding the president, his secretary, and General Clintock a formal

Chapter Thirty-Nine

farewell, and with a casual nod to the other people in the room, they walked over to the door of the adjacent Oval Office. When they were out of sight of the assembly, they gently embraced and teleported up to their ship still hovering above the White House. As soon as they had materialised on the flight deck, Jon's first words were, 'And now we will have a little time to ourselves, so off to our island, Jamaica, Jacob Bernstein, and a little shopping trip, all in that order. Lana, you're the navigator, set the course and speed for paradise.'

It was an order that she carried out with alacrity.

Chapter Forty

On arrival in the Caribbean, following what was now their normal procedure, they docked their craft twenty miles above their island, well above the altitude of commercial aircraft, but easily within teleporting distance of the deserted beaches below. Lana opened the viewports to allow them to gaze through, looking toward the horizon obscured by the heat haze. 'Not a lot to see from this altitude, Jon, is there?'

'No,' he agreed with a chuckle, 'the only way to get a really clear view is to use the on-board scanners, which will eliminate all the distortions caused by the heat of the day and our altitude, but even better, now, don't think I'm pushing you, but we could teleport down to the beach and have our first taste of freedom in days, just us, the sea, and the sand.'

Clasping Jon's arm firmly in anticipation of the pleasures to come, Lana smiled as she said, 'Just give me a moment to get out of this uniform, and I'll be ready to go.' She added coyly, 'Do you need any assistance peeling off that tight clothing, Jon? It must be very uncomfortable at times.'

'If I were to allow you to do that for me, Lana, my dear,' he replied with a laugh, 'it could delay our trip to the beach for some considerable time, so I would suggest that we undress quickly, on our own, then drop down to our favourite location on the beach and get some sand between our toes.' Within a very short space of time, they were walking along the seashore, like a modern Adam and Eve, but with the difference that this Adam was a product of Earth, while

Chapter Forty

his Eve was a child of the planet Zel. Even so, to a casual onlooker, they looked like a match made in heaven. A tall man with a physique like a Greek god of old, albeit with hair that glowed silver in the reflection of the sun, and his Eve, almost as tall, but of a more slender build, the personification of a man's perfect woman, just two people in love.

They only spent a little more than one hour in the pleasant environment of the beach, because Jon reminded Lana that it would take a little time to acclimatise to the tropical surroundings and strong sunshine again. 'Don't forget; we're here for nearly seven days, so there's plenty of time to relax and enjoy ourselves, but not get sunburnt.'

It was with some reluctance that they returned to the ship, but were compensated by the pleasure they both gained in assisting each other to dress in their tight-fitting uniforms, a process that took several hours. 'But we're in no hurry, my darling,' Lana giggled, 'and we can do this every day, can't we?'

'Whatever pleases you, pleases me,' Jon replied with a contented smile. For the remainder of the day, they spent some time talking about their respective lives up to and until Jon had come aboard Captain Jara's spacecraft,, and his agreement to become a Teacher on behalf of the Zel.

'I can understand why you were so easily persuaded to undergo the indoctrination process under Mort's guidance and care. Incidentally, it was much longer than anyone, human or Zellian, has experienced, which is why you are so mentally and physically superior to any of either species. To have lost everyone in your previous life has made it easier for you to adapt to the role of a Teacher and the longer life you will now have before you.' She smiled as she reminded him, 'Five hundred years, Jon, longer than any human has ever lived before.'

Chapter Forty

The prospect of an extended life was not something he had given a great deal of thought to until Lana mentioned it. Compared to her expectation of life had she remained on her own planet, about one thousand years, five hundred years for a Zellian was a comparatively short lifespan. It was his turn to smile as he replied, 'However long we are together, I shall be content to perform my duties as a Teacher to the human race, and if we were to formalise our relationship, according to the customs of my people, I would make you my wife.'

'Wife?' Lana was aware of that concept from her familiarity with knowledge of the ways of humankind. 'I am already your wife,' she said. 'We live, eat, and sleep together, and mentally, we are conjoined at all times.' She frowned slightly as she continued, 'Are you suggesting that we go through a ceremony of joining? That is something that doesn't happen on Zel, as life is considered too long for two people to be bound together for a thousand years or more. Some will stay together as we will do, but then find a new companion, or even another two or three, but as always, any separation is always amicable.'

To gain an insight into Lana's innermost thoughts, Jon probed into her mind and was pleased that the ceremony of joining was pleasing to her. First, because it would symbolise their commitment to a life together, but also, it would be a union between a human and a Zellion on an official basis, which had never happened before, mating yes, but not a recognised ceremony in the eyes of Jon's people or hers.

Her eyes gleaming with excitement, Lana embraced Jon fervently. 'If you wish to go through such a ceremony, I shall be equally happy, but when will this happen and where and who will be present at that time?'

In answer, Jon said quietly, 'When we get back to the States and get this war game demonstration over and done with, I'll ask George K. Lane to organise everything for our wedding, our joining

Chapter Forty

ceremony. I can't think of anyone better than the secretary of state of the United States to arrange it. No doubt, all concerned will be pleased that two Zellians have decided to adopt one of their customs, if only they knew,' he added under his breath, 'one Zellion and a modified man of Earth.

'In the meanwhile, I think it's time to contact Jacob Bernstein, if he's at home. He may have some news regarding the sale of the diamonds and the acquisition of a suitable island for our permanent home.'

For the moment, Lana's attention was concentrated on the matter of communicating with the jeweller's premises in Kingston. The telephone system was not a problem for them to hack into. 'Better to arrive by appointment nowadays,' she said. 'Jacob's shop may now be a rendezvous for the wealthy, and we don't want to frighten the life out of any of his clients, do we, Jon?'

'Not until he has concluded any financial transactions,' Jon agreed with a laugh, 'but if he's not available today, there's always tomorrow, since time, for once, is on our side.'

After a few minutes, Lana responded to the voice of their friend. 'Yes, Jacob, it has been some time since we last saw you, but we've been very busy attending to Jon's commitments. We are now taking a few days to relax before undertaking yet another mission, but I won't go into any details on that score.' As she was talking, she unconsciously transmitted and shared her thoughts with Jon, so it was almost like a three-way conversation. She continued, 'If it's convenient for you, Jacob, we would like to give you a personal visit, personal and business, if you wish.'

Jacob's answer could be heard quite clearly in Jon's head. 'It's always convenient to see my two best friends and to talk business at the same time is even better.'

Jon smiled at that remark, sensing that Jacob had something important to tell them. Interrupting Lana's conversation briefly, he

Chapter Forty

leaned over and spoke into the radio-telephone. 'We will be with you in ten minutes, Jacob, and bring some more merchandise for you to dispose of for us. I suspect we are going to need a great deal of money in the near future.'

They could hear Jacob chuckling at that statement. 'You already have a great deal of money, my friend. You are the richest man I know personally, although I'm not complaining as you have also made me one of the richest merchants in Jamaica, if not in the Caribbean. However,' he continued, 'we will wait until you are in my office before we discuss any further business, so until you arrive, I'll be sorting out some paperwork for your perusal.'

As the radio link went dead, Jon turned to Lana, and said, 'I do believe Jacob has some interesting, possibly exciting, news for us, so we won't keep him waiting, but before we go, let me select a few more diamonds to take with us.' For the next few minutes, he rummaged in the box of jewels, then with a sigh of satisfaction, he said, 'These will be more than satisfactory, another delight for Jacob.' With that, he took Lana by the hand. 'Shall we drop in on him now?'

Moments later, they were walking into the workroom at the rear of the premises to find Jacob sitting at his customary position at his workbench, looking very thoughtful, but pleased with himself. 'My friends,' he exclaimed as he stood up. 'It seems such a long time since you flew off to the States, and so much has happened in that time.' He sat down again with a sigh of satisfaction, then continued. 'No doubt your duties as a Teacher or diplomat have been keeping you busy, and I look forward to hearing about your trip to Washington and wherever else you've been, but first, I must confide in you what I've been doing during the last few weeks.'

Both Jon and Lana were reading their friend's mind and were aware that he could barely contain his excitement. 'I sold the diamond you gave me in lieu of an advance commission, which is why I said that Jacob Bernstein is probably the richest merchant in

Chapter Forty

the Caribbean, but even more amazing, although there were no buyers wealthy enough in Kingston, I travelled to New York, London, Amsterdam, even Paris in order to secure a buyer, but it was in an exclusive auction house in Amsterdam, naturally, that one of the agents of the wealthiest man in the world bid for the set of all six diamonds. The deal was secured with no problems whatsoever, other than that mega-rich man is now several billions of dollars poorer, while you and Lana are correspondingly that much richer.'

While the mention of how much the diamonds had been sold for made little impact on Lana's mind, since arthly values still had only a vague meaning for her, Jon, however, couldn't help gasp. 'Several *billion* dollars, did you say, Jacob? That's unbelievable. I was thinking in terms of millions of dollars, but billions, that's astounding.'

Giving a smile that was almost triumphant, Jacob said, in a manner as relaxed as he could contrive, 'Everywhere I showed the diamond collection, the experts were astounded by the size and quality of the stones. They also pressed me to reveal their origin and who the lapidary was responsible for the cutting process. While there was only one person wealthy enough to purchase the complete set of six gems, I was assured that, should I obtain any further stones of the same quality, there would be no shortage of prospective buyers.' Again he smiled in a self-satisfied manner. 'The name of Jacob Bernstein is now known throughout the world markets as a purveyor of quality gems, so if you should have any more diamonds to sell, I would be delighted to act as your agent, and as to my commission, I leave that to your generosity.'

While Jon was recovering from the shock of having become a billionaire as a result of Jacob's success in selling the merchandise, he was mentally trying to convey to Lana the difference that material wealth would make to their life here on Earth. Their first priority was to purchase a suitable location to build their new home, preferably a private Island in the Caribbean where climatic conditions were similar to Lana's home on Zel. Lana smiled in

Chapter Forty

delight at Jon's obvious pleasure at being in a financial position to provide the lifestyle they both had only been able to dream about, but now was a reality in their grasp.

Still on a telepathic level, since thought transference was so much quicker than speech, she approved of Jacob's venture into the world markets and the sale of their diamonds. Although she confessed that millions or billions of dollars had little meaning for her, other than knowing that this kind of wealth made it possible to lead a life of luxury and seclusion for as long as they wished. After all, they expected to be together in their new island sanctuary for at least five hundred years. *If the sale of just a few of our trinkets has provided us with so much wealth,* she transmitted, *how much more would we acquire if we were to sell all of them? We still have a box full, dozens of them, and many as big as those Jacob has just sold.*

Jacob, meanwhile, was unaware of the mental exchanges between Jon and Lana, but since the possibility of further diamonds being for sale in the future had already been mentioned, he took the opportunity to remind them, 'You are now among the wealthiest class of people in this part of the world, and with the prospect of selling further quality gems at some time in the future, you are now in a position to purchase your own island anywhere in the world, or indeed, here in the Caribbean, if that is what you desire. That is a matter that I've been delving into during your absence these last few days, since I returned from Amsterdam.' With a smile, he beckoned them toward his work table where he had a number of documents neatly spread out in front of him, inviting them to look at each separate sheet of paper in turn. 'These are the details of a number of privately owned islands here in the Caribbean; surprisingly, there are dozens of them. Some are quite large, but with a resident population, which I don't think you want, and others vary in size and character, which would be more in keeping with what I imagine you have in mind.'

Chapter Forty

Together, Jon and Lana began sifting through the leaflets, which contained the details and photographs of the various locations on offer, and very shortly, Lana gave a gasp of amazement. 'Jon, this is our new home. It's exactly like my parent's home on Zel. There's a mountain in the background with a waterfall, surrounded by lush jungle, and here,' she said, pointing at the photograph, 'open meadowland in the foreground, which appears to be extensive.'

As Jon read the details of the property on offer, he felt cautiously excited. He waved the paper in the air and exclaimed, 'And where exactly is this location, Jacob? It's called Buccaneer's Point, presumably because of the mountain, and it's one of the US Virgin Islands.'

Jacob smiled. 'I think the area is exactly what you are looking for, Jon. It's on the same latitude roughly as Jamaica, but several hundreds of miles to the east, past Haiti and the Dominican Republic, and is one of a large group of islands. Buccaneer's Point has all the requirements you said you wanted. Remote perhaps, but transport is not likely to be a problem for you. And it's comparatively small.' He added with a laugh, 'The mountain and jungle take up most of the land on the island, but it still leaves you with several thousands of acres. Oh. And on the plus side, apparently, there is still an old colonial mansion on the site, which hasn't been lived in for fifty years, but the agent assured me that it would be quite easy to import a labour force from the other islands to restore it to its former glory. It wouldn't cost more than a million dollars or thereabouts, which is small change for a man of your wealth, Jon.'

'Apart from the price of the island,' Jon enquired cautiously, still not accustomed to the thought of his newfound wealth, 'what else should we know about the house, and any facilities such as water and power? The other details here . . .' he waved the paper with the information, 'don't say much about the geography of the island.'

Again, Jacob smiled as he flourished a second paper. 'I thought Buccaneer's Point would be the place to meet all your requirements,

Chapter Forty

so I took the liberty of making my own private assessment of the island. I hired a helicopter to fly me over the property, and I must say, it is not only beautiful, but spectacular.'

As he recalled his surveillance flight, the memory of the views around The Point and its coastline brought a smile of pleasure to his face. 'While Buccaneer's Point is far from being the largest property available in the group, you will find it will afford you the greatest degree of privacy, which was another of your stipulated requirements.'

'Why do you say that our island will be more private than any others in the region, Jacob?' Lana enquired. 'From these photographs accompanying the written details, everything looks so beautiful that tourists must flock to the beaches in droves.'

'Ah. But that's it.' Jacob sighed. 'There's a beautiful beach in front of the house lined with palm trees, as you would expect, and the waters offshore are crystal clear, ideal for all kinds of water sports, which would normally attract many private sailing boats and cruisers. But to reach the beach, they have to negotiate a narrow channel and go into what is, in effect, a large lagoon. It's not a difficulty in itself, but from the air, I could see that the entrance is obscured from the seaward approach. To anyone familiar with the island, like the previous owner, or going back in time, the buccaneers who apparently used that beach for careening their ships or as a safe haven in a storm, this would have been the perfect safe haven.'

'And what of the rest of the island?' Jon asked cautiously. 'Don't the tourists land elsewhere?'

'No,' Jacob replied. 'At the eastern end of the property is Buccaneer's Point itself which, while it is only about one thousand feet in height, provides a sheer drop into the sea, and the rest of the coastline around the island is of a similar nature, so the lagoon is the only place with a beach. It would be your own private playground,

Chapter Forty

but it is quite extensive and in common with other islands in the region, the sands are of a dazzling white and a pleasure to walk on.'

Jon and Lana exchanged glances and both thought, *Sand between the toes, darling.* 'Tell me more about the house that is already on the site,' Jon said to Jacob. 'Is there any history to it, and what services are provided; is there water and a power supply?'

'My understanding,' Jacob began, 'is that the house was built by a seventeenth century plantation owner, and the cost was not a consideration for him. He had to ship in practically all the building materials from the other islands in the region. He didn't want to scar the landscape by quarrying for stone and felling trees, but labour was cheap, and the fact that the house is still in reasonable condition today speaks for the quality of the workmanship of the slave tradesmen at that time. And I'm sure that the same quality of craftsmanship will be available today. The previous owner of the island married a much younger woman than himself, but apparently, one of the conditions of the marriage was that they should move to London, where the lady originated from. In fact, that was some fifty years ago, but the wife had survived until quite recently, which is why the island has now been put up for sale. The family in London would rather have money in the bank than a piece of rock in the Caribbean.'

'What a sad story,' Lana commented. Turning to Jon, she said, 'We are going to buy his island and we won't be leaving it during our lifetimes, will we Jon?'

'Indeed we won't,' he replied with a soft laugh. 'Apart from my ambassadorial duties and to perform my function as a Teacher, we shall stay put.' After a moment's reflection, he added, 'No doubt we will be expected to entertain our friends and political acquaintances from time to time, but if the access to the island is going to be a difficulty, something will have to be done about that.'

Chapter Forty

'No problem there, Jon,' Jacob suggested. 'They can do as I did, fly in by helicopter, or for a modest outlay, you could have a small landing strip for light aircraft built. Alternately, they could come by boat and anchor in the lagoon.'

Although their minds were already made up with regard to the purchase of this island of their dreams, Jon thought it prudent to consult with Jacob about the vendors' asking price.

When the subject was raised, his friend replied by saying, 'Ah. moie, ah moie,' his favourite expression of pleasure.

'My friend, I was so sure that Buccaneer's Point would be your final choice that I began negotiations with the lawyers representing the family in London, who have no idea what kind of jewel they are selling, only what money they will be able to put into the bank. Subject to your approval of course, you will be able to conclude the purchase for the trifling sum of one hundred million dollars.'

Thinking back to his life as an air traffic controller at the Manchester Airport and the salary he had earned at that time, Jon admitted with some irony that one hundred million dollars was not exactly a trifling sum by any standards, but nevertheless, it was easily affordable in his present circumstances. His thoughts were clearly read by Lana, their telepathic communication saving any unnecessary discussion, so the purchase was silently but mutually agreed to by both.

'Very well, Jacob, when we go back to the States, if you will act as our agent for the purchase of Buccaneer's Point, we would be most grateful,' he said, adding with a laugh, 'for a small commission, of course.'

Jacob appeared to seriously consider the offer for a moment and then sadly announced, 'I couldn't possibly accept any commission for this transaction.' Then laughing hilariously, he added, 'What would my ancestors say to hear Jacob Bernstein refuse to take money for an honest business transaction.' Then he held up his hands as if in

Chapter Forty

protest. 'You have already made me a very rich man by your generosity, my friends; now let me do something of a practical nature to help you to realise your dream of an island of your own in the Caribbean.'

'That settles it then,' Jon exclaimed. 'All we have to do now is to have a good look at Buccaneer's Point to confirm that it is all that we are hoping for, although, from the details you have provided, Jacob, I'm sure that it will more than live up to our expectations. However, one thought does occur to me.' He scrutinised one of the descriptive leaflets in his hand carefully. 'It says that the property, the house of the previous owner, hasn't been lived in for the past fifty years, which would imply that there is likely a lot of renovation to be done. Not a problem,' he hastened to add, 'so long as the skilled labour force is available, since a little time and money will soon give the old house a new lease on life.'

'A lot of time and a lot of money,' Jacob added with a grin. 'But undoubtedly, your acquisition will serve as your permanent home for many years to come, and you will find that Buccaneer's Point itself will shelter you from the main force of the hurricanes that we experience every year in the Caribbean, although the house itself is of a more solid construction than the present-day buildings and will withstand anything the elements can throw at it.'

'Well, I think we can safely leave all the business details to you, Jacob,' Jon said with an approving smile. 'Although I would suggest that you employ a project manager and an architect to remain onsite until completion of the project. Also, I would imagine that provision for power and water supplies will have to be made, but that is something we can discuss on conclusion of the legalities, and of course, subject to our personal inspection of Buccaneer's Point itself. That is something Lana and I will do within the next few days before we return to Washington to conclude some other business arrangements with the President, so in the meantime, if you can show me the location of the island on the map, the US Virgin Islands

Chapter Forty

you said, did you not? We can then complete our shopping trip here in Kingston, collect a number of items from my tailors, spend the rest of the day at leisure on the beach, and then do the inspection flight to our island, something we are now looking forward to, aren't we, Lana?'

The prospect of becoming the owners of their very own island paradise was making Lana feel more excited than on any other occasion that she could ever remember, and there would be much more to come when they had their first sight of Buccaneer's Point, a green-emerald isle surrounded by sapphire-blue seas, a scene of beauty and tranquillity, and a further reminder of her home planet, Zel, which she might never see again, unless fate decreed otherwise.

As they stood up to leave the premises, Lana communicated silently with Jon. *The diamonds, Jon, don't forget; we may require more money to spend on our house on the island, since we want it to be a dream home in idyllic surroundings. Apart from that, Jacob will have a great deal of pleasure inspecting and valuing this latest collection of stones. No doubt he will take the opportunity to revisit Amsterdam as soon as he has concluded our island purchase.*

Acknowledging the reminder with his usual smile, Jon turned to his friend. 'If you would look at these diamonds, Jacob, when you consider that the time is favourable to market them, would you again act as our agent?' He added with a laugh, 'But on this occasion, I insist that you accept a commission on the sale; after all, we don't want to upset your ancestors, do we?'

After a cursory inspection of the merchandise, Jacob raised his eyebrows, blew out his cheeks, and said. 'Ah moie. Ah moie. How many more of these have you got? You will be the richest landowners in the whole of the Caribbean, and I will be the wealthiest diamond merchant.' Nevertheless, having first of all deposited the merchandise in the new secure safe, he then accompanied them to the door, opening it for them with the remark, 'I don't often get the opportunity to see you off the premises, you usually just disappear

Chapter Forty

like a puff of smoke.' But he was still smiling when he closed the door after the departure of his friends.

It was a further two hours before Jon and Lana had completed their visit to the tailor's premises, much longer than Jon would normally have tolerated,. Being fussed over by a number of female assistants was not necessarily a pleasure, even though they were all very attractive and willing to please.*Too willing*, Lana thought.

Finally, however, laden with boxes and parcels, they were able to leave the shop behind with the voices of the excited young lady assistants ringing in their ears. 'Do come back soon, Jon.'

Feeling the heat of the afternoon sun beating down on them, by mutual agreement they made for a small garden area just off the main shopping boulevard, and when they were satisfied that they were not being observed, holding on tightly to their assorted packages, they bade a temporary farewell to Kingston and teleported back to their ship in its docking position twenty miles above the city, arriving on the flight deck with a sigh of relief. 'I never did like shopping for clothes,' Jon exclaimed, 'but now I have a sufficient wardrobe to cope with all possible official functions that we may be called upon to attend. All that remains is to provide you with a few more dresses and gowns, Lana, although you look perfectly stunning in those that you purchased on your last shopping trip, but the ambassador's lady will always be in the forefront when we are in public.'

'And I do believe,' Lana added, 'there is a certain custom among your people that, when taking part in the joining ceremony, the bride normally wears a special dress for that occasion . . . When do I buy that and where?'

'Ah.' Jon said with a smile, 'I hadn't forgotten about your wedding dress, although it will have to wait until the war games are out of the way. Then we will give New York another visit where you will have a choice of trousseau to match the best salons of London

Chapter Forty

or Paris. You are going to be the most beautiful bride this world of mine has ever seen.' He then drew her close and kissed her tenderly, their minds and bodies in a long embrace.

Chapter Forty-One

As they were both impatient to visit the island of Buccaneer's Point, their future place of permanent residence, instead of dallying on the sands of the beach of what they had always loosely regarded as their island, they found themselves returning to the ship after only a short time, and setting a course for what was to become their home. *For the next five hundred years,* Jon reminded himself.

'It will only take about half an hour,' Lana said, taking a course almost due east over Jamaica, Haiti, and the Dominican Republic. 'They are all beautiful islands in themselves, but far too crowded for our purpose, whereas from the way the island of Buccaneer's Point is described, it's doubtful if many people have visited the place in the last fifty years.' As she busied herself with the navigation controls, with a few graceful moves with her hands, the course was set, and in a short time, they would be above what was to be truly their island.

As ever with the spacecraft, there was no sensation of speed or movement, so they were only aware that they had reached their destination, a predetermined position five miles above the island, by the computer announcing, 'The island of Buccaneer's Point is now directly below, daytime temperature 28 degrees Celsius, a light westerly breeze, a most pleasant environment.' They both hurriedly switched on the viewing screens to get their first glimpse of this precious jewel in the Caribbean, a dream island only made attainable by Lana's father's gift of jewels of another kind, diamonds that were in themselves so beautiful and perfect that their friend Jacob had

Chapter Forty-One

been able to acquire a fabulous price for them, thus ensuring that Buccaneer's Point would soon be theirs. 'And then the work to restore the house will begin,' Jon reminded Lana. 'The place may not even be habitable for some time, but on an optimistic note, let us view the island first of all from this altitude, then I suggest we actually land the ship near the house. There appears to be plenty of open space nearby.'

From their present altitude of five miles, it was possible to see the entire island, showing the mountain or point at the east end, where the rocky cliffs created a natural barrier to the uninvited, and although their view was somewhat hazy, they could make out the large lagoon with its sandy beaches, with the outline of a large structure nearby, which had to be the house.

'Please, Jon,' Lana urged excitedly, 'let me land the ship now; I can't wait any longer. I must see our future home now.'

Smiling in understanding, he felt the same sense of urgency despite the fact that he knew that until all the legalities were completed, they couldn't even begin any construction work or renovations on the house. 'We can visualise and plan how we want the house to be, and yes, Lana, we will land the ship at what appears to be the rear of the building and take our first walk around our own private piece of the planet Earth.'

A few minutes later found the craft nestled to the ground, surrounded by a large expanse of what was presumably the rear garden of the house, although there were no obvious boundaries, just open land up to the edge of the jungle at the rear, and equally open land between the front of the house and the lagoon. Despite their ship being about one hundred feet in diameter, there was more than enough ground space available to provide a permanent parking space when they eventually took up residence on the island. 'After all,' Jon confided to Lana, 'we won't need a car for transport, but do as the previous owners probably did, that is, use horses to tour our estate.'

Chapter Forty-One

'That is a problem we will deal with when the time comes,' Lana laughed, 'but in the meanwhile, I suggest we disembark and go and have a look at the old house. This close it looks fascinating, but obviously neglected.' Having opened the exit door, they stood at the threshold, arms encircling each other as they gazed out over the landscape with the point in the background. 'It's so beautiful,' Lana breathed, 'it's almost like my parent's home on Zel. The house, of course, has an architectural style relating to the aristocracy of this part of the world in days gone by, but with a few changes and improvements of our own, we will give this place a new lease on life and transform it into a place where we can be content to live for the rest of our lives. It will be a home to be proud of, a home befitting your status of ambassador of the planet Zel, Jon.'

'Just looking at the landscape and the background,' he replied, 'it already stirs my imagination as to how we can transform the building into something elegant but modern, but we will retain the openness of the original gardens so as not to be enclosed in any way. We'll want to keep the grounds as open parkland, as I'm sure was the original intention of the previous owner.' With that, now holding Lana's hand, he descended the short ramp in order to leave the ship, a different mode of exit from their usual practice. *One that our passengers a few days hence will be using,* he reminded himself.

'It seems strange to be walking through tall grass again,' Lana remarked. 'I haven't done this for several years, not since I left my parent's home.' There was a note of sadness in her voice at this recollection, but then she immediately brightened up. 'But every time I walk over our land here at Buccaneer's Point, it will remind me of my happy childhood days. I was only forty years old when I left home for the first time, would you believe, and here I am about to become the joint owner of a marvellous estate with parkland, jungle, and our very own mountain, only a very small one, but ours nonetheless.'

Chapter Forty-One

As they swished through the tall grasses, they headed toward the old house and became aware of its neglect as they drew near, but they surmised that fifty years of vacancy had only superficially damaged the structure. 'A little cosmetic treatment will be required,' commented Jon as they walked around the perimeter of the building. Having satisfied themselves regarding the exterior, together they opened the massive double doors leading into the darkened interior, where they stood for a few minutes to allow their eyes to adapt to the gloom, taking in the musty smell typical of many old and unused habitations.

Despite the accumulated dust of half a century and the faded decor, Jon, at least, was able to appreciate that this must have been a beautiful home, and the original owner must have lavished a considerable fortune in building and equipping the house to the highest standards. As they stood hand in hand, peering into the gloom of their surroundings, Lana said with a smile, 'It will take an army of craftsmen and cleaners to return this house to its former glory and to make it habitable again.'

As Jon mentally agreed, he also added thoughtfully, *That's true, but once the island is legally ours, I'll press Jacob to hire an architect and project manager to recruit a workforce to get on with restoring the house. It's surprising how quickly an army of dedicated craftsmen can transform a neglected old place like this.*

For the next hour, they toured the interior of the house, exclaiming at the spaciousness of the reception rooms, what must have been a banqueting suite and ballroom, a grand staircase leading to the upper floor, and the many bedrooms and en suites, storage areas, and finally, another level where the household servants must have been quartered. 'It appears from the accommodation on this level,' Lana commented, 'that a large number of servants were responsible for running the household.' She then paused in thought. 'Will we have to have servants of our own, Jon?'

Chapter Forty-One

'Yes,' he replied. 'We couldn't possibly manage without a fairly large number of people of our own, at least a dozen I would think, and that would include the house servants and several grounds men and gardeners.'

With a frown of concern, Lana exclaimed, 'I've never had a servant of any kind before; how will I know what to do?'

Jon gave a quiet laugh of amusement at the idea of Lana trying to organise a household of servants. A flight deck and personnel on a spacecraft she could cope with efficiently after years of experience, but the domestic routine of a large household was far beyond her understanding. 'That is something you won't have to worry about, Lana,' he hastened to assure her. 'In very large houses like this, it is normal to have one servant who will organise all the indoor servants on your behalf; he is called a butler. You will have a housekeeper, cook, kitchen staff, and maids to do your bidding as well.'

'But that means we won't be on our own, Jon,' Lana wailed. 'I do so want to spend as much time together as possible.'

'You won't have to worry about the presence of the servants, my dear,' he said reassuringly. 'Well-trained servants can be quite unobtrusive, I assure you, but always on hand when needed. I promise you that when the house is nearly ready for occupancy, I will get Jacob to contact an agency to recruit the necessary staff, well trained, and discreet, but as that may be several months away, while we remain on the island, we will use the ship as our living accommodation until all the building work is complete, and only then will the servants occupy their quarters.'

Having spent a considerable time inspecting the interior of the house, and letting their imaginations run riot regarding what they would like to do to modernise, decorate, and furnish their new home, Jon suggested that they should inspect an outbuilding discreetly positioned a short distance away from the main house

Chapter Forty-One

which they had ignored earlier. 'If I don't miss my guess,' he declared, 'that was where a generator was probably installed to provide all the electrical power for lighting and other services; it will be interesting to see if it has survived after fifty years.'

Accordingly, they walked over to the small outbuilding where it immediately became obvious that at some time in the past, many years ago, the door had been forced open and was now hanging on its hinges, open to the elements. Without making any comment, Jon walked into the powerhouse, and after a brief inspection, he turned to Lana and said, 'As I thought, this was the source of the electricity supply for the house, but it is of little use now. It appears that after the house was abandoned, thieves must have attempted to steal the diesel-powered generator, ripped it out of its mounting, found it too heavy for them to handle or transport, gave it up as a bad job, and just left it as it is now.

'However,' he continued, 'I will install something more suitable and reliable, something that doesn't require fossil fuels. A small atomic power pack from the ship will provide for our needs for years to come with only replacement rod' every fifty years or so, and it will have the benefit of being completely silent, not like this old thing.' He patted the diesel generator. 'While I'm at it, I might as well complete the job the thieves left undone, and put it outside in readiness to install the new power pack when I get the opportunity. Stand clear, Lana.'

Waiting until Lana had stepped out of the building and was standing well clear of the door, Jon exerted his telekinetic power and lifted the generator effortlessly from the floor, and walking slowly, he made his way to the door, where he then guided his burden outside. When he was well clear of the building, he allowed it to sink down onto the grass, where its own weight caused it to sink several inches into the soft surface. With a grin he said, 'When the workmen are due to arrive, I will move the generator down to the edge of the lagoon; no doubt, they'll salvage it for use elsewhere.

Chapter Forty-One

But if they try to move it without heavy lifting equipment, there will be a few strained backs in the process.'

As they were returning to the ship, the inspection of their future home completed, Lana had a suggestion before they left the island behind. 'Why don't we do a low-level reconnaissance around the coastline and get a really close up view of our property from the air, not with the scanners, but through the open viewports.'

Jon was more than happy to agree, since the beauty of Buccaneer's Point already held him entranced. As they had plenty of time before they needed to return to Kingston and Jacob Bernstein, another pleasant hour would be spent circumnavigating the island.

In due course, Lana set the controls to allow the ship to follow the coastline, at a minimal speed and height so as to give them time to enjoy the spectacular scenery. They were flying so low that it was possible to see the reefs and rocks surrounding the island, magnified by the clarity of the waters in the shallows, and the different colours indicating where the sea varied in depth. "It's a scuba diver's paradise, I would think,' Jon commented with interest, 'although it isn't something that I've ever tried.'

For the most part, Jon was content to look down on the rocky cliffs, which would deter all but the most determined uninvited visitor to the island with its natural security. When they gained the most easterly end of Buccaneer's Point, the peak appeared to soar above them, although it was only some thousand feet in height, and where the base of the mountain merged with the sea, it continued to plunge into the depths, briefly visible through the opaque waters before rapidly disappearing into the darkness of what probably was an abyss. As the ship silently cruised along, still at a very slow speed, Jon marvelled at the ability of the craft, at the moment not doing more than forty miles per hour, and yet capable of speeds of up to forty thousand miles per hour when unfettered from the gravitational effects of Earth. They reached a point where almost having circumnavigated the island, they found themselves passing

Chapter Forty-One

over what appeared to be a large luxury motor cruiser with a number of people on board, As their approach had been so silent, most of the passengers were unaware of the presence of the spacecraft above them until a young woman, who was sunbathing on the upper deck, happened to look up. Both Lana and Jon laughed at the look of astonishment on her face as she gesticulated at the craft above, and although it was not possible to hear what she was saying, it was obvious that she had the immediate attention of her companions as they all looked up, some looking scared, others waving frantically, and a few lounging nonchantly on the decks as though a passing spacecraft was an everyday occurrence.

Within a few seconds, they had left the tourists far behind and now approached the most westerly point of their island. With a smile, Jon commented, 'Well, Lana, my darling, we have seen all there is to see of Buccaneer's Point, its lagoon, land, and of course, the house itself. All in all, I think if Jacob can secure the sale for the price he mentioned, we will indeed have the island of our dreams.'

Lana's answer was to embrace Jon gently, with their minds once more in accord. 'I can't wait to see Jacob and confirm our decision to purchase the island. Don't forget, you will have to authorise him to contract an architect to supervise any building work required, and what you called a project manager to ensure that the necessary labour force is employed.'

'All these things we will do together, Lana, but even so, it will probably be some time before the legalities are completed, unless the family in London gives us permission to go ahead with the renovations straight away. I'm sure that if Jacob were to offer a few million dollars on account, they could be persuaded to waive some of the customary procedures regarding the sale of Buccaneer's Point.'

Lana smiled as she held him close to her. 'Once we have these war games out of the way, Jon, I want to return to our island and spend much more time in deciding what needs to be done,

Chapter Forty-One

preferably with the architect to advise us.' She gave a little laugh as she declared, 'Do you think Jacob could be persuaded to accompany the architect on another helicopter ride? He might be able to give some useful ideas as regards that airstrip for light aircraft he mentioned before; after all, any guests we may invite in years to come may not relish the thought of a long sea voyage, or a noisy helicopter for that matter. I know I wouldn't.'

'That's because you've been accustomed to the comfort and technology of the Zellian spacecraft for all your travelling requirements, unless of course,' and his voice quieted at his next thought. 'How far could we teleport ourselves? When I went from New York to Washington, that was no difficulty and that was a distance of several hundreds of miles.' But sensing the unease in Lana's mind at the prospect of teleporting more than her customary twenty miles to and from the spaceship's docking position, he resolved to experiment with increasing distances for his own satisfaction. After all, he had been told that the Zellian adepts could transport themselves thousands of miles at a time; it was all a matter of experience and confidence. *However.* he thought, *that is something that can wait until after the war games are over and we can finally take up residence on Buccaneer's Point. Who knows, I may attempt a little island hopping on my own.*

As expected, the journey back to Kingston didn't take long, and they were soon back in their usual docking position above the town. By this time, the sun had dipped below the horizon and all that could be seen of the city below were the lights of the busy streets and shopping areas, with the occasional private dwelling glimmering in the darkness. 'Somehow or other,' Lana said, 'I think we should wait until tomorrow before we call on Jacob; he won't be expecting us so soon, and may not have contacted the solicitors in London as yet. Besides, I have to radio Captain Jara and Mort to arrange our rendezvous above Washington. I hope all the other arrangements for the trip to Arizona are finalised.'

Chapter Forty-One

'I have every confidence that the secretary of state will have invited the appropriate personnel and dignitaries to view the war games, Jon said patiently, 'and no doubt General Clintock knows which of the politicians will be most influential in giving a report to Congress on the results of our demonstration.' He added thoughtfully, 'I have the knowledge instilled in my brain on how to operate all the weapons systems on this ship, but have never utilised that knowledge in any practical way, so I hope Mort's indoctrination treatment will prove to be just as effective for this exercise as everything else has been so far. The ability to teleport has been proven without a doubt, and telekinesis has been useful on a number of occasions, although mind reading and control of other people's minds has only had a limited application so far, and the telepathy between us, Lana, seems so natural, it is as though our minds have always been as one.'

'When Jara and Mort selected you to become a Teacher, Jon,' Lana replied soberly, 'they must have instinctively sensed that you had the potential to become some kind of super-being, a man of intellect, a man capable of great power, and yet ruled by compassion. Similar in some ways to another Teacher of great wisdom two thousand years ago, with the difference that the world is now a far different place, and you are quite invulnerable to the threats of humankind in general; you're a man to bring about peace on Earth and knowledge to the benefit of all.'

Chapter Forty-Two

The reference to the Teacher of some two thousand years ago made Jon feel slightly uneasy; he knew of the person involved, and while he had never been a particularly religious man in his early life, any comparison to the man called Jesus of Nazareth was not welcome. He had been a man who had only come into prominence a few years before his own death, and despite being hailed as the Messiah by the Jewish people, he had also been labelled a troublemaker and rabble rowser by the Roman rulers in that part of the world, the penalty for which had been death by crucifixion, a death from which there had been no escape, a fate that he could not avoid because the Zellions had not given him the powers that successive Teachers possessed.

'Whatever Jara and Mort sensed about my future potential as a Teacher, Lana,' Jon said quietly, 'having undertaken the indoctrination procedures and acquired my newfound powers, I will be able to perform my role as a Teacher for several hundreds of years, with you by my side. As you say, I shall be invulnerable to any threat of a physical nature that any man or government can throw at me, and so long as I wear my force field belt, even a surprise attack against my person will be futile, and the same goes for you, my dear.'

'It's just as well that the belts are so unobtrusive, they look as though they are just part of our uniforms,' she replied with a smile. 'Of course, when we wear our new civilian clothes, we can still wear our belts underneath them, although it might prove difficult for me

Chapter Forty-Two

when I have to wear feminine attire or my wedding dress,' she added with a giggle.

'That's something to think about when the time comes,' Jon remarked with a grin, 'but in the meanwhile, my first commitment as a Teacher is to ensure that I can bring some semblance of peace to the world in general. Getting rid of the nuclear weapons was a good start, and now I have to prove the futility of armed aggression by conventional means. I'm sure our war game demonstration will convince the politicians and military chiefs alike on that score. Assuming the whole episode is filmed and televised to the rest of the world, perhaps the various governments will divert their resources and provide sustainable prosperity for their people, convert the swords into ploughshares.' He had to explain that metaphor to Lana.

'And when will you bestow your technical knowledge and scientific skills on the people of Earth?' Lana enquired.

'Not until they have proven they can live in peace and are worthy of advancement, and want to have a culture like the Zel,' Jon replied soberly, 'but as that is likely to be many years in the future, first we must secure peace on Earth. Then we'll endeavour to remove the potential reasons for conflict such as power supplies, and increase agricultural output to feed the masses, and then make the planet a healthy environment by reducing pollution of the atmosphere and the seas.' He pulled a grim face as he continued. 'I rather think that eliminating global conflict will be the easiest part, as many of the so-called superpowers have already had to add the cost of losing their nukes to their economies, and diverting money and manpower to other things will cause even more upheaval in order to improve the lives of their populations. History should have taught them that wars, once fought, become meaningless, and the so-called victors often find themselves having to support the vanquished for many years after the event, so that quite often it is difficult to define who won the war and who lost.'

Chapter Forty-Two

Probing into Jon's innermost thoughts, Lana said, 'I have no knowledge of such things on a personal level as wars were eliminated on Zel millions of years ago, although other civilisations on other planets have been observed undergoing similar problems to those experienced here on Earth, but always with the same outcome, eventual peace. But it was only after the intervention of the Zellian government and with help of Teachers such as yourself, Jon. Sometimes it took centuries to reach a successful conclusion to the peace missions.' At this point, Lana reached over and as she held Jon's hand firmly, she said, 'But they never had a Teacher as determined and powerful as you; I'm sure your vision for the future will enable you to stop all global conflict, especially after the war games, and no doubt, if you can then introduce the Zellian technology to the scientists and people of Earth in order to create a pollution-free environment to clean up the planet, then a better life will be had by all, young and old alike.'

Although he felt gratified at Lana's faith in him as a Teacher, Jon had little optimism for any sudden changes economically or scientifically in the world; they were not likely to happen any time soon. He smiled as he explained, 'Scientific and environmental issues may well go hand in hand, but education of the masses is not a viable option, since that may well take centuries to achieve. No, one problem I intend to resolve within the first few years of my term as a Teacher is in regard to one commodity that is likely to make countries to go to war in the future, with or without nuclear weapons, and that's oil.' He paused for a moment to read Lana's mind, but the significance of oil to the planet and peace was not registering at that moment, so he decided to explain briefly.

'When Earth and its people were largely an agricultural society, oil was used sparingly for cooking purposes, lighting and lubricating various implements and farm machinery. But when the Industrial Revolution happened, and such things as the motor car came on the scene, the large-scale production of machinery required oil in the production processes, Not only oil for lubrication, but there was an insatiable demand for fuel products such as petrol and diesel, fossil fuels which are responsible, in part, for the contamination of Earth's atmosphere and a gradual increase in global warming, which is slight at the moment, but with far-reaching consequences to the flora and fauna of the planet.'

'If I can persuade the governments of Earth that alternative technologies can be introduced over a comparatively short period of time, dependency on oil will become a thing of the past and relegated to history and not worth fighting over.' He shook his head as he added, 'There are, of course, many nations whose economies are dependent on oil production, and who will undoubtedly oppose the introduction of any new technology. They will be the ones to lose out, but of course, even now, they realise that the future of their oil fields is very limited; therefore, new technologies will have to be introduced, and until then, they will have to learn to diversify and explore other fields of commerce.'

'There is one source of power that will have to be delved into and that is nuclear. As yet, progress in that field of energy supply is being held back due to fears for its safety and stability. That is where the knowledge of the Zellian experts in that respect can be applied comparatively quickly, twenty or thirty years at most, making nuclear energy available to most of the civilised world, and again, making the use of fossil fuels redundant.'

As he reflected on the concerns expressed by many of Earth's scientists, such as how to dispose of the waste product of radioactive material that they thought would remain active and a threat to humanity for a thousand years, he mentally confided to Lana, *The Zellians overcame that particular problem many thousands of years ago; they found a way to recycle the waste product and to utilise it for further energy production, leading to more efficiency in producing more power, sufficient to meet the needs of the whole planet.* He smiled as he added, *If it had been possible, they could have exported the surplus amount of nuclear capacity available.*

Chapter Forty-Two

Jon noted that Lana's attention was wandering. She was more interested in what was to happen in the very near future. 'The day after tomorrow, in fact,' she reminded Jon. 'Now is the time to communicate with Captain Jara and Mort to ensure that we rendezvous above Washington at the time we arranged with the Secretary of State and the President; it would never do for us to be late in picking up all our distinguished guests who wish to witness the war games.'

Nodding in agreement, Jon simply said, 'In that case, I'll let you get on with your radio call to Jara to make the final arrangements for the rendezvous and the procedure for taking our passengers on board. We will land first, and then they will come on board immediately afterwards. There won't be sufficient ground space available in the White House gardens for two flying saucers to land simultaneously.' Then laughing, he added, 'The day after tomorrow is going to be a great day for tourists in Washington.'

As she turned toward her control console and radio, Lana was smiling as she silently agreed. *A great day.* Shortly afterwards, having confirmed the rendezvous for the day after tomorrow, Lana once more sat down close to Jon, and snuggling close to his side, said, 'Now, let's talk about our meeting with Jacob Bernstein tomorrow and how we intend to purchase our island, Buccaneer's Point. As I have no idea of financial dealings, that I will leave to you entirely, Jon, but as to renovations and designs for the old house, I rather think that I will be somewhat more involved than you, Jon darling.'

Smiling indulgently, he replied, 'And so it shall be, all decisions will be shared, and all ideas mutually agreed upon, so that in the end, our island will be our very own paradise on Earth. But until tomorrow, this ship is our home, the first that we have ever shared, so we can be content to be on board, as ever sharing minds and bodies. Tomorrow can wait, for Buccaneer's Point will be ours soon enough.'

Chapter Forty-Three

The following day, they waited until the morning was well advanced before going to Jacob's shop. Jon said, 'I'm sure millionaire jewellers won't be up and about too early.' But as soon as they thought it reasonable to call on their friend, they teleported down to the town of Kingston and its pulsating atmosphere. The streets were already crowded with the native population and a fair sprinkling of tourists as well. As there was no particular urgency for their social call, they dawdled through the crowds, enjoying the happy holiday atmosphere until eventually they arrived at the doorstep of the jeweller's shop, but were surprised to note that the name of Jacob Bernstein was no longer displayed above the entrance and windows of the establishment.

'What has happened here?' Jon declared, 'It was only a few days ago that we met Jacob, and there was no mention of him going off anywhere at that time.'

Lana smiled as she replied reassuringly, 'Perhaps our friend has decided to spend some of his money and is going to refurbish the premises, something more in keeping with his being a millionaire.'

'Or maybe it's still too early for him to be up and about,' laughed Jon. 'Whatever the case might be, we will go in by the door like normal customers, or if it's locked, teleport in as we usually do.'

As it happened, they were able to walk into the shop, like normal customers, to find Jacob collecting his many pieces of display stock, some of which were not only beautiful and of his own design, but quite valuable; whereas, much of the merchandise on

Chapter Forty-Three

display was strictly for tourist consumption, but still of excellent quality. As he became aware of their presence, he looked up. 'Welcome back, my friends, I take it that you enjoyed your visit to Buccaneer's Point, and would I be correct to assume that you have already made up your minds regarding the purchase of the island, another Caribbean gem.'

'We'll come to that in a moment, Jacob,' Jon said severely. 'Why are you alone with all this valuable jewellery lying around? You have already had an incident quite recently with would-be thieves, don't you think it's tempting providence? We could have been potential robbers walking in on you just now.'

Jacob laughed in genuine amusement, or was it relief. 'Not to worry, my friends, since that last encounter, I have arranged to have a constant minder with me when I'm carrying valuables or when here in the shop. Where I go, she goes. In fact, I wouldn't be surprised if she didn't have a gun trained on you the moment you walked in the door.'

With an effort to keep a straight face, Jon enquired, 'Did I hear you say that your minder is a she, a female?'

'But of course,' Jacob replied with a chuckle. 'If I'm to have a constant companion for security reasons, either here or when travelling abroad, then I might as well have someone who is not only trustworthy and reliable, but whose company I can enjoy, business and pleasure.' With that, he turned and called out, 'Come out here, Miranda, come and meet my good friends, Jon and Lana.'

At that moment, a young, coloured woman, probably in her mid-thirties, walked out from behind a partition where she had apparently been concealed. Jacob had been right; she was still holding a gun in her hand in a way that suggested she knew how to use it. 'Jon, Lana, this is Miranda, the lady who is going to be my constant companion from now on.' Noting the enquiring looks on their faces, but unaware that his mind was being probed, by Jon in

Chapter Forty-Three

particular, Jacob then gave a brief account of his previous acquaintance with his newly hired protector.

'Miranda was employed by the police department here on the island of Jamaica, so she has had plenty of experience dealing with crooks and violence in her career, and part of her job was calling on businesses like mine as a matter of routine, which is how I got to know her.'

Jon was smiling inwardly as he continued to read his friend's mind. *I'm way ahead of you Jacob,* he thought, *I can see that you were attracted to this beautiful ex-police officer in more ways than one, and as you say, if you're going to have a constant minder, having one as attractive as Miranda will make life so much more interesting for you, but where will it all lead, and for how long?*

As Jacob finished his explanation and introduction to his future companion, Jon and Lana silently conceded that the old rascal was going to find life very different from now on, so it was no great surprise when Jacob continued talking about his plans for the future. 'As you may have gathered from the fact that I've removed the sign from above the shop front, and I'm gathering up all my stock, I'm vacating these premises as from today. Now that you've made me a very rich man, and with the promise of more to come, I can afford to live the life of a millionaire and travel the world if I so wish. Indeed, I shall have to in order to conclude the sale of the diamonds you left with me, was it only a day or two ago? Ah moie, ah moie! So much has happened in such a short time.' He paused briefly, his face flushed with excitement as he recalled the pleasure of examining the stones. 'Such perfection I have never seen before, and I'm sure that when I show them at auction in New York and Amsterdam, possibly even in London, they are going to add to your already considerable fortune, my dears.'

Having given Jacob time to discuss his future plans of closing his shop and travelling the world, with his beautiful bodyguard to protect him, it was Jon who brought his attention back to the other

Chapter Forty-Three

reason for them being there. Apart from being assured for his security, they wanted to know what progress, if any, had been made in contacting the solicitors in London regarding the sale of Buccaneer's Point.

'Ah, my friends,' Jacob exclaimed, 'you have made your minds up already; you are intending to buy the island of your dreams?' Without waiting for a reply, he continued, 'I knew that once you had inspected the location, you would fall in love with the place. As I said before you left the last time, I have already begun a preliminary enquiry through the agents and solicitors for an early occupancy of the island, with the assurance of a deposit of several millions of dollars as security. Payable immediately, Buccaneer's Point will be yours with their blessing. Handing over that kind of money before exchanging legal contracts is, of course, highly irregular, but in your case, Jon, and you, Lana, you will then be able to return to the island as soon as is convenient and begin to realise your dream.'

Feeling highly elated by this good news, but with an important question in mind, Jon then enquired, 'Up to this present time, Jacob, I have left all the financial issues in your capable hands, the marketing of the diamonds, in particular, as a result of which you have assured Lana and me that we can easily afford to buy the island and renovate the old house. But how do we access the money to do so?' With a laugh, he added, 'Even with Miranda as your constant companion, you can't carry that kind of money around with you.'

Jacob had no difficulty in assuring his friends that he, Jacob Bernstein, had arranged not only the sale of the first consignment of diamonds, but had taken all necessary steps to secure their financial future and security of their funds. 'All your money is, at this moment, earning thousands of dollars in interest.' He smiled at such a pleasant thought. 'I opened an account in your names, a joint account, with a bank that specialises in real estate investments, an American bank by the name of Merrill Lynch, so when you wish to clinch the deal to buy Buccaneer's Point, it will be a simple matter of transferring the funds, electronically of course, from your own account to that of the solicitors.' He laughed. 'A few phone calls to the right people, and you will potentially be the new owner of your own small island in the Caribbean.'

Lana's happiness at such a prospect was evident by the expression on her face, and as her mind and thoughts blended with Jon's, she giggled with delight, the laugh of an eighty-year-old girl, which was very young for a Zellian. 'The sooner you make those phone calls, Jacob,' she exclaimed, 'the sooner our dream will become a reality. Then after our next mission to Washington, we can start planning for the future of The Point. Jon frowned slightly at the mention of Washington and the forthcoming mission, the war games.

To keep Jacob and Miranda in the conversation, he said, 'We intend to give the President and senior members of the government a demonstration of military tactics, something you will no doubt see at some time in the near future on your local TV channels, so I won't go into any detail at this time. It is more important to us that you arrange the money transfer to secure the sale of the island.'

Jacob's mind was focussed on his friends' financial situation and the legal practicalities of the impending purchase of Buccaneer's Point, the prospect of having to travel abroad with his lovely minder, and the sale of the last batch of perfect diamonds, so any kind of military tactics were far removed from his thoughts. *Let me get on with my work,* he thought, *It's time for me to earn my commission, by making a few phone calls, and then my friends will find happiness on their island paradise.*

His mind racing ahead, thinking of the problems to be encountered in setting up a new home in such a remote location, he turned to Jon. 'For a wealthy couple like yourselves, buying the property may be the easiest part; it only requires money, a commodity that you have plenty of, but may I suggest that when you

Chapter Forty-Three

have completed your trip to Washington, that you hire the services of an architect to supervise the renovation of the old house. I know just the man to advise you, and he can hire the necessary labour force for all the work involved.' He smiled as he added, 'In fact, he is also in a position to select some first-class servants when you are ready to move into your new home; they are reliable and trustworthy people.'

'You seem to think of everything, Jacob,' Jon remarked, 'but how can I ask you to get so involved with our project when you are contemplating travelling abroad with the lovely Miranda, your attendant,' he added teasingly. 'Are you sure you will have the time?'

There was a moment of confusion in Jacob's mind as he realised that Jon somehow knew that he had more than his personal safety in mind when he had hired the services of the delectable Miranda as his minder. After all, Miranda might be coloured, but she was a very attractive, intelligent and charming person, and ah moie, he could already imagine her as his soul mate. He was Jewish and she was, well, what did it matter what religion she practiced, she could practice voodoo for all he cared.

Jon was reading his friend's mind again, so he didn't attempt to embarrass him with any further personal questions. He simply added, 'We will again be indebted to you, Jacob, for all your help in procuring Buccaneer's Point.'

Relieved that there was no need for further evasion from awkward questions, Jacob answered happily, 'It is I who am indebted to you both, Jon and Lana. Since our first meeting a few months ago, my life has been changed around completely. From being a simple jewellery craftsman at that time, I am now a wealthy man in my own right, a respected diamond merchant, and purveyor of precious gems.' He smiled and nodded at Miranda. 'And I'm protected by the most beautiful escort in the Caribbean.' The warmth of his tone of voice was not lost on any of them, especially Miranda.

I do believe she blushed, Jon, Lana declared telepathically.

I do believe you're right, he conceded silently. With further assurances from Jacob that he would contact all the people involved, the banks, the solicitor for the vendor, and the architect for the project, everything was arranged so that on completion of his mission to Washington, Jon would find that he would be able to return to Buccaneer's Point and begin the serious business of making the island a suitable residence for an ambassador of the Zellians. It was secure, remote, and beautiful, and strangely reminiscent of Lana's home planet where she had spent her early childhood.

After spending this time with Jacob and his guard, Lana reminded Jon that they should return to their ship on the pretext that they had much to do in preparation for their trip to Washington. Although she knew the journey would only be of short duration, and the on-board weapons systems were always fully operational, she again simply wanted to be alone with her man, her Teacher.

Knowing what was in her mind, Jon was happy to comply with the reminder, so turning to Jacob and Miranda, he said, 'No need to see us to the door this time, my friends, we will take the quickest way back to our ship.' Then holding hands, as lovers do, they smiled at each other, and then disappeared like the proverbial puff of smoke.

It was to Miranda's astonishment, as this was the first time she had witnessed anyone teleporting. 'Well, I never,' she exclaimed breathlessly.

Meanwhile Jacob said nonchalantly, 'They do it all the time!'

Chapter Forty-Four

Knowing that they were in for a busy day, Lana and Jon were awake earlier than usual, so much so that they had had breakfast before the sun had risen above the horizon. With the viewports open, they watched with fascination the first lightening of the sky, then the appearance of the golden orb as it apparently rose out of the sea in the East. They enjoyed the gradual transition from darkness to a dark blue sky, then again from every shade of blue to purple, and finally, as the sun lifted above the horizon, the warmer shades of orange, followed with the familiar paler blue of the subtropical skies and daybreak.

They gazed out of the viewport for another ten minutes before the town of Kingston below them became illuminated by the early morning sun, and what few lights had been left on overnight were extinguished. It was a sign that the inhabitants were up and about, and ready to go about their daily lives, some to open their businesses and shops, others to promote the tourist industry, and the lucky ones to enjoy a carefree lifestyle without any kind of responsibilities.

From their altitude of twenty miles above the city, once the early morning haze had been dispersed by the warmth of the sun, it was possible to see for a distance of fifty miles or more before the sea and the sky appeared to blend into one, making the horizon difficult to define. Even so, it was possible to pick out a surprising number of ships and smaller craft already out at sea. No doubt some were local boat owners making their way out from the island in search of deeper waters for fishing, or taking parties of divers to the

Chapter Forty-Four

wrecks of ships, which abounded in these waters. Alternately, there were several cruise liners apparently on course for their anchorages off Kingston itself. Jamaica was without a doubt one of the many jewels of the Caribbean and a popular tourist destination.

Although there was no particular urgency to begin the flight to Washington, since it would only take an hour, Jon suggested they ensure that they were on station above the White House prior to their rendezvous with Captain Jara. 'I would like to finalise what I intend to do with regards to the demonstration of the war games. Jara has the same weaponry on board his ship as we have, but as to when he last used the necessary equipment is debatable, and to be effective, we will have to fly in close proximity to each other, at no more than one thousand feet, and at a very slow speed, so the effect of the energy beam will be devastating to any potential ground force. Personnel and equipment in the form of tanks and other mechanised transport will be completely annihilated within minutes.' The images in his mind, a disturbing picture of destruction on a massive scale, were, of course, picked up by Lana telepathically.

'I'm glad that this will only be a demonstration of the power that you will have at your disposal, Jon,' Lana said quietly. 'As a Zellian, the potential loss of life in an exercise of this nature is completely abhorrent, although I can accept that, in extreme circumstances, such action might become necessary to restrain a would-be aggressor.'

With a hint of irony in his voice, Jon replied, equally quietly, 'Once our distinguished guests and observers have seen this demonstration, and they realise that no army on Earth can resist our technology, they might just as well scrap their armaments, nuclear or otherwise.' Then he added with a grim laugh, 'Swords to ploughshares.'

Lana was clearly impressed with the forthcoming demonstration, but was curious to observe the the practical demonstration of the annihilation of the enemy forces as envisaged in Jon's mind.

Chapter Forty-Four

'I'm sure that Captain Jara has never had occasion to use the technology of this weapon you intend to use, Jon, and I've never heard of any other Zellian spacecraft deploying the energy beam that you describe; what exactly does it do to be such an effective weapon?'

With a thoughtful frown on his face, Jon hesitated before replying. 'When I was undergoing my initial training or indoctrination, I was taught many things. Apart from the many languages of Earth, your language also, Lana, I received a comprehensive history of your people and how they achieved peace and prosperity with their benign influence on the people of the hundreds, no, thousands, of planets they have visited in the past millennia, or should I say, millions of years. But during the time that the Zellians were helping the inhabitants of those planets, they had to recourse to physical force before being able to impose their benign influence; it was a bit like dealing with a rebellious child. This energy beam that I intend to deploy has been used quite a number of times in the past, but the reason that you have not been aware of its existence before is simply that it can only be used effectively on planets such as Earth.' Realising that Lana was listening attentively, but still didn't fully understand how the energy beam could only be used on some planets, but not others, Jon continued to explain slowly and in the simplest terms.

'From your basic training as a cadet, Lana,' he said with a smile, 'you, no doubt, were informed that all the planets and life forms were by no means identical. The Zellian people, in common with human beings, are water-based, and they even use silicon as an alternative. As for this planet, it has something unique in the solar system, a molten iron core, which among other things, emanates a constant magnetic field, which gives the Earth protection from the harmful solar stream, but I'm sure I don't have to go into detail about that?'

Chapter Forty-Four

'No,' Lana conceded, 'but what has all this to do with the energy beam and what it can do?'

'Coming to that Lana,' Jon said with a laugh, 'Earth's magnetic field is not something we can feel as individuals, although scientifically it can be measured, and it has been used for hundreds of years for navigational purposes. But to get to the point, the weapon itself emits a beam of electronically charged positive and negative electrons, which interact with Earth's own magnetic field, causing a local collapse of the flux. As this takes place literally hundreds of times per second, it causes solid matter to vibrate and disintegrate to the consistency of water, making it unable to support anything of greater density, such as the vehicles we will be targeting.'

The dawning of understanding showed on Lana's face as she commented, 'Does that mean that the terrain the tanks and lorries are sitting on will become like quicksand and swallow them up?'

'Yes, precisely, Lana,' Jon replied, 'and that would also include all infantry, lock, stock, and barrel, as they say, if there were any taking part in this exercise.'

'But if all the enemy are to sink into the ground,' Lana persisted, 'how long will that take and how deep will the tanks and other vehicles go?'

With a grim smile, Jon replied, 'For the purpose of this demonstration, I want every trace of the potential enemy to be removed from the face of the earth. This has to be seen as the fate of any aggressor foolish enough to wage a war in the future. We have eliminated all nuclear weapons already, now so-called conventional armies will be proved impotent against the power at my disposal. The technology of the Zellians will be used to convince the nations of Earth of the futility of making war on each other.' A certain wistful note crept into his voice as he added, 'Once the war game is over, perhaps I can begin to fulfil my role as a Teacher. There is so much knowledge to teach the scientists and engineers of Earth, so

Chapter Forty-Four

much so, that once humanity has learned to live in peace, the work of educating them can begin.'

Feeling slightly in awe of her man, this Teacher, Lana probed his mind, but was dazzled by the thoughts going through his brain at that moment, visions of the future that would entail many years of dedication to further the advance of science, and the cooperation of all the governments of Earth. Nevertheless, she voiced the same question. 'How far will the enemy sink into the ground and how long will it take?'

It only took a moment for Jon to refocus his mind on the forthcoming war game and how it would be conducted. 'Fortunately, Lana,' he replied, 'the area where all the armoured vehicles, tanks, and trucks have been assembled is mainly desert and scrubland, so the effect of the energy beams will be more quickly apparent. The ground will become like a morass within seconds, and as we are passing over the area quite slowly, the magnetic vibrations will penetrate for a depth of ten feet at least, more if necessary, just by reducing speed as we fly over the battle area. The slower our speed, the greater the penetration and destruction of the enemy force.'

With a frown on her face, Lana's curiosity prompted her to ask another question regarding the effectiveness of this weapon she knew nothing about. 'Would this energy beam give the same result if the terrain was mountainous and rocky? After all, the enemy won't always choose a convenient landscape such as the desert area where this mock demonstration is to be held, would they?'

'That's true, Lana,' Jon replied quietly. 'All that we would have to do is to fly lower to increase the density of the magnetic charge and hover over the target area a little longer. Even solid rock will disintegrate within seconds, but to be realistic, in normal combat situations, it wouldn't be necessary for us to wait until the enemy had completely disappeared from view. They would be immobilised and ineffective even if they were submerged or bogged down into the landscape by only a few feet.'

Chapter Forty-Four

With the intention of changing the subject of conversation, Jon laughed and said, 'I'm going to do the US government a favour today by getting rid of all their surplus and scrap vehicles by burying them forever, and at no charge for the service. But I think it's time to make our way to Washington and our rendezvous with Captain Jara and Mort.'

With his arm still around Lana's shoulders, he activated the viewport windows to close them and gently guided her to the control console. He said with a smile, 'Today, you're going to be in charge of flying the craft, which will impress our distinguished guests, I'm sure, and that will leave me free to demonstrate the effectiveness of the magnetic energy beam.'

With a matter-of-fact tone of voice Lana replied, 'And that, I'm equally sure, will impress our guests even more so.'

Within minutes of activating the flight controls, they had left Kingston and Jamaica far behind. With the ship gradually accelerating to their usual atmospheric cruising speed of two thousand miles per hour, the journey to Washington DC was accomplished with ease within their estimated time, allowing Lana to dock in their usual position high above the White House, where they would wait for Jara to rendezvous with them as arranged.

'Punctuality was said to be "the politeness of kings" on Earth,' Jon quoted with a smile, but with the Zellians, it was also a virtue to be admired, so it was no surprise when Jara's ship showed up alongside, and his smiling face beamed at them from the control console.

'I take it that it's too early to pick up our passengers for the day, Jon,' he said, 'so is there anything you wish to discuss or any plan of action you intend to follow during this demonstration we are going to do today?'

Deliberately, Jon put his first question. 'As our ships are identical in every detail, Jara, and the weapons systems are the

Chapter Forty-Four

same, are you aware of a magnetic energy beam at your disposal, and more to the point, have you ever used it?'

Captain Jara visibly raised his eyebrows in wonder before replying. 'Yes, Jon, it is a standard piece of equipment on this type of craft, but in all my years in the service, I have never been called on to use it myself. Indeed, I have never seen it demonstrated, although from descriptions in our training when I was a cadet, and that was hundreds of years ago, when used effectively, it is regarded as a formidable weapon. Why do you ask?'

Jon then went on to explain his plan for the demonstration of the war game when they reached the prepared site in the desert in Arizona later that day. He emphasised the need to shock and impress the military and government representatives with the power and destructive force that only two Zellian craft could inflict on a large-scale invasion by a hostile enemy. Nothing less than complete annihilation would convince the sceptics among the spectators. The scenario to be enacted would replicate a type of war never seen before.

Waiting until Jon had outlined his plan and explanation of how the two ships would work together on the battlefield, Jara commented dryly, 'I'll have to make a few notes for future cadets to read based on our practical application of the magnetic energy beams. I must say that I look forward to helping the US government clear the landscape of all their junk. But I'm even happier that, on this occasion, we won't be called upon to inflict any real casualties.'

This was a sentiment quietly shared by Jon and Lana. As the plan of campaign had been simplified to the satisfaction of both crews, Mort and Lana would pilot their respective craft, while Jon and Jara would be in charge of controlling the weapons systems. They conceded that, while neither of them had ever used this technology, both of them were completely familiar, at least in theory, as to how to operate the energy beams. The Arizona battlefield would be a good proving ground.

Chapter Forty-Four

Conscious of the fact that the politicians and military personnel would be gathering in the White House below, Jon gave a wry smile as he said to Captain Jara, 'Time to go, I think. I'll drop down to the grounds of the White House and pick up our passengers and the government photographer, then I'll lift off and wait until you have done the same.'

Jara acknowledged his agreement with a nod. He pursed his lips as he commented, 'After you, Teacher.'

They broke radio contact as Lana began the slow descent to the White House. The early morning sunshine cast the city in sharp relief as the saucer sank gracefully to the manicured lawns below.

Chapter Forty-Five

'They've arrived, Mr. President. They're just sitting on the lawn outside,' remarked George C. Lane, 'punctual to the minute.'

'In that case, let's not keep them waiting,' was the reply. 'I take it that all the observers have already been assembled and are ready for boarding?'

The secretary grinned as he commented, 'Some of them have been pacing up and down like expectant fathers at a maternity ward.' He continued with a laugh, 'I suppose there is a similarity in this situation, though, since none of them know what the outcome of this event will be.'

'Neither do we, George, neither do we,' replied the president, 'but by the end of the day, I feel sure that our ambassador of the Zellians will have convinced us that wars, as pursued by earthly forces, are futile against superior technology.' He added as an afterthought, 'But how to deal with the imbalance of manpower may be another factor to consider.'

General Clintock, as an old-style military man, snorted in derision. 'Men against machine guns—give me a thousand, properly equipped, well-trained soldiers, and I'd take on any enemy ground force, and win!'

'Well, I'm no military man,' retorted George C. Lane, 'but as I see it, this demonstration or war game that we are about to witness is all about a superior invading ground force, more than a thousand men with all the hardware, up against just two Zellian spacecraft

Chapter Forty-Five

using whatever advanced technology or weapons at their disposal. It's an airborne attack against a massive ground force.'

General Clintock pulled a wry face as he replied, 'I admit that we would likely sustain heavy casualties in a conventional shootout between aircraft and ground forces, but against two flying saucers, if some of our divisions were equipped with heat-seeking missiles, I think we could soon bring them down.'

Davis Cooper gave a polite cough to attract the attention of his secretary of state and the general. 'Gentlemen, I believe we should wait until we have seen this demonstration Jon has prepared for us before we jump to any conclusions regarding methods of attack or defence. In the meanwhile, I suggest that we make our way downstairs and get on board our allocated craft. I believe that we will be with Jon and Lana, along with an assortment of politicians and other military personnel.'

'Don't forget we'll have a cameraman along for the ride,' added George with a humourless grin, 'to record the event for posterity, and to convince the worldwide audiences that they may have to bend to the will of the Teacher in pursuit of world peace.'

By the time the presidential party were ready to board the spacecraft, having been preceded by the cameraman and the other passengers, Jon was waiting at the threshold with a smile of welcome on his face. 'We will take off as soon as you are safely on board, Mr. President,' he said. 'Then the other craft will come down and pick up the remainder of the observers.'

As he joined the rest of the group, Davis Cooper smiled as he noted the expression on their faces. 'Is this what they had expected to see inside an alien spacecraft?' He recalled his own amazement at the size of the interior of the vessel, which was much bigger than its outside appearance suggested, and the complexity of the flight deck control consoles with their myriad flashing lights, reminiscent of a

Chapter Forty-Five

certain rocket launch site that many of them had visited quite recently.

Raising his voice to still the babble of conversation going on, Jon announced, 'We will raise the viewport windows during the flight to Arizona so you may enjoy the scenery. We will be travelling at a comparatively slow speed for this craft, about one thousand mph, so it will also prolong the pleasure and give you an insight into some of the many technical innovations that Zellian technology can bring to you; that is, once the people of Earth have been persuaded to live in peace.' Jon knew that now was not the time to hold out the prospect of education for humankind. His audience clustered around the viewports, excitedly pointing out to each other landmarks they recognised below, but completely unaware of the speed of the ship, which was far in excess of the speed of any other aircraft that most of them had ever flown in before, except for possibly one or two ex-military pilots on board. Jon and Lana merely looked at each other, their minds as ever aware of the mixed emotions of those around them, but they smiled indulgently at their behaviour. They turned their attention to the radio in order to contact Captain Jara who was, by this time, airborne with his group of dignitaries and following the same flight path to the desert in Arizona.

Jara's thoughts mirrored the thoughts of Jon and Lana. *They do get excited easily, don't they? Wait until they see what's in store for them.*

In due course, after their slow flight to the South, they arrived over the target area, and descended to their operational height, some one thousand feet above the massive array of military hardware. There were literally hundreds of obsolete tanks, relics of bygone wars, armoured vehicles of every description, transport for military personnel, and presumably to make it even more interesting, or simply to get rid of them, a number of World War II aircraft on the fringes. Without attempting to count them, Jon estimated there

Chapter Forty-Five

must be close to a thousand potential targets for them to deal with or annihilate.

Turning to General Clintock, he said with a confident smile, 'Well, General, do you think this represents a formidable task force?'

'It would, if they were shooting at us,' General Clintock replied with a scowl. 'But at the moment, they're just sitting ducks and no threat whatsoever. What kind of defence would you offer in the event of a combined land and air attack?'

Acknowledging that the target was indeed a sitting duck, Jon said quietly, 'First, we will dispose of the enemy on the ground; then, if we can arrange with the president's permission an attack by one of your squadrons of fighter aircraft, a live fire assault on both of our spacecraft, you will see how we choose to defend ourselves.' He added in a severe but taunting tone of voice, 'But do order the pilots not to pull any punches; make it look like the real thing for your benefit, and to impress our other guests.'

Noting the incredulous look on the general's face, he added, 'I will deter the attack, but not damage the aircraft or harm the pilots themselves. That I promise you.' Then turning to one of the control consoles on the flight deck, he continued, 'How would an enemy force of this size attack, General, in columns in line, or in line abreast?'

Without even considering the question, General Clintock answered, 'In open country like that,' he said, pointing down at the arid desert below, 'line abreast would be the most effective tactic to achieve a victory.'

At that point, Davis Cooper butted into the conversation with his own comment on the distribution of the enemy forces. 'Since they are already positioned in line abreast, they present a very wide front, at least half a mile wide, and while I'm no military tactician, I would think it nearly impossible to stem their advance by conventional means.'

Chapter Forty-Five

Confident in what was to follow, Jon smiled. 'Working together as a team, Captain Jara will keep his craft about two hundred yards away from us as we sweep across the head of the advancing column, cutting a swathe of destruction across their path, then we'll turn around and repeat the manoeuvre across the following columns, a bit like using a scythe on a field of wheat.'

'So, you intend to be the grim reaper,' Davis Cooper intoned grimly.

'You could say that, Mr. President,' Jon replied, 'but fortunately, as I said before, there won't be any human casualties during this demonstration, although some of your military advisors may have nightmares as a result of what they are about to witness.' Pausing for a moment, he again spoke quietly to General Clintock. 'General, I would think that by the time we have completed our task and eliminated the enemy on the ground, with Lana's help, you can call up that squadron of aircraft, so if you will excuse me, I will prepare for our first pass over the enemy, then when you have confirmed your call for reinforcements, we will begin.'

Some five minutes later, having conferred with Captain Jara in the other craft, they began the methodical sweep from side to side of the massed vehicles on the desert floor below. 'Watch carefully what is happening to the ground below and the effect it is having on the enemy,' Jon advised the president and the general in a tense tone of voice. Although he knew what the magnetic energy beam was capable of, this was the first and hopefully the last time that he would have to use it; nevertheless, he was fascinated by what was happening to the sandy scrubland below. To improve the view and to bring it into close perspective for everyone on board, himself included, he adjusted the scanners to full magnification, and in doing so, it seemed as if they were hovering just a few feet above one of the ancient battlefield tanks. As they watched, the vehicle seemed to sway violently and plunge about like a boat in a rough sea. Looking at the ground on either side of the tank, it resembled a misty morass of constantly moving mud. Even as they watched, they realised that the vehicle was rapidly disappearing from their view, sinking like a stone into what moments before had been a solid landscape. It was an awesome sight that was repeated each time the Zellian craft swept over the assembled armada below.

Davis Cooper and the general watched in horrified fascination as the destruction of the entire assembly of vehicles was completed in less than twenty minutes, with no trace remaining of what had been one of the biggest scrapyards of military vehicles in the country.

The general shakily commented, 'There's no answer to that technology, Jon.' He tried to appear very matter of fact in front of the other dignitaries and the cameraman who had been filming the entire incident, and he jokingly said, although not very convincingly, 'That's saved the government an expensive clean-up job.'

George C. Lane went one further as he observed what was now nothing but sand and scrubland below. 'Apart from getting rid of all the junk, in effect, the magnetic beams liquefied the ground, and like water, has found its own level. Look at it now. It looks like a huge lake, perfectly smooth and not a ripple in sight.' With a nervous laugh as he tried to break the silence and tension among the observers, he said, 'If that surface down there has reformed to its original hardness, we'll have another potential Bonneville Flats at our disposal.'

Davis Cooper had been visibly shaken by the sight and manner of the destruction of the potential enemy invasion force—no bombs, explosions or fires—just the rapid disappearance of everything in sight into the maws of the earth. Luckily, he had not had to witness the fate of living beings in the demonstration provided by the Teacher. Although, he could well imagine the catastrophic result of the magnetic energy beams controlled by just two Zellian craft. *What,* he asked himself, *would a greater number of such craft be able to destroy? And what defence, as the general has stated in so many*

Chapter Forty-Five

words, could be mounted against the Zellian technology? None that he could think of.

It was at that moment that General Clintock reminded everyone on the flight deck that the squadron of fighter aircraft he had requested were due to begin their scheduled attack to test the defences of the spacecraft. Jon and Lana were the only ones on board completely at ease with that prospect, knowing that they would be completely invulnerable with their force field activated, but Jon took the opportunity to remind the president that he and all the other passengers on board would be perfectly safe. 'In fact,' he said by way of reassurance, 'I will keep the viewports open to let you see what is happening outside, but you won't be able to hear any noise of any description. It will be like watching a silent movie, but you won't be in any danger.' He then continued, saying to Davis Cooper, 'If you remember the occasion of our arrival at the White House the first time, we came under fire from some of your military jets, and one of them ventured too close to our force field, and as a result, was destroyed.'

He smiled as he again continued, 'To prevent such an unfortunate occurrence happening again, I will contract the field to a minimum for the safety of the pilots. They will still be able to attack with cannon and rocket fire, but unless they are intent on suicide, they won't get too close to us, and therefore, the force field.'

Lana's voice was the next to be heard as she said, 'There are a number of aircraft approaching, Jon. They should be here in two minutes, and then the fireworks will begin.'

To show his lack of concern, Jon stood beside George C. Lane at one of the viewports, and with his feet wide apart, placed his arm in a friendly fashion across the secretary's shoulder. 'This will be your first time to experience being under enemy fire, will it not, George?'

With a nervous nod of affirmation, the secretary quietly replied, 'It is, but I have every confidence that, by the manner in which you

Chapter Forty-Five

and Lana conduct yourselves in the face of this attack, all will be well.' As an afterthought, he added, 'I wonder if the pilots were briefed regarding who their targets were going to be on these craft? Are they aware that they will be firing at the president and some of his senior advisors?'

'I think not,' replied Jon with a laugh, 'to make this defensive exercise more realistic, the attack has to be equally realistic. However, when all is said and done, none will die, although the pilots are going to be somewhat frustrated when they return to base, out of ammunition and without having made a kill.' He paused for a moment as he glanced out of the viewport and exclaimed, 'And here they are, on time and on schedule, hoping to destroy two sitting ducks with their missiles before we can evade them. Well, I'm going to make it easy for them, neither Jara in his ship nor myself will attempt to flee. We will effectively invite them to try their luck, but as you will soon realise, George, we are quite immune to any kind of weaponry on this planet, so just stand here and watch the action. As Lana said, the fireworks are about to begin.'

Feeling assured by the apparent confidence of Jon and the secretary of state standing so close to the viewport, the president, General Clintock and the other members of the government were soon persuaded to gather around to share the sight of the fighter jets attacking in force, in an attempt to finish off the motionless spacecraft as quickly as possible. The first choice of weapons to be used was their most powerful one, the air-to-air missiles. The group watched each incoming aircraft release its rockets then banked hurriedly to avoid a collision, and they had a head-on view of the missiles trailing a tail of fire and vapour, a sight to make any man blanch or wince in anticipation of death or destruction. Then, they felt sudden relief as the force field around the spacecraft detonated the missiles before they could impact on the target itself, which momentarily blinded all of them, despite involuntarily closing their eyes at the last moment, as many of them would later testify. It was

Chapter Forty-Five

like defying death, knowing that they would not die. Again, it was thanks to the Zellian technology and the impregnable force field.

As Jon watched the afterburners of the jets receding in the distance, he turned to the photographer standing nearby and said with a smile, 'Did you record all the action of the last ten minutes?'

The cameraman grinned with satisfaction as he replied, 'Every detail, I guess the public will be amazed at how close the jets came to us during the attack without scoring a hit.' He then laughed as he added, 'But I won't recommend that the film is produced in 3-D. Otherwise, heart failure rates across the country will soar.'

Looking around the flight deck, Jon observed the reactions of the various military personnel, General Clintock included; their faces mirrored feelings of relief that the attack was over, which had been a scary experience even for battle-hardened veterans.

Davis Cooper remained at the viewport until the last of the attack force had completely disappeared, and only then did he turn around to address Jon. 'Well, that was an exciting ten minutes wasn't it. I would never have believed that a top squadron of our air force could engage an enemy in such a sustained offensive without scoring a hit. In fact, if such a report had landed on my desk on a normal day, I would've been tempted to say, you've got to be kidding.'

General Clintock was also shaking his head in disbelief, despite having witnessed the determined attack by the fighter aircraft. 'Is there anything that can break through this force field around your ship, Jon?' he asked incredulously. 'You said that you had deliberately contracted it to allow the pilots an easier target, so if it were to be extended, how far would your safety perimeter then be?'

Taking one question at a time, without revealing the true nature of the force field, Jon replied, 'No, General, no physical body can penetrate our force field. We could withstand even a nuclear attack, if an adversary possessed such weapons, and there are none left on this world,' he reminded the general and all the observers on the

Chapter Forty-Five

flight deck. 'As to the protective range of the field, while it is not infinite, it could be extended to several miles if necessary, as is the case when there is a danger of collision with space junk or asteroids when travelling between our mother ship and the planets.'

Having waited for a suitable opportunity to make his voice heard, George C. Lane said, 'Well, Mr President, with our personal testimony of the events of today, of the complete destruction of a potential enemy task force, an awesome sight against which there would have been no defence, then the inability of our own aircraft to breach the defensive energy shields of the two spacecraft, all of which has been recorded by the cameramen on board the two ships, there will be little difficulty in convincing the politicians and the military of all nations of the futility of waging war on each other. Especially, if Jon, with the backing of the Zellian mother ship and however many flying saucers they may have at their command, says desist.'

Davis Cooper shrugged his shoulders and gave a sigh. 'As you say, George,' he replied, 'with our own report to Congress and the televised reports that will be shown around the world, there will be little doubt in the minds of civilian and military administrations alike, that like it or not, peace will be enforced on the all nations of Earth for the first time ever.'

For his part, the general was thinking about his own future in a world where armed conflict was relegated to the history books. The military would become peacekeepers acting as policemen, dealing with violations of civil law; they'd be law enforcers. It was not a prospect to please a professional soldier who, over a period of many years, had experienced the challenges and excitement of action in wars on every major continent on Earth. But reluctantly, he had to accept that, after thousands of years and millions of fatalities, wars would now become redundant, and he and others of the same ilk would have to accept a way of life that was going to be hugely

Chapter Forty-Five

beneficial to humankind. *Perhaps I may live to see the changes that universal peace may bring,* he thought with a rueful smile.

One by one, Jon quickly probed the minds of everyone on the flight deck, the president, the secretary of state, all the military personnel, the politicians, even the cameraman, and within minutes, he found that the war game had had a profound effect on their prospects for the future. While it hadn't really sunk in as yet that it was possible to live without fear of aggression, probably for the first time since man had walked the earth, nevertheless, all on board would be prepared to embrace the changes that a new way of life would bring. Hopefully, their changed outlook would soon be shared by the civilian populations throughout the world, and once a lasting peace was assured, then as the Teacher, his real work could begin.

His goals were prosperity for all, elimination of disease and poverty, the advancement of science and engineering, to put humans on the path that the Zellians had chosen to follow millions of years ago. But one item he had already resolved not to interfere with was the religious beliefs of the people of Earth; they were too diverse and had contributed to more bloodshed than any other cause in the past. *Besides,* he mused, *if the leaders of the various religions—Catholics, Buddhists, followers of Islam, and any others—were aware of the beliefs shared by the Zellians and many other ancient races throughout the galaxies, I don't think they could be persuaded to live a peaceful, God fearing life, and thus preserve a reasonable degree of harmony. After all, who am I to inflict such a change in the minds of untold millions of people? It has been tried before, but with only limited success, so I will try a different approach. Hopefully, if my vision for the future can be met over the next five hundred years, I may well be the last Teacher to live on Earth.*

The observers talked excitedly among themselves about the success of the war game and its aftermath, the defensive force field that protected the Zellian spaceships, and how the attacking aircraft had proved completely impotent, despite the lack of retaliation from the two spacecraft. However, the question in the minds of many was that if the magnetic beams were so effective in annihilating the enemy ground forces, what weaponry was available to the Zellians to repel or destroy any future airborne attack against their ships?

Both Jon and Lana were aware of the doubts and fears in the minds of these representatives of the military and government of the United States, but for the moment, they silently agreed that the demonstration or war game had been effective in convincing all the observers on board of the power of destruction that the Zellian spacecraft possessed. It still left questions in the minds of General Clintock and the president. What other unknown weapons could be used to subdue any government's intent on pursuing a state of war against other nations? Furthermore, would Jon be ruthless enough to quell any military uprisings?

Davis Cooper thought that even though Jon seemed like a gentle-mannered person, there was a fist of iron underneath the velvet glove. He was also certain that this Teacher was like none other before him, and would be successful in bringing about a lasting peace on Earth. Whether Jon acted on his own with just one ship or called on the mother ship for reinforcements, he was determined to change the course of history on this planet Earth, and Davis would do everything in his power to persuade the other world leaders to go along with Jon's teachings.

Chapter Forty-Six

Completely unaware that his thoughts were being read by Jon and Lana, Davis Cooper continued to speculate on the many changes that could occur as a result of improved technology—food production would be more efficient, there'd be advances in the field of medicine, and new power sources would be discovered that wouldn't contaminate Earth's atmosphere. *Almost as good as the Holy Grail,* he thought with a derisory internal laugh.

At that moment, the sincerity of the president's thoughts convinced Jon that here was one political leader who would be a dependable ally in the crusade for peace among the nations, and as such, he should be rewarded and encouraged to embrace the advanced technology of the Zellians. But where to begin?

Ever since he and Lana had visited their island and inspected their future home, he had given some thought as to how they should replace the original diesel generator for their electrical power supply. One possibility was to remove a power unit from the ship, which was more than adequate to provide enough power for a small town, but while that would be quite easy to do, it wouldn't be of direct benefit to the scientists and technicians of Earth, or the president of the United States in particular.

With that thought in mind, drawing on the knowledge instilled in his brain during his indoctrination procedure on Captain Jara's craft, now his own, he reminded himself, he had requested the on-board computers to prepare all the information and specifications for a number of atomic-powered generating units. The first and

Chapter Forty-Six

easiest to manufacture would also be the smallest, for his own use on Buccaneer's Point, or for smaller installations or towns. But for installations for producing energy on a grand scale, such as was already used on Zel, these would be far more complex to build, but also far more efficient than any currently in use on Earth, and cause no harmful emissions into the atmosphere.

Lana was, of course, still in mental union with Jon, following his thoughts and approving the course of action to be taken in promoting the shared technology of the Zellians. 'All you have to do now, Jon,' she said aloud, 'is to put your proposals to the president and his secretary of state with regard to the production of the smaller unit for our own use. Hopefully that can be completed by the time we are ready to begin work on Buccaneer's Point. As for the bigger installations, it could take a few years before they are ready to generate enough power to satisfy all industrial and commercial needs, but once established, energy costs will be greatly reduced and be utterly reliable.'

'No doubt,' Jon replied with a grin, 'this will be an offer they can't refuse. Unlimited energy at a price industrialists and public alike will easily be able to afford, and once the scientists have got to grips with the new technology, I will then assist them to develop even smaller units for the automotive industry. That will have a dramatic effect on CO_2 emissions worldwide and solve many health problems also.'

At this point, Davis Cooper turned directly toward Jon and Lana, just in time to catch the end of their conversation, but not fully aware of its content. 'So, now that you've convinced everyone on board that even conventional warfare is outdated, and you have the means to enforce peace throughout the world using your advanced technology,' he added with a laugh, 'and this flying saucer is literally fireproof, all that remains now, Jon, is for us to return to Washington, report to Congress on what we have witnessed this day, and

Chapter Forty-Six

recommend total compliance with your plans for the future of Earth.'

George C. Lane was, as ever, following closely behind the president. *Another good man,* Jon thought soberly.

George smiled as he contemplated the reaction of the politicians in Congress and the House of Representatives when they received the verbal report they would be given first of all, but then assured that any dissent would soon be dispelled when the televised report was broadcast to the nation and the world at large. 'We will owe you a great deal of gratitude, Jon, for all that you have done in promoting peace on our planet, and for the promise of other benefits in the future, but what can we do for you and Lana in return?'

Before answering, Jon had two requests in mind, but chose to deal with the subject of the power plant for Buccaneer's Point and the proposed construction of the superefficient atomic energy power stations for the future. He explained that the technology involved was far in advance of what humankind had attained so far, but with the information and drawings provided by the on-board computers of the ship to guide them, the scientists and engineers would be able to manufacture and construct the smaller power plants with ease, while the rest of the project was likely to take several years to complete, which was a mere tick in time for a Zellian, of course.

Davis Cooper voiced the concerns of the dangers perceived by some scientists and politicians with regard to the use of atomic energy as a power source. Lana stressed, 'Their fears will be allayed when they know such power has been in use on Zel for countless millennia, and without incident of any kind. The same technology will be implemented here on your planet, Mr. President. With our guidance, the mistakes that have previously happened in different parts of your world will never happen again. The age of unlimited power will become a reality within a comparatively short period of time, possibly twenty years at most.'

Chapter Forty-Six

This was good news for the president and a number of the other politicians and military personnel who, by this time, had gathered round to listen to the conversation. Some already nodded their heads in approval at the mention of unlimited power and the benefits that that would bring to the people, the voters. One further question was forthcoming from General Clintock. 'And how do we dispose of all the waste products from all these power stations?' he asked. 'Do we have to bury it for a thousand years until it is no longer radioactive?'

'A good question, General,' Jon replied with a smile of assurance. 'What you regard as a dangerous waste material can be reprocessed or recycled and used in smaller power plants, and converted into energy sticks to power small machines such as trucks, automobiles, or even small ships. One stick provides enough energy to last for months.'

Such a concept was beyond the imagination of most of them, but because Jon was making these statements, they believed him. He was tempted to tell them that it was these same by-products of nuclear energy production on Zel that powered the spacecraft they were in at this moment, and once fully charged, they could fly for the lifetime of a Zellian, a thousand years or more, but he decided that his passengers would have even more difficulty accepting that information. With a smile of anticipation, he decided to put his next request to George C. Lane himself.

He began by placing his hand on George's shoulder in a friendly manner. Then, with a disarming smile, he said quietly, so as not to be overheard by everyone on the flight deck, 'George , as you are now aware, the Zellians have been observing the people of Earth for millions of years, and one aspect of your social structure is similar to that of the Zellians. I refer to your custom of marriage, which is similar to that of the Zellians, but whereas in your country, it's partly founded on some kind of religious belief, for the Zellian

Chapter Forty-Six

people, it is a commitment for two people to live in harmony for most of their lives, although not necessarily forever.'

George nodded in agreement. 'Forever is a long time, Jon.' He added with a grin, 'Even fifty years can seem like forever to us.' Waiting for Jon to continue, he wondered where the conversation was leading to, but was soon to find out.

Lana was, of course, aware of what Jon was going to ask the secretary of state to do for them in return for the services rendered to society in general, and the world in particular. *Being a telepath has its advantages in these situations,* she thought.

'As Lana and I intend to remain on Earth for the remainder of our lives,' Jon continued, 'we would like to conform to your customs as much as possible, and marriage, no doubt, would make us more socially acceptable to your religious leaders. Otherwise, I do believe that some of your people would regard our union as sinful, not a concept shared by the Zellians, I may add.'

'I don't think anyone on Earth has given a thought to your personal relationship, Jon. They accept that you're from a different planet and a different culture, end of story. But,' he grinned 'if you want to get married quickly, you can always make a quick trip over to Vegas to tie the knot.' While this conversation was meaningless to Lana, Jon was, of course, worldly wise, and the prospect of a quickie wedding was not what he had in mind. He wanted his marriage to Lana to be a dignified and moving experience for them both, an occasion for them to remember for the next five hundred years. 'That was not what I was thinking of, George,' he replied. 'I would like you to take charge and arrange our wedding for us, bearing in mind that Lana will become the wife of the ambassador of the Zellian people, and as such, the ceremony should be given the attention of the top government officials from as many countries as possible.' As he warmed to the subject of the forthcoming wedding, he continued, 'Expense is not a problem, and I give you a free hand

Chapter Forty-Six

with all the arrangements, assuming that you will accept the commission of such an important occasion, important to us, that is.'

For a moment, the secretary of state was about to take the hand of the Zellian ambassador as a token of sincerity, forgetting that, on previous occasions, this had not been acceptable, but he remembered instead to give the alternate salute of hand on heart as used on some ceremonial occasions in the recent past. One day he would find out why physical contact was not possible, unless Jon and Lana were to enlighten him at some time in the future.

'Jon,' he said, 'for you to ask me to get involved with your wedding arrangements is quite a surprise, but nevertheless, I am more than delighted to accept that responsibility.' Then, with a laugh, he continued, 'If expense is not a problem, then I can assure that the guest list for the occasion will be a lengthy one and will include heads of state and no doubt a few kings, queens, and princes of royal blood. Your debut to the politicians at the United Nations has assured the world that you are already a public figure, and after these war games today are broadcast worldwide, your face will be instantly recognisable to millions of people, as the ambassador of the planet Zel.'

'But don't forget,' Jon said reprovingly, 'that Lana is equally important to my mission on Earth, and as my wife, she, too, will attract the attention of the media. Besides, her beauty alone will make her one of the most photographed women on the planet and instantly recognisable wherever she goes.' George K. Lane was only too happy to concede that together Jon and Lana were of a striking, if alien appearance, and likely to turn the heads of the public wherever they chose to go. When their wedding was publicised, invitations to the ceremony would be greatly sought after by the great, the rich and the famous.

Jon smiled inwardly at the reference to his own alien appearance, but had to admit that apart from his exceptional physique, it was his mass of silver, glowing hair that set him apart from everyone else.

Chapter Forty-Six

By comparison, Lana, who was a true alien, had dark hair similar to many of the women around her, but it was the perfection of her slim figure, her height, and her facial beauty that set her apart and made her the perfect partner for the ambassador of the Zellians.

Having happily accepted the role of organiser of what was likely to be the wedding of the century, the secretary of state then enquired, 'How much time do I have to complete all the arrangements, Jon? Normally a ceremony such as you envisage would take months of preparation.'

Jon was relieved that he would not have to be involved in the wedding arrangements. *I provide the finances, a few millions of dollars, no doubt,* Jon thought, then smiled as he scrutinised George's face. He said, 'We leave everything to you, George. Do whatever you deem necessary to ensure that the wedding ceremony will be an occasion for us, and the public to remember, but,' he added with his usual smile, 'we have another project to complete before our big day, so you can take three or four months to ensure that all the preparations are completed. When everything is finalised, just say the word, and we will be ready.'

While they had been engrossed in their conversation, Lana, in the meanwhile, had already set course for the flight back to Washington. As there was no sensation of acceleration or speed within the spacecraft, many of the people on board, George C. Lane included, were unaware that they had departed the scene of the war games, which was now a long valley with a surface as smooth and level as a lake, and an area to be used for something quite different from its original purpose, no doubt.

'And what is this project to be Jon?' George enquired. 'Not another demonstration to deter the warmongers, I trust?'

Smiling calmly, Jon replied. 'Far from it, George, with the help of a very good friend, Lana and I have found the perfect haven to live and settle down to our life together on Earth.' He then went on to describe their search for a secluded island in the Caribbean, a place that would remind them of the planet Zel, with lush green forests, open meadows with a mountainous background, and that their search was now completed. Buccaneer's Point was that perfect place, meeting all the requirements specified.

By the time he had answered the many questions put to him by the secretary of state regarding this idyllic retreat from the public eye, the president had come over to join them, and Lana was announcing their arrival over Washington, which was yet another surprise for the passengers at the short duration of the flight. *Supersonic speeds for civil aircraft are not, as yet, the norm, but given time*, Jon thought, as he read the minds of some of the civilian passengers, *the aviation industry will be transformed. Flying at twice the speed of sound will no longer be the reserve of military aircraft.*

While all the observers, military and civilians alike, gathered around the viewports, fascinated by the smooth descent to the pristine green lawns of the White House, Lana smiled as she concentrated on making the landing as gentle as possible. She succeeded to such a degree that it was only when she announced, 'You're home, Mr. President,' did Davis Cooper realise that this historic day was over. It had been a flight of thousands of miles, and he had witnessed the destruction of a mock enemy force, had survived a ferocious airborne attack at the hands of one of America's top fighter aircraft squadrons and now was able float like thistledown onto his own backyard. *What a day, what a day*, he reminded himself.

After thanking Lana and Jon for such an interesting day, Davis Cooper and George K. Lane were the first to disembark, followed in order of seniority by the military and government officials. As they were strolling across the lawns, the president said, in a undertone so as not to be heard by those behind them, 'I've been thinking, George; after what we've seen today, and in view of the fact that our Zellian ambassador has effectively removed the threat of nuclear

Chapter Forty-Six

war against this and any other countries, I think he deserves some kind of recognition, an award of some kind. What do you think? Any ideas?'

After a moment's hesitancy, the secretary of state replied, 'Well, Mr. President, we can't present him with the Nobel Peace Prize, that's out of our jurisdiction, and we can't give him the Congressional Medal of Honour, that's purely a military award, but I do agree that Jon does deserve some kind of formal recognition.' Both men stopped simultaneously as they pondered the question for a moment. 'How about a Presidential Peace Medal and honorary citizenship of the United States,' George declared enthusiastically. 'I think Congress would go along with that, Mr. President.'

At that moment, they both turned and looked back at the spaceship, which was just in the process of taking off. 'Yes, I think that such an award would be appropriate, and one that would be acceptable to the ambassador, George," Davis Cooper declared. Without waiting for the second spaceship to land, he turned and entered the White House, well satisfied with the day's events and the decision to award Jon for his services to the nation, and to the world. He wondered, *Which will be more appreciated, the medal, or the honorary citizenship, or both?*

Chapter Forty-Seven

When Jon and Lana returned to Kingston and resumed their normal docking position high above the island, their first attempt to contact Jacob Bernstein was not successful. First of all, they tried to use the telephone link, and although the phone was still live, there was no answer, suggesting that Jacob was simply not available at that time. So, they determined to spend a few days of relaxation back at their original island retreat, but to attempt to get in touch with Jacob by phoning occasionally on the off chance of catching him in. After several days, they were rewarded for their perseverance by the sound of Miranda's voice. 'This is Mr. Bernstein's assistant, can I help you?' she asked in a matter-of-fact tone.

'Well, this is a pleasant surprise to hear your voice, Miranda,' Jon replied with a smile on his face. 'I take it that you have settled down in your role as protection officer for Jacob and that you are both well?'

With a giggle, the minder assured Jon that she had indeed adapted to the task. 'Jacob is very happy with the level of protection he now enjoys,' she said, adding with a suggestive laugh, 'I never leave his side, night or day.'

Lana, who had been listening to the conversation, simply raised her eyebrows, pouting her lips as she commented quietly, 'I can well believe that Jacob is now more contented than he has ever been. More money than he has ever had in his life, and now with a beautiful woman by his side, night and day.' While she didn't giggle

Chapter Forty-Seven

as Miranda had done, she was secretly delighted that Jacob appeared to have found a soul mate.

Mentally agreeing with Lana's observation, Jon continued his conversation with Miranda, enquiring after Jacob's whereabouts. 'At this moment, he is on his computer, making various enquiries relating to the purchase of your island, Jon,' she replied. 'And yesterday, he was in contact with some American and European diamond merchants with a view to travelling overseas in order to procure the best sale price for the merchandise.' She added in a slightly awestruck tone of voice, 'I can appreciate the beauty of the gems, any woman would, but as to their value, Jacob is really excited at the prospect of showing them to his professional counterparts.' She then continued. 'He keeps telling me that the diamonds he has already sold on your behalf and also the latest collection of stones are unique, or out of this world as he keeps saying.'

Lana and Jon simply exchanged smiles at that comment, but this was not the time to elaborate on the true origin of the diamonds. *Not so much out of this world,* thought Jon, *not even this universe, but from a different galaxy many light-years in distance away. Perhaps I will let Jacob into the secret one day, but not yet,* he decided. In the meanwhile, at the mention of the purchase of the island, he then focussed on that matter, it being the most important item in their minds. They knew that Jacob could be relied upon to negotiate an appropriate price for the sale of the gems, and in doing so, secure not only the necessary funding for the purchase of the island, but to rebuild the house and provide the finances for their wedding and a lifestyle suitable for the Zellian ambassador and his wife.

At that moment, Miranda interrupted his thoughts by announcing, 'Oh, here's Jacob now. I'll hand you over to him, Jon.'

A moment later, Jacob's voice was heard booming down the phone. 'Good to hear from you again, Jon. I trust that your trip to the States had a successful conclusion?' Without waiting for a reply, he continued excitedly, 'I can report good news on all fronts regarding

Chapter Forty-Seven

negotiations for the island of Buccaneer's Point, and the same applies to the sale of the diamonds.' He could be heard taking a deep breath before continuing unabated. 'But first, the diamonds. I have assured my contacts overseas that this last collection of gems that you have commissioned me to sell are far and away the biggest and least flawless stones that they are ever likely to see in their lives. On closer examination, I've come to the conclusion that each diamond is even more valuable than the Cullinan, and at the last estimate, that was worth sixteen million dollars. At the moment, Jon, I've got six stones of immense value sitting in my safe. At a conservative estimate, because of their size, quality, and rarity value, two white, two blue and two pink, if anyone is rich enough to buy them as a set, they can expect to pay a reserve price of one hundred million dollars.'

The sums of money mentioned were almost incomprehensible to Jon. In his previous life, as an air traffic controller, even one million pounds or dollars would have been more than he would have earned in a lifetime, and now, here was Jacob talking about one hundred million dollars for the sale of a few chunks of carbon from some far-flung planet in a strange galaxy.

Lana was, of course, aware of his thoughts at that moment, but the enormity of the sums of money mentioned had little meaning for her, although Jon smiled at the recollection of Lana's ability to enjoy spending money on her last shopping expedition in Kingston.

Fortunately, as the conversation had been somewhat one sided up to this point, by the time that Jacob got round to asking Jon for any comment regarding the sale of the diamonds, Jon had regained his composure, and was prepared to follow on with his enquiries about Buccaneer's Point. 'From the sound of things, Jacob, I take it that we will have no difficulty in paying the final price for our island, and refurbishing it as well?'

'No difficulty whatsoever, Jon,' was the reply. 'The original owner may have appreciated the beauty of the island, but his family

Chapter Forty-Seven

in London were only interested in a quick sale to get their hands on the money.' Jacob then continued by pointing out that there had not been a great deal of interest from the public when the private island had come on the market. 'It's a pretty remote area of the Caribbean and well off the normal tourist routes. In addition, The Point itself dominates the island, and the coastline is quite forbidding, all those rocks and high cliffs, and as you saw on your first inspection, there's only one entrance to the lagoon, and that's practically invisible from the sea. Although, it has to be said that once you are ashore, the beach, the grasslands, and the jungle make it an idyllic place, a little piece of heaven, I would say.'

'And did you manage to finalise the price of the sale, Jacob?' Jon asked with a feeling of apprehension in his mind. 'I know that it probably wouldn't appeal to many buyers, because from the sea, it does tend to look somewhat forbidding, just a long, wedge-shaped island with a one-thousand-foot mountain at one end and high cliffs everywhere else. It's only possible to realise the beauty of the island when you have passed through the entrance to the lagoon, only then can the house in that glorious setting with the mountain and the jungle in the backdrop really impress a prospective buyer, unless you do a complete survey by helicopter as we did.'

'Again, good news, Jon,' Jacob replied with a laugh. 'As there is no agricultural potential on the island, and the original estate covers more than a thousand acres of meadowland and jungle, I was able to convince the London owners that the price you were prepared to pay was more than reasonable for what was on offer.' He nodded as though in agreement with his own statement, then continued. 'I simply pointed out that the dwelling place itself had fallen into a state of disrepair after fifty years of neglect, and that it would be a difficult and expensive undertaking to restore it to a habitable condition.'

He laughed in amusement as he added, 'Perhaps I did exaggerate a little about the house, but I still believe that it will need at the very least a million dollars to repair and refurbish it. That is money you can well afford, if you don't mind me saying so, Jon, so for the princely sum of $35 million, you are now the owners of Buccaneer's Point, once the papers are all signed.'

'Well, I have to agree that that is all good news, especially the sale price,' exclaimed Jon, 'but I have some other issues to raise with you, which will require a more lengthy discussion, so if you don't mind, Jacob, Lana and I would like to drop in on you as soon as possible or when convenient.'

'No time like the present,' was the instant reply from Jacob. 'Miranda is going to get used to your comings and goings before long, I'm sure,' he added with a chuckle. 'We're standing by for you as of now.'

Within minutes, Jon and Lana teleported into the middle of what had been the main display area of the shop, which was now stripped of all the goods and furniture, and ready for Jacob to vacate the premises. No sooner than they had materialised, Jacob stepped forward to embrace his friends with his usual greeting of pleasure. 'Ah moie, ah moie! It is so good to see you both again.' For the next hour, the conversation alternated between the sale of the jewels and the purchase of the island, and in conclusion, Jacob decided that he would be leaving Kingston within the next few days with the intention of meeting a syndicate in Amsterdam, a group with a firm interest in what had been described to them as a collection like no other. 'As I said earlier, Jon, to encourage other bidders at the auction, we will begin at a very reasonable price of one million dollars for each individual stone, but I fully expect to get a much higher price than that,' adding with a laugh of delight at the prospect of being at the centre of a bidding frenzy. 'I rather think we are going to see a few records broken during this sale, and you can rest assured that you will end up a very wealthy man, rich enough to buy two islands such as Buccaneer's Point.'

Chapter Forty-Seven

'So far, so good, Jacob,' Jon said, placing his arm around Lana's shoulder. 'And what progress has been made regarding the procurement of the services of an architect to oversee the renovation and building project?' As he put this question, he was aware of the tension in Lana's body, as well as her mind, as they both waited for some reassurance that their future home would indeed be refurbished under the supervision of the best architect in the Caribbean.

'I have everything under control, Jon,' Jacob exclaimed enthusiastically. 'I was able to persuade one of the most reputable men in the business to undertake this commission, at a price, of course, and he, in turn, will be responsible for employing the necessary craftsmen to complete the project.' Jon didn't offer any comment at that moment. He could read the thoughts in his friend's mind, the pleasure that he was helping Jon and Lana to realise their dream, although with some reservations regarding the cost.

Jacob continued excitedly, 'The architect is a man named McDonald, Howard McDonald,' he added with a laugh of merriment. 'As you may gather from the name, he is not Jewish. But a fine man nevertheless, and more to the point, he has been responsible for the design of some of the most prestigious homes in this region of the world. You may safely leave the entire project to him, everything from the survey, the design, hiring the local workforce, the materials and all the supplies for the duration of the build.'

'And when will I meet this Mr. McDonald?' Jon enquired. 'He sounds as though he must be a very efficient administrator as well as architect.'

'The very best,' Jacob agreed with a grin, 'and you will find that he has a wonderful personality as well. I'm sure that you will take to him like a brother. Ah moie, ah moie! I can give him no better recommendation than that.'

Chapter Forty-Seven

Jon laughed as he agreed. 'Yes, he seems to come with a pretty good pedigree, and from what you say, I believe he could be the man to get this building project on the move fairly quickly.'

Out of curiosity, Lana enquired, 'Is Mr. McDonald a native of this country or of some other nationality, and how soon will he be able to inspect the house on Buccaneer's Point with a view to starting the reconstruction and refurbishing?' Smiling at Lana's excitement about the events for the future, understandable for an alien who was about to take up residence on a strange planet many light-years from her own, Jacob nevertheless tried to answer all her questions.

'Howard McDonald is truly a native of this country,' he answered. 'He was born and bred in Jamaica, although he was educated at one of the top universities in the States, and with a name like McDonald, you might suspect that somewhere in his ancestry lurks a trace of Scottish blood.' Jacob added with a humorous smile, 'Not that you would guess that from his appearance, apart from being bigger than most Jamaicans, he is still quite dark with the usual curly hair. As for when he will be able to assess the building project,' he continued, 'I suggest that I contact him today and arrange for you all to give Buccaneer's Point a visit. Then you can outline your vision of what you would like your new home to be designed like, possibly after the colonial style as the original owner had envisaged, but with a more modern touch, perhaps?'

At the suggestion of designing their new home, Jon could already read Lana's kaleidoscopic thoughts regarding the alterations to the interior of the building, the décor, and furnishings, even the layout of the gardens surrounding the house. Essentially, the building would retain much of its old colonial outward appearance, but inside would be redesigned to mirror Lana's old home back on Zel. Ultra-modern with generous use of marble on all the floors, and where interior walls were removed to create the impression of space, all supporting pillars would also be of marble. It was too early to decide on how to furnish their new home, but Jon decided

Chapter Forty-Seven

ruefully that Lana would undoubtedly make all the decisions in that department.

'Howard has assured me that he will hold himself available should you want to visit Buccaneer's Point within the next day or so,' Jacob said. 'He has his own helicopter and can arrange to meet you on the island, if you wish to use your own transport.' He grinned as he added, 'I didn't tell him that you had your own flying saucer, so that will be a surprise, I've no doubt.'

'We'll try not to give Howard McDonald too many surprises, Jacob,' Jon replied, 'especially when it comes to our requirements for the house and its surroundings, although one thing I've already decided against is a landing strip for light aircraft. Too intrusive and a temptation for a casual flyer to drop in. A helicopter landing pad would, I feel, be more appropriate for the island.'

'I think you're probably right about that decision, Jon,' Jacob agreed. 'After all, in that remote location, you're not likely to be inundated with visitors, are you?'

'Not unless they're invited,' Jon replied, 'as they will be on the odd occasion, as part of my duties as ambassador, but that is a long way off from the moment. Mr McDonald will have much work to do to transform the old house into a dwelling fit for the ambassador of Zel and his wife.'

As ever, Lana had been following Jon's train of thought and was happy in the knowledge that she would be given virtually a free hand in the specification for the interior decor and furnishings of their new home. *I may never go back to Zel,* she thought, *but as far as possible, we can recreate the same environment on Buccaneer's Point, and make it a true home away from home.*

'As you intend to jet off to Europe within the next few days, Jacob,' Jon said thoughtfully, 'if you inform Mr. McDonald that we will meet him on Buccaneer's Point in two days' time, that will give us time to envisage the changes we would like to bring about and

Chapter Forty-Seven

give the architect some definite ideas to work on. One extra item is the power plant for the electrical supply. I was assured that a unit would be manufactured and ready for installation by the time the house is ready for occupation; hopefully, some time in three or four months' time.'

'I think Howard may be able to give you a surprise on that score, Jon,' Jacob retorted. 'Knowing how he works on a project, he will flood the site with labour, promising the workers a handsome bonus to finish the project early, so if you look at a time scale of two months, that could prove realistic for the build, although the finishing could take a little longer, since it usually does. But it's not as though you will be homeless in the meantime; you still have your spacecraft to live in.'

'Quite so, Jacob,' Jon replied. 'I have also decided to wait for a period of two months before returning to Washington to get a report from the president's office regarding the outcome of the war games and the reaction from the various governments around the world.' He then gave a smile of pure pleasure. 'I'm also hoping that George K. Lane will have completed all the arrangements for our wedding by that time.'

'And I'm hoping that Captain Jara and Mort can get a message back to Zel to inform my father of our impending marriage,' Lana said emotionally. 'I would so like him to be with us on that day, but,' she added wistfully, 'for a commander to travel the width of several galaxies for a wedding is unheard of, so I can only hope.'

Jon placed his arms tightly around her to comfort her. He said, 'If it's possible for your father to come, Lana, Jara will let us know, but in the meanwhile . . . .' He turned to include Jacob and Miranda in his scrutiny, 'Let us all be happy for our immediate futures.'

Chapter Forty-Eight

As arranged, it was two days later that the spacecraft arrived over the island of Buccaneer's Point. From their vantage point several thousands of feet above the original dwelling place, Jon and Lana could clearly see a helicopter close to the old house; undoubtedly it was the architect waiting for them to appear to keep the rendezvous. 'Take us down, Lana,' Jon said with a smile. 'We won't keep Mr McDonald waiting any longer.'

Although the architect had been expecting them to arrive at this time, his first sight of a flying saucer descending majestically and silently toward him was breath-taking, and as it sank lower and lower, its sheer size filled him with wonder. *How can a craft weighing presumably thousands of tons be suspended in the air without any apparent power source, silently floating down as gently as thistledown?* When the craft came to rest a short distance from the helicopter, he realized he had been holding his breath until the moment of touchdown. Only when the hatchway and a ramp appeared in the side of the spaceship was he able to breathe normally again.

With Lana walking beside him, Jon approached McDonald with his hand raised in salutation, but he avoided the possibility of an attempted handshake as always. 'Good morning, Mr McDonald,' he said quietly. 'I've heard a lot about you from our mutual friend, Jacob. He speaks very highly of you, both as a person and your abilities as an architect, and as you have presumably had a quick look at the house already,' he gestured toward the once elegant mansion nearby, 'you may already have conceived some ideas as regards what work may be required to restore and further improve the building.' He added with a touch of humour, 'Subject to Lana's inspiration and approval.'

Howard McDonald had already been briefed by Jacob Bernstein as to what to expect when he finally met his new clients, the ambassador of Zel and his wife-to-be, Lana, but nevertheless, it was still a surprise to meet them face to face for the first time. Naturally, as a man, his eyes were turned to Lana and her exceptionally tall and perfect figure, her exquisite features and alien beauty, and although he was by no means a romantic, he could see that here was a woman who would command the adoration of most men and the envy of all women.

Reluctantly, he tore his gaze away to concentrate on the ambassador, who as now was only a few paces away, his right hand raised in greeting rather than extended to shake hands. *Ah, well,* he conceded, *different people, different customs.* As he quickly appraised his alien client, he noticed the physical appearance of Jon. Exceptionally tall, well over six feet, and obviously a muscular build, and his face of almost angelic appearance emphasised by a halo of glowing silver hair, rather like a saintly prophet of old.

Now here's a man who will command respect wherever he goes, with or without the title of Ambassador of Zel, and from what Jacob has told me, this couple are fabulously wealthy and know what they want from this project. Perfection in all things, and I'm just the man to deliver on that score

Unknown to Howard McDonald, Jon and Lana were scanning his thoughts and appraising him. With a smile of approval, they acknowledged that Jacob had provided an architect for them worthy of his name and trustworthy, a man they could have confidence in, an administrator who would see the project through to its conclusion and to their full satisfaction. The fact that he was black and local to the Caribbean implied that employing the labour force

Chapter Forty-Eight

required would not be a problem. No doubt he was well acquainted with all the kinds of craftsmen who would have to be hired and brought to the island to begin the work within the next few days.

Knowing that a good working relationship was essential to a project likely to last two or three months at least, Jon resolved to put his architect at ease by introducing himself not as ambassador, but as Jon, and suggested that first names be used at all times, other than on any formal occasions that might arise at a later date. This was an arrangement that McDonald was only too happy to accept.

'In which case, Jon,' he said with an infectious laugh, 'let me show you around the house and point out the different features worth retaining, and if you and Lana have any comments to make regarding changes in design and materials to be used, I will take note, of course.' Although it was now the hottest part of the day, the thick walls of the old building helped to retain a fair degree of coolness, and as they went from room to room, Howard had his notebook in hand, listening to Lana's ideas of what she wanted incorporated into the new interior of her future home. *Attention to detail is essential to the satisfaction of my clients,* McDonald thought as he continued with the tour of the building, still giving his professional advice regarding the practicalities involved in removing some walls and creating a more spacious interior. Extensive use of marble for the floors and supporting pillars or columns were required. 'No problem,' was a phrase that he repeated from time to time, although he was aware that everything about the build would have to be designed and planned for at an early stage of the reconstruction to allow for delivery of materials.

Other than that, with the labour force that he would recruit, Howard assured them that two or three months would finish the main building work to be done, leaving only cosmetic work to be completed. 'You'll be surprised how much work can be done with a well-organised workforce, Jon,' he said with a grin, 'especially with the promise of a big bonus at the end of it all.'

Chapter Forty-Eight

McDonald went on to explain that he would employ some twenty or so craftsmen directly from Jamaica itself. 'They are all people who have been employed in the luxury building industry on the island, and all are acquainted with the standard of workmanship required, so there will be no concerns in that respect. They will be working six days a week, with time off for church on Sunday,' he said with mock reverence.

'And where will you accommodate these twenty or so workers?' Lana enquired, not liking the thought of her house being used as a barracks by the workforce.

Guessing what was on her mind, Howard hastened to assure her that this was a situation that had occurred frequently in the past, a building project in a location far from home and with no accommodation on site, a problem that had been easily overcome by the expedience of buying an old sailing vessel, a schooner, and using that to transport the workforce and provide them with facilities to live and sleep, an arrangement that had proved hugely popular for the men involved.

'The lagoon here will ensure that all on board will have a tranquil anchorage for the duration of their stay,' Howard said with some satisfaction. 'And it will give the workers their own space when not at work; a happy worker is a productive worker, Lana, mark my words.'

By this time, their tour of the house was complete, and it was Jon's suggestion that they have a quick look at the outbuilding where the old diesel generator had been sighted, with a view to establishing whether it would be suitable for the installation of the new power plant, albeit it would not be available for another two months. When McDonald was informed of their purpose for visiting the outbuilding, he voiced his concern at the lack of an electrical supply, but suggested that he could ship in a replacement generator before the work was begun. 'Just another delay, unfortunately,' he added.

Chapter Forty-Eight

Having already given some thought to such a possibility happening, and the outbuilding being suitable for the installation he had in mind, a temporary one, Jon said, 'No need to worry, Howard, I can utilise a power unit from the ship that will give you all the power you need for your tools and equipment. In fact, I can have it ready to transfer to the outbuilding tomorrow morning, connect it to the house, and test it before the heat of the day sets in.'

'Won't you need a few men to assist you with this unit you talk of, Jon?' Howard enquired. 'How heavy is it?'

Jon smiled. 'I suppose it would be quite heavy if you were to try to lift it physically, but that won't be necessary, Howard, just you wait and see.' As they had completed the tour of the house itself, Jon led the way to the point where the helicopter was parked and indicated to Howard the obsolete diesel generator still lying where it had been left close to the edge of the lagoon. 'That's the original power plant, which I removed on my first visit to the island. To facilitate loading it into a boat to get rid of it, I dumped it close to the shoreline for convenience.'

Howard looked askance at the heavy piece of machinery. 'How did you manage to move it on your own, Jon? Did you lift it with a block and tackle and then use some kind of truck to bring it this far?'

With an amused smile, Jon shook his head in firm denial, 'No, my friend, there is another way. As I said before, wait and see.' Then turning toward the lagoon and the cast-off generator, he indicated that Howard and Lana should follow him. He walked to a point quite close to the old piece of machinery then stopped.

Without any further explanation or warning, he stood silently looking at the object of their attention, and for a fleeting moment, mentally communed with Lana. *This demonstration will undoubtedly be a surprise to our architect, but it will also convince him that nothing will be impossible when it comes to any heavy lifting that may need to be done during the construction and alterations to the house.*

Chapter Forty-Eight

Howard, in the meantime, was also gazing at the old generator and wondering why Jon seemed so intent on this piece of junk. Then not daring to believe his eyes, he noticed an almost imperceptible movement of the object as it lifted slowly off the ground, only a few inches at first, allowing him to see the grass underneath. Then, as he watched in amazement, it rapidly rose higher, knee high at first, then shoulder height, then well above their heads until he had to crane his head backwards to keep it in view.

To complete the demonstration, Jon took a few paces toward the edge of the shore, taking the piece of machinery with him as he used his telekinetic power, then finally, he lowered the generator gently until it was in a position where it could be easily loaded into a boat for further transportation when the time came.

Howard had watched this feat of telekinesis without a word, mouth agape and his eyes popping out of his head, and it was only when the demonstration concluded that he could bring himself to speak. 'Wow.' he exclaimed. 'That was some trick, or was it magic or voodoo perhaps?'

'No,' Jon replied with a smile of satisfaction, 'control of the mind over matter, a science that some of your people are aware exists in theory, but that none of you has mastered.' Pausing for a moment, he added, 'Although there is evidence to support a suspicion that certain cultures in the past were capable of telekinesis, and the success of some building projects in the ancient world were attributed to the use of that science, but that is another matter. I only demonstrated my own ability to assure you that, should the need arise, I will be available to assist you with any heavy lifting during the building project.'

Still unable to believe what he had seen, Howard commented, 'Some of my boys are skilled craftsmen, but if they see you performing tricks like that, Jon, they will put it down to some kind of voodoo magic. Basically, they are simple people who are good with their hands, but have no knowledge of science.' He grinned. 'The

Chapter Forty-Eight

only kind of tele they are familiar with is the kind you sit in front of for entertainment!'

'I can well believe it,' Jon replied with a laugh. 'So, break it to them gently at some point that the ambassador, or the big boss, has some magical power; then they won't be too surprised, and hopefully we won't scare them off.'

'And they ain't got nowhere to run,' Howard observed, lapsing into the patois he used when dealing with his workforce. 'But it's likely to be some time before the real construction begins, a week or two at least. As always, it's the preparation and planning that comes first, but from what I already know of your requirements, I can now go back to my office in Jamaica, start preparing the drawings, the work schedules, and recruit the workforce ready to start the preliminary work within two or three days. After that, it will be all go until the project is complete.'

'But don't forget that they'll need time off for church on Sundays,' Jon reminded him with a laugh.

On that genial note, all three of them strolled over to the helicopter in readiness for Howard to return to his main office in Jamaica. He piloted his own aircraft, so there had been no other witnesses to the lifting demonstration. 'I'll be back as I said, Jon, in two or three days' time,' Howard commented, 'and the schooner with all the men on board should be here shortly after that. In the meanwhile, do you intend to remain here on the island for the next month or so?'

Looking at Lana for confirmation and sensing her agreement, Jon nodded to confirm that unless any other situation were to develop, they would indeed remain on Buccaneer's Point until it was time for them to return to Washington for their wedding, an event that they were both looking forward to. Although for Lana, in particular, two months seemed a long time, even for a Zellian. As there was little more to discuss at this time, Howard climbed into

Chapter Forty-Eight

the helicopter and assured them that he would begin organising the building project and all the supervision it would entail the moment he got back to his office. With a casual wave to his clients, the craft lifted off noisily and within minutes was only a speck in the sky, skimming over the blue seas of the Caribbean.

Chapter Forty-Nine

For three full glorious days, Jon and Lana enjoyed the peace and tranquillity of the island of Buccaneer's Point, sometimes walking along the shoreline of the lagoon hand in hand, scuffing the sand with their feet, remembering that sand between the toes sensation they had so enjoyed on the first island they had experienced in the Caribbean. Alternately, they paddled along in the shallows, splashing each other and laughing like children at play. In the afternoons when the sun was high and the beach proved to be too hot for comfort, they took advantage of the shade provided by the luxuriant jungle, only a short walk from their future home. After the departure of their architect, they had only spent a short time, possibly an hour in the building, but it was so different from what they envisaged for the home of their dreams, it was mutually agreed that they would wait until the first stages of the reconstruction were complete before accompanying McDonald on any future inspections. In the meanwhile, they had the choice for the next few days, the shore of the lagoon when it was cool or the jungle with its wildlife, of which there was an abundance, or as a complete contrast, walking along the length of the island, keeping to the grassland, which was knee deep and emitted the smell of crushed grasses. 'An aroma that reminds me of my childhood days on Zel,' Lana stated wistfully.

Their brief period of isolation was over all too soon as Howard McDonald arrived on the afternoon of the third day, the noise of the helicopter shattering the tranquillity of the island. Not for the first time Lana thought, *How can people enjoy travelling in these primitive conveyances?*

Chapter Forty-Nine

Jon merely smiled as he assured her, *Because they have never known anything different, Lana, but given time, perhaps we can improve their technology to a point that you won't have to rely on our own spacecraft.* He reminded her of the alternative, *Or instead, using our ability to teleport.*

Lana smiled at that suggestion, still unsure of what she was capable of in that respect.

As the helicopter settled to the ground and the blades of the rotor came to a standstill, Mc Donald clambered out of the cockpit, patting a large briefcase. With a cheerful, 'Hello, I'm back again,' he strode toward his hosts with a broad grin on his face. 'With a bit of luck, the boat and the building squad should be arriving sometime tomorrow,' he said amiably. 'But in the meantime, I've got all the drawings required for the project, and subject to the approval of the owners to begin the work, we can get started straight away. No need for planning permission from any local authority.' His light hearted and jocular mood must have been infectious, as Jon and Lana shared his laughter at the thought of asking permission to undertake the transformation of the old house, the ambassadorial residence on the island of Buccaneer's Point.

Little time was wasted in further conversation as the first thing to establish was where Howard would live and sleep during his stay on the island. 'Would you prefer to remain on the schooner with your workforce, Howard, or does the thought of living on board our craft appeal to you instead?' Jon enquired. 'I'm sure you will find it somewhat more luxurious, not to mention less cramped than a small ship shared with at least twenty or so other men.'

Howard's response was immediate. The offer to go aboard a flying saucer was not something to be refused, and the prospect of actually living on one for several weeks was undreamt of. Jon was already reading the architect's mind, knowing that his curiosity had already determined his answer to the invitation.

Chapter Forty-Nine

'You're right, Jon,' Howard replied with a chuckle, 'to share the crews' accommodation is something I've had to do on the odd occasion in the past, and yes, it can be very cramped, despite many of them preferring to sleep out on deck.' He paused for a moment as he looked over in the direction of the spacecraft parked a short distance away, its size even more obvious at ground level. 'This will be something for me to recount to all my friends and future clients,' he said, 'how I lived on a spaceship with the ambassador of a distant planet.' Then shaking head as though in sorrow, he said, 'They'll never believe me.'

'Then you'd better put your camera to good use, Howard,' Jon retorted with a laugh. 'Seeing is believing, is it not.' With the question of where their architect would live during his stay with them resolved, Jon and Lana made their way over to their craft with Howard following close behind, his long flight from Jamaica and the heat of the day forgotten as the ramp of the space vessel loomed closer. Moments later, all three of them were aboard, and the door silently closed behind them, insulating them from the heat outside and the noises of the wildlife emanating from the jungle.

It was several long minutes before Howard could bring himself to speak. He simply dropped his briefcase to the deck and slowly turned around full circle, his professional eye taking in as much detail of the flight deck and control consoles as possible. He did not understand any of it, but he was appreciative of the advanced technology of this Zellian ship. Neither Jon nor Lana interrupted his train of thought, which they could see so clearly, giving their guest time to come to terms with being surrounded by this alien environment. In due course, the first words he uttered were brief and to the point, 'Big, isn't it?'

'And this is only the flight deck,' Lana said quietly, impressed by the architect's response. *A man of few words on this occasion,* she confided mentally with Jon. Then beckoning Howard to follow, she said, 'And now we will show you to your quarters, where we hope

Chapter Forty-Nine

you will be comfortable for the duration of your stay.' Leading the way through to the living quarters and into the sleeping cabin area, she activated the door into the room selected for their guest, then standing aside, she ushered Howard into his personal accommodation. It prompted him to again exclaim, 'Big, isn't it.' Jon and Lana's response to this understatement was quiet laughter.

'Well, you won't be as cramped as you would have been on the schooner,' Jon said with a smile, 'and you'll have some privacy as well.'

'Talking of privacy,' Lana exclaimed, 'I'll leave Jon to show you around your quarters, Howard, and to explain how to operate the various facilities available, some of which are unlike those you are accustomed to.' Noting the look of curiosity on Howard's face, she added, 'Like using a shower without water.' She smiled at his mental response to that statement.

For the next half hour, Jon acquainted his guest with the hygiene amenities in his cabin, many of which were hidden from view, even the bed, and electronically controlled by a small computer. When Howard declared himself satisfied with his ability to use all of the equipment, Jon suggested that he might like to freshen up after his long flight during the heat of the day, and to then join Lana and himself on the flight deck. 'We can then show you around the ship, after which it will then be time to discuss dinner.'

Leaving the architect to his own devises, Jon rejoined Lana on the flight deck, and after embracing her fondly for a moment, he said, 'Our own privacy may be slightly curtailed while we have a guest on board; unless, of course, we retire to our own quarters from time to time.'

With a giggle of delight, Lana answered, 'We may have to do that quite often, my love.' What passed through Jon's mind at that moment made Lana giggle even more.

Chapter Forty-Nine

Jon had left one of the viewports wide open to take full advantage of the scene outside. The helicopter was a short distance away, and beyond that, the area of grassland adjoining the beach and lagoon, which at that moment was calm and tranquil, something that was likely to change after the morrow with the expected arrival of the schooner and the twenty or so builders and crewmembers. 'I can see that over the next few weeks we will be exploring every inch of our island, Lana,' Jon said dryly, 'not only to satisfy our curiosity about what we own and anything interesting that we may find, but to be truly alone again.' Then with a grin of amusement, he added, 'We can even begin practicing your teleporting skills, moving around the island in short hops to begin with, then the ultimate challenge, to the top of The Point.' Noting the look of doubt on Lana's face, he reminded her, 'It's only one thousand feet in height, whereas you have frequently teleported from the ship down to ground level, and that has been twenty thousand feet, in some cases.'

'You're right as always, Jon,' she replied quietly. 'I don't know why I'm being so silly. Lack of confidence, and yet, I know that it might become an essential ability at some time in the future.' Then brightening up with a laugh, she continued, 'It could be fun to try different locations as we teleport. I assure you that, within a week, we'll be up there on the Peak, looking down on our very own island, without having to climb up. We will teleport together, and after that, we will try something much more ambitious.'

At that moment, as though to remind them that having a guest meant a certain loss of privacy, Howard McDonald rejoined them on the flight deck. Noticing the open viewport, he went over to gaze out at the early evening tropical sky, which, even as he watched, quickly changed colour, rapidly going darker as the sun dipped below the horizon. Although he was a native of the Caribbean, he never ceased to be impressed by this display of Mother Nature's beauty. When Jon and Lana came over to the window to share this moment, he

Chapter Forty-Nine

remained motionless, oblivious to their presence until the last vestiges of light had gone and the tropical night was all around them, unrelieved by any lights of civilisation. Only then, with a sigh, did he turn away.

'Although I've lived most of my life in this part of the world,' he said, 'this is my first experience of such solitude. Buccaneer's Point is a small island in comparison to Jamaica and is way off the usual tourist routes, miles from the nearest inhabited country, and as such, you're unlikely to get many uninvited visitors.' As Howard settled himself comfortably in one of the seats on the flight deck, he continued, 'But I already begin to share your dream and vision of what life will be like living in your beautiful home in this remote location, inaccessible to the general public and giving you the privacy you both want.'

Both Jon and Lana smiled as they followed the architect's innermost thoughts, pleased that he did indeed share their own vision of what the old mansion house would become as the building and renovation work progressed. As to what would be done to the rest of the island had not received any serious consideration, although Jon suspected that they would simply let nature take its course and let it return to the wild, with the exception of a helicopter landing pad and a cultivated area around the house itself.

McDonald had been thinking along similar lines during the last few days. His brief was the complete renovation of the old mansion house itself, but he was well aware that Jon and Lana would want their home and surroundings to reflect their status as representatives of the distant planet Zel and its people, not to mention their considerable wealth. *On reflection, with regard to expense,* he mused, *they've never mentioned any limit on the money that I have at my disposal for this project as a whole.*

While appearing to be totally relaxed in the company of their guest, Jon, in particular, was still reading his guest's mind. He decided that, as the night was still young, before going on a tour of

Chapter Forty-Nine

inspection of the ship with the architect, he would broach the subject of their finances, not to flaunt or boast of their wealth, but only so that Howard would not in any way feel restricted by any financial boundaries in this project.

Having made that decision, he mentally communicated with Lana, and as always, she responded positively, assuring him that as they both wanted their new home to be perfect in every way, money would be of no consequence. After all, they were probably the richest people in the Caribbean, if not the world. She even reminded Jon that they still had a hoard of diamonds available for sale at some future date. With that thought in mind, Jon gently steered the conversation away from Howard's immediate curiosity about the flight deck and its controls, instead asking what a breakdown of costs had revealed. As the architect answered, somewhat hesitantly at first, fearing that the sums involved might be a deterrent to the quality and financing of the renovation, it was Lana who hastened to assure him. 'So long as our home meets with our expectations, Howard, the costs will be fully justified.'

Jon smiled as he added, 'Yes, Howard, there will be no constraints on how much it costs to bring the old house back to life and perhaps to even exceed its former glory as befits the residence of the ambassador of Zel.' He was laughing as he concluded this last statement, knowing that otherwise it could be construed to be a pompous declaration, not in keeping with his personality as the Teacher, or his old self as Jon Bradbury, air traffic controller at Manchester Airport.

With the issue of the financial outlay required for the project clarified to his entire satisfaction, McDonald's elation at the prospect of being able to give free reign to his imagination in designing and renovating the old property knew no bounds. 'I've already prepared a selection of drawings for your perusal and approval. No doubt we can discuss them after another inspection of the site tomorrow, by which time the schooner and the workmen

Chapter Forty-Nine

will have arrived.' He added with a grin, 'After a day to recuperate from the voyage, they are going to be hard at work for the next two or three months at least.' At the mention of the project commencing within the next few days, Jon took the opportunity to inform the architect that, as promised, he had transferred a power unit from the ship into the outbuilding where the old diesel generator had previously been housed. 'You will find that your workmen will have all the electrical power they need to carry out their duties, although I was only able to carry out a limited test on the lighting facilities.' He added dryly, 'After switching on the power, the initial surge blew every bulb and fuse in the system. Not entirely surprising given that it was the first time in fifty years that anyone had tried the electrics.'

McDonald grinned as he replied, 'I'll make it a priority to get the power and lighting up and running within the first day or two, then we can work well into the evenings, if necessary.'

'I can see that you intend to make your men earn their bonuses,' Jon declared with a laugh. But he was inwardly delighted that the architect was showing some initiative in getting the project started in earnest. 'And now, Howard,' he continued, 'Lana proposes to prepare dinner for this evening, nothing elaborate, of course, but something in keeping with the climatic conditions in this part of the world, while I give you a brief tour of the rest of the ship.'

As both men were leaving the flight deck, Lana murmured quietly, almost inaudibly, 'Don't be long, Jon. Remember, it only takes a short time to programme any kind of food, and Howard no doubt will be hungry after his trip from Jamaica this afternoon.'

Jon glanced back over his shoulder as he passed through the door leading to the other control centres and living accommodation, telepathically assuring her that unless Howard started asking too many in-depth questions about what he was about to see, they wouldn't be more than half an hour. As it happened, the architect was only vaguely interested in the technical aspect of the spacecraft, although he did stop from time to time to inspect the workmanship

Chapter Forty-Nine

and structural design of the various compartments that he was shown. When it came to viewing the weapons and defence systems, Jon only glossed over their functions and the same applied with the central power source. 'The ship depends on nuclear power for inflight and static use,' was all he volunteered, and Howard seemed to be happy to accept that explanation. As a result, they were able to rejoin Lana much earlier than she had expected.

'Well, that didn't take long,' she exclaimed as they reappeared. 'Dinner is ready to be served any minute now, but we will go through to the crew dining area.' Whereupon she indicated that they go through to yet another compartment adjoining the flight deck. With a little flourish of pride, she invited them to be seated at a small table in the centre of the room, which she had obviously taken some pains to prepare. 'After all, you are our first friend to stay on board with us, Howard,' she said. 'I only hope that my choice of food will suit your palate.' As it happened, the meal consisted of many dishes common to the Caribbean islands, and their guest was intrigued to learn how Lana had known how to prepare them. She laughingly explained that the chef was, in fact, a machine that could be programmed to provide any kind of food to order. 'Just programme the computer with the necessary information, punch a few buttons, and within a short space of time, you would have the right kind of food for the area that you are in, in this case, the Caribbean, compatible with the climate and for the designated number of people to be served. Of course, I can't take any credit for cooking the meal, I wouldn't have any idea as to how to begin,' she said apologetically, smiling ruefully at this confession.

'Nevertheless,' Howard replied gallantly, 'it was delightfully presented, and I thoroughly enjoyed it, just like home cooking.' He paused reflectively as he looked at Lana, a thought forming in his mind, a thought that his hosts were aware of before he uttered a word. 'It occurs to me that when you engage the staff to run your household, an ordinary cook may suffice to serve your daily needs,

Chapter Forty-Nine

but for more important social occasions, a really good chef will be a necessity. I know just the man who would welcome such an appointment to your household.' He hesitated a moment while he gauged the response to this statement, but apart from a slight inclination of the head from Jon, he was not interrupted, so he continued. 'The man in question is one Julian, a superb chef in one of Jamaica's top hotels who feels that he is getting too old for the demands of his job, but doesn't want to retire completely as he loves his work in the kitchens. I'm sure that that I could easily persuade him to come to Buccaneer's Point and work for you on a permanent basis with one cook as an assistant or possibly as a trainee chef.'

Jon raised an eyebrow as he caught Lana's attention, again telepathically, before answering. 'It will, of course, be several months before the house renovations are complete and we are ready to receive guests, but if this Julian is prepared to rough it for a time, as soon as there is accommodation available in the main house, you could invite him to make the trip out here, presumably in your helicopter, Howard, and he can then assess his working environment before making any decision about permanent employment.' He added quietly, 'I'm sure that on your recommendation, he would be the ideal person for the job, and if he can come out early enough, he could also organise the layout and equipment for his kitchen.'

McDonald nodded in agreement. 'No doubt I will have to return to Kingston in the near future to chase up supplies and materials, but in the meanwhile, I'll get my men to prepare a small apartment area in the main building as a priority, then in about two months, you could have your personal chef move in, providing, of course, that he likes the prospect of working for the ambassador of the Zel. I daresay I'll have to explain who you are.'

'I wonder how long it will take for Lana and me to be instantly recognised by the people in this part of the world? So far, events

Chapter Forty-Nine

have been confined to the war games in Arizona, but we didn't seek or obtain much publicity on that occasion. However, the time will come when I shall seek to address the people of the world at large via television media, outlining my vision for the future of humankind.' He smiled ruefully at the thought of how such an address would be received by the masses and reflected on his experience with the world leaders at the UN in New York, which was scepticism at best and disbelief in general. Was he another Messiah perhaps?

Ah, well, he thought. *I may have another five hundred years to convince them that the changes I envisage will be for the benefit of the world at large. Its people, the environment in which they live, technology in general, and above all, the survival of the earth, which at the moment, is heading for self-destruction.* Putting aside the thoughts of what would have to be done in the years to come, Jon once more gave his attention to McDonald and his suggestion regarding the employment of a chef, a necessity if the ambassador intended to socialise with politicians, world leaders, and no doubt celebrities and other public figures.

'Buccaneer's Point might well become as famous as some of the bigger islands in the Caribbean, and no doubt Lana and I will become the focus of attention as a result.' Again, he smiled ruefully. 'My image as the Teacher is not likely to be enhanced if I'm seen to be just another rich playboy, but once my presence is established and the serious work has begun, starting with the results of the war games and their consequences, the world will begin to take notice.'

'So tomorrow,' he said to McDonald with a grin, 'we can begin by doing an assessment of the work that has to be done as a priority, the chef's accommodations, and a building programme for the rest of the project. Lana won't be involved in the early stages, but do expect her to take a lively interest in the final stages, the finishing and fittings for the house, which will no doubt be influenced by her early life on Zel.'

Chapter Forty-Nine

'In that case,' McDonald replied with a smile, 'we can expect the finished product to be out of this world in more ways than one.'

'Quite so,' Jon agreed happily. 'But for the moment, Howard, may I suggest that we now retire as no doubt an early start tomorrow will give you time to sort out your team of builders and craftsmen and check on the power supplies for the house.'

As they were rising from their seats McDonald commented, 'After their leisurely cruise from Jamaica on the schooner and their inactivity, my men will be raring to go, no doubt spurred on with the thought of a big bonus at the end of the job.'

'In which case,' Jon exclaimed, 'Lana and I will delay our breakfast until you can rejoin us.'

Chapter Fifty

True to his word, at dawn the next day, McDonald went on board the schooner to find the ship's crew and his own men still asleep, some in the cabins down below, but many sprawled on the decks with nothing more than a light mattress to provide for their comfort. Laughing at the prospect of what was likely to follow, he tiptoed around some of the inert bodies on the deck, then seizing the lanyard of the ship's bell, he rang it with an enthusiasm and gusto not normally applicable to its daily use and was rewarded to see the majority of the sleepers on deck leap to their feet, dazed and confused by the sudden confusion, But they quickly realised who was responsible for their rude awakening, the boss.

With a few groans of mock despair, but nevertheless grinning as they went about tidying up the deck, most of the men simply splashed their faces with a little water to freshen up, but otherwise had no need to dress, since protective clothing would be worn on the building site. But that would wait until they had breakfasted.

Within the hour, the architect had allocated the men with their respective tasks under the supervision of a foreman, an experienced stonemason and craftsman in all the building trades. Having satisfied himself that he could safely leave them to get on with their work, he returned to the grounded spacecraft, rejoining his hosts for breakfast, but without the need to awaken them with the clamour of a ship's bell.

Chapter Fifty

As he sat down at the table, he was surprised to see a selection of everyday cereals and fruit on offer. Raising his eyebrows in disbelief, he enquired, 'Courtesy of the chef?'

To which Lana replied with a laugh, 'But of course, you name it, and the machine can provide it.'

Joining in the laughter, Jon commented. 'However, Julian won't have to worry about the competition; there is a limit to the capacity that our on-board chef can provide at any one time. It couldn't cope with a banquet for instance.'

'Glory be for that,' Howard replied with a smile.

As Lana had stated earlier, she didn't want to go into the old mansion house until most of the reconstruction work had been completed, so Jon and Howard left her on her own while they made a quick survey of the building, deciding which areas required immediate attention and what materials would be necessary to complete the work. As Howard was an architect experienced in this type of work in the tropics and with all the drawings for the project ready to hand, it was very much a routine matter to lay out a program for the initial stages of the renovation work.

After a little more than two hours, he turned to Jon and said, 'Well, we've covered all the different aspects of your requirements for the renovation project, and unless Lana has any changes to propose at a later date, you can now leave it to me, Jon, to get the work under way, and I will then give you a daily progress report of course.'

With a satisfied smile, Jon nodded as he turned away, saying, 'There should be no further need for me to intervene with your work, Howard, unless you have difficulty in lifting anything too heavy for your men to handle, in which case, just shout.'

Left to his own devises, McDonald watched his employer enter the spaceship a short distance away before turning to look at the old mansion house. Its one-time splendour was still recognisable, but

Chapter Fifty

waited for the creative breath of life to transform it into a residence that would reflect his own architectural genius, and the culmination of Jon and Lana's dream.

As Jon stepped onto the flight deck, Lana left her seat at one of the control consoles and quickly walked toward him, embracing him with her usual affection and enthusiasm, then urgently led him to the viewing screen that she had been watching during his absence. 'Do you think this situation is likely to affect us in any way?' she asked, pointing at the screen.

As Jon leaned forward to gaze at the data shown, he saw information regarding the approach of a tropical storm to their area of the Caribbean. It was not yet of hurricane force, but building in strength as it approached Buccaneer's Point with projected winds of eighty mph. 'I don't think so, Lana. As the storm is approaching from the southeast, its force will be deflected by the height of The Peak, so it will probably go around the island and out to sea again.' He added with a laugh, 'But it's just as well that the schooner has a safe anchorage in the lagoon. Anyone caught out in open water is likely to experience a rough ride. Even a sizeable vessel could have a difficult passage.' For a few more minutes, he continued to watch the projected path of the storm and the forecasts of the torrential rains it would bring, then with a satisfied smile, he fondly put his arm around Lana's shoulders. 'We have nothing to worry about, my love. By tomorrow morning, the storm will have passed and McDonald and his men will be able to continue with their work, although it will be a different story for any small ships out there. I imagine the seas will be pretty rough for a few days even after the storm has passed by our island.'

After being assured by Jon's demeanour and his statement that the work on the old house would continue unaffected by the storm, Lana paused to reflect on some storms she had observed from above some planets in other galaxies. These had been storms where wind velocities of three hundred mph were commonplace and

Chapter Fifty

where the surface of these planets constantly changed and reformed even as they watched. By comparison, the storm approaching Buccaneer's Point would be a benign influence on the island, the rains refreshing the vegetation, encouraging the already lush grasses, bushes and trees to produce further growth, to rival the habitat she had known as a child on her home planet of Zel.

After a light lunch, courtesy of the chef, Lana suggested that they should have a little private time on their own, away from the house and workmen, who appeared to be swarming all over the building. Jon, of course, readily agreed. Not only would it give them the opportunity to explore their island a little further, but being out of sight of McDonald and his workmen would give them a chance to practice Lana's teleporting ability. With that thought in mind, they made their way out of the ship, closing the door securely behind them. 'McDonald is going to be fully engaged with the project until near sunset,' Jon observed, 'so that gives us plenty of time to be on our own and do our own thing.'

They were well out of sight of the old mansion house and any curious eyes that might have been watching before they stopped, knee deep, in the tall grasses of the meadowland with the afternoon sun blazing down on them. Jon turned to Lana, took hold of both her hands and said gently, 'Now, my dear, it's time to build up your confidence in your ability to teleport.' Noting her look of apprehension, he continued, 'When we were over Kingston, you used your ability on several occasions without difficulty, so today, we will begin with a few short hops, then when you feel that your natural ability is under control, we will lengthen the distance we jump, and then the frequency of the exercise.' Then with a reassuring smile, he said, 'Are you ready? Hold my hand for the first hop, and aim for that point near that tree.' He indicated their objective about a hundred yards ahead. Seconds later found them both standing, still hand in hand, close to their objective.

Chapter Fifty

'That was quite easy,' Lana said with a sigh of satisfaction. 'It is truly a matter of confidence, so now I must try again, but on my own.' So saying and without further warning, she teleported to a distant point on the meadowland, so far ahead that Jon had some difficulty in locating her. Nevertheless, he was grinning with delight when he joined her again. For the next half hour, they repeated the exercise, increasing the distance travelled each time until Lana declared herself quite confident in her ability again.

By this time, without realising it, they had reached the lower slopes of The Point itself, the tropical jungle forming a impenetrable barrier to all but the most determined assault. As they stood looking at the thousand foot summit towering above them, the top of which was denuded of any kind of vegetation, Lana gripped Jon's arm tightly, and with a note of determination in her voice said, 'This is much sooner than I would have thought possible, but now that I'm feeling more confident in myself, I must prove that to teleport to the summit is easily achievable.' A moment later, she was gone, leaving Jon craning his neck to catch sight of her, but at that distance from the top of the mountain, it was difficult to verify that she was indeed waiting for him, leaving him with no option but to follow.

A moment later found them reunited and spontaneously embracing, Lana with a feeling of relief and satisfaction that her natural ability to teleport was proven, and Jon with pride that Lana's determination to reassert her willpower and overcome her doubts in herself would now make it possible for them to travel to any part of Buccaneer's Point. The thought passed through his mind, *The distance that it is possible for one to teleport is only relevant to one's confidence.*

As always Lana knew what he was thinking, she replied, *I'm now quite happy to move around on our own island, Jon, but as to teleporting from here to any other point hundreds of miles away, well, that is something I don't think I want to attempt, not for a time anyway.*

Chapter Fifty

Jon was more than happy to let the matter rest for the moment, but mentally reassured Lana that, although she was not a natural adept, with practice and more experience, teleporting would become a function that would enable them to travel without relying on their spacecraft or flying in Howard's helicopter or any other primitive mode of transport. 'In which case,' she replied verbally, 'I will take every opportunity to move about the island by teleportation, starting as of now. Shall we go back directly to the ship in one jump, or just go back to the bottom of The Point where we started from?'

Pleased that Lana was now feeling confident enough to propose a jump of several miles back to the ship, Jon laid a restraining hand on her shoulder. 'I think going back directly to the ship sounds like a good idea, Lana, but before we go, let's enjoy the view over our domain.' Gesturing toward the horizon to the southeast, 'In particular, look at those storm clouds approaching. That is the tropical storm that was forecast for this region, and no doubt, it will reach us in a few hours.' As they continued to watch for a while, it became apparent from their elevated position on the top of the mountain that the seas around the island were already being whipped up by the gale force winds, the whitecaps on the waves extending to the horizon in every direction. 'I'm glad that we don't have to travel on a boat, my love,' Jon declared. 'I was never a good sailor.'

'And I have never been on such a craft,' Lana replied, 'but from the picture in your mind, your experience of such a journey was not a pleasant one.'

They continued to watch with fascination the raw forces of nature and its effect on the seas and the forest below them. On their approach to The Point earlier, all had been calm and pleasant, but now it was becoming evident that the trees were bending and being lashed by the ever-strengthening winds. 'I think now would be a good time to return to the ship,' Jon said with a grimace. 'It looks like we're in for a good storm before long. We can give Howard and

Chapter Fifty

his men some warning to get under cover, and give the captain of the schooner time to secure his ship. Even in the lagoon, they can feel the effects of the high seas as the waves come crashing in through the narrow channel.'

As they held hands again in readiness to teleport together, Jon said quietly, 'Just focus your mind on the flight deck of the ship, Lana.' Then with a reassuring smile, he squeezed her hand gently and the next instant found them in the central area of the flight deck, far removed from the mountain top and the threat of the storm. As they moved over to one of the viewports, the scene that met their eyes was one of bustle and activity around the house as the workmen were going about their duties. Looking toward the lagoon, they saw the schooner tied up alongside the jetty. In all, it was a scene of normality, but one that would change once the storm hit.

As yet, there was no urgency to take cover, but Jon decided to give the captain of the schooner warning of the impending storm approaching. *He might feel the need to put extra braces out to secure his vessel,* he thought with a smile. *And Howard would be well advised to get his men accommodated in the house for the night, or certainly, until the storm has passed.* The thought of twenty or so men enduring the cramped conditions on board the schooner while it was pitching and rolling about in the expected heavy seas aroused his feelings of sympathy for their plight, and he recalled a similar experience that he had had to endure in his past life. *Not a pleasant one.*

Lana decided to accompany him while he visited the ship, and then the area around the house where McDonald could be seen in discussion with his foreman. As Jon interrupted them and told them to expect the arrival of the tropical storm within the next hour or so, both men grinned, but Howard said, 'It's no great surprise, but we'll be ready for it and finish work a little earlier than intended.' He

Chapter Fifty

added with an even wider grin than usual, 'But we'll make up for it tomorrow, never fear.'

There being little more to say at this time, Jon and Lana turned back to their own ship with a reminder to the architect that dinner would be served a little earlier than usual. 'Then we can sit and watch as the storm goes by,' Lana said with a laugh.

Chapter Fifty-One

The schooner and her crew rode out the storm despite the tropical downpour through the night and the terrifically high winds. 'No trouble for my ship,' the captain boasted after the weather had abated, while the occupants of the spaceship had hardly been aware of the passing storm, secure within the comfort of the flying saucer. At breakfast the following morning, Jon enquired if their guest had been in any way disturbed by the elements.

'Not at all,' Howard declared. 'In fact, I was only aware of the storm when I looked out of the viewport before I turned in; otherwise, I didn't hear a sound.' Then he added thoughtfully, 'It made me think about the possibility of providing some kind of sound insulation to the bedrooms in the house for your future comfort, as a full-blown hurricane can be extremely noisy, and they can quite often last for twenty-four hours before moving on.'

'A point worth considering,' Jon agreed. 'But now that we've had a comfortable night, shall we go and check on the workforce, Howard? They may not have had a quiet night sleeping in the old house.' He added with a laugh, 'Although it would have been much worse for them on board the schooner.'

Again Lana declined the opportunity to accompany the two men; she didn't really approve of the workmen using her future home as a dormitory, storm or no storm. *It will be some time before I can appreciate the transformation taking place within the building,* she thought, *but when the time comes, I shall be just as eager as everyone else for the project to reach a successful conclusion. In the meanwhile, there is so much yet to be done.*

Jon was smiling as he read her mind. *Yes, Lana,* he communicated telepathically in deference to Howard's presence. *Once the building and renovations are well on the way to completion, we will have to return to Washington for a report on the consequences of the war games and reports from the world's leaders, and of course, don't forget,* he added with a teasing grin, *to find out how our wedding arrangements are progressing.*

As this mental interchange had been taking place, Howard had made his way to the door and was ready to descend the ramp out of the ship. 'Lead the way, Howard,' Jon quipped. 'Let's see how your merry men have survived the night.' As both men reached ground level, they turned naturally in the direction of the old mansion house, striding over the flattened grasses of what one day would become a manicured lawn, which would be the pride and joy of some native gardener, no doubt.

Even before they entered the house, the sounds of activity could be heard, knocking and banging, and the voices of the workmen shouting to make themselves heard above the noise, but as Howard commented, 'They all sound very happy and industrious, don't they?'

Jon only smiled in agreement and continued into the building, curious to see where the workmen had spent the night. *No doubt on the ground floor where all the windows were still intact,* he thought.

His suspicions were soon confirmed after a short tour of inspection. On board the schooner, the men would have been somewhat cramped if they had all tried to sleep below decks during the storm, but with plenty of space available in the old house and the ability to ignore fifty years of neglect and debris, they had spread out, occupying several rooms on the ground floor, evidenced by their personal belongings scattered untidily about. 'Looks like a

Chapter Fifty-One

typical bachelor pad, doesn't it, Jon,' Howard commented with a grin of amusement. *But,* he thought, *good job Lana isn't with us. I can imagine how horrified she would be to see the shambles in here.*

Jon, of course, knew precisely what was going through the architect's mind and could only agree. However, while he was in full accord with Howard's assessment of the state of the temporary living accommodations, he quickly hastened to point out that this was probably a one-off arrangement, since the men would no doubt be happy to return to the ship, and a more familiar environment for them when working away from home. And hopefully, there would be no further storms or hurricanes during whatever time it was going to take for the completion of the reconstruction and refurbishment project on the old house.

For the next hour, accompanied by the foreman of the building crew, Jon and Howard walked around the old mansion house, which was already showing the scars of the first intended renovations or alterations. Some of the internal walls had been demolished, which left bricks and plaster lying everywhere. *A scene of organised chaos,* was the phrase that came to Jon's mind.

No doubt guessing what his employer was thinking, Howard volunteered a comment. 'It's the preparation that takes all the time, but it is also the messiest part of the project, too. Given a few weeks, you'll begin to see the transformation within the building and realise that your dream home is becoming a reality. It is then, no doubt, that Lana will take an interest in the final details of the structure.'

As there was nothing they could do of a practical nature, with no heavy lifting required, the next thing was to go to the schooner and check how the crew had coped with the storm. As they drew closer to the ship, it soon became obvious that the captain was supervising his first mate and a deckhand in some obscure task that only a seaman could appreciate, but they all sounded happy in their work. 'Very harmonious,' Howard commented with a laugh. They

Chapter Fifty-One

spent a pleasant hour on board the vessel, chatting with the captain, or 'Sharkey,' as he liked to be called, and the two crew members, one of whom was no more than fifteen years of age, but already knowledgeable in the ways of the sea.

With a little questioning by Jon in particular, they learned that the lad was one of a large family back home in Jamaica who depended on his income to sustain them. 'Poverty stricken, in common with so many people on the island, but of a naturally happy disposition, a common heritage of the population of the Caribbean islands, and one shared by the boy himself.'

In due course, it was decided to take a walk along the shore of the lagoon and take in the view of the house and the backdrop of the luxuriant jungle and The Point, Buccaneer's Point itself at the far end of the island. They had barely set foot on the shore when they heard the loud roar of a marine engine coming from the entrance of the lagoon, and as they turned to stare in that direction, they observed a vivid red powerboat with its bow high out of the water, speeding toward them, leaving a frothy wake in the otherwise calm of the lagoon. Even as they watched, the person steering the boat slewed the craft around in a tight circle without any apparent loss of speed, causing the other occupants to yell out in delight at the thrill of such a dangerous manoeuvre, and at the same time, it sent a huge wave crashing onto the beach, causing the schooner to rock violently at its mooring.

'Well, well, look at what the wind's blown in,' Howard commented bitterly. 'If it isn't Red Rodriguez himself.'

While he had no need to question his friend's statement, Jon, nevertheless, encouraged him to enlarge on his statement. 'Sounds like you know these people, Howard, and you don't approve of them or their present behaviour in that boat, which to me looks reckless and dangerous.'

Chapter Fifty-One

'Rodriguez and those men with him are the scum of the earth. They are known throughout the Caribbean for their criminal activities. Everything from murder, extortion, rape and blackmail. You name a crime, and they're guilty of it, and the one thing that has virtually guaranteed them immunity from the law is their wealth. Wealth that has been created from one activity in particular, and that is drug smuggling.' He snorted in disgust as he viewed the occupants of the boat, as they raced off down the lagoon, where they again turned at high speed, narrowly avoiding capsizing the craft, but apparently unaware of the danger involved.

With a note of anger in his voice, Howard continued, 'Judging from their behaviour, they must all be high on drugs at the moment, so there's no telling what they might do next, although they seem intent on having a good time.'

'In which case,' Jon replied, 'so long as they only endanger themselves, they can carry on making fools of themselves.' Even as he spoke, the powerboat raced toward them once more, Rodriguez standing up at the helm and his three companions hanging on desperately, but all of them appeared to be brandishing weapons of some sort.

Grimly, Howard retorted, 'Looks like they mean business, Jon. If they run true to form, they will be using pump action shotguns, not very accurate at a distance, but devastating at close range, and let's face it, they will only be a short distance from the ship and the beach when they pass us.'

As they watched the powerboat intently, it appeared to swerve into the shallows to get nearer to their intended targets, the two men standing near to the edge of the beach. 'You don't have to be a telepath to read their minds,' Jon murmured quietly. Urgently, he said, 'Get down and take cover behind that old generator, Howard,' as he indicated the discarded piece of machinery that had been lying on the edge of the beach for some time now.

Chapter Fifty-One

'Me take cover,' Howard yelled, 'what about you? You're a bigger target that they can't miss.' But nevertheless, he hastily crouched down in the hope that he would be protected from the murderous blast of several shotguns at close range.

As he did so, he was amazed to see Jon walk to the very edge of the beach, almost into the shallows, offering himself as a target for the approaching powerboat and its crazed occupants. As he did so, unknown to Howard, Jon adjusted his personal force field belt that he always wore, the control being on his waist. *A radius of forty feet should suffice,* he thought with a calm smile. *Howard will then have more than enough protection from these mad dogs.*

As he was doing this, Rodriguez shouted to his companions, 'Look at that white-haired honky; he's just asking for a load of buckshot, ain't he?'

As the boat drew level with Jon, he calmly waited for the expected fusillade of fire from the junkies. He shouted at the top of his voice in the hope that he would be heard. 'Back off, Rodriguez, while you have the chance; get of my island' It was no surprise, however, that he was ignored. By way of reply, the men in the boat, with hoots of derision, discharged their weapons in a ragged volley as they passed as close inshore as they could without grounding their craft.

At that moment, it was difficult to tell who was more amazed that Jon was completely unscathed by the hail of fire at such close quarters, Rodriguez or Howard, who had watched the attack from behind the safety of the discarded generator, an obstacle that had taken much of the force of the blasts from the weapons of the criminals, a murderous assault by any standards. Not to be thwarted by their failure to destroy the honky on their first attempt, the occupants of the boat, still shouting excitedly, decided to make a rerun. They described another tight turn in the lagoon and came racing back toward their target, who was still standing at the water's edge, completely unruffled by the threat of another attack.

Chapter Fifty-One

I will allow them one more chance to get out of the lagoon and leave us in peace, Jon decided. *After that, I may have to teach them a lesson that they and others like them won't forget.* With a wry smile, he mentally added, *After all, I am the Teacher.* Within seconds, the boat once again swerved even closer inshore to afford a more devastating firepower from the deadly shotguns, and when it came within a few yards from Jon, he could see that Rodriguez was also brandishing a hand gun.

Not much chance of hitting anything with that, he thought, *not at the speed the boat is travelling and bouncing about on the water.* The thought was no sooner in his mind than another salvo was released by the occupants of the boat as they raced by. The bow of the boat was high out of the water and its wake crashed onto the beach, immersing the Teacher up to his knees. At that moment, a loud shriek of terror was heard coming from the schooner, the crew of which had witnessed the attacks of the criminal gang. They had let their curiosity get the better of them by not taking cover, with the result that a stray shot had claimed at least one victim.

It was the young boy whose voice could be heard. Panic stricken, he was yelling, 'Cap'n, old Ben, the first mate has been killed, and those murdering bastards are getting away with it.' As the blue acrid smoke and cordite fumes slowly cleared away, looking in the direction of the schooner, Jon could see the body of the old man draped over the side of the ship, his lifeblood already spilling over and running down the side, and Captain Sharkey and the boy trying to pull his body inboard. Whereas the attack on his own person had left him unscathed, and Howard had come through the ordeal shaken, but otherwise unharmed, the sight of the distress of the crew of the schooner aroused a feeling of fury in Jon's breast. It was a life taken needlessly by a bunch of drug-crazed hoodlums. 'This is something that calls for the most drastic form of punishment that can be meted out,' he murmured to himself, while outwardly, his feelings were reflected by the look of fury on his face.

Chapter Fifty-One

In the meanwhile, Rodriguez and his men had circled the lagoon once more and were standing off the shore in the deepest part of the channel, bemused that they had killed an innocent old man, but had failed to hit such an obvious target as the white-haired honky. By now, Howard had come out from behind the cover of the old generator and joined Jon at the water's edge. They gazed out at the powerboat, now motionless, but with the engine still running in readiness for another possible foray against them. He muttered quietly, 'As I told you, Jon, those men are the scum of the earth, and they have proven that point by murdering that helpless old man and endangering the lives of all of us. Who knows what else they are going to try next?'

Still burning with anger, but now fully in control of his emotions, Jon concentrated on the powerboat some twenty yards away, with Rodriguez and his men still shouting abuse, liberally sprinkled with expletives, Jon turned to the architect and said, 'Now is the time of retribution for those men. What I am about to do will be witnessed not only by you, but the captain of the schooner, the boy and . . . .' He gestured toward the old mansion house, from whence the entire workforce had emerged and were now advancing toward the shoreline, confident in the belief that the danger was now past. 'Everyone present will be able to testify that those criminals,' he said, pointing again at the boat, 'got their just desserts.'

With a grim smile, he turned his attention once more and focussed his mind on the boat, now sitting quietly in the water while its occupants continued with their drug-controlled ranting. As Howard watched in wonder, the face of the Teacher appeared to change, an expression of benign calm replaced his normally animated self, and whether it was a trick of the light or the sun high in the sky he could not afterwards be sure, but the Teacher's mass of silver hair seemed to glow and sparkle as he extended his arms over the waters of the lagoon. *This is how Moses would have looked*

Chapter Fifty-One

when he parted the waters of the Red Sea, he thought, recollecting his early years in Bible classes.

By this time, practically everyone on the island, with the exception of Lana, had gathered on the beach to witness Jon's punishment of the smugglers. Lana had no need to be physically present as she was mentally aware of Jon's intentions and was following his actions telepathically. As they all watched in fascination, the first sign of anything happening was that the boat ceased its gentle bobbing action on the water, then it rose imperceptibly, inch by inch, until there was a clear space between the underside of the boat and the surface of the lagoon. As the propellers cleared the water, the engines of the craft, unfettered by the drag of the propulsion system, roared into life once more, accompanied by the cries of alarm from the crew, Rodriguez included.

Even from the shore, their terror was more apparent as the boat lifted inexorably higher and higher, with all the occupants hanging on for dear life, their cries of distress becoming louder as the distance above the water increased. *Will any of them jump for it before they get too high?* Howard thought. But by this time, the paralysis of fear had them in its grip, and they could only await their fate.

'Let me down, you bastard honky,' Rodriguez shouted in panic. 'I'll kill you for this.'

Although his facial expression didn't change as he raised the boat ever higher, fleetingly Jon did think, *Yes Rodriguez, I'm sure you would like to try again, but for you, this is the end.*

To the amazement of Howard and all the onlookers, amidst the screams and curses of the crew, Jon finally relaxed his telekinetic power when the boat was at a height of nearly a hundred feet. Immediately, Red Rodriguez and his henchmen plunged downward into the lagoon, hitting the surface of the water with such force that the boat disintegrated upon impact. The engine and fuel exploded,

Chapter Fifty-One

ensuring that if the fall didn't killed the men, the blast and the ensuing fire most certainly did. As the smoke and debris settled, there was an awestruck silence from the onlookers as they gazed out over the lagoon at the charred remains of one very expensive powerboat with no bodies visible anywhere.

'Well, justice has been done,' Jon quoted dryly, aware that this episode would be recounted in many homes, bars and hotels when the workforce had completed their tasks on Buccaneer's Point. 'And it has saved the authorities the cost of a trial for those rogues.'

'Something which was long overdue,' Howard said, still finding it hard to believe that what he had witnessed was for real and not a biblical memory from his boyhood.

As a last humanitarian gesture, Jon indicated his intention to go aboard the schooner to speak to Sharkey and his one remaining crewmember, the fifteen-year-old boy. By this time, Old Ben's body had been stretched out in a shaded spot on the deck and covered with a tarpaulin to protect it from the heat of the afternoon sun. As the captain, in a subdued manner, welcomed his visitors aboard, he simply commented, 'A sad day, a sad day indeed.'

'But at least you had the consolation of seeing his killers brought to justice,' Howard said with a grim smile, taking Sharkey's shoulder in a firm grip of sympathy.

'That's true, Mr McDonald, and now I've got a new readymade first mate,' he said, gesturing toward the fifteen-year-old boy. 'They don't come much better.'

'And now, you will no doubt wish to bury the old man pretty quickly,' Jon intervened. 'If you wish, you can use that spot where the headland juts out by the entrance to the lagoon. Old Ben will then be in a position to see all the comings and goings at all times.'

'If you don't mind, sir,' Sharkey insisted, 'if Mr McDonald can spare a couple of his men for a few hours, I'm sure a more fitting end for Ben would be a burial at sea, not too far out, mind you. He

Chapter Fifty-One

was never a landlubber and the sea is kinder to a body than rotting in the ground.'

As Jon and Howard exchanged glances of agreement, the captain nodded in satisfaction. 'If I can have two men within the hour, we can put out to sea and lay Ben to rest in a deep-water canyon where he won't be disturbed ever again.' He concluded by saying, 'Poor old Ben,' and wiped a genuine tear from his eye. 'My old shipmate.' As there was nothing more to say at this time, the Teacher and architect took their leave with the promise that two men would be provided to assist with the burial at sea, and with the work crew following, they returned to the old mansion house. There was still much work to be done.

Chapter Fifty-Two

Work on the renovation of the old mansion house continued apace during the following days, during which time Lana and Jon explored every glade in the grasslands, every cliff top around the island's perimeter, even venturing into the jungle areas in search of local wildlife, where they found different species of birds in abundance and even a small herd of wild pigs. 'They were probably brought to the island by the original owner,' Jon declared with a knowing smile. 'Then, when he returned to London with his young wife, the animals were left to fend for themselves and subsequently returned to the wild.'

'They seem to be a very placid and contented animal,' Lana ventured as they viewed the small herd rooting about in the undergrowth. 'We have nothing like them on Zel. Probably my ancestors hunted anything similar to extinction in the same way that your people have done to various species of land and sea animals in the recent past.'

Jon could only agree with a wry smile, adding, 'That is another aspect of education that will have to be addressed if the planet is to retain its animal population, which is diverse at the moment, but dwindling rapidly in some cases.'

Lana didn't pursue the subject of conservation of the species; she was content that the Teacher was aware of the many problems facing him in the future and that he would, in time, resolve all the issues relevant for the good of all humankind, and the planet itself. *After all,* she reasoned, *he will have a lifespan of some five hundred*

Chapter Fifty-Two

years, and he has been endowed with more powers and wisdom than any other Teacher ever before in the history of humankind. But for the moment, she thought, *our immediate concerns are the completion of the work to the house to make our home not only habitable, but as beautiful as any on Zel, and of course, the preparations for our wedding ceremony in Washington.*

As she let these thoughts pass idly through her mind, Jon monitored the mental pictures, which he could see clearly, and being aware of the subject of their wedding coming to the fore, he suddenly realised that time had been passing by unnoticed while they had been enjoying this peaceful interlude on the island. The encounter with Red Rodriguez was now all but forgotten, *But now we must return to the reality of my responsibilities as the Teacher,* he thought, *and our return to Washington also.'*

Turning toward his wife-to-be, he drew her gently to him in a tender embrace, murmuring, 'My love, I think we can safely leave McDonald in charge of the workforce for a month or so while we return to Washington. Not only is it necessary to confer with George K. Lane with regard to the arrangements for our wedding, something we are both looking forward to, but I must set up a meeting with the president and the heads of governments again. I need to discuss the outcome of the war games and to prepare a broadcast to the people of the world regarding my intentions to improve their way of life . . . and that's only the beginning.'

With a sigh, Lana conceded, 'Yes, I suppose we will have to leave Buccaneer's Point and our idyllic existence here for a time, for you to resume your duties as the Teacher, and for me to prepare for our wedding.' She added as an afterthought, 'I wonder if Captain Jara or Mort have had any success in contacting my father in recent weeks. At the last report, the commander was in another galaxy, many light-years from Earth,' but she smiled proudly as she continued, 'he will use all his skill and technology to bring his ship back to the solar system in time for our wedding, if that can happen, I shall be the happiest woman in the Universe.'

Giving her a gentle squeeze of assurance, Jon said with a grin, 'When the mother ship is detected approaching Earth, every telescope and every radar installation on the planet will be focussed on it, and there will be those who will think, the Martians are about to invade.' Laughing at such a thought, he continued, 'Instead, it will be a proud father whose intention is simply to attend an earthly ceremony of union between his only daughter and one very lucky man of Earth, but a man who has to deny his origins in order to promote his role as a Teacher and representative of Zel.'

'Do you find it difficult to think of yourself in that way?' Lana asked, shaking her head in wonder. 'I haven't detected any sign of your being unhappy that you no longer have any emotional ties with family or friends from your previous existence. Since you were selected and picked up by Captain Jara and Mort all those months ago, your physical and mental persona have made you a very different man to the Jon Bradbury of old.' Wistfully, she continued, 'Would you like to go back to your previous way of life as a normal man of Earth, without the mental and physical powers you now possess, unable to do anything to change the lives of your own people, or can you now accept that it is your destiny to be the last Teacher on Earth, the only man who has ever had the opportunity and the ability to improve the lives of his own people worldwide, and in so doing, save the planet Earth from destruction?'

Now it was Jon's turn to shake his head in denial. 'No, Lana, my darling, by the time I was found by Jara and Mort and persuaded to become a Teacher, I had already come to terms with the loss of my own family and accepted that my life would never be the same again.' He smiled ruefully. 'I couldn't imagine how different I would be as a person, for want of a better word, transformed into some kind of super being with mental and physical powers far beyond those of normal men.'

Chapter Fifty-Two

Still holding her gently, he continued quietly, 'Since falling in love with you, I haven't had a moment of unhappiness, and the thought of an extended life together fills me with contentment, albeit there is much to be done to improve the lives of the multitudes of Earth, with or without the cooperation of the various governments concerned. Once I've had the discussions in Washington, I then intend to meet the heads of science and technology and begin educating them in the matter of providing power, unlimited power, for industry without causing pollution to the atmosphere and subsequent damage to the planet.'

Knowing how Jon's mind was working toward the challenges that lay ahead, Lana still found it difficult to grasp the mental pictures of the many changes he envisaged for the future, especially more sources of electrical power and transport that was no longer dependant on oil. Road vehicles, in particular, would have with tiny nuclear energy cells to drive them instead of the old-fashioned internal combustion engines that choked the atmosphere with noxious gasses. And this, of course, would change the adverse effect that the economies of the industrialised nations that had been dependent on oil over the years had had, and for the immediate future, it would remove the threat of war from the equation of desired change in the present-day world. In all, it was a very definite challenge for a Teacher to be confronted with, even for one with abilities never before seen in mortal man.

Lana shared Jon's thoughts regarding his role as the Teacher and accepted that life for them both was likely to be busy over the next few months, especially with the prospect of the visit by the interstellar mother ship and her father, an event not yet confirmed by Captain Jara, but one that made her pulses race with excitement.

Being very much aware of her emotions at that moment, Jon enquired softly, 'How long has it been since you last saw your father, Lana?'

Chapter Fifty-Two

'Well, I'm just a little more than eighty years old now, and my training as a cadet is almost complete.' She paused for a moment's reflection before continuing, 'So, it must be about ten Earth years since he had me transferred to another commander's ship for the final instruction in space technology, in general, and diplomacy, in particular, a requirement for anyone who would aspire to a higher command at a later stage in her career.'

Jon was again laughing as he replied, 'Well, Lana, my darling, when it comes to all kinds of technology, your knowledge is far in advance of many scientists here on Earth, which being the case, you will be of great assistance to me when it comes to teaching them about how to improve every aspect of mechanical engineering and harnessing atomic power for the benefit of humanity.' He was still smiling as he continued with gentleness in his voice, 'As for the requirements of diplomacy for higher command in the space service, that will be something that you will now be able to apply to your duties as First Lady of the Ambassador of Zel.'

It was Lana's turn to smile as she replied, 'With Earth people, diplomacy is quite easy. Their minds are like an open book, and generally, if you know what they are thinking, then it's only a matter of telling them what they want to hear.'

'Always assuming that they know their own minds,' Jon cautioned. 'I find that when dealing with many of them, their thoughts are so confused and devious that I have to probe deeper into their minds to get a clearer picture and that is not always a pleasant experience. But so far, you have proved that you are well prepared to adopt the role of wife to the ambassador and to be my assistant in some of my teaching duties.' Then, laughing heartily to lighten the tone of the conversation, he continued, 'As well as being pilot, navigator, communications officer, advisor on matters dealing with Zellian commanders, and of course, my companion and soul mate.'

Chapter Fifty-Two

'I take it that I meet with your approval in all aspects of our future together, Jon,' Lana said in a teasing tone of voice, 'especially the constant companion relationship part of it.'

By way of reply, Jon drew her close to him, and nuzzling her ear gently, whispered softly, 'I'm always happy when we are as one, mentally and physically.'

This statement caused Lana to blush with pleasure. 'Then I think we should be making our way back to Washington,' she said with a giggle, 'and see what arrangements George K. Lane has made for our nuptials, and also, I must communicate with Captain Jara, wherever he may be on the planet, as he may have some news of my father's ship.'

Reluctantly releasing his embrace on his soul mate, Jon turned away, saying, 'I will now go and inform Howard that we are going to return to Washington within the hour. He will be in sole charge of the project until our return, hopefully as man and wife, and optimistically, when the renovations are nearing completion.'

'No doubt he will want to transfer his personal belongings to the schooner before we go,' Lana said as she laughed at the thought of the architect having to share the cramped conditions on the ship and the comparative discomfort after the luxury of his lifestyle on board their own ship, the saucer.

'I think it would be advisable if McDonald utilises the space in the house that is being prepared for our chef, remember?'

'Perhaps you're right,' Lana conceded. 'As the man in charge, he deserves a little privacy and extra comfort.'

It only took a short time for Jon to find the architect, who was busy supervising and directing a group of workmen in the old house. After informing Howard that he and Lana intended to return to Washington immediately, he suggested that he accompany him back to the spaceship to collect his personal belongings and transfer them to the small apartment adjacent to the kitchen in the main

Chapter Fifty-Two

house, which fortunately, had been given some priority in readiness for the arrival of Julian, the chef, although that was not likely to happen until the return of the ambassador and his bride. Nevertheless, Mc Donald was more than happy with the new arrangement, a small luxury apartment of his own was a perk that he hadn't expected, and while it didn't compensate for the novelty of living aboard a flying saucer, it did offer accommodation far superior to a berth on the schooner.

After a short discussion relating to the intended program of work to be done in his absence. Jon received assurances from the architect. 'You're going to see a big difference to the old place when you come back, Jon. Another week and we will be starting on the internal rebuild, with new walls, columns and marble everywhere as specified by Lana.'

Smiling in satisfaction at the prospect of leaving the renovation project in a safe pair of hands, Jon said his farewells to McDonald and joined Lana on the flight deck. With a last look out of the view window to ascertain that all was clear for take-off, he gave Lana the order. 'Okay, pilot, take me to Washington.'

Grinning with delight, she answered, 'Aye, aye, captain!'

Some two hours later, after a leisurely flight at high altitude, well above the ceiling height of commercial and military aircraft, Lana put the spaceship into docking position directly above the White House, but maintained what was now considered their normal height above ground level, twenty miles or so. It was high enough to be safe from accidental collisions with other aircraft, but low enough for their scanners to pick out every detail of what was happening down below.

As she changed from propulsion to hover mode, she said, 'All we can do now is to try and contact Captain Jara to find out what has been happening in the world while we have been enjoying our

Chapter Fifty-Two

break in the Caribbean, and also, if he has any news of my father's ship.'

'All in good time, Lana,' Jon replied patiently. 'If there had been anything urgent to report, Jara would have contacted us before now. In fact, he might have taken the opportunity to join us on the island out of curiosity to see Buccaneer's Point and to see how our new home is shaping up. Although it's not yet up to the standards of your family home on Zel, if McDonald's assurances are anything to go by and he follows your instructions to the letter, the transformation of the old manor house will make you believe that you are once more back in your original home, even complete with the mountain, jungle, and our own private and idyllic lagoon.'

Lana leaned back contentedly in her chair in front of the control console, relaxed now that the flight controls were no longer required and allowed her mind to go back to her far-off childhood days, a time of happy memories with her mother in the beautiful surroundings of the family home, and the very occasional visit of her father when he returned from yet another voyage into the depths of space and some far-flung galaxy. Knowing that Jon would be following her thoughts telepathically, she said aloud, 'But there will never be any need for us to be separated for more than a few days at most, will there, Jon?'

As he hastened to assure that it was unlikely that would ever happen, he added, 'Wherever I go, I daresay you will always accompany me.' He added as an afterthought, 'Unless it happens to be a particularly dangerous situation beyond my control.'

Recalling other incidents where Jon had been subject to attack by aggressors who had been well armed and dangerous, she only smiled as she said, 'But if we both utilise our personal force field belts, how could we come to any harm, Jon?'

'That is true, my love. When Red Rodriguez and his men were trying their best to gun me down on the beach, I wasn't in any kind

Chapter Fifty-Two

of danger, and the same would apply if we came under a similar attack in future. We would be immune from harm, so long as we wear our force field belts at all times other than on board this ship. Come to think of it,' he added thoughtfully, 'they are so much a part of our everyday uniform that the only time I don't wear mine is when sleeping or bathing.'

'That's true,' Lana agreed. 'I find that my belt is so unobtrusive that it's almost like a fashion accessory, decorative perhaps, but so important in times of danger.'

'In which case,' Jon retorted, 'wear it at all times when outside this ship. While it may be our intention to help the people of this planet to develop into a progressive and happy culture, there will be those who will resent us because they regard us as aliens, and as such, a threat to the existence of humankind and someone to be destroyed.'

With that warning ringing in her ears, Lana resolved that the people of Earth might appear to be civilised in the main, but just like the animals they were descended from, some of them would always be a danger to the ambassador and herself. *Why,* she thought, *even in America, a civilised society, they have killed several of their own political leaders, presidents, no less.* Pushing these sombre thoughts to the back of her mind, she rose from her seat and gently led Jon over to the viewport to look down on the city of Washington far below, sometimes obscured by clouds, and the next moment bathed in sunshine, which threw the city into sharp relief against the surrounding countryside.

They stood at the viewport for some considerable length of time, observing the effects of the alternating shades of light and darkness caused by the hazy cloud cover and the sunshine, almost a kaleidoscopic change of scenery. It was fascinating for a time, but other thoughts distracted their attention. Jon thought, *I must try to contact George K. Lane and find out what progress he has made with the arrangements for the wedding ceremony,* while Lana was still

Chapter Fifty-Two

thinking, *Is my father anywhere near the solar system as yet, or has Captain Jara had any contact with him?*

Since Lana was more experienced in handling the communications system, she took the initiative by sitting down again at the main control console. 'Who do you wish to contact first of all, Jon, Captain Jara or George?'

'Jara, I rather think,' Jon replied, 'because without knowledge of your father's estimated time of arrival, we can't really fix a date for the ceremony. As you haven't seen your father for ten years, I know you are just as excited about that as you are about the wedding. Besides, once you know that the commander is nearing Earth's orbit, I daresay it won't take long to finalise the details and arrangements for both occasions, your reunion with your father and our ceremony, which I have no doubt George will have organised down to the last detail.'

Lana lost no time signalling, flooding the airwaves on the prearranged frequency in her efforts to make contact with Mort, who would be in charge of communications on his ship. As luck would have it, either Mort was aware of their presence above Washington, or the automatic alert radio system had informed him of the incoming call, and he responded within minutes. 'Good to hear from you again, Lana,' were his first words. 'I trust you and Jon are both well and that you have enjoyed your trip to your island in the Caribbean, Buccaneer's Point, I believe you called it.' A few more pleasantries were exchanged before Lana could bring herself to ask the most important question about her father. With bated breath, she waited for Mort's reply.

'The commander? Oh, yes, his ship is, at this moment, already in orbit around Earth's moon and has been for several days now.' It sounded as though Mort was having a quiet chuckle of amusement when he added, 'In fact, he has suggested that, as this is your first meeting for several years, he would prefer that you meet in privacy on board his own ship, away from public gaze. He would also like to meet the Earth man to whom you intend to commit the rest of your life.' Without waiting for Lana to reply, he continued. 'The commander says that while he is impatient to meet you both, he is aware that it will take you about six hours to cover the quarter of a million miles in your little craft, so do what you have to do about your other earthly arrangements, meaning this ceremony of union, then head for the moon, just like that.'

Chapter Fifty-Three

'Once a commander, always a commander,' Lana laughed with delight, 'but in this case, I'm happy to do as he commands.' Then turning to Jon with a smile, she said, 'Now I'll try to get into the White House communications system and try to contact George K. Lane, a busy man, no doubt, but by now, our presence above the White House has already been reported, and he is probably waiting for our call at this very moment.'

In that respect, she was absolutely correct. Within seconds of the moment of contact, the secretary of state answered in a tone of voice that betrayed his pleasure to hear the sound of Lana's voice. Once again, the dialogue consisted of the expected questions concerning their welfare, what progress had been made regarding the building and renovation of the ambassador's residence on the island of Buccaneer's Point, and finally, 'Are you both ready for the wedding ceremony that we have arranged for you?'

Rather than answer all the questions herself, she simply said, 'I'll let Jon answer all your questions, George, but I thank you for all your efforts regarding the ceremony; it will be a unique experience for me.' She added somewhat breathlessly, 'And my father will be in attendance in his capacity of commander and a member of the High Council of Zel.'

For a moment there was silence as the secretary of state absorbed the importance of what that would mean to the guest list for the wedding. 'Wow.' There was again a moment's silence as George continued with the conversation, but he changed the subject

Chapter Fifty-Three

to Jon's impending meeting with Davis Cooper. 'There has been a great deal of discussion at the highest level with regard to Jon's assistance to the world community at large, and on a more personal level, how he saved the life of the president and members of his party during the last visit to the United Nations assembly in New York. Do you remember the occasion, Lana?'

'But of course,' she replied. 'Even by Zellian standards, Jon is a remarkable man, and his abilities are far greater than any other Teacher to walk this Earth. I have personally witnessed several occasions when he has saved lives in circumstances similar to those in New York.'

'Be that as it may, Lana,' George K. Lane replied, 'it's not every day that someone saves the life of the President of the United States, not to mention his secretary of state and other dignitaries.' Lana and Jon could sense that while they couldn't see George's facial expression at that moment, he was smiling at the recollection of the would-be assassin dangling from the ceiling in the hallway of the hotel, having been elevated by Jon's telekinetic powers. 'However,' George continued, 'during your absence these last few weeks, we, that is, the president and a number of congressmen representing politicians and several senior military personnel, General Clintock included, of course, have met a number of times to discuss how best to reward Jon for his intervention in matters of global importance, the promotion of peace worldwide, and the promise of advances in scientific projects to the benefit of humanity.'

Jon, in the meantime, had been listening to the comments made by George K. Lane, and of course, Lana's supportive replies, and while not wishing to give the impression of false modesty, he simply said, 'George, everything I have done since I was placed in my role as Teacher is only what I was trained to do.' He did not, however, reveal that his origins were of Earth, and that his own preparation and training had been received at the hands of Zellian aliens, a process that had already been repeated over countless generations

Chapter Fifty-Three

of humanity. He didn't add that it was envisaged that after his work was completed over the next five hundred years, there would be no further intervention by the Zellians. *I am to be the last Teacher.*

'You know, that's what I like about you, Jon, and Lana, you make your achievements sound so ordinary, and yet, to us mere mortals, you are capable of such extraordinary powers that we can only watch and wonder.' Jon and Lana smiled at each other at the mention of their respective mental powers. Teleporting was something that by now had been demonstrated a number of times, and Jon's ability to exercise his telekinetic power had been proven during the incident while in New York, and which apparently had been discussed at a higher level in their absence. No doubt it was now well known to a number of people in the White House that they could also disappear in an instant by using their teleporting abilities, something that would be to their disadvantage in the not-too-distant future.

George continued the conversation regarding the outcome of the discussions between the president and members of the government, but without disclosing what may have been agreed as a suitable reward for the Zellian ambassador. 'I can only say at this moment that in recognition for your services in the recent past, it's been decided to honour you, Jon, and you too, Lana, in a way that is unusual for our country, but in a manner that you will find most gratifying. More than that I won't say at the moment, but as you are now back in Washington, or should I say, above Washington,' he added with a laugh, 'with your permission, I will arrange your meeting with the president and a select group of the government and the armed forces, plus quite a few diplomats from other countries who will no doubt clamour to witness this unique occasion.'

Although curious as to how he was to be rewarded for his services to the nation, Jon only said, 'I'm only performing my role as a Teacher.' Nevertheless, he didn't press the secretary of state for

Chapter Fifty-Three

any further information, although he did question Lana mentally. *What can they have in store for us?*

Meanwhile, the question uppermost in Lana's mind, which she could no longer hold back was, *The wedding arrangements?*

'While we have been away, George, we have seen many changes on Buccaneer's Point, and there has been much progress in the renovation of our future home, but we have also been wondering how you have managed with our ceremony of union, the wedding ceremony?'

When George K. Lane replied, he sounded quite excited. He had never been involved in such an occasion, either for a member of his own family or indeed a close friend, so it had been a steep learning curve for him. The date and time had still not been finalised, but he had been assured by the management of the chosen venue that if given about two weeks' notice, all the arrangements could be put in place, so now it was up to the bride and groom to name the day. As for the guest list, that was another matter. He was aware that Lana's father was the only member of her family who would attend, so he took the opportunity to enquire if there would be any other Zellians likely to be invited as guests or witnesses.

'We have a custom in our wedding ceremonies, Lana, that the father of the bride walks his daughter down the aisle and gives her away to her groom.' He then laughingly explained that this didn't mean that he literally disposed of her, but also that many members of her family would be present. 'In your case, however, it's more likely that members of your own space fleet could attend, if that is what you would wish?' Lana hastened to assure George that she would provide him with the names of several crewmembers of her father's ship, senior officers no doubt, and top of the list was Captain Jara and his first officer Mort, the two Zellians largely responsible for the recruitment of the last Teacher. But this was a fact that she didn't disclose as Jon's earthly origins would and must remain a

Chapter Fifty-Three

secret, if he was to carry out his duties without bias from the many different nations of Earth.

With a smile, George K. Lane continued, 'Well, that leaves us with enough places for the rest of the heads of government, royalty, and no doubt, the sensation-seeking celebrities who would like to attend, although the numbers will be limited to a little more than three hundred, and that is due to the size of the venue.' He laughed as he said, 'I think if we had arranged to hire a football stadium for the ceremony, I'm sure we could have filled it.'

Although Jon had an idea of a baseball or sports stadium, Lana, of course, had no knowledge of such places, and again had to question George about where the venue for the wedding was located. 'Now that is a question that is easy to answer, Lana,' he replied. 'I take it that you can see the whole of Washington below you right now?' Lana affirmed that she could, since her viewing screen was already focused on the White House and surrounding areas. 'Well,' George calmly replied, 'we, the White House that is, is positioned on what is called Pennsylvania Avenue, and your venue is just a short distance away, in walking distance in fact, and is called The Willard Intercontinental Hotel, the best in Washington and famous worldwide for its luxury and ambience, and a setting worthy of the weddings of the very rich and famous,' and again laughing gently, he said 'and the ambassadors of Zel.'

Feeling pleased that the secretary of state had taken the time and trouble to make all but the final details for the wedding, Jon and Lana together thanked him profusely and assured him that they would talk over the details as soon as possible. But Jon had one further question to raise, 'What about security? From our previous experience in New York, George, is it possible that such a situation could occur again?'

'Our security arrangements have been improved since that last incident,' George declared, 'but with so many heads of different governments and royal guests, there will be dozens of armed

Chapter Fifty-Three

bodyguards, including the president's men hovering about, not to mention surveillance cameras constantly zooming in to check the identities of everyone present, but even so....' He hesitated, leaving Jon to his own conclusions.

Talking in an undertone, Jon murmured to Lana, 'Personal force field belts will be our surest means of protection, my love,' to which she nodded in agreement, although on her wedding day, would she still agree to wear this important piece of uniform equipment? Or would the appearance of the belt compromise the appearance of her wedding dress? That was a decision to be made on the day.

After making a few further enquiries regarding the ongoing renovations to the house on Buccaneer's Point, the secretary of state reminded Jon and Lana that he would now finalise the date of the wedding with the management of The Willard, draw up the guest list, and arrange for accommodations for those who would be travelling from other parts of the world. 'And the thousand and one details I didn't know about before taking on this job,' he declared with a cheerful laugh. 'So, if you will excuse me, I'll also go and set up this meeting with the president and the rest of the top brass, which should take place well before your wedding day. See you soon,' he said and immediately broke off radio contact.

Chapter Fifty-Four

The prospect of meeting her father for the first time in ten years, a mere blink of the eye in the lifetime of a Zellian, some would think, to Lana, the enforced separation at such an early age from both her parents had been slightly traumatic. Even now, it bothered her when she was eighty years old, with the difference that she would soon be considered a fully-fledged member of the space fleet, something she was sure her father would confirm at their impending meeting. As her mind turned toward this joyous event, she wondered, *Will my father, Commander Rega, notice that I've changed very much in these ten years?* Smiling inwardly as she sensed Jon's mind probing hers, she thought, *I've not only been trained to a high degree of efficiency in all matters relating to the command of a spacecraft with all the technology that entails, but I've also developed as a woman as a result of meeting you, Jon.*

Mentally, she was giggling with delight at the recollection of her additional training and the prospect of the years to come while perfecting that aspect of their lives. 'Better not let your father read your mind too deeply, Lana,' Jon spoke out aloud, 'remember, he will probably still be thinking of you as his little girl. In fact, he may not have yet adjusted to the idea of your joining ceremony, especially to a man of Earth.'

Lana smiled as she replied verbally. 'When my father meets you, Jon, he will realise that although you were nurtured on the planet Earth, you are more like a Zellian than many of our own kind. Mentally, you are as powerful as any of our space commanders,

Chapter Fifty-Four

physically you are far superior to any of our race, and that also applies to your own kind as well. As to your appearance, although I know that you wouldn't agree with my description, as a man, you have been likened to an angel, almost beautiful, and as everyone is aware, your hair sets you apart from all Zellians and humans alike.'

Although he felt somewhat embarrassed by Lana's flattering description of his physical attributes, sincere as it most certainly was, Jon had to concede that he probably had more in common with the Zellian race than he had with humankind in general. 'I hope Commander Rega will approve of your choice of a lifelong partner or earthly husband, Lana,' he said to disguise his discomfiture. With the thought of the rendezvous with the Zellian mother ship now uppermost in both their minds, it was decided that as George K. Lane would be going ahead with the organisation of their wedding ceremony, they could now concentrate on the reunion with Lana's father and Jon's introduction to the commander of the mother ship. *Do the Zellians recognize the expression father-in-law or son-in-law,* Jon wondered in amusement. *This is going to be an interesting meeting of minds.*

There being little reason for further delay, and since Lana felt slightly impatient to be off on their journey to the moon, it only took a short time to set the coordinates to traverse the quarter million miles to Earth's satellite and their rendezvous with the mother ship. *And father-in-law,* Jon reminded himself with a smile, while Lana tried to relate his amusement to meeting Commander Rega.

As expected, it took their small craft six hours to complete the journey to the moon, during which time several observatories on Earth were watching their progress right up to the moment that they disappeared from view in their telescopes. They went behind the blind side of the moon where the mother ship was waiting for their arrival, with its entry port opened up, ready to engulf them. *Like a mother welcoming her child,* Jon thought, *or in this case, a*

Chapter Fifty-Four

father embracing a daughter who has been missing from his life for ten long years.

As their own craft completed the entry procedure without mishap, no doubt under the watchful eye of Commander Rega, Lana breathed a sigh of relief. 'Now the tractor beams can take over and select a berth for our ship. It would appear that the hanger deck is nearly empty for whatever reason.' It took a few further minutes before they felt the slightest tremor as the tractor beams locked down their craft, which was Jon's second experience of docking in a mother ship.

They didn't have to wait long before the internal communications screen slit up to reveal the face of one of the ship's junior cadets, a young girl. *Somewhat younger than Lana, I would think, probably no more than fifty years of age,* Jon thought with a smile. Self-consciously, knowing that she was addressing an ambassador for the Zel and the daughter of her commander, the cadet formally welcomed them aboard the mother ship, and in the same breath, she requested that they report immediately to Commander Rega in his private quarters. 'You will be provided with an escort, ambassador,' she said with a smile.

The internal transport facilities ensured that they were conveyed into the presence of Lana's father without any delay, no more than ten minutes. *Pretty good considering the size of these interstellar ships,* Jon mused. *I suppose this one is about two miles in length, with at least twenty decks, enough to dwarf any ocean-going ship on Earth.* As their escort ushered them into the commander's living quarters, their first impression was how palatial the surroundings were. A life of luxury was only one of the compensations that the commander, senior officers, and crew enjoyed while traversing the far reaches of space.

The officer, who had escorted them to this part of the ship, had barely excused himself and withdrawn, when they sensed the approach of the commander as his telepathic aura reached out

Chapter Fifty-Four

before him, communicating with his daughter and Jon, her chosen partner. When he finally appeared in person, his face was radiant with joy as he approached Lana with his arms outstretched, ready to embrace her. 'My little girl, come to me.'

Jon had to smile at those words, but was careful to screen his thoughts from the commander and Lana also. He was sure that had he not done so, she would have had a fit of the giggles, which was probably not very becoming on this reunion with her father.

Once the initial embrace was over, father and daughter drew apart, the better to appraise each other. Lana thought, *You haven't changed much in the last ten years, Father, slightly heavier and the first signs of a few grey hairs, but still very distinguished in appearance, every inch a commander in the space Fleet of Zel.*

Meanwhile, the commander viewed his daughter with parental pride. Ten years in the life of a Zellian would not normally result in any great change in their physical appearance and wellbeing, except for the very young, as in Lana's case, but as Rega continued to gaze silently for a few moments longer, he noted that his little girl had changed greatly since their last meeting, more so than he would have expected after a mere ten years.

Being careful to screen his thoughts for the moment, he continued his visual appraisal of Lana. *Whereas you were a very young and immature cadet, a very young adolescent, when you left my command to accompany Captain Jara on your training mission, now what do I see? Physically, you have developed into a fully developed Zellian woman of exceptional beauty, so like your mother, and mentally, you have matured surprisingly in such a short space of time.* As he delicately probed Lana's mind, and avoided having his mental presence felt, he realised that she had indeed changed far more quickly than he would have expected of one so young. Physically poised and mentally confident. *I wonder if this transformation has anything to do with your liaison with this young Earthman, your chosen partner?*

Chapter Fifty-Four

Jon, in the meanwhile, had been aware of the separate thoughts of father and daughter. Lana's mind was as ever like an open book to him, although the commander was trying to screen his thoughts from both of them. To block Jon's mental intrusion was something that he would soon be aware was difficult to do. The Teacher had also matured since his indoctrination all those months ago and was now capable of meeting the Zellians as an equal, and that included the commanders of the space vessels and the members of the High Council of Zel.

Their initial reunion and appraisal of each other happily completed, Lana and her father embraced each other again with a warmth that would not normally be displayed in public, hence the reason for this first meeting in the commander's private living quarters. 'And now, Lana,' Rega said with a smile, 'protocol demands that you introduce me to our ambassador to the planet Earth, but as we are also to be united as a family in the near future, we don't have to be too formal, do we?'

Making no attempt to disguise her mental and physical attraction to Jon, her love for him being apparent to her father in any case, Lana went through the motions of introduction in a light hearted manner. If there had been any doubts about her choice of a lifetime partner in her father's eyes, those doubts were now dispelled as he acknowledged Jon as a worthy ambassador and a very welcome addition to the family. 'I have already been informed by Captain Jara of your selection as a Teacher, and the length and manner of your indoctrination procedure, which is unprecedented so far as I am aware. And that you are more than adequately equipped mentally and physically for the task ahead of you.' He smiled gently. 'No doubt, as a man of Earth, you still find it difficult to envisage a lifespan of five hundred years. But judging from the behaviour of your fellow men during the last few centuries, you will probably need all of that time to educate and change these people so that their way of life is acceptable to the Star Federation, not to mention the hope that your planet will survive the damage already inflicted on its flora and fauna.' Looking fondly at his daughter, he added, 'But with Lana at your side, I'm sure she will make you happy and provide wise counselling from time to time. After all, she is a Zellian, with millions of years of culture and civilisation behind her. Need I say, if you do experience any difficulty in persuading some of your people to accept your teachings, and no doubt that is quite likely, you only have to request assistance and I, with my ship and its technology will be available to help you in whatever way may be necessary.'

He thought of the war-like nature of humankind and the history of destruction only too evident during the preceding two or three hundred years, wars of a localised nature in many cases, but more recently escalating into global warfare causing the deaths of millions of people, and for what reason? As Jon quietly reflected on his future role as the Teacher, he grimly conceded that he just might have cause to ask the commander for assistance, if only to quell the troublesome nations who would not be prepared to live in peace with their neighbours. From his experience with the leaders of the United Nations, he knew that to gain the cooperation of all of them was unrealistic; therefore, he would probably have to use the-iron-fist-in-the-velvet-glove approach to drive home the message that wars on a grand scale would not be tolerated.

As these thoughts were passing through his mind, he made no attempt to screen his views of the future possibilities from Rega and Lana, but became aware of their approval for his approach to the question of wars, famine, and death, or peace, prosperity, and knowledge. It was a future that would guarantee a happy life for everyone on the planet, if they would accept Jon's teachings.

'As I'm sure they will, Jon,' the commander exclaimed. 'As soon as the more advanced nations have benefitted from the advanced technology that you will bring to them, their example will be followed by the poorer countries, who will no doubt strive to better

Chapter Fifty-Four

themselves. Within a hundred years, wars, starvation, poverty, and disease will be eradicated, although I think that their life expectancy is unlikely to be anywhere near yours.' He added with a smile, 'The next hundred years is going to seem like a long time as you deal with all your problems, Jon.'

Given that Jon had only made the acquaintance of the commander so recently, less than one hour ago, he reminded himself, perhaps it was because of their telepathic openness to each other, but he had to concede that he felt that they had known each other for years. Or was it Lana's latent memories that impinged themselves on his subconscious mind?

In due course, Lana managed to steer the conversation to include a description of their past life on Zel, and her mother, who preferred to remain at home, while her husband roamed the universe, despite the opportunity to live and enjoy a life of luxury aboard the mother ship, and of course, her own upbringing and education prior to becoming a cadet in the space fleet.

During the course of their conversation, Jon was able to question Rega regarding the construction and technology involved in building the mother ship, with a view to applying the same skills for a similar project on Earth, albeit not for another century at least. When other subjects were discussed, he was very much impressed by the commander's knowledge of all things, his meetings with the various aliens from other galaxies, many of whom were of humanoid appearance, and a few who were of grotesque appearance to the eyes of a Zellian or human.

In due course, Lana brought up the subject of her joining ceremony. She had waited patiently for her father to mention it, but having listened to his far-reaching discourse with Jon, she decided that the commander was intentionally avoiding the subject. *Is it because he somehow believes that he will lose me as his child?* However, once she drew his attention to the ceremony to be held in Washington, his curiosity regarding this ritual or wedding

Chapter Fifty-Four

ceremony had to be satisfied, which Lana was more than happy to explain.

'In every detail,' Jon noted with a grin.

When she anxiously enquired if he would indeed make an appearance and attend, her father hastened to assure her that having crossed at least one galaxy as a result of the request to give the bride away, he would accompany Jon and Lana back to Earth in their little craft. 'My first time to fly in one of those for about two hundred years,' he admitted ruefully, which apparently was not something he was looking forward to.

Knowing of Jon's earthly origins and being aware that the joining ceremony or marriage between certain races and cultures was based on certain superstitious or religious beliefs, Rega enquired, 'Do you wish to adhere to the customs of your own people, Jon, and have the ceremony performed by a priest or some such person? No doubt that would be pleasing to the governments and people that you associate with on Earth, but I have to observe that it would have little meaning for Lana as she has no religious beliefs. If we Zellians worship anything, it is probably nature and science respectively.' He smiled indulgently for a moment before continuing. 'I believe that many of the beliefs of what you term Christianity are shared by many cultures throughout the known universe. They have been proved to provide a basis for peaceful coexistence and harmony between different types of societies and cultures for millions of years, and so predate your quaint beliefs in some kind of prophet on Earth, a belief shared by more of your other religions, Buddhists and Muslims also.'

'That is true,' Jon conceded, 'and it is one aspect of life on Earth that I have no intention of trying to influence. Too many wars have been waged in the name of different religions in the recent past, but it has to be said, Rega, that I believe such beliefs will change to some extent as the populations all over the world come to live in harmony. Starvation and disease will be consigned to history, and

Chapter Fifty-Four

the politicians will be persuaded to help educate the masses to accept the many changes to technology and science that will benefit all humankind.'

Again Rega smiled as he put his hand gently on Jon's shoulder. 'I can see that you have the welfare of your people at heart, Jon, and I applaud you on your ambitions for the future, but having seen similar situations on other planets in the past, I would urge you to be patient with your own kind. They have come a long way in the last thousand years, but the next few short years may well see greater changes in science and technology than has ever been experienced before in the memory of man. You will have to guide them along this road patiently and firmly, Jon.'

Then relenting from his sober mood for a moment, he continued, 'But from what Captain Jara has told me about your transformation from a normal man of Earth into a Teacher, and now that you are officially recognized as the ambassador of Zel, with the assistance of all our resources and technical knowhow, you will be able to bring about all the required changes that I see in your mind. But enough of such things, Jon.' He laughed. 'Let us discuss your joining ceremony with my beloved daughter.'

Aware that Rega had been probing his mind during their conversation, but not resenting the intrusion of a fellow telepath, Jon smiled as he replied, 'The type of ceremony that we both would wish for will not be based on any religious format. As you said, Rega, that would be meaningless to Lana. We do recognize a form of civil marriage, which depends more on a declaration of love and commitment to each other between the two people involved. It is a declaration made in front of family and friends that is every bit as sincere and binding as any religious ceremony, and will be accepted as lawful to all who are present on the occasion, and indeed to the society of men.'

Lana was, at this moment, showing signs of excitement at the mention of the joining ceremony. *What does it matter if it has some*

Chapter Fifty-Four

religious overtones as practised by the people of Earth, she thought, *since a civil declaration is considered normal on my home planet.* Then a wonderful thought occurred to her, and she said, 'Father, as the commander of a mother ship and a member of the High Council of Zel, would you do us the honour of officiating at our joining ceremony?'

Rega pretended to deliberate before answering, blocking his innermost thoughts for a moment in order to keep Lana in suspense. 'But of course I will,' he said, 'If I'm expected to travel across the width of at least one galaxy to give my only daughter away to an alien, albeit a man of Earth, who is more like a Zellian than a Zellian, then I would have insisted that I'm the one best qualified to perform the ceremony.' As he embraced Lana and Jon simultaneously, he laughed again as he said. 'What would your mother say if she could see the man you have chosen to be your lifelong partner, a perfect specimen physically and mentally, but whose appearance would certainly cause much comment at home. He is so much more muscular, but is as tall as any Zellian, and that hair. None of our people have hair that shines like a silver beacon.'

'Perhaps the people of Earth will come to regard Jon as a beacon of hope for the future, Father,' Lana stated. 'He is revered in some parts of the world already and is respected by many of the governments of Earth.' She added, 'Although depriving them of their nuclear toys did cause some initial resentment.'

Rega again smiled as he recalled the report he had received from Captain Jara regarding the location and destruction of every missile in every country of the world. 'Your wisdom in dealing with that particular problem, Jon,' he said dryly, 'was commendable and bodes well for any future crisis that may occur. But in your role as the Teacher, you will no doubt benefit from experience as you deal with your own people, some of whom will resent whatever action you take. Such is the nature of emerging nations on all the planets that the Zellians have nurtured in the past. I personally take comfort

Chapter Fifty-Four

in your future, knowing that you have received far more training and education than any other Teacher in the past, and that your abilities will protect both you and Lana from the physical dangers that you will undoubtedly encounter during the next five hundred years.'

Jon found himself grinning at the recollection of one incident and the physical danger of the attack by Red Rodriguez back on the island of Buccaneer's Point. 'I do believe we will survive to live to a relatively old age,' he said with certainty. 'Our one concern will not to become victims of one of Earth's many diseases and become ill and die.'

'You can rest assured on that score,' Rega stated, 'whereas you have been trained in so many skills to fulfil your role as a Teacher, Lana is not only a trained scientist and space pilot, but she had to undergo some medical studies as part of her duties on board your own little craft. If you recall, she assisted Mort in your indoctrination process and medical aftercare, and if ever the need were to arise, you will find that her knowledge is at least equal to that of any of Earth's medical people, probably more so,' he added with parental pride.

'Well, that is a comfort to know,' Jon replied, not the least bit surprised to learn of yet another of Lana's repertoire of abilities. 'She is truly a remarkable woman.'

Rega again smiled as he acknowledged his daughter's unique personality. 'Yes, Jon,' he replied, 'you are going to be the last but most effective Teacher on Earth, the only human ambassador for the Zellian people, and Lana will give you comfort and support for however long you both may live on Earth. Unless, of course, you decide to take up residence on Zel once you have completed your mission on your own planet.' He added with a touch of elation in his voice, 'That would undoubtedly increase your life spans by at least another hundred years.'

Chapter Fifty-Four

Jon and Lana looked at each other for a fleeting moment, their minds communicating their innermost thoughts, and Lana replied for them both. 'Father, when you have been to where we intend to live during our lifetime on Earth, you'll appreciate how similar in appearance it is to our family home on Zel—subtropical climate, green pastures, and jungle surrounding our home, a mountain in the background, and we even have a waterfall to complete the illusion.' Then wistfully she added, 'But perhaps you could arrange for us to be transported back to Zel, perhaps in another hundred years' time in order to see my mother and,' she said with a laugh, 'to introduce my Earthman, who is more of a Zellian than a Zellian, apart from his hair!'

Once more Rega embraced Lana as he replied, 'After your joining ceremony, I would most certainly visit your island sanctuary. From your description, it sounds very much like our own home, and if it is, then I can understand why you are prepared to live out your life on Earth.'

At the mention of the ceremony again, and a possible visit to Buccaneer's Point by the commander, Jon was prompted to remind Lana and her father that it was time to consider their return to Washington. 'We may have to finalise certain arrangements for the wedding,' he said quietly, 'and I believe the president intends to recognize our services to the Unites States and the peace process in general. In what way, I don't know, for when I looked into his mind, he was still contemplating an appropriate award, subject to agreement with his advisors and government officials.'

'Well, it has been many years since I last set foot on your planet, Jon,' Rega said with a smile. 'If I recollect, that was the occasion when I took a quantity of rough carbon-like stones, a product of the planet Ka to one of one of your excellent craftsmen, a man of unique skills who transformed them into what you term diamonds. Pretty trinkets, which I understand, are of some commercial value to you. In fact, I still have in my possession a quantity of those finished

Chapter Fifty-Four

stones, which you may have as a wedding gift.' Turning to Lana, he said with a laugh. 'I believe these diamonds can be exchanged or bartered for almost any commodity on Earth, even your own island paradise.'

Mentally, Jon had to concede that it would be difficult to keep a secret of any kind from a powerful telepath such as Rega, but equally fortunate that they could all be open minded with each other. *Keep it in the family,* he thought wryly. The origin of the diamond hoard already in their possession having now been verified, and with the offer of yet another gift from Commander Rega to bolster their already immense worldly wealth, smiling with amusement, Jon turned to Lana and said, 'Jacob didn't know the truth of it when he said the beauty of the diamonds was out of this world. Now perhaps we can satisfy his curiosity regarding their origin, but sadly, the craftsman or lapidary who cut and polished the stones to such perfection is presumably long since dead. A pity.'

Embracing her father affectionately, a gesture only possible between them in the privacy of Rega's living quarters, Lana thanked him for the promised gift, assuring him that the trinkets would undoubtedly be useful in providing every luxury that the ambassador of Zel and his wife could possibly wish for.

Passing over the matter of the commercial value of the diamonds as of no consequence, Rega turned the conversation to their intended return to Earth. 'We will wait another twenty-four hours before we leave the mother ship. We are only waiting for a number of the shuttle craft to return to base, the flying saucers as your people refer to them, Jon.' He smiled. 'You probably noticed that the hangar deck was almost empty when you docked into position on your arrival.' Jon nodded. 'They were on a separate surveillance mission of Earth to satisfy my curiosity that all nuclear weapons have indeed been destroyed,' Rega added, 'and I'm glad to say it would appear that that part of your mission was entirely successful.' Smiling in satisfaction, he continued, 'When the last of

Chapter Fifty-Four

the craft are back on board, we will make our departure. We mustn't keep the president waiting too long; after all, you'll want to know what he has in store for you both.'

'I can't even begin to guess,' Jon replied with a laugh, 'but whatever he has in mind, I'm sure that Lana and I are in for a pleasant surprise. But one thing's for sure, he can't offer us any financial rewards since we will now have more wealth than any other individuals on Earth, thanks to the wedding gift you intend to bestow on us.'

Lana too had to make a comment about the additional hoard of diamonds. 'What will Jacob think when we show him another collection of rare stones, collected on Ka and transformed by an unknown lapidary into those scintillating jewels that he admires so much?'

Rega made no effort to suppress his laughter as he exclaimed, 'What would your friend Jacob think if he could see Ka? It is almost ten per cent compressed carbon, and these crude diamonds litter the surface of the planet as do the pebbles on a beach on Earth.'

Both Jon and Lana could appreciate why Commander Rega regarded his intended wedding gift as mere trinkets, but for themselves, they knew that with the help of Jacob and his connections with the jewellery markets of the world, they represented untold wealth on Earth. 'Anyway, Father,' Lana said with an appreciative smile, 'Jon and I thank you for your gift. You may not realise their perceived value on Earth, but having experienced what influence they can have on the minds of men, we can assure you that in terms of material wealth, there is nothing more valuable that you could give us, so what the president intends to bestow on us must be very rare indeed.'

As there was little more to add about the trinkets and wedding gifts, the subject of conversation again turned to other matters of mutual interest to three highly intelligent individuals. The galaxy in

Chapter Fifty-Four

which they lived, or in Jon's instance, the solar system and its planets, the furtherance of space exploration and how it was necessary to bend or warp time itself in order to traverse the enormous distances between the various star systems or galaxies, something which the Zellians had been doing for millions of years already. Rega continued with his own observation on the subject. 'That is something that we Zellians have been doing, as you surmise, Jon, for millions of years already, and we're still exploring the so-called frontiers of space, space that has no beginning, space that has no end.' Shaking his head in wonder, he added, 'Even with our extended lifespan and the technology available to us, no one in our recorded history has ever reached the end of the universe. It is truly infinite.'

Chapter Fifty-Five

After a time, they discussed the subject of Jon's plans for the future of the people of Earth, and as Rega revealed his extensive knowledge of Earth's history, it gradually dawned on Jon that it was going to be a very slow process to make any meaningful changes to the attitudes of people in general. The technology wouldn't be difficult to implement. That could be possible within the first hundred years of his term as the Teacher, but to teach them to live in harmony with each other for any length of time was something that had eluded all social groups on Earth.

The commander finally conceded that while Earth and its people had reached the stage ready for change, it was going to take a strong, perhaps even a ruthless, leader, someone who could make the decisions for those changes. 'And you, Jon, are that person. But I have no doubt you will have to request the assistance of my ship in military matters from time to time. Your one little craft has enormous potential for destruction, but it can't cover a very wide area at any one time, whereas when my fleet has returned from their mission, I will have at least eight craft at your disposal, and no nation on Earth can resist that amount of persuasion.'

Jon voiced his concerns regarding the use of force, quoting a very old proverb, or something similar, that he doubted Rega had ever heard before. 'You can guide a donkey easily through a hole in a wall, but you would find it difficult to push it through.'

This was a concept that Rega was quick to grasp as he replied wryly, 'And no doubt you will come across many donkeys in your

Chapter Fifty-Five

quest for progress, Jon.' With a thoughtful expression on his face, he continued. 'Another demonstration of your military strength would subdue the more war-like factions who might challenge the measures necessary to bring about a lasting peace on Earth.'

'That won't be long in coming, Commander Rega. There is at least one region that comes to mind where there has been almost continuous conflict over the last fifty years.' He only took a moment's reflection before continuing, 'but I won't initiate any immediate action, as I have other concerns on my mind.' Nevertheless, he resolved that the problems of the fanatical beliefs of certain tribes in the mountainous regions of Asia would require his attention.

'Ah. Religion,' Jon frowned as he reflected, 'most of them preach love of their respective Gods and their fellowmen, and yet, they still kill and wage war to impose their own brand of religion on their neighbours. Such futility.' He dismissed the petty conflicts of man from his mind for the time being and returned to the matter of going back to Earth and the subsequent introduction of Commander Rega to the President of the United States. He also pondered the prospects of Rega meeting the politicians of that country as well as the many heads of state who would be visiting Washington for the wedding ceremony. *Not very far away now,* Jon reminded himself. The trip back to Earth would only take about the usual six hours to complete. That was certainly not long enough for Rega to experience any real discomfort with the cramped conditions of the small saucer spacecraft, but Jon had to concede that for a lengthy stay on Earth, much more suitable accommodations would be required, something more in keeping with the luxurious surroundings of the mother ship.

As his gaze took in the opulent appearance of the commander's private living quarters. He could only compare it with some of the more exotic and expensive hotels he had stayed in during his journeys on Earth as Jon Bradburn, air traffic controller at the City

Chapter Fifty-Five

of Manchester Airport, and those hotels of the far-flung reaches of western civilisations, which were only outdone by many in the Middle East and Far East countries, some of which were breathtaking in their splendour. *Well,* he thought, *Washington has The Willard Intercontinental, which compares favourably to what the best in the world has to offer, and I think that the commander will find the accommodation there to his satisfaction. And security should not be a problem.*

As always, Rega had been following Jon's thought processes. He smiled as he remarked, 'I haven't always been privileged to live in such comfortable surroundings,' gesturing to the area in which they were seated. 'As a young Star Fleet officer, I had to spend months and years at a time on a craft such as yours. Not exactly a hardship, as you well know, but not to be compared with life on a mother ship where every comfort and luxury is provided to make life in space compatible for every crewmember, from the most junior officer to the commander himself.'

With an easy smile, he continued, 'From what I see in your mind of our accommodation in Washington, it should prove to be more than satisfactory, almost the same standard of comfort that I have here on my own ship, and as for personal security, Jon, any Zellian who leaves the confines of one of our ships, is aware of any personal danger from the native species or animals, and is always equipped with the usual force field belt, which incidentally has proved so useful to you on a number of occasions already.'

Jon grinned at the recollection of those occasions and replied, 'Yes, Rega, I wouldn't go anywhere without it in the outside world. Earth itself is not a dangerous planet, but its inhabitants are.'

He then briefly explained that physical contact with the president, shaking hands in particular, was not possible while the force field belt was activated, but otherwise, as a means of personal protection, it was invaluable. He added ruefully, 'It has also been improvised as a weapon of death and destruction on several

Chapter Fifty-Five

occasions.' There was no need for explanation regarding that statement as Rega could read Jon's memories of those events quite clearly, almost as though they were his own.

'If very close personal contact with your friends on Earth is important to you, Jon, such as this custom of shaking hands with each other, very quaint,' he said with a laugh, 'then that can easily be arranged. I will ask one of our technicians to fine-tune your individual belt so that it will feel as if you are in physical contact with your friend, with the president, or anyone else you trust. But even so, a minimal amount of force field will remain around you to protect against a projectile of low velocity should such an attack occur.'

Raising an eyebrow in question, Jon asked in disbelief, 'You mean an assassin's bullet or knife?'

'Most certainly,' Rega replied. 'There have been several instances in the history of your people where politicians and world leaders have had their lives terminated as a result of assassination, is that not so?'

'That's true,' Jon admitted ruefully. 'History has been changed several times as a result of such happenings, even in very recent times.' For a fleeting moment, he paused while a sudden thought passed through his mind. 'Rega, in the person of the president, Davis Cooper, we have a potential ally to assist me in my work for peace on Earth, if he lives long enough. If I could ensure that he could survive unharmed for at least another two years, until the end of his current term of office, that would give me the opportunity to make some of the necessary changes to industry in particular, and the energy problems of the world more feasible.'

Not doubting that the commander had already anticipated his next request, Jon continued quietly, 'Although the Zellians have probably never intervened in such a way before, I would ask you as the representative of the High Council and a commander of the

Chapter Fifty-Five

mother ship, would you consider giving Davis Cooper a modified force field belt that would only protect against an assassin's bullet or knife. There would be no need for the belt to be as powerful as our own. It would only be used for his limited protection.'

Rega nodded sympathetically at this suggestion, knowing that Jon regarded Davis Cooper as a friend as well as one of the most powerful politicians in the world, a very useful ally in the coming years ahead. 'Yes, Jon,' he replied. 'I see no difficulty in providing the president with the means to protect himself from assassination. By wearing the belt continuously night and day, he will be immune to any low level physical attack, although,' he smiled grimly at the sudden thought, 'he would still feel the blow if a bullet were to hit his force field, but at least he would only be bruised, not dead. I will also see that your own belt is modified, too, to allow hand contact with your friends. It will be like having a very thick skin on the whole of your body, but in your case, the force field can be extended at will as at present. In the meanwhile . . . .' Rega looked fondly at Lana, who had been holding on to Jon's arm while this discussion had been taking place. 'I will give orders for these modified force field belts to be prepared and ready for our departure. I did say within twenty-four hours, and also I will be accompanied by two of my crew members, junior officers I think, to act as my stewards during our trip to Washington.'

Lana intervened with a laugh. 'And don't forget, Father, that apart from what will be a diplomatic visit to Earth in general and Washington in particular, we will no doubt be making a visit to Buccaneer's Point immediately after our joining ceremony.'

'In that case,' Rega replied with mock severity, 'I'd better instruct my stewards to pack my best uniforms for the duration of this extended visit.'

Still laughing, Lana retorted, 'Don't worry, Father, if some extra clothing is required for your stay on our island we can always stop en route in Jamaica.' Again with a mischievous giggle, she added,

Chapter Fifty-Five

'We know of a shop in Kingston where the staff will be delighted to fit you out with all your clothing requirements; they will be most meticulous in taking your measurements.' As she said this, she looked pointedly at Jon, recalling their last visit to the tailor shop and the attentions of the assistants, all females, of course.

With his preparations for his visit to Washington in mind, Rega excused himself and left Lana and Jon to their own devices, with the suggestion that they spend the time until departure having a thorough exploration of the mother ship and all its wonderful design and technology, the result of the ingenuity of millions of years of the advanced civilisation of the Zellians. This they were more than happy to do. However, after some three or four hours walking around the various departments and living quarters on board, they both agreed that while the mother ship was only some two miles in length, with so many decks stacked one above the other, twenty-four hours didn't possibly allow enough time to see more than a fraction of the interior of the ship. So, in due course, they conceded that they were both physically weary of their exploration, and it was now appropriate to retire to their quarters to refresh themselves. After which, who knew? There was still a long time until departure.

Chapter Fifty-Six

As Jon and Lana entered the hanger deck, they noticed that every parking bay was occupied by a sleek and shimmering craft, identical in every way to their own flying saucer. These craft made up the mother ship's full complement of patrol vessels, and including their own, a total of eight in all. 'A formidable force should they ever have to be used to assert a military presence at any time in the near future,' Jon reflected. If persuasion to live in peace became necessary to subdue those areas of Earth where most of the problems occurred, at least with the assistance of Commander Rega and his battle fleet, it would take a matter of days, not months or even years as it had done in the past. It would be a lesson delivered in such a manner that there would be no defence, of short duration, and possibly with few survivors on the ground. As he recalled the outcome of the war games in the Arizona desert, Jon smiled grimly at the picture of total annihilation of the supposed enemy, and how the landscape below had completely changed, and that had only involved two of the small Zellian craft.

Jon's thoughts didn't dwell on the possibility of taking action against any insurgents or opponents of his teachings, which could happen in the weeks or even months ahead. The first thing was to get aboard his own ship and prepare to receive Commander Rega and his stewards, with all their personal belongings. Then finally, they'd leave the confines of the mother ship and set course for Earth.

Chapter Fifty-Six

Lana, as ever, had been tuned in to his thoughts, but it was only when they were on the flight deck of their own ship that she spoke aloud. Her first comment was, 'I can see what Father meant when he said that he wasn't looking forward to travelling in one of these small craft.' Looking around, she said with a smile, 'This has always seemed comfortable and cosy to us, but after the luxury of his own mother ship, he will understandably be glad that he has only a six-hour journey with us.'

Jon grinned as he replied, 'We will all transfer from ship to shore as soon as possible after making our rendezvous with Captain Jara and Mort.' He then continued, 'When we're about one hour from Washington, I'll contact George K. Lane with our ETA, and he will then confirm our reservation with the management of the Willard Intercontinental Hotel.' He couldn't help but suppress a laugh as he said to Lana, 'They will believe that they are being invaded by aliens, especially when they see how tall and slim all the Zellian males are.' He added as an afterthought, 'But they will undoubtedly be assured by the perfection of their speech and decorum.'

They had only been aboard their own ship a little more than an hour, and had completed all preflight checks in readiness for departure from the mother ship, when Commander Rega, accompanied by his two stewards, came aboard without any announcement or ceremony. To Jon's surprise, the stewards proved to be two young female cadet officers of exceptional beauty by Zellian standards, tall and willowy, and as would no doubt be demonstrated on closer acquaintance, were extremely intelligent and efficient in their duties, as one would expect from the commander's immediate staff officers.

At the sight of her father coming aboard with his personal flight attendants, Lana couldn't hide her surprise that she was to have some female company for the duration of this visit to Earth. Meanwhile, Jon noted with wry amusement, 'Will these young

Chapter Fifty-Six

ladies find love with a man of Earth or return to the mother ship leaving a few broken hearts behind?'

Rega had caught this last thought, which Jon had not attempted to screen, and answered with equal amusement. 'Very doubtful, Jon. My stewards are even younger than Lana, barely sixty years old, and have shown no inclination toward the opposite sex as yet, but,' he continued with a smile, 'if the atmosphere on Earth has the same effect on them as it apparently had on Lana, it may be that they will mature more rapidly and blossom into full womanhood much earlier than usual.'

In a bantering tone of voice, Lana said to her father, 'Your stewards are unlikely to meet any men on Earth like Jon. He is unique and one of a kind in every way, physically, mentally, and a Teacher who will live for at least five hundred years. Apart from his physical attributes and beauty, he is now going to be the richest and most powerful being on the planet.' She paused for a moment before continuing in a more serious tone. 'Despite all of that, Father, you, more than anyone else, can look into his mind and see that he is a man of compassion and has the welfare of humanity in his heart. He has a desire to achieve what all Teachers before him have been unable to bring to the Earth, peace between the different races and cultures, the elimination of starvation, poverty and disease, in essence, to herald a new age for humanity under his guidance and leadership.'

Commander Rega replied with sincerity, 'Yes, my daughter, not only can I see that you have chosen a worthy lifelong partner, but I have to concede that Captain Jara and Mort selected the finest candidate on Earth to take on the role of the last Teacher. Whatever kind of life he had before, since his indoctrination and transformation. after being picked up by the search team, yourself included, of course, he has shown a willingness to learn and adapt to his new life, to leave the past behind, and look only to the future. And with you beside him, his extended lifespan of five hundred

Chapter Fifty-Six

years may not seem enough. Perhaps you may both decide to return to Zel one day, where you could both live for another century, at least.'

Soberly, Lana replied, 'We will make that decision in five hundred years' time, when Jon has achieved his purpose on Earth.' Then on a lighter note, she continued, 'Are you going to introduce your staff officers to us, Father? They are rather young to be part of a diplomatic mission, or were you thinking of company for me in the days ahead?'

Rega smiled indulgently as he replied, 'Yes, Lana, they are both very young cadets, much the same age as you were when you left the space academy at the start of your career, and look how you have progressed since then. You will be a perfect role model for them, and yes, I did consider that a little Zellian female company would help you to keep in touch with your own culture for the time being.' At that moment, the stewards returned to the flight deck, after apparently stowing away, temporarily at least, all the personal belongings of Commander Rega and their own considerable baggage, which, judging from its quantity, must entail a protracted stay on Earth.

With an inclination of his head, the commander said in a jovial tone of voice, 'Ah. Here they are. My staff officers, cadet Asa and cadet Rea, whom I shall place in your care, Lana. You will find them willing pupils, and I'm sure attentive to their duties.' He added with a laugh for Jon's benefit, 'I believe you have a saying on Earth, they are bright young things and are good for the morale of an ageing space voyager like myself.'

Jon relaxed with a smile. 'They will also be good for the morale of the many young men of Earth that they are destined to meet in the days and weeks ahead.' He paused for a moment before continuing. 'Judging by the amount of personal belongings your stewards brought aboard, I get the impression that you intend to remain with us for some time, weeks or months perhaps?'

Chapter Fifty-Six

Again Commander Rega spoke quietly, although in his mind he was also communicating with them both telepathically. 'Having been parted from my only child for some ten years, I feel that I have much to catch up on. The occasion of assisting the last Teacher on Earth to fulfil his role in completing the education of humankind in itself warrants my presence for as long as several months at least.'

Then with a flash of parental pride, he added, 'And I'm sure the Grand Council of Zel will approve of my staying on Earth until my daughter's joining ceremony. And I shall establish diplomatic links with the many leaders of what I believe you refer to as the United Nations.' He was obviously contemplating with some pleasure the events likely to occur in the weeks ahead. 'Although I have visited Earth a number of times before, it was always a stay of short duration, a matter of days to complete whatever business was required, with no time to appreciate the undeniable beauty of some parts of the planet, and certainly, with little opportunity to mix with the present-day race of humankind.' He laughed as he conceded that the Zellians of five million years ago were the ones who had integrated with early man in the broadest sense, educating and improving the species. Now, it was going to be Jon's turn to complete the transformation of what had been the primitive creatures of this planet into something akin to the Zellians, very similar physically and much improved from a mental point of view. Although, when he looked at Jon standing next to him, he realised that Lana's declaration that Jon was unique could not be disputed. He was more Zellian than most Zellians were. He was stronger and mentally equal to any commander or member of the High Council, himself included. As he looked at the man who was to change the destiny of humankind, he felt an inward glow of pride that Jon was to become a member of his own family as a result of the joining ceremony. As his thoughts turned to that happy event, he embraced Lana gently with one arm, while he grasped Jon's shoulder firmly and said, 'As captain of this, your own ship, Jon, I would like to see you take command of the bridge and take us out of the mother ship and set

Chapter Fifty-Six

course for Washington and Earth.' He added with a laugh, 'You can utilise the services of your latest crew members, Asa and Rea. They are still only cadets, but have received basic training for this type of craft and will no doubt be eager to demonstrate their usefulness to you and Lana on board this ship, as well as when we are all on your home planet.'

Jon raised an eyebrow quizzically as he looked at Lana, as if to say, *I hope my training was more than basic as this will be my first experience in leaving a mother ship, especially under the eye of the commander himself. However, here goes.* With that, he sat in the command chair with all the instrumentation before him, noting the array of flashing lights and symbols informing him of the state of readiness of the ship, since the before-flight inspections had been carried out prior to Rega and his stewards coming aboard. As he calmly observed all the data before him, he requested the two cadets to be prepared to standby the communications system and visual awareness instruments recording the outside activity on the hanger deck. On being informed that all systems were ready, and it was clear for them to go, Jon, first of all, requested permission from the mother ship's control centre to leave the confines of the ship. The operator duly gave the required permission, adding that the tractor beams holding them in their docking station were now disengaged and that they could officially take their leave. As before, when he had piloted this craft, Jon found that it wasn't necessary to actually touch any of the controls, only to pass his hands over them, and in some instances, with the simpler commands, he could relay them by thought or mind control, something that even Lana had never achieved. Under the watchful eye of Rega, now every inch a professional commander of the Zellian space navy, Jon gave his orders to his crew in a calm and assured manner until the undocking procedure was completed and they were well clear of the mother ship. Only then did he relinquish the con to Lana, with the order to set course for Washington, Earth with all speed.

Chapter Fifty-Six

Commander Rega was nodding his approval. 'A textbook display of the command required to control a departure from the mother ship to whatever the destination, in this case, Washington.' Then with a wry smile of amusement, he added, 'I'm glad that it will only take a few hours to arrive. After my own ship, yours does feel rather constricted, even though a few hundred years ago, I was content to be captain of a similar craft, proud of it, in fact. One thing I did notice, Jon. You seem to give many of your commands telepathically and the ship responds as though it was an extension of yourself. Is that a result of your indoctrination procedure all those months ago, or is it something that you've trained yourself to do?'

Jon's response to that question was immediate as he was, and had been aware for some time now, that his mental control in all things was gradually getting stronger. His telepathy, reading the minds of others even when they attempted to block his probing, would not be denied. As the commander had observed, his control of the ship was almost completely a reflex mental exercise. *Telekinesis? That remains to be tried during a suitable occasion, and when it is, that will prove to be a moving occasion.* He smiled inwardly at the pun. *Teleporting? How far can an experienced Zellian travel with the power of the mind? I'm told that an adept can project himself in space thousands of miles at a time, in which case, I will try the same feat at some time in the near future, perhaps from Washington to Jamaica, and then on to Buccaneer's Point. Now that would be an achievement for a man of Earth.*

While these quiet musings went through Jon's mind, Commander Rega was aware of every thought, and he conceded that, *For a man of Earth, you have far surpassed the abilities of any Teachers before you; indeed, few Zellians to my knowledge can equal you at this present time.* At that, he placed a friendly hand on Jon's shoulder and said, 'What does the future hold for the last Teacher on Earth? I wonder if I shall live long enough to see how powerful you will

Chapter Fifty-Six

become Jon.' He added with a smile, 'But looking into your heart, I'm sure that, in your case, absolute power will not bring corruption, as it did for so many other rulers on Earth in the past.'

With the prospect of another six hours before making landfall over Washington, and the ship now under automatic pilot control, Jon and Lana then engaged the cadets Asa and Rea in conversation with a view to becoming not only their superior officers, but their friends. Class distinction was unknown among the Zellians. Only respect for experience, knowledge, and Jon had to smile at the thought, old age. Looking at his companions on the flight deck, he realised that, although he was second only in rank to Rega, he was also the youngest person on board, still only thirty-two Earth years in age. By far, he was more junior than the sixty-year-old cadets.

Lana had been following his innermost thoughts with some amusement, but the commander made the most relevant comment. 'In your comparatively short life, Jon, you have gained more experience and education than it has ever been the privilege of mortal man, or Zellian for that matter. Your achievements, as a result of your extended indoctrination process on this very vessel . . .' He gestured toward the adjoining cabin where the medical centre was located. 'Was as a result of what was, in fact, a gamble to see how much knowledge could be instilled in a human brain.'

He smiled as he continued. 'Lana assured me that she watched over you throughout the procedure, as your mind absorbed all the programming, your body changed, and your physique was enhanced to its present state of perfection. Had there been any sign that there was a danger to your life during the procedure, the experiment would have been terminated immediately.' Rega smiled at his own thought. 'It would appear that the only outward sign of distress to your person was that your hair changed to that very unusual, but distinctive texture and colour, something that Lana and all the ladies undoubtedly admire, even Asa and Rea seem to find it attractive.'

Chapter Fifty-Six

Jon grinned at his recollection of the first sight of himself in a mirror after his awakening. 'My own mother won't know me, I've changed so much. In fact,' he added, 'I may yet have to meet old friends or colleagues at some time in the future and as Jon, ambassador of the Zel, they are quite unlikely to recognise me. Until a few months ago, I was just like any other mortal man of Earth, but now so very different in many ways, physically and mentally.'

Rega again touched Jon lightly on the shoulder, a gesture showing his respect for this young man of Earth. 'There is nothing ordinary about you now, Jon, ambassador of the Zellians.' He then laughed to lighten the moment. 'And soon to become a member of my own family, and that is far from ordinary.'

They continued their conversation for some hours, sometimes in serious dialogue, occasionally exchanging bantering comments about life in the space service and its effect on their individual lives. Even Asa and Rea were encouraged to talk about their experiences as children, how they were educated and their subsequent recruitment into the space service. Having such an attentive audience of senior officers, they were delighted to be able to express their views of life as they had found it so far and their hopes and aspirations for the future. Teasingly, Jon asked them. 'From what you have seen of the men of Earth, albeit from a distance, do you think you will find them physically attractive?'

Lana gave Jon a reproving look as she commented, 'The girls are far too young for such thoughts.' But she was unprepared for Asa's answer.

'If we could meet men like Jon, then yes, we would find them attractive.'

Rea then went a step further as she addressed Lana directly. 'If the daughter of the commander of a mother ship and a member of the High Council is going to take part in a joining ceremony with a man of Earth, then surely, we too will find them attractive.'

Chapter Fifty-Six

It was Rega who decided to change the subject to less personal issues, by asking his stewards to retrieve a certain package from his effects in his temporary living quarters. 'A flat box, with my seal on it,' he said. Rea went in search of the package, returning a few minutes later holding the item carefully, not knowing what it contained. Accepting it with a courteous, 'Thank you, Cadet Rea,' Rega then turned to Jon and said, 'This is the energy belt that you requested for your friend, the president. It has been greatly modified from the likes of your own, which has a force field that extends for quite a large area and can be activated manually or by your own mental awareness of danger, in other words, telepathically.' He handed the package over to Jon as he continued with his explanation of the limited power of the belt. 'No doubt you will have to persuade Davis Cooper that this apparently ordinary belt has the power to save his life, if an assassination attempt should be made on his life. Once placed around his naked body and locked in position, which I suggest you do for him, it will immediately be energised and will remain so until it is released sometime in the future. Again, only you will be able to perform this function as the radiation of the belt is tuned into your personal brainwave pattern.'

Jon smiled at the thought of the president submitting to the procedure of having the belt placed around his naked body. 'I wouldn't like to speculate when anyone last saw him naked,' he said. 'But perhaps we can compromise. To strip to the waist will probably suffice.'

Rega also smiled as he agreed. 'Again, a wise decision, Jon. Spare the president's modesty, but do ensure that you impress on him the necessity that he begin to wear the force field belt as soon as possible.'

As Jon inspected the belt and turned it over in his hands, he had to concede that it looked like an ordinary belt as worn by the normal adult males on Earth to hold up their trousers, but at such close proximity, he could sense the pulsating radiation source, the

Chapter Fifty-Six

latent power only distinguishable to himself. 'I think the President will need a small demonstration of his personal force field before he will be convinced of its practical ability.' As he thought about how to explain the practical protection afforded by the belt, a picture formed in his mind of the chainmail worn by medieval knights of old, which had been comparatively light in weight, but impenetrable to any light projectile, a veritable lifesaver. *Yes, that explanation should convince him, together with a demonstration of an object thrown at him across his office.* Again, a smile crossed his face at such a thought. *Shall I carry out the demonstration myself, or shall I let the General have that privilege?*

Lana intervened with a laugh. 'I think General Clintock would welcome the opportunity to take part in a demonstration of that kind, although he might have to be assured that no harm will come to the president.'

Again, Rega stated his opinion that Davis Cooper should begin wearing his protective belt as soon as possible and that it should also be clearly explained that it couldn't be removed without Jon's assistance, but once fitted, it would quite unobtrusive to the wearer in any circumstances. 'Even in the shower,' he added with a smile of amusement.

While they had been discussing the issue of the president's personal safety, the spacecraft had been drawing nearer to Earth, which now loomed large on the forward viewing screens. It was a familiar sight to all on board, but to Jon in particular, one that made him appreciate the beauty of Earth as seen from space. They were now only about one hour from their estimated time of arrival over Washington, but still far enough away for the planet it to appear as a brilliant, multi-coloured globe suspended against the velvet blackness of space. The blue oceans and weather systems were evident by the cloud formations swirling slowly, casting shadows over the oceans, then moving gradually to reveal the various landmasses below.

Chapter Fifty-Six

As he gazed at this spectacle of nature, Rega came and stood quietly beside him, and after a moment's silence, said, 'Yes, Jon, Earth is one of the most beautiful planets in the universe, very similar to Zel in many ways, but with one difference. Whereas Zel has an assured future and its people are happy and content, your people have been heading for self-inflicted destruction for many years.' He continued soberly, 'But you have already taken one major step toward altering the destiny of humankind by eliminating all the nuclear weapons on the planet. But now you have the task of educating your people to live responsibly and together to strive toward peace and prosperity.'

Jon smiled calmly as he replied, 'When the advances in technology I have in mind are seen to improve the prosperity of those countries that cooperate with me, then those factions, who would otherwise rebel or resist peaceful change, will soon change their minds given the appropriate incentives, such as improvements in technology and unlimited sources of energy to power industry without polluting the atmosphere of the planet. And increasing food production to feed the masses, thereby eliminating starvation and disease. Those points can be achieved within a comparatively short period of time, say the first fifty years.'

'Is that being a little optimistic?' Rega said. 'To bring about such changes, I think will take at least a hundred years.'

Jon grinned. 'Humankind can be impatient when it comes to making progress. They want to see any changes taking place within their own lifetime, which, as you know, is very short.' He frowned slightly as he continued. 'We will have one problem that won't be easy to address in the future. As health is improved and food supplies become more plentiful, populations throughout the world are likely to increase dramatically.' He turned to Lana and her father. 'In some of their religious teachings, a quotation attributed to their God instructs them to go forth and multiply, something they have done enthusiastically, with the result that now the world is already overpopulated. That will have to be part of their education for the future. To limit their procreative activities will not be very popular, but it will have to be done in such a way that they are not aware that responsibility for the regeneration of the species is no longer under their direct control.'

Chapter Fifty-Seven

Rega nodded his understanding of the problem. 'We had the same difficulty on Zel many generations ago, but it soon became apparent that the planet could only support a given number of inhabitants if life was to be sustained. It would appear that a method of birth control will have to be introduced among your people, Jon, but as you say, without their knowledge, which is a difficult choice, since you won't be able to rely on any voluntary participation by many of the less educated men and women of the different races.'

He smiled briefly as he indicated Lana standing nearby, listening attentively to their conversation. 'With Lana's medical knowledge regarding how the Zellians controlled population growth without causing distress to the inhabitants of the planet or depriving them of their physical pleasures, no doubt you can be guided by her advice on this important matter, thus allowing you to concentrate on the other important issues you intend to initiate as soon as possible.'

Then, to lighten the tone of the discussion and to change the subject, he added, 'This will happen after your own joining ceremony, of course.' Then he reminded Jon to contact George K. Lane of their ETA since they were within an hour of Earth. 'No doubt our arrival will require a certain protocol to be observed,' he declared. 'The presence of two Zellian spaceships above Washington won't cause any panic nowadays, but we must decide if we are actually going to land our craft, or will we all teleport down to the president's office for our first meeting?'

Turning to Lana once more, Jon requested that she make the personal call to the secretary of state, not only informing him of their time of arrival, but that initially, Commander Rega, Lana, and he would teleport down from their ship at a given time to be arranged by the president when convenient.

There being little more to do as they approached Earth except watch the scene on the viewing screens, Jon gazed in fascination as the curvature of the earth disappeared gradually, and was replaced by what appeared to be a flat landscape below. As their altitude decreased, the velocity of their craft diminished, until they were barely doing two thousand miles per hour, a speed suitable for the atmospheric conditions of Earth.

Jon reflected on the method of approach to the planet by his flying saucer. There was no need to circumnavigate the earth in order to lose speed or approach at a precise angle to avoid burning up on re-entry to the dense atmosphere. Theirs was a direct descent once over their designated landing or docking position, in this case above the White House in Washington DC. Even as he watched, the details of the landscape below grew clearer, until he could make out with clarity the city below. As they continued their descent, he observed that Captain Jara was already in his docking position, hovering a mere thousand feet above the White House. 'Another spectacle for the tourists, no doubt,' Jon remarked idly to those standing nearby.

Within a few minutes, their craft took up a position close to Jara's spaceship, which, to the people below, was a sight never to be forgotten—two alien craft that posed no threat to humankind because they knew that Jon, the ambassador of the Zel, was on board. *What will all the American people think when the Zellians appear together for the first time in public?* Jon thought with a smile.

Chapter Fifty-Seven

As he contemplated that event with some amusement, Captain Jara appeared on the communication screen, with Mort close by in the background. 'Greetings, Jon, ambassador of the Zel, and may we extend a welcome to Commander Rega, Lana, and your two new assistant crew members, Asa and Rea.' He continued without waiting for a response. 'We only arrived several hours before our designated rendezvous time, and to occupy ourselves whilst waiting for your arrival, Mort has been doing a close-up survey of the people in the city below using one of his favourite toys, a mobile aerial camera which he perfected for exploring the more hostile environments of other planets in other galaxies.'

'And has he found the survey of some interest?' Jon enquired after acknowledging Jara's greeting.

'We both have,' Jara replied with a smile on his face. 'The camera is so small, no bigger than a human's eyeball, and it can pick up amazing data whilst traversing the city unnoticed. In effect, it mingles with the people unobserved.'

The image on the communication screen was enlarged to include Mort, who was holding a tiny object in his hand. 'My surveillance camera, my toy,' he declared with a grin. 'While I've landed on Earth many times before in the past, my visits have always been of a covert nature and short lived, such as when we picked you up, Jon, some time ago. However, with this device, it is possible to come into close proximity with the subject to be observed, in this case, the citizens of Washington.'

Jara again took up the story of their exploration of Washington and its people. 'The cities of Earth are so much larger and their populations much greater than ours on Zel. Having had time to study the people at length, and at leisure, we have to conclude that they are far more diversified than our own race. On Zel, we are all dark haired, the adults are fairly uniform in height and physique, and we live in excess of a thousand Earth years. Also,' he said quietly, 'we don't live by superstitions such as the religions practiced by the many Earth people of whatever race and creed they belong.' He paused for a moment as he looked at Mort for confirmation of the observations he had just made, and after a nod of agreement, he continued. 'In this one city alone, the stature of the adults varies enormously. Some are veritable giants, even compared to a Zellian, while others are of such stunted growth as to suggest some physical deformity.'

Looking at Jon rather pointedly, he exclaimed, 'Your hair is unique among the people of Earth and Zel also, but in the city below, we have seen examples of many different colours among children and adults alike. Some have hair similar to your own, but not so vibrant and without a glow like yours. Others have various shades of dark hair, red hair, and we've even seen a number of young people with multi-coloured hair, like certain species of bird that you have in different regions of the planet.'

Jon laughed at the bewilderment evinced in Jara's voice at such diversity. 'You mean parrots. Yes, we do have all different kinds of people. Different coloured skins as well, quite a mixture, unlike your home planet, Jara. But for the most part, when you begin to mix or socialise with them, you will find that they all have one thing in common, they are human.'

As both ships were now in docking position above the White House, where they were expected to remain until after the meeting with the president and whatever ceremonies were to be conducted on behalf of the American government and people, all the normal power systems used in flight were closed down, leaving only the residual mechanisms functioning. The protective energy shields around the ship was constantly energised on Commander Rega's insistence, and of course, sufficient power was sent to operate the magnetic field that enabled the Zellian craft to remain suspended above any planetary body for an indefinite period of time.

It was shortly after their arrival at the rendezvous that Cadet Rea reported a signal from the White House. Jon took the call on the

Chapter Fifty-Seven

visual monitor as the face of George K. Lane appeared, smiling broadly in greeting. 'Well, ambassador, it's great to see you again.' He then continued by exchanging the customary pleasantries between old friends, adding a warm welcome to Commander Rega. 'The father of the bride,' he quipped, 'as well as a member of the High Council of Zel and commander of the mother ship.'

Jon resolved to acquaint the secretary of state at the first opportunity, in private, just how important the father of the bride was equal to any president or royalty on Earth, and by far, more powerful in every way.

When all the introductions were over, George announced the purpose of his call. 'Mr President is standing by in the Oval Office for your visit. Just say the word and drop in on us.' He laughed at his intended pun, remembering the many occasions that Jon and Lana had done exactly that, appearing in the White House at a moment's notice.

Aware that the casual invitation was, however, a sincere one, Jon hastened to reply. 'Commander Rega, Lana, and I will, as you say, drop in on you in ten minutes' time, just as soon as we have briefed our junior officers regarding their duties during our absence.' This he knew to be a unnecessary precaution. Asa and Rea were well trained and reliable cadets, capable of manning the spaceship in the absence of their senor officers, but the interim period of time gained was a courtesy to the president and his staff. 'Give them time to brace themselves for our arrival, and of course, we don't know who will be waiting for us.'

As the visual contact with the White House was broken off, Commander Rega said, with his customary smile when he was pleased, 'You handle the niceties of diplomacy quite naturally, Jon. Is that a result of your Zellian training, or is it an inborn quality of your earlier life?'

Chapter Fifty-Seven

Jon grinned as he replied, 'I would like to think that I've always been polite and courteous to other people, regardless of rank or station in life.' Still smiling, he continued. 'There is one difference in my personality that has become more noticeable as time passes by, and that is, while I can respect people in authority, such as yourself Rega and President Cooper, I no longer feel in any way subservient, as I presumably was when I was just plain Jon Bradbury, the air traffic controller at Manchester Airport.'

With a frown of concentration on his face, the commander replied thoughtfully. 'That is because, Jon, as a result of your training, indoctrination, and education, you are now in possession of the cumulative knowledge of the Zellians and much more besides. During the month you spent in an induced coma on board this ship, your brain absorbed more data than any computers are capable of storing, and now, although you are not consciously aware of it, that knowledge is still in a latent form and will only be released as and when it is required. As the commander of a mother ship and a member of the High Council of the Zel, knowing what your powers are capable of now, mentally and physically, and knowing that your powers are still developing and getting stronger day by day, it is I who am in awe of you, the last Teacher. For you to feel subservient to any Zellian or man of Earth is the last thing that I would expect.'

With the now familiar pressure on Jon's shoulder, Rega continued, smiling in understanding. 'But, despite all of that, your concern for all the people of Earth and their welfare, will guide you in the path of destiny, and when, in five hundred years, you have completed your task of saving humankind and the planet itself, I sincerely hope that you will consider coming to Zel with my daughter.' Then, realising that the conversation had become a little heavy, he laughed and added, 'And perhaps you can bring your children with you, a daughter like Lana and a son like you, Jon. But will they have dark hair or hair that shines like a beacon?'

Chapter Fifty-Seven

It was Jon's turn to laugh as he returned the commander's grip, their hands on each other's shoulders, their friendship evident to everyone present. Lana beamed with pleasure at the sight of her father and Jon so obviously in accord with each other. 'First we have to conduct the joining ceremony, Rega, and as to having children in the future, that is something Lana and I have never discussed.'

'Oh, but I do wish to have children, as soon as we have established our home on Buccaneer's Point,' Lana interrupted. 'After all, the women of Earth bear their first child at a very tender age compared to the women of Zel.' Then turning to her father, she asked, 'How old was my mother when I was born, one hundred years? Our shortened lifespan, if we stay permanently on Earth, makes it more desirable to start our family much earlier than that.'

Rega smiled and said to Jon, 'I have a feeling that Lana is going to have her way in that matter, despite her own tender years, but she does have a point with regard to longevity of life on Earth.' He then embraced them both as he chuckled contentedly. 'I shall look forward to being a grandfather.'

Chapter Fifty-Eight

As time had passed by quickly as they conversed, Jon indicated that it was now appropriate that they make their appearance in the White House below. He said, 'To be punctual is to be polite.'

Rega nodded in agreement. 'After you, Jon,' he said, 'I will follow with Lana in a moment.'

Upon that, Jon teleported the short distance down to the president's Oval Office and found Davis Cooper, George K. Lane, and the familiar figure of General Clintock already assembled and waiting for the arrival of the Zellian contingent. They all rose from their seats and were about to give the salute, hand on breast, as they had done on previous occasions, but Jon remembered that his personal force field had been modified for just such an event and forestalled them by reaching out with his hand, shaking each of theirs in turn. He explained, 'We have now established our friendship to such an extent that your custom is acceptable to all Zellians,' which paved the way for the future introduction of Rega.

No sooner had they exchanged courtesies than the commander and Lana appeared behind Jon. It was with some sense of amusement that Jon read the general's thoughts as he appraised the commander for the first time. *Handsome old guy, but as skinny and tall as a beanpole.* Knowing that Rega would know what was passing through General Clintock's mind, although he might not be familiar with the description, as skinny as a bean pole, to avert any misunderstandings at this meeting, Jon quickly intruded into the general's mind telepathically, cautioning him to be more

Chapter Fifty-Eight

circumspect in dealing with any Zellian in personal matters. It obviously came as a shock to the general to find his own mind invaded, but he was shrewd enough to realise that Jon was demonstrating another of his powers. *What else is this man capable of?* Jon simply nodded amiably at the portly figure of General Clintock.

Commander Rega was an imposing figure. Tall even by Zellian standards, but as was common with all the inhabitants of that planet, he was what could only be described as being of slight physique. Lana was, of course, slender by Earthly standards, but being female, she was shapely and rounded, emphasising her beauty and femininity. So far no one had commented on the fact that Jon was so different to others of his race. When further comparisons were made with Captain Jara, Mort, and the cadets Rea and Asa, they did. *Is diversity of the Zellian race a plausible explanation for his uniqueness? Perhaps, but was he not also unlike his fellow human beings,* he had to ask himself.

Davis Cooper, as President of the United States of America, arguably the most powerful man on Earth, went to great lengths to welcome Commander Rega to the planet Earth and Washington, in particular. He was unaware that the Zellians had been visiting Earth for millions of years in the past. Indeed, it would have been a surprise for him to learn that Rega had visited Washington after cessation of hostilities after the American Civil War, albeit in a covert manner, hence, no record of such an event had ever been recorded.

As Jon, Rega, and Lana communed silently with each other for a moment, it was their turn to reflect that present-day man had much to thank the Zellians for, especially their intervention in the affairs of the many civilisations in the distant past. Now, finally, man was almost ready to be accepted into the Federation of the Stars, but it would all depend on Jon's success as the last Teacher.

Chapter Fifty-Eight

When all the introductions were completed, Davis Cooper invited them all to be seated, and proceeded to explain what was intended to happen during the next few days. First, there was an informal dinner in the White House in honour of the member of the High Council of the Zel. That would take place the next day. 'If that's okay with you, Commander?' the president asked. Rega confirmed his acceptance with a nod and his customary smile.

George K. Lane then took up the conversation, and turning to Jon and Lana, he said, 'During the time since we last saw you, all the arrangements have been completed for your wedding ceremony. It has been a little hectic in this office as you can imagine, but the date has been set. You did say that it wouldn't be too difficult for you, whatever time or date, didn't you?'

Jon grinned his approval. *The sooner the better,* he thought in satisfaction, which was echoed silently by Lana.

George then continued, 'So, two months from today, Washington will come to a standstill to celebrate a wedding like no other, a joining ceremony between the Teacher and his Zellian bride, two beautiful people.'

Steady on, George, thought Jon, unconsciously reverting to his former modest persona, but nevertheless, he said, 'Thank you, George, for all the effort you have been putting into all the preparations for our big day. We both thank you sincerely.'

The secretary of state was only just getting into his stride as he continued briefing the happy couple with the details of their wedding day. Not wishing to sound too long winded about it all, he explained that the venue for the ceremony would not be in the White House itself, since that was being prepared for another ceremony of a different kind for the following day. 'But more of that later,' he said with a conspiratorial smile at the president and General Clintock. 'The best place for an event like this is the Willard

Chapter Fifty-Eight

Intercontinental, where you are already booked in for the duration of your stay as of now.

'The accommodation is first class and the management have had plenty of experience of handling important events like this. Many of the guests, some three hundred of them, will take up residence a few days before and after the ceremony, so you'll have time to get acquainted with them, the only drawback being that they are all from different countries and speak different languages.'

'I'm sure we'll cope,' Jon said modestly, knowing that his linguistic abilities had not yet been fully put to the test.

In a satisfied tone of voice, George continued. 'Security is the only concern in such a public place, but we will have so many government agents mingling in the crowds that you will be able to feel perfectly safe.'

Jon reflected on his and the Zellians' force fields, which gave them immunity from attack, and recalled his intention to advise Davis Cooper to begin wearing his modified version of the belt. *Before I leave the White House and before I go to the hotel*, he reminded himself.

It was now that General Clintock came into the discussion. 'You'll remember, Jon, that not so long ago, we were all feeling pretty sore, an understatement, that you rendered all our nuclear weapons obsolete, along with every other country with such a capability. Well, after some deliberations among the various members of government, along with our counterparts elsewhere in the world, we've come to the conclusion that the world has suddenly become a safer place to live and . . . .' He paused for a moment to contemplate his next observation, 'The technical information and drawings you gave to our scientists and engineers regarding power units for industry at all levels, have been received and progress in manufacturing the prototypes is already underway.'

Chapter Fifty-Eight

Davis Cooper then took the advantage as the general stopped talking for a moment, Clintock was, after all, a soldier, and not an industrialist or politician used to talking at length. 'Yes, Jon,' he said, 'you have already begun your crusade to make the world a better place to live, and although it's early days, you have shown, by the introduction of new technology and the destruction of nuclear weapons, that the road to peace and prosperity is the one you will guide us along, willing converts to your teachings. No doubt we will have to make many adjustments in our way of life and attitudes toward our fellow men, but would I be right in assuming that you have some grand plan as to how you intend to proceed? Obviously, the destruction of the nuclear weapons was your first priority, and then there was your demonstration of the futility of conventional war against the technology you have at your disposal. Even the General here,' he said, indicating General Clintock sitting quietly nearby, 'was devastated to see how a conventional army could be wiped off the face of the earth in such a short space of time. So, the next question I would ask is, how can we assist you in whatever you deem necessary to achieve world peace?'

As he looked at Lana for support before answering, Jon then replied with just a hint of a smile. 'Mr, President, for the immediate future, all we would ask you to do is be patient. Keep us informed regarding the manufacture of the prototype power units. I will have the assistance of another Zellian colleague to further advise you on how to adapt them to various functions. Some will be to generate electrical power on a fairly small scale at first, but later versions can be modified to supply a whole city. One issue regarding the global pollution of the atmosphere,' he continued, 'is something that can be addressed within the next ten years, by adapting the entire automobile industry to use the smallest units you are even now manufacturing, albeit in prototype form.'

George K. Lane nodded to confirm that the scientists and engineers were indeed actively engaged in building a variety of

Chapter Fifty-Eight

atomic-powered units suitable for many civil projects. 'But,' he said thoughtfully, 'a ten-year period, as you suggest, might be somewhat optimistic. Much as we would like to reform the automobile industry and reduce the pollution of millions of cars poisoning the atmosphere, change of this magnitude will cause worldwide upheaval in manufacturing generally. Engine manufacture in itself will be adversely affected due to the simplified design and manufacture of the components in their assembly. Fitting the new power units into a modern automobile's shell doesn't appear to be much of a problem, but the engines are of a revolutionary design, atomic powered with zero emissions, which is good for the planet, but what of the oil industry? Will they revert to supplying oil for lubrication purposes only, as used to be the case hundreds of years ago?'

Jon looked steadily at George, then the president as he put a question of his own. 'These are problems which you would have to resolve within the next few years as the oil reserves throughout the world dwindle and run out. How long do you think it will be before the oil dries up completely? Twenty years perhaps, fifty at the most? But as I have noted already, little preparation has been done as yet to herald the day when petrol and oil for vehicles will no longer be available, so you now have the opportunity and a ten-year interval to switch over to the use of a new technology, which will bring benefits to the entire world, and incidentally, reduce the dependence on oil for your economies and any possible conflict as a result of your desperation for fuel some time in the not-so-distant future.'

Davis Cooper and his secretary of state exchanged a quizzical look at each other as though to ask, *Well, what are we doing to avert a future crisis when the oil runs out?* Silently, they had to concede that very little was being done.

Although George tried to defend their position by saying, 'We have greatly improved the design of our automobile engines and made them more efficient than ever in their use of fuel, but we do

Chapter Fifty-Eight

acknowledge that the time when alternative technology will have to be introduced is sure to come.' Turning to the president, he continued, 'This could be the time for us to bite the bullet and apply all our resources to promoting the use of these atomic-powered units for industry over the next ten years.'

Davis Cooper had no hesitation as he replied, 'I'm reliably informed that some of these prototype engines are nearing completion, and with a little help from you, Jon, and the technician you mentioned, we could be ready to carry out some initial tests quite soon.'

With a confident smile, Jon addressed both the president and his secretary of state together. 'When your preparations are completed, the technician in question, who is called Mort, a scientist who you will be introduced to you before the wedding, both he and I will be available to advise you on how to utilise the new power units to the best advantage.' Then sensing that Lana was mentally reminding him of the event uppermost in her mind, he added with a laugh, 'But that will be only after the joining ceremony. Until then, continue manufacturing a variety of the units suitable for the purposes we specified, power for domestic and industrial consumption, automobile and marine engines, and I'm sure that some of your industrialists will come up with ideas for further uses for these nuclear units.'

Rega, in the meanwhile, had been sitting quietly listening to the dialogue between Jon, the ambassador, and the president and his secretary of state. He concluded that, *Yes, the selection of the last Teacher was indeed opportune for us, the Zellian race and the people of Earth. Jon has all the qualities to succeed in bringing about the transformation in the minds of men, and in the process, to save the environment of the planet and secure its future in the Federation of the Stars. Earth can then determine its own future without any further help or interference from the Zel.*

Chapter Fifty-Eight

Jon was, of course, well aware of Rega's musings, and quietly thanked him on a telepathic level for the confidence he was showing for the ability of the Teacher. Then verbally, he turned his attention to include the rest of the occupants of the Oval Office, all males with the exception of Lana. 'For the moment, Mr. President,' he said soberly, 'if we can leave the problems of the world to one side and leave the organisation of the wedding and hotel arrangements to George, who has been doing a wonderful job of it so far, I have to bring up the matter of security, not only for the duration of the next few days, but in the weeks and months ahead. No doubt Agent Spencer, your head of security, has already briefed you regarding the difficulty of protecting you personally while you are so publicly exposed at times like these.' Jon laughed openly for a moment, contradicting the seriousness of what he was about to suggest. 'If you can overcome your reluctance to undress in front of a group of friends such as these,' indicating the general, George K. Lane and Lana, of course, 'or at least strip to the waist . . .' He paused for a moment as he caught Davis Cooper's thoughts of confusion, not because he was bashful, on the contrary, he often took part in social events, sailing, swimming, and other sports, which necessitated exposure of his upper body.

I'm in pretty good shape, he thought, *but what kind of game is Jon playing at?* Nevertheless, he knew that the Teacher wouldn't be asking him to do something just for fun; there had to be a very good reason for the request, so he grinned good-naturedly as he peeled off his upper garments.

Knowing what was about to happen, Lana brought forward the package containing the modified force field belt and handed it to Jon just as Davis Cooper completed his impromptu strip tease act.

With a smile of encouragement, Jon withdrew the belt from its wrapping, and holding it out to the president, he said, 'I want you to place this belt around your waist, next to your skin, where it will remain for as long as there is any risk to your safety. Only I can lock

Chapter Fifty-Eight

or unlock this belt, but while you are wearing it, you will be completely immune to any attempt on your life.'

He noted the look of incredulity on the president's face. 'You will be protected by a force field of a very limited nature, part of the Zellian technology, but sufficient to protect you from knives or bullets in any assassination attempt.' He added, 'If you remember, an attempt was made on your life when we last visited New York.' That recent event was indelibly imprinted on Davis Cooper's mind, but he still had to question the effectiveness of this innocent-looking belt as Jon placed it around his waist, adjusting it until it was a comfortable fit, which was then locked. 'A permanent fixture now,' Jon reminded him with a smile.

'And it doesn't even hold up my pants,' the president commented. 'And now that it's locked on, I can't even feel it. Does this mean that I have to sleep with it on and even take a shower while I'm still wearing it?'

'Quite so,' Jon said quietly. 'You will find that the belt is unobtrusive in use, and as I said, only I can remove it from your body; therefore, you will be protected like no other president has been protected before.'

General Clintock gave a humourless laugh as he said, 'Your grouchy security man, Spencer, is going to feel decidedly unwanted if you tell him that you don't really need him now. On second thoughts, it would be advisable not to let anyone know that you're wearing that gadget, otherwise there will be some crank or fanatic who'll try to take you out just for the hell of it.'

Rega had been watching and listening to the comments made during and after the fitting of the belt and was inclined to agree with Clintock. 'You will find that even now,' he remarked, 'you're not aware of the device permanently around your body, and no one outside this room needs to be informed that you have your own force field protection. Live with it and forget it, safe in the

Chapter Fifty-Eight

knowledge that you have a future whereby you can escape the fate of some of your presidential predecessors.' He smiled as he continued. 'Live long Mr. President and go down in history as the politician who helped to make the world a better place for all humankind.'

As he fingered the belt now strapped around his waist, Davis Cooper reminded himself that it was now a permanent fixture that could only be removed by Jon, and that was not likely during his own lifetime apparently. *But to what extent can this innocent-looking belt give me protection?* His mental question was immediately answered by Jon, who addressed Davis Cooper with a smile to put the president at ease.

'Mr. President, understandably, you may have doubts regarding the usefulness of the gadget you now have about your waist, but as it has already been explained, it is, in fact, something to give you protection for the rest of your life. Protection, that is, from any physical assault on your person.' Noting the look of doubt on Davis Cooper's face, he continued. 'This is your own personal force field device, which will protect you from an assassin's bullet or knife attack.' Jon reminded him briefly of the assassination of President Kennedy, then he added, 'Your own force field will protect you from thrown objects, knife attacks, or even hand guns used at close range.' He could still read the doubts in the president's mind regarding the effectiveness of the device around his waist, so Jon spoke quietly to quell Davis Cooper's anxiety and doubts. 'I think it is time for you to be convinced of the power of your protective device,' Jon said with a laugh. 'You may recall that on a previous occasion, in this very room, your security men tried to gun me down, but failed spectacularly.' The president nodded to affirm that recollection. 'In the same way,' Jon continued, 'if someone were to shoot you or throw a knife as a means of killing you, you would feel the impact of the object, but your force field wouldn't be penetrated; in other words, you wouldn't be injured or killed.'

Chapter Fifty-Eight

At that moment, General Clintock, who had been listening attentively to Jon's reassuring words, and who had great faith in Zellian technology based on his recent experience of flying saucers and teleportation, decided that this was his opportunity to convince his president of the effectiveness of his protective device. 'Mr. President,' he bellowed with laughter, 'I'm more than willing to help you to try out your protective barrier. Just tell me what form of attack you would like me to adopt.'

Davis Cooper looked at Jon for reassurance. 'What would you suggest, Jon, a thrown object doesn't sound very realistic, but there again, a gun would be more convincing, but scary.'

Turning to the general, Jon said gravely, 'If you could bring yourself to turn a gun on your own president and friend, General, then everyone will have confidence in the force field's ability to protect the wearer.'

Turning to Davis Cooper, Jon said calmly, 'I suggest that you sit down to give yourself solid support while you undergo this test. As I said before, a bullet cannot penetrate the force field, but you will still feel the impact, and no doubt you will be bruised in the process, but otherwise unhurt.' Everyone in the room turned expectantly to look at the general, who was already standing with pistol drawn, facing the president. He took deliberate aim, and with a look of apprehension on his face, he pulled the trigger. The single shot rang out, and when the smoke cleared, all eyes turned to Davis Cooper still sitting on his chair, feeling his body for any sign of injury or blood, not believing that he could possibly be unscathed after being shot at such close range.

With a grimace, he looked down at a bruise already appearing on his chest, and weakly laughed. 'I think that was a convincing demonstration of my security belt, Jon, although in future, I'll just let things happen naturally and in the course of normal events.' He added with a shaky laugh, 'I wouldn't like the General to have to undergo such a trial again.' He was obviously relieved that the

Chapter Fifty-Eight

ordeal was over. 'To shoot one's friend was not a pleasant experience for him, even knowing that there would be no fatality.'

General Clintock merely grinned. 'Spencer would've been having kittens if he'd been here.'

His reference to the security chief was completely lost on Rega, until he scanned Jon's mind for clarification, and then he merely smiled.

The demonstration over, Davis Cooper said calmly, 'Well, gentlemen, and Lana, if you will excuse me, I will get properly dressed again.'

While he was doing so, Jon could sense that Lana still had thoughts of the joining ceremony uppermost in her mind again, so turning to George Lane, he remarked, 'That's something I've never had to do myself, but I presume it has taken a great deal of your time?'

The secretary of state smiled as he replied pleasantly, 'Affairs of state can be pretty complicated, but to organize the wedding of the year for the Zellian ambassador and his lady is something very different.' He continued with a slight frown of concentration. 'The venue is already booked, of course, the guest list is drawn up and we're in the process of sending out the invitations. In fact, we've had a number of requests from several heads of state from around the world for accommodation in the Willard Intercontinental so as to be near you. In all,' he continued, 'the arrangements are gradually falling into place, but unfortunately,' he said to Lana in particular, 'it will be about two months before the ceremony can take place, a disappointment for you, Lana, but we can't let the public, in this case, the people of the world, feel that you are keeping them out of your lives. They believe that you belong to them.'

Knowing Lana's thoughts regarding the joining ceremony, Jon hastened to express his own disappointment at the two-month delay, but to soften the blow, he said coaxingly, 'It will give you

Chapter Fifty-Eight

more time to arrange your wedding dress, do more shopping for other clothes, and of course, to return to Buccaneer's Point to check on the progress on our new home.

While the ceremony was something Lana was looking forward to, this was to be an experience that no other Zellian had gone through, and she was more excited at the prospect of having her wedding gown fitted, and further shopping expeditions, not to mention their return to the Point. 'Ah, well, what is two months out of our lifetime, Jon? In the meanwhile, all your other technical projects for the good of humanity can be making progress.' She kissed him affectionately and smiled contentedly.

Chapter Fifty-Nine

Some days later, Lana and Jon teleported to join Rega in the Willard Intercontinental Hotel. There had been little point in giving any advance warning of their intended visit or the purpose of the visit. The telepathic link between father and daughter, and now Jon, was so strong that only if they deliberately chose to block their thoughts from each other could they evade their innermost thoughts; it was as though a physical contact existed between them. As they materialised in the sumptuous suite of rooms provided for the Zellian commander, Jon nodded approvingly as he noted the luxury of the surroundings similar to Rega's mother ship.

'Yes, Jon, this was a good choice of accommodation, fit for one of your earthly kings at least, and comparable to my home on Zel.'

Jon smiled appreciatively at that remark and mentally made yet another note as to the final interior design of the house being renovated on Buccaneer's Point. He then grinned as he replied, 'Many of the so-called kings on Earth have never been in such surroundings in their lives. Should any of them come to our joining ceremony, they will be going home with some new ideas on how to make improvements to their own palaces or homes.' Then as an afterthought, he added, 'Unfortunately, that doesn't apply to the welfare of their people.'

Rega had to agree with the vision in Jon's mind. He was already aware of the poverty that existed in many of the countries of Earth, and much of it existed in some of the so-called developed countries, even here in the United States. 'Yes, Jon, as a Teacher, it is part of

Chapter Fifty-Nine

your intention to eradicate this problem, I know, but it will take many years to achieve that goal.' Knowing that Rega was sincere in his observation of life for many of the people on Earth made Jon resolve that he would strive to improve the living standards of his fellow men as soon as technology could help to improve the situation.

As I said before, Jon, Rega communed silently, *be patient, as you have much to do.*

With their physical contact now established by an affectionate embrace among all three, Lana brought up the subject of being measured and of choosing the design and materials for her wedding dress. 'No need to worry about that, Lana,' Jon reassured her. 'Our friend George has already arranged for a team of designers to visit the hotel this very afternoon, so you'll be in expert hands. As a result, you will have a gown that will be the envy of every civilised woman in the world.'

As Lana exchanged glances with Jon, physically she couldn't contain her excitement, and she clapped her hands and jumped up and down in very un-Zellian display of emotion. 'It will be like a dream,' she exclaimed, 'the dress, the ceremony and the occasion. I won't be able to contain myself for another two months of waiting.'

Both Jon and Rega had to smile at Lana's outburst, and Jon said, 'We will have much to do during that time, but at least when you meet the team who will be preparing your wedding dress, you will know that you are on the countdown to our big day.'

It was several hours later that the telephone rang, and a message was delivered from the reception desk. 'Would it be convenient for the dressmaker and designers to come up to the suite?' After the arrival of a group of four women, Jon and Rega decided that what was to follow was woman's time and promptly left them to it with Lana talking excitedly to her dressmakers. The men joined the other members of the Zellian contingent and several other guests, including George K. Lane in one of the downstairs reception rooms.

Chapter Fifty-Nine

As they mingled with some other hotel guests, George took the opportunity to introduce the bridegroom-to-be and Zellian ambassador simply as Jon. After overcoming their surprise at the physical appearance of the ambassador, many of the guests proved to be of foreign origin, staying at the hotel for business or diplomatic reasons, and were even more surprised that after their introduction, Jon addressed them in their own native language. Arabic, Russian and Mandarin Chinese were the most common tongues among them. It was likewise a revelation for the secretary of state as he listened and noticed the reaction and comments of the guests later on. His opinion of Jon as an ambassador, already high, reached stratospheric proportions.

In the meanwhile, upstairs in Rega's suite, Lana was in a state of undress and was being measured for her wedding gown amid the comments about the perfection of her figure by the seamstress in charge. When it was mentioned that the gown would be a figure-hugging creation to show off her Zellian physique to perfection, so as not to spoil the effect in any way, Lana insisted that she would remove her force field belt, so not even a ripple in the fabric would then show.

As though this was a prearranged signal, it was at this moment that a group of masked men burst into the room, and the apparent leader levelled a weapon at Lana and fired. As she went down, she was immediately unconscious, having been darted with a tranquiliser gun. The other women were terrified, believing that they were about to be killed. Instead, the leader of the group barked an order, 'Get down on the floor and you won't get hurt.' They immediately complied while two of the gangsters took hold of Lana's limp body by the wrists and ankles and unceremoniously carried her out of the room.

As soon as they had gone, the women scrambled for the phone to raise the alarm. It had only taken a matter of minutes for the abduction to take place, and very shortly, members of the hotel staff

Chapter Fifty-Nine

along with Jon and Rega appeared on the scene. While the ladies were giving a very garbled account of what had taken place, the kidnappers were already on the roof of the hotel, preparing to make their getaway in a private helicopter. They wanted to make sure that there wouldn't be a pursuit by a convoy of police cars.

Having surmised that Lana had indeed been kidnapped by a group of unknown people, Jon and Rega then tried to make a telepathic connection with Lana, but found that they could only pick up a very faint echo of her thoughts. 'She must be drugged or still unconscious,' Jon declared. 'It's almost impossible to locate her whereabouts. All we know is that in the short time since her abduction, her kidnappers can't have gone far.'

By this time, the presence of the helicopter on the roof of the hotel had been discovered and reported to the management, who in turn had informed the police and the FBI. Despite the number of officials who flooded into the hotel, there was an air of impotence with regard to the course of action to be taken. The only certainty in the minds of the police was that the abduction of the wife of the Zellian ambassador had been carried out by a group of unknown criminals, and that even now, they were using a helicopter to make their escape to an unknown destination.

Despite the confusion of the people around them, Jon and Rega were concentrating on the problem of locating Lana's whereabouts telepathically. Rega gripped Jon's shoulder as he said, 'If we join our minds together, it will give us more power to get through to Lana in her present state and enable us to find her.' With that thought in mind, literally, they each pressed their fingers on each other's forehead and concentrated their combined powers to pick up Lana's rapidly fading brain emissions. Within a few moments, Rega gasped, 'I can feel her presence. She is still only a few miles away, but we will have to act fast before we lose all contact.'

Jon then replied, 'This is something that I must do.' He smiled grimly as he continued. 'These people must be shown that criminal

Chapter Fifty-Nine

activity will not be tolerated in the society of the future. If I must, I will teach them a lesson they will never forget, and it will be an example to others of their kind as well.'

'What do you intend to do now, Jon?' Rega enquired doubtfully.

Jon replied brusquely, 'As the helicopter is well within range, I will teleport directly into the craft, and with Lana's signal as a guide, I will be close to her when I materialise, which will be a shock to the crooks on board,' he said with a grin. As an afterthought, Rega reminded Jon that, as Lana was no longer wearing her own force field belt, she would be vulnerable to any violence that might occur when he suddenly appeared, so therefore he should exercise diplomacy and caution.

Now that a decision had been reached with regard to Lana's recovery from the gangsters, the plan of action seemed quite straightforward to Jon, so much so that he was again able to grin as he said to Rega, 'I'll be back before you know it,' and promptly teleported, guided by Lana's muted brain signal.

A moment later, as expected, he found himself close to Lana in the cramped confines of the helicopter, and facing one of the kidnappers, who, despite the fact that Lana was not yet fully conscious, was nevertheless holding a gun trained on her recumbent figure. At the sudden and seemingly miraculous appearance of a giant of a man in the cabin, he almost dropped the gun, but within seconds, he had regained his composure and continued to point his weapon at his supposed captives.

'Well,' he drawled sarcastically, 'what have we here? I don't know how you got here, but one thing's for sure, your little lady has been as quiet as a mouse, and I suggest that you do the same. Then we'll all be happy and no one will get hurt.' He smirked and added, 'Now we have two for the price of one.' He obviously realised Jon was the Zellian ambassador and likely to be a valuable hostage for ransom.

Chapter Fifty-Nine

There was a hatch between the passenger compartment and the aircraft's cockpit, which he slid open. 'Hey, you guys, we've got company. I don't know how he got here, but it's that Zellian character we've been hearing about lately. He's just sitting here quietly with his arm around his lady love, and I've got him covered in case he tries any funny tricks.' His announcement was received with gasps of astonishment by the other gang members.

One of them said jubilantly, 'How many millions do you think they are worth to the government for their safe return? I guess we could name our own figure,' he added with satisfaction.

Jon listened to their conversation with disdain, and thought, *How can these fools think they can get away with this heist. I will give them the opportunity to return to the hotel with us and to hand themselves into the authorities so that justice may be done.* By this time, Lana was now almost recovered from her drugged state, but not yet capable of teleporting out of the helicopter and to safety, so Jon resolved to give the gang one more chance to take them back to the Willard Intercontinental Hotel.

Addressing himself to the hoodlum still sitting in front of him, with his gun still aimed at him, Jon said calmly and dangerously politely, 'I must request that you give up this foolish escapade immediately and return Lana and myself back to our hotel.' With a disarming smile, he continued, 'Failure to do so will have serious consequences for your safety.'

Their captor couldn't believe what he was hearing. 'Hey, you guys,' he shouted through the hatch to the other gang members, 'this guy is a comedian. I'm sitting here with a gun on him and he's telling me to take him back to his hotel, or else.' The sound of raucous laughter could be heard through the bulkhead of the aircraft as this warning was received.

Jon then decided that their cooperation would not be forthcoming, so it was time to take positive action to get out of their

Chapter Fifty-Nine

present predicament. Tightening his embrace on Lana's body, he whispered quietly so that only she could hear, 'I've given these people the chance to return us to the hotel, but they've refused, so I intend to teleport both of us out of the aircraft to safety.' He added, 'Don't be alarmed by what is going to happen next; you'll be back in the Willard before you can say Zel.' With that comment, Jon concentrated on teleporting back to the Willard, and at the same time, he activated his force field to maximum. He and Lana were only aware of the slight feeling of being in limbo for the briefest period of time, usual in the process of teleporting, but completely unaware of the scene of complete destruction they were leaving behind.

As the force field expanded to maximum in a split second of time, the helicopter disintegrated into tiny pieces and exploded in a ball of fire, sending plumes of smoke into the sky and showering the countryside below with burning wreckage. It created a spectacle worthy of the Fourth of July. Before Lana had time to catch her breath, she realised that they were back in Rega's suite in the hotel.

With a smile of reassurance and a gentle kiss for Lana, Jon said, 'Well, did I hear you say Zel?'

Lana gave a brave laugh as she replied, 'No, but I'm glad to be back with friends.' Her father was the first to embrace her and to thank Jon for his intervention in returning Lana to safety. This sentiment was echoed by George K. Lane and the officials who were still in the room at that time. Despite the ordeal that she had just undergone, Lana insisted that she would continue the fitting session for her wedding dress the following day, adding quietly, for Jon and Rega's benefit, 'But I will be wearing my force field belt. I've learnt my lesson that on Earth, we can't be completely safe from potential harm from animals or humans.' Jon and Rega smiled approvingly in agreement.

Chapter Sixty

The following day, Lana returned to the Willard Intercontinental in order to continue with the appointment with her dressmaker, and it was no surprise to note the large numbers of Secret Service personnel present, who tried to blend in with the ordinary guests, but to Lana, were completely visible. It only took a short time to complete the measuring session that had been started the previous day, although it took a greater time to choose several other outfits to be worn for other less formal occasions, and of course, the choice of materials. Although she was enjoying the experience on this occasion, the thought did occur to her that as a result of always wearing a uniform normally, the choice of how to dress as the ambassador's wife was going to be interesting.

Confident that Lana was now wearing her force field belt and perfectly safe again, Jon joined Davis Cooper and George K. Lane again in the president's office to discuss the progress of the implementation of the technical innovations supplied by the Zellian technology. George did most of the talking as he explained that, with the constant presence of Mort to guide them, rapid progress was being made by the engineers and scientists who had gathered from various countries on Earth to develop the prototypes of various nuclear devices, which would, in turn, be converted into generating plants suitable for installation in road vehicles and ships. With notable enthusiasm, George went on to explain that within another six months, a certain car manufacturer, always in front with technology, would have a working model of one of their vehicles to test on the road.

Chapter Sixty

Davis Cooper listened quietly to his friend's progress report, and with equal enthusiasm added, 'Although on a much larger scale, our engineers are working on the beginnings of a new type of nuclear reactor, a generating station, which, although basically similar to our existing power plants, has many innovations unknown to our own people. I don't know anything about that kind of technology, but I'm told it will improve the safety issue that has concerned our scientists by 100 per cent.' He grimaced as he added. 'With such a big project, I'm told that it will be at least five years for the first of this type of reactor to be commissioned.'

Jon listened carefully to the debriefing and remarked genially, 'That, Mr. President, is all the good news, and as for it taking five years for the first of the power stations to come online, ask yourself, how long did it take to build Boulder Dam? How many lives were lost in the process, and at what cost to the taxpayers?' With a smile, he continued. 'While it will take many years to build all the new power stations your country requires, without studying the design of the existing plants, have you considered adapting them to meet the demands of the new technology?'

Davis Cooper sat back in his chair, obviously pondering the question, and after a few moments' reflection, he replied, 'That's something the boffins may get round to thinking about after comparing the differences in the technologies involved. And yes, no doubt the taxpayers and the voters will be happy to reduce the costs of all these projects.' He added, 'I rather think that we are going to ask you to help us even more with this transition to full nuclear power.'

Again, Jon smiled, and with a gesture of spreading his hands wide, he remarked, 'I'm here to teach you as much as possible.' Then with his usual good humour, he laughed and said, 'And now, my friends, I must get back to my ship. Knowing that everything is under your control, I will take my leave of you for a number of weeks in order to check the progress of the renovation of my house

Chapter Sixty

on Buccaneer's Point.' As ever, having made his excuses and without further ado and without any further word, he teleported back to his ship, hoping that Lana would there also.

And so it proved to be. Lana had made her choices clear regarding the bridal dress, a dazzling yet simple gown, which she was assured would enhance her natural beauty, and not reveal her force field belt. Also, a complete wardrobe to fulfil all the social occasions as would befit the richest woman on Earth, at a cost that would have made many a rich man wince if they had to pay a similar sum on their wives' behalf. But to Lana, cost was never something that she had to consider. As it was now some seven weeks to the wedding day, she had been given a guarantee that the gown would be completed in plenty of time, although the complete trousseau would likely take a little longer.

After some discussion, Lana and Jon agreed that they would retreat to the privacy of Buccaneer's Point immediately after the wedding reception at the Willard Continental, and the Point was their next port of call. As soon as the craft was in motion, Lana hesitantly asked, 'While we are on our way to The Point, can I suggest that we stop above Kingston and give Jacob a visit?' Excitedly, she went on, 'I would like to collect the ring he was going to make for me, then I will feel completely ready for the joining ceremony.'

Jon smiled good humouredly as he said jokingly, 'I had completely forgotten all about that small matter, but yes, we need only stop for an hour, collect the ring, and then Buccaneer's Point, and home.'

With the usual graceful movement of her hands over and above the flight controls, Lana changed the navigational coordinates for their usual docking station above Kingston. Having done so, she turned to Jon, and with a flirtatious tone of voice, she said, 'Do you know, this is the first time that I have felt that we are completely alone again.'

Chapter Sixty

'In which case,' he replied teasingly, 'what would you suggest we do to pass away the next two hours that it will take to get to Kingston?' But there was no need to say another word; it was a complete union of minds and bodies.

Chapter Sixty-One

As the spacecraft hovered above Kingston, it was difficult to get a clear view by normal visual means, although it was much clearer using the scanners, but otherwise, the heat haze was impenetrable. As always, they decided to teleport directly into Jacob's premises, hoping that there would be no customers present. 'It wouldn't do to frighten a valuable client by our sudden appearance, would it?' Lana remarked.

With a nod of agreement, Jon said, 'Well, let's go visit Jacob.' A moment later found them standing in the outer display room of the premises, now strangely clear of all the display cabinets, with the exception of one large unit with several examples of Jacob's handiwork. These were items that were his own creations, each worth a small fortune, obtainable only to the extremely wealthy and those who would appreciate priceless beauty. Of Jacob there was no sign, so assuming that he was in the workroom at the rear of the premises, Jon gave a loud shout to announce their presence before opening the curtain to the inner sanctum.

Sure enough, Jacob was sitting at his worktable with Miranda close beside him as ever, both enthralled by an object in front of them. As they drew near, Jon and Lana could see the object of their attention, a piece of jewellery, a ring. Looking up, Jacob exclaimed with a smile, 'Come closer, my dears, that you may better appreciate my masterpiece.'

As they did so, Lana gave a soft cry of delight. 'Ah, it's so beautiful.' With the object of their delight lying in its presentation

Chapter Sixty-One

case in full view before them, all four of them were transfixed by the hypnotic splendour of the magnificent diamond mounted in a ring of platinum and surrounded by ten blood-red rubies. It was some time before anyone could speak. Finally, Lana whispered in awe, 'Jacob, when I wear this ring, even the ladies of Zel will be envious of such a gem. They will all be asking their commanders to provide them with similar trinkets for their adornment. It isn't customary to wear jewellery on our planet, but this ring is exceptional!'

Jacob was obviously gratified that Lana was so impressed with not only the beauty of the ring, but also his workmanship in the final polishing and mounting of the stones. 'Ah moie, ah moie,' he sighed ecstatically. 'Never was a merchant such as I so privileged to work with objects of such beauty and rarity.' He continued with a self-satisfied smile, 'And also of such immense value.' He then held up the jewel case containing the ring for all to see. 'Here we have a ring, which is so rare that I couldn't put a price on it. If it were to be offered at auction on the open market, I could only say that it is worth more than a king's ransom.'

Again, it was Lana who commented, 'And that will never happen, Jacob.' As she spoke, she reached out and retrieved the ring from its presentation box and tried it on her middle finger of her left hand, only to find that it was too tight, and so transferred it to her ring finger. As she waved her hand in the air, admiring the scintillating diamond and ruby ring, she purred with pleasure, and said, 'This ring will be on my finger forever. No one will ever buy it at any price. It will remind me of the happiness I have enjoyed and the friendship of so many people here on Earth.'

Again, Jacob expressed his satisfaction that Lana was so pleased with her trinket, but had one more surprise for her. Reaching into a drawer underneath his worktable, he pulled out yet another small box. He opened it to show everyone what it contained, and said quietly, 'Knowing that you intend to go through a joining ceremony with Jon in a few weeks' time, not only can you wear your beautiful

Chapter Sixty-One

diamond ring now, but you should know that many people in the Western Hemisphere observe the custom of giving and receiving rings from each other during the joining ceremony as a symbolic gesture of becoming one.' With a smile of affection for his alien friends, he said, 'I would like you to accept from me a small gift as a token of my friendship and gratitude.' And opening the box, he displayed two gold rings.

Jon accepted them and curiously inspected them, and then turning to Lana, he explained that they were commonly referred to simply as wedding rings, plain bands of the precious metal, but on closer scrutiny, Jon and Lana saw inscriptions on the inner faces of both rings, which read, *Love Eternal*. 'That is so apt for Lana and me,' Jon said, thinking of their expected five hundred years of life before them. Holding Lana's hand, he placed the rings in front of her to view, at the same time turning to Jacob and thanking him for his kind and appropriate gift.

While the presentation of the rings and talk of the joining ceremony had been going on, Jon had caught, quite unintentionally, a fleeting glimpse into the mind of Miranda, who was still standing close by. With a smile of amusement on his face, as he shared the thought with Lana, he mentally noted that Miranda was having similar ambitions toward Jacob. *With such an attentive minder, Jacob, your bachelor days are numbered,* he mused.

Now that the rings were in their possession, Lana was eager to get back to the ship and renew their flight to Buccaneer's Point. 'I'm impatient to see what progress has been made in transforming the old house into a home fit for a Zellian ambassador, and a rich one at that,' she laughed. Having said their farewells to Jacob and his minder, they promptly teleported back to the ship hovering high above Kingston, unobserved by the people of the city. Within minutes of their arrival on the flight deck, Lana, as navigator and pilot, set the course for Buccaneer's Point, and within minutes, the ship was cruising silently at two thousand miles per hour, heading

Chapter Sixty-One

for what was to be their home for the next five hundred years. At this speed, their journey seemed of short duration. When they neared the island, the computer announced their imminent approach and requested permission to land near the residence in its former parking position.

Moments later, they stepped out of the craft and walked excitedly over the grassland toward their new home, which was already beginning to look like a very impressive structure. Despite the silence of their approach and landing, a group of people led by McDonald, the architect for the project, were already coming forward to greet them. With a broad smile on his face and a cheerful, 'Hi, folks,' he stopped a short distance away and allowed Jon and Lana to close the distance between them. He was wearing a open-necked shirt and shorts, appropriate for the heat of the day and the working environment, although the hard hat perched on top of his head looked somewhat out of place.

With a smile, Jon and Lana greeted McDonald genially and turning toward the residence, continued slowly forward toward the residence. It soon became obvious to them that many changes to the old structure had taken place during their absence. They didn't attempt to enter the house, as Lana had said earlier that she would rather wait until the renovation was near completion before making a tour of the project, apart from which, McDonald reminded them, hard hats had to be worn by all personnel at all times. Although, as far as Jon could see, the workmen weren't wearing any kind of headgear. *So much for health and safety,* he mused.

The architect confided that during the past few weeks, as well as the renovations to the design and structure of the house in general, as suggested by Jon, the accommodations for the chef, Julian, had been completed and that was where he himself was living. 'And very comfortable it is too,' he grinned.

Chapter Sixty-One

'Well, if you're happy with that arrangement,' Jon remarked, 'you might as well enjoy your new quarters until the completion of the entire project.'

The short inspection over, and having renewed their acquaintance with McDonald and the workforce, Jon and Lana walked away from the house, over the broad grasslands toward the edges of the green and inviting coolness of the jungle. The tranquillity was only disturbed by the sounds of the birds in the trees and the sounds of a wild pig rooting in the undergrowth. Holding hands as they walked, Lana talked using voice contact instead of telepathy and said, 'This is so much better, to be away from the clamour of other peoples' minds and the noise and bustle of so-called civilisation.'

Squeezing her hand gently, Jon replied, also verbally, 'Yes, I'm looking forward to the day when we will finally take up residence on our island. My duties as the Teacher will no doubt be demanding for the first few years, but as we will be able to return to Buccaneer's Point as and when possible, I can predict that life here will be like paradise on Earth, or almost like being at home on Zel for you, Lana.' After contentedly strolling along the edge of the jungle for a time, they turned into the broad grasslands, and with mutual consent, they continued their walk back to the ship. It was parked near the house, where it would serve as their home for the next few weeks.

'Until we're ready to go back to Washington for our joining ceremony,' Lana reminded Jon. During the following days and weeks before their return to Washington, they received daily reports from McDonald regarding the progress of construction and the materials being shipped to the island. The schooner was the means of transport as well as providing accommodation for the majority of the workforce. The promise of the generous bonus that they would receive on completion of the ambassador's residence,

Chapter Sixty-One

spurred the workmen on, and they worked long hours, but with skill and dedication to their respective crafts.

All too soon, the time for their return to Washington drew closer, and McDonald was able to report that work on the house was now almost complete, and that after a final clean up, was now ready for their final inspection and approval. Lana, in particular, having restrained herself from continually looking into the house while the renovations had been taking place, was eager to now tour the residence, which, from the outside, was looking most impressive, despite the fact that an army of gardeners had been imported and were even now landscaping the grounds of the ambassadorial mansion.

Accompanied by McDonald, Jon and Lana spent the next two hours examining the house, starting from the spectacular entrance hallway, then systematically going from room to room, admiring the elegant design and workmanship throughout the entire building. On completion of the tour, Jon turned to Lana, and said, 'If this is like your home on Zel, then Rega will be content to visit us, and possibly stay with us for a time before continuing his journeys across the galaxies of the universe.'

With a sigh of obvious pleasure at the prospect of taking up residence in the splendid surroundings of this first permanent home of their own, Lana giggled like a young girl and exclaimed, 'After our joining ceremony, darling, we'll have to go shopping again for all the furniture and fabrics for the house.'

With an indulgent smile, Jon said, 'I would suggest that we have a design consultant with us on that occasion, although I rather think it will be several months before we can say it is now perfect for us.'

Having delayed their departure from the island for as long as possible, they finally took their leave of McDonald and his workforce, with the instruction to begin recruiting the necessary domestic staff to enable the smooth running of the household when

Chapter Sixty-One

they took up residence on their return. The architect walked with them toward the saucer, stopping only a few yards away, and waited until Jon and Lana were aboard the craft and out of sight. He remained there until, without a sound, the craft rose vertically for several thousand feet, turned westward and streaked across the sky, lost to sight within seconds, leaving McDonald standing with his arm still raised in a gesture of farewell.

Chapter Sixty-Two

Shortly after they arrived over Washington, their presence was announced to the relevant authorities. The spaceship was left in hover mode while Jon and Lana teleported down to the Willard Intercontinental Hotel and into the presence of Commander Rega, who happened to be entertaining George K. Lane, to whom he had formed a certain bond of friendship. They were two men of different cultures, but with similar aspirations for the promotion of peace and prosperity for the people of Earth.

'Lana, Jon.' It was Rega who was first to greet them, holding his arms wide to embrace them both. 'Life on your island must be good for you, or is it the prospect of your joining ceremony tomorrow that has caused you to blossom, Lana?' he commented. 'And you, Jon,' he continued with a smile, 'look every inch an ambassador of the Zellian people, albeit you're bigger and mentally stronger than most of us!' He was careful not to refer to Jon's earthly origin in front of the secretary of state. That would have to remain a secret for another five hundred years.

'And a welcome return Lana and Jon,' remarked George. 'You'll be happy to know that all arrangements are in place for the big event tomorrow. There are some five hundred guests already assembled in Washington, two hundred of them accommodated in this hotel alone.' He then added with a grin, 'This town has never seen an event like your wedding is going to be. What a party!' His enthusiasm was catching.

Chapter Sixty-Two

Lana quickly enquired if her wedding dress was available for her to try on, and having been assured that it was, she expressed her desire to call in the dressmakers to ensure that it would be perfect in every detail.

In her excitement, she took the opportunity to show her father how their Jewish friend, Jacob, had transformed one of the trinkets into a work of art and beauty, a ring like no other on Earth, or even on Zel. After admiring the striking piece of jewellery, Rega quietly but mentally resolved that he would commission Jacob to fabricate something similar for his wife back home on Zel, knowing that any woman's heart would melt at the sight of such beauty. This thought was mentally approved by both Lana and Jon.

The new day dawned, and all the preparations for the joining ceremony were complete, so all the guests in the hotel and those from the surrounding areas, the media reporters and cameramen, and of course, the many security people involved, began to assemble in the reception room where the ceremony was to take place. As the room in question couldn't accommodate such numbers, even had they tried to squeeze in, seats were allocated according to status. This included the president and senior government officials, politicians, royalty from many different countries, Commander Rega and members of the second spaceship, including Captain Jara and Mort, the technician. In addition to these expected guests, the two young cadets, Rea and Asa, had been included as companions of Lana and stewards of Rega's personal staff. And last but not least, a place was reserved for Jacob and Miranda, now regarded as personal friends of the bride and groom.

Elsewhere in the hotel, television screens had been installed in every available room in order that as many people as possible would be able to see and hear the historic ceremony to take place. Anticipating the public interest in the event, giant screens were already erected in a number of open parklands in the city, and of

Chapter Sixty-Two

course, media camera crews were assembled all around the hotel, hoping to relay the spectacle to the masses all over the world.

The air of expectation was electrifying as everyone waited for the appearance of the Zellian ambassador and Lana. Many people were aware of the striking appearance of the Zellian couple, having already seen them, if not in person, then on the few public appearances they had made on television in previous months. As this was not to be a religious ceremony, but wishing to retain some semblance to a normal wedding, George K. Lane had consulted with Jon regarding the music for the ceremony, particularly the entrance of the bride. They agreed on the traditional "Here Comes the Bride" because it sounded rather grand, and Lana would appreciate that. As to any other music for the ceremony, he was quite willing to leave that choice in the hands of his friend George, the organiser of the whole day's proceedings.

When the bridal anthem rang out, Jon and Lana appeared together, the first deviation from normal tradition, and as they came into view, many of the guests gasped with surprise at the sight of two such equally beautiful people. The bride was much taller than the average Earth woman, over six feet, with a slender yet firmly rounded form, exquisitely defined by her figure-hugging white bridal gown, and to the fortunate few who were in a position to see her left hand, wearing a ring that flashed and reflected the many lights above and around her. A number of cameras zoomed in closer to catch a glimpse of such a fabulous gem, soon to become famous the world over.

As always, Jon was a man who turned the heads of most men and certainly all women. Apart from his height, even taller than Lana by a good six inches, his physique and sculpted figure, enhanced by his all-white ceremonial uniform of a Zellian ambassador, was an impressive figure. The eyes of the world were fixed on these two majestic people as they slowly came to a halt before the father of

Chapter Sixty-Two

the bride, Rega, commander of the mother ship and a member of the High Council of Zel.

The ceremony that followed was simple and sincere, a simple statement before the congregation of the commitment between one man and one woman, and that they would love and live with each other for the rest of their lives, although only the Zellians present knew how long that would be. As the newlyweds made their way out of the room used for the ceremony, to the strains of a well-known classical piece of music chosen by George K. Lane, they were repeatedly congratulated by dozens of well-wishers, and as Lana confided to Jon later, 'I had to close my mind to everything that some people were thinking.'

To which Jon replied. 'So did I. Many of their thoughts were complimentary, and others I wouldn't like to discuss with a young woman like you!'

Lana, in her innocence, wasn't too sure what Jon meant by that.

For the remainder of the morning and into the afternoon, Jon was always accompanied by Lana, now officially recognized in the eyes of the world as the wife of the Zellian ambassador. They mingled with many of the guests, most of whom were, of course, complete strangers to them both, but who were shocked that this giant of a man, an alien, seemed to know the name of every person he was introduced to, and even some of their personal history.

George K. Lane continued to hover close behind Jon on the pretence that he could introduce the ambassador to royalty and celebrities alike, and as he listened to the conversations, he mentally noted how many languages Jon seemed to be familiar with. As one famous member of the Saudi royal family later commented to his friends, 'He spoke like a true son of the desert.' Fortunately, they were not aware that Jon could read their minds like an open book.

Chapter Sixty-Two

Eventually, the time came for all the guests to take their places in the massive dining room where the wedding feast was to take place. Again, places were allocated in order of family and friends, royalty and the favoured few. The dinner was a sumptuous affair, with so many courses it took several hours to consume, and of course, there were all the congratulatory speeches to the bride and the groom with best wishes for their future happiness.

But as the proceedings appeared to be in the final stages before the reception ended, the master of ceremonies called the attention of the assembly to Secretary of State George K. Lane, who wished to make an announcement. After the noise in the room had abated, George stood up and said with a smile, 'Don't worry, folks, I'm not going to make any lengthy speeches, but President Cooper has something he would like to say.' With a theatrical gesture, he threw his arms wide, inviting the president, who was sitting close by, to address the attentive guests.

Davis Cooper slowly stood up to loud applause from the expectant guests, and quietly and in a sincere manner, began to talk. 'You are all aware that the bridegroom is the official representative and ambassador of the Zellian people, a race of an ancient civilisation on the other side of one of the many galaxies in the universe.' He paused for a moment and then continued. 'Although we were not aware of it, the Zellians have been our benefactors for millions of years, guiding humankind from our primitive beginnings up to the present day when we like to think that we are truly civilised people.' Turning to Jon at his side, he added, 'The nations of our planet have ravaged and destroyed much of our natural resources and have been the cause of the extinction of many species of animals on land and in our seas and oceans. But now, with the help and guidance of the Zellian people, represented by Jon, we are on a path to a new way of life. We can live in harmony with our fellow men and preserve the ecology of our planet, and before it's too late, ensure the continuation of all living creatures on the planet.'

Chapter Sixty-Two

Davis Cooper continued his address. 'Jon has been designated as our Teacher and will be our mentor for many years to come.' He smiled wryly at the thought of his own schooldays and a very different kind of teacher. 'He will no doubt have to teach us discipline as well as many new subjects. That process has already begun by confiscating many of our toys or weapons of war, but he has introduced new technologies to improve the way in which we can live a more secure life in the future, and enjoy peace and prosperity for all nations and all peoples. Because of the work already done and also for the task that lies before him, Congress has decided to make an award to thank him and to encourage him to be patient with us as we strive to improve the actions of governments and the people of this planet.'

Then turning to Jon, he raised his voice slightly to ensure that his words would be heard by everyone present, including the members of the media. 'Jon, representative of the Zellian people, ambassador to our planet, we, the government of the people of the United States of America, wish to present you with this award.' Davis Cooper turned to his secretary of state, who handed him an object. 'The Presidential Humanitarian Medal,' he stated, and held it up for all to see.

Jon stood up, towering physically over the president, and bent forward to facilitate acceptance of the award, which he did with pleasure.

But the president was not finished. Despite the solemnity of the moment, he laughed quietly as he said, 'For the benefit of all the guests present and the millions of people undoubtedly watching this event on television, what else can we do or give to a man or Zellian who already has everything he can possibly desire? After much discussion among senior members of Congress, it was decided to honour your status as Teacher. We offer you something that money cannot buy: honorary citizenship of the United States of America.'

Chapter Sixty-Two

Amid rapturous applause by all the guests, and the cheers of the citizenry in private and public venues everywhere, Davis Cooper handed Jon a prepared scroll to which had been affixed the Presidential Great Seal, which Jon promptly held aloft for all to see.

Then, not wishing to prolong the wedding reception further, Jon made a very short but sincere speech expressing his appreciation of the honour accorded to him by the president and the people, but he reminded everyone that Lana, as his consort, had played a major role in the past and would continue to do so in the future.

As the day wore on, Jon and Lana mingled with the guests until they decided to slip away, making their last farewells to their immediate friends and family. Once in the privacy of Rega's apartment suite, holding Lana firmly to him and nuzzling her ear, Jon enquired, 'Now what do we do?'

'First, let me get out of this dress,' she replied, 'and into something less formal. Then, Mr Ambassador, it's back to the ship, where we'll set course for Buccaneer's Point.' Within the hour, the spaceship was well on its way to the Caribbean and the Point.

Chapter Sixty-Three

Several months passed after Jon and Lana returned to Buccaneer's Point, during which time, back in the States and several other European locations, work was still progressing in the manufacture of the atomic power plants required to drive the wheels of industry and the civilisation of the future. With the constant guidance of Mort and other Zellian technicians who had since been allocated to the project, success had been achieved in harnessing the smaller power units for the purpose of installation into road vehicles of all sizes, with cars and trucks the priority.

There were now a number of vehicle builders running their prototypes on every continent in the world. Equally, the design and construction of huge nuclear power stations in various parts of the States, in particular, were looking more viable to the many sceptics who had initially opposed their construction. As the advantages of the new technologies became more evident to the masses, the transformation of industry, the main cause of atmospheric pollution and global warming, was more readily accepted, so much so that Jon's task as the Teacher became easier. He only had to point the way, and the scientists and engineers of Earth were happy to follow.

The construction work on the ambassador's residence had long since been completed, and with the help of a team of designers, Jon and Lana had visited some of the most elegant fashion houses in various parts of the world. Their desire was to create a home that would be as elegant as any on Earth, or even on Zel. While their mansion was not as pretentious as some of the palaces and castles

Chapter Sixty-Three

of their earthly counterparts, no others could claim to have such a happy place to live; it was heaven on Earth.

Rega was one of the first people to visit the island after he was informed that his daughter was eagerly looking forward to seeing him. He was accompanied by his two delightful flight attendants, Asa and Rea, of course. It was on this occasion that Mort decided to tag along, as he felt that he was in need of a respite from scientific duties, having worked continually since the joining ceremony on the various construction projects all over the world. Their unanimous opinion was one of delight in the choice of location of the island, the external appearance of the house, and of course, the fabulous interior. As Rega entered the portal and into the main hallway, he looked around appraisingly and breathed, 'This is indeed a home away from home, Lana.' He could not have given a better compliment to the ambassador and his wife.

Elsewhere in the world, for the most part, peace did prevail, but in one area in Asia, in particular, local wars continued unabated, despite having been warned of the consequences of refusing to live in peace. As a certain US General Clintock put it, 'They've been at it for generations, and no matter what has been tried, first by the British, then the Russians, then the United Nations, it still goes on. The only way to put a stop to it is their extermination.'

Jon was disappointed that persuasion and incentives to live in peace had all failed over the years, and taking Rega to one side, he explained that the people concerned in that particular part of the world had been waging war against all comers and even themselves. Religion was one of the most divisive factors that motivated them, which, in many other cases, had also been responsible for some of the bloodiest wars in the history of mankind. Clintock's reference to extermination made Jon think that since persuasion had so far failed to bring peace, now was the time for the iron fist to be deployed, and he had a plan for that. Taking Rega into a room he used as a library and an office, he spread a map of central Asia on a

Chapter Sixty-Three

table and pointed out the area of Pakistan and Afghanistan, with a large river running through what appeared to be a mountain gorge.

'This is the area populated by the tribesmen who have been making war for centuries,' Jon stated, 'and all attempts to drive them out have so far failed.'

Rega noted the inhospitable terrain and conceded that for the primitive type of warfare employed by such men, it would be difficult to oust them from their habitat. 'I take it that you have some kind of plan, Jon, something that has never been attempted before.'

Soberly, Jon replied, 'Yes, while I don't wish to destroy all the women and children who live on the plains and in the valleys of the region, the men must be driven out or captured, then educated to appreciate a peaceful way of life.'

Rega smiled and said, 'It has been the experience of many military commanders in history to drive an enemy out into the open, but to educate those who have no wish to learn is quite another thing. However,' he continued, 'obviously you have a plan in your mind as to how to drive this enemy out of his stronghold, Jon.'

Without hesitation, Jon replied, 'I know you can read my mind, and if it seems a little confused, it is because what I propose to do will entail your cooperation and the use of the entire battle fleet from the mother ship.'

Rega continued to read Jon's mind, but what he saw was something beyond his personal experience, so he asked for clarification of the intended action Jon was proposing to take. Recalling the war games carried out several months earlier when only two of the saucers were deployed in the annihilation of an entire mock army, Jon outlined his strategy to drive out the entire population living in this particular region with a minimal loss of life.

With a thoughtful frown, he said quietly, 'I propose to target this area.' He pointed at the map in front of them and said 'Where the river passes through a deep gorge in the mountains before

Chapter Sixty-Three

emerging onto the plains, where incidentally, the majority of the people are peace-loving farmers.' He continued in a firmer tone of voice. 'On both sides of the river, the mountains rise thousands of feet, sheer cliffs for the most part, an area which has proven to be a haven for the war-like tribesmen for centuries.' Even now, Jon was contemplating the course of action that the battle fleet would pursue. 'I intend to lead two columns of the saucers, four on each side of the gorge, with disintegrator beams on full power, and about two thousand feet above the river.'

Rega nodded his head, understanding the purpose of this strategy. 'Yes,' he remarked, 'you intend to cut a swathe into the rock face of the mountain and let natural gravity collapse the mountainside.'

With a smile of satisfaction that he and Rega were of like minds on his strategy, Jon enlarged on his plan. 'With the two columns of craft deployed and moving slowly through the gorge, and with their force fields activated for their own protection from falling rock, the swathe that's cut into the rock face will become deeper until the weight of the rock causes the spontaneous collapse of the mountain above, resulting in an avalanche of epic proportions.'

As he visualised the aftermath of this operation, he explained that this should not cause any immediate loss of life in the local community, but with millions of tons of rock falling into the gorge, this would immediately create a natural dam hundreds of feet in height, blocking the river in its tracks. With nowhere to go, although it would take many months or even years, the water would back up and eventually flood the valleys for many miles upstream. That would give the population ample time to evacuate the area.

Rega again nodded in approval. 'As always, Jon, your concern for your people is commendable, as is this strategy that you propose to use to drive out the troublemakers.'

Chapter Sixty-Three

Jon couldn't help but grin with amusement as he remarked, 'This will probably create the largest series of lakes in Asia, and the people will have to take up fishing rather than fighting in the future.' Rega could appreciate the irony of that statement.

Chapter Sixty-Four

Several days later, having informed Davis Cooper, who was an interested party, of their forthcoming foray into the mountains of Asia, Jon, Lana, Rega, and Mort, making up the full crew of the spaceship, departed from Buccaneer's Point and headed for the rendezvous with the other ships of the battle fleet. Because they were in Earth's atmosphere, their speed was limited to two thousand miles per hour, so it took several hours before they made contact with the other captains, who were already in position several miles above the target area.

The mountains below provided a spectacle of beauty and grandeur that, Rega conceded, was more magnificent than anywhere else in the universe. As luck would have it, the weather was perfect. The sun blazed down, reflecting the blinding whiteness of the snow-covered mountains far below, although Jon smilingly reminded them that the outside temperature could kill them if exposed to it for more than a few minutes.

With the fleet being assembled, Rega opened the communications channel in order to brief the captains of the other spacecraft. He described how they would enter the gorge at an altitude of two thousand feet and slowly traverse the side of the mountain, each ship cutting a deep swathe into the rock face. This would only be done for about a quarter mile of the length of the gorge, to bring down that much of the mountainside would be more than enough to achieve the desired result, the damming of the river

Chapter Sixty-Four

below and the flooding of the ravines and valleys for many miles upstream.

With a smile of approval, Jon indicated to Lana that, as pilot of their craft, she would now lead the way into the gorge with the other saucers flying slowly in convoy, as they watched for any premature rock falls. As each ship progressed gradually through the gorge, they kept the viewports open and watched in fascination as their own disintegrator beams began the process of gouging a deep cut into the sheer face of the mountainside. As Jon observed mentally, *it was about ten feet wide and even more in depth.* It was fascinating to watch the displaced rock, now reduced to nothing bigger than pieces of gravel, pour down the mountainside. *Almost like a solidified waterfall,* he noted.

As each of the ships followed them, deploying their own beams, the scar across the mountainside became deeper and deeper, and it wasn't long before the rock face began to crumble. With an air of expectancy, they watched as the sides of the gorge split several hundred feet above them then down to the level of the river itself. The spectacle of the collapse of the mountainside held them in a hypnotic grip, and they were unable to move as they watched, as in slow motion, the disintegration of massive slabs of rock and falling boulders crashed into the river below.

The avalanche continued for what seemed an eternity, bringing down more rocks and thousands of tons of snow from the higher peaks. *Something else to add to the flooding effect,* Jon mused, a thought that was echoed by the other occupants of the cabin. The deed being done, there was no need to hurry away, so all eight ships hovered above the scene of devastation wreaked by their own efforts and the Zellian technology. Already, the first signs that the stoppage of the river was having an effect became obvious to the observers. The waters of the river foamed and churned where they met the impassable barrier of rock piled high for several hundreds of feet.

Chapter Sixty-Four

Jon concluded that, while it might take years to flood the region, the waters would form the deepest series of lakes in this region of Asia. He was already thinking about the possible benefits that could be derived from this situation.

Rega was again reading Jon's thoughts. *One thing at a time, Jon,* he cautioned. *There is still much to do elsewhere in the world, even though you may have solved the immediate problem of the conflicts in this region.*

Lana also communed telepathically, agreeing with her father, and she urged Jon that it was now time to return home, to Buccaneer's Point.

As commander of the Zellian force, Rega gave the order that the other spacecraft should return to the mother ship since their work was now done, while Lana, with Jon's approval, set course for their return to The Point. As soon as they were safely under way, she also made a point of communicating with the White House and Davis Cooper, and of course, George K. Lane, that their mission was accomplished.

The news of the success of the mission in Asia was relayed around the world, and the media film crews lost no time in gaining access to the mountainous region where the action had taken place, in order to bring the graphic scenes to the attention of worldwide audiences. As one commentator observed, 'The Teacher is a man who can move mountains.' This was a phrase not lost on the people of that region, and it was notable that peace soon returned to the region. The iron fist had had the required effect.

After this event, the scientists and engineers continued their work to improve and perfect the projects to enable the transition to a pollution-free atmosphere of the planet, the results of which were to become evident within the first five years. There was cleaner air, better health for the people, less devastating weather patterns, and stabilising temperatures throughout the world. Although it was yet

Chapter Sixty-Four

to be introduced, Jon also had a ten-year plan for the introduction of an economy that was not dependant on the production of oil, but that was still to be in the future. It would be somewhat more difficult to gain acceptance by those countries which would be adversely affected , the oil-producing nations, and would have to be gradually introduced over a period of time. It would mean that their economies would have to diversify in order to survive, to diversify into other lines of commerce.

One more difficult problem remained, the one which would be the most difficult to resolve in Jon's opinion, and that was the overpopulation of the planet that now numbered in the billions. As one Zellian scientist observed, 'The healthier the people, the faster they breed.' As a consequence, a meeting between representatives of the World Health Organisation, scientists, and different governments was scheduled to debate the issue. Jon, as the Teacher, in conjunction with some of the Zellian scientists, resolved that the populations must be allowed to dwindle naturally, without causing distress within the different cultures and societies. 'We did it on Zel millions of years ago,' declared one eminent scientist from the mother ship. 'And while it may take many generations to achieve, it will improve the outlook for future generations of mankind in the long term.'

Jon was aware of the method used to control the Zellian population that had eventually reduced that population many aeons ago. He counselled himself, *Better that they don't know. Let it appear to happen naturally and gradually, since ignorance, in this situation, will be better for all concerned. Nature will always take its course.*

As the world grew more peaceful and prosperous for its population, Rega and the mother ship continued on its patrol of the galaxy. Whenever he returned to Earth, his now favourite planet, to visit his daughter (and his son Jon, he reminded himself with a glow of pride), he noted the changes that were gradually taking place, and he was pleased.

Chapter Sixty-Four

Yes, it was always good to return to Buccaneer's Point. It was so much like Zel that it was almost like being at home.

Epilogue

It was some two years after Jon and Lana took up residence in the mansion house on the island of Buccaneer's Point in the Caribbean that they announced to the world in general that Lana had given birth to a son. Among the first to know were their friends, Davis Cooper and George K. Lane, who had at that time also concluded their terms of office and were now retiring from the political scene after being hailed as the most successful administration in the recent history of the United States of America.

Lana's son was a healthy boy who showed every sign of being a mirror image of his father, even down to the mass of glowing silver hair that he had inherited from Jon. Everyone who saw him commented, 'He is such a beautiful child!' A simple but memorable name was chosen for him, Jolan, derived from Jon and Lana. It was by coincidence that Rega made one of his frequent visits to Earth, and was delighted to be told he was now a grandfather.

All over the earth, people were experiencing the ongoing recovery of the planet's ecological system in the form of cleaner air and healthier crops, although it was conceded that there was still a long way to go before a full recovery of the planet would be achieved and be what nature intended. It was also observed that the scientific progress toward the development of the atomic power units for the automobile industry and other aspects of their development was continuing apace, to the delight of the government and industry moguls alike.

Epilogue

There was, however, one continuing source of irritation for Jon, and that was the continuous squabbling and fighting, even bloodshed, among the people in a certain region of the Arab world, a situation from which there appeared to be little chance of resolution. It was always a potential source of violence that could erupt and spread throughout the entire region at the slightest provocation, as had happened many times before, but that he would not permit to happen again.

After the actions taken against the warring nations of the Middle East on a previous occasion, and since these conflicts continued to rage spasmodically despite Jon's repeated warnings, he resolved that he must take action, and thereby avoid the risk of future wars in this or other areas of the world. It was again time for the iron fist to be used as had been done before in an Asiatic country. It was time to strike fear into the hearts and minds of all who opposed his teachings. Remembering the biblical lesson of Sodom and Gomorrah, he resolved that nothing less would teach the religious zealots the lesson of living in peace or suffering death.

Accordingly, he called on the services of Mort, the Zellian technician who was still assisting him with the transformation of earthly technology, to carry out a punishment of truly biblical proportions, one that would deter mankind from future folly and acts of war, and defiance of their Teacher. They left the island of Buccaneer's Point, and after a lengthy flight, arrived over the principal city of the rebellious region. No warning of his intention was given, and the spacecraft climbed to an altitude of one hundred miles above the densely populated area. After a lengthy deliberation of his planned strategy, he instructed Mort to focus the weapon of death, a heat-producing ray many times hotter than the heat of the sun itself, so that the city below was completely engulfed in the all-consuming blast of heat, burning everything in its path. Death was instantaneous for all living creatures. Men, women, and their children, even all animals and livestock perished. The spacecraft hovered over the city until every vestige of civilisation had been destroyed and reduced to nothing more than smouldering ashes. Sodom and Gomorrah had been repeated in a lesson for all others who would defy the Teacher in future. With such a threat to curtail any further war-like behaviour, peace was observed throughout the world, until all wars were consigned to the history books as ancient history.

Some ten years after the time that Jon had been persuaded to become a Teacher on behalf of the Zellians and for the benefit of the human race, he reflected on the changes that had occurred during that period. The health of the planet had much improved, and although the global population had not been reduced, it had at least stabilised. It was too early to expect otherwise. *Give it another hundred years,* he mused. It had been necessary to intercede on many occasions for the benefit of less fortunate people in some of the poorer and domestically backward countries. Many had been reluctant to give up or change their traditional lifestyle. *But at least,* he smiled grimly at the thought, *it has not been necessary to again use the iron fist to assert my will on the people. That lesson has been learnt.*

Jon and Lana lived a happy and contented life on Buccaneer's Point, and Rega visited them from time to time, always eager to see his grandson Jolan, who was growing into a sturdy young lad. On one such visit, Rega made a comment that Jon found amusing. 'It's a bit early for a young woman like you, Lana, to be a mother; you're barely a hundred years old.'

Many more of their friends, such as Davis Cooper and George K. Lane, Jacob and his wife, Miranda, came to visit them, but they were all growing older, as is the way of humanity. However, Jon still appeared to be a young man in his thirties, and Lana, of course, was a radiant young mother. Both had the prospect of another five hundred years of life before them. Whatever changes might have to

Epilogue

be initiated for the good of humanity, the Teacher would have more than enough time to bring them about.

A further twenty-five years passed, and the world learned that dependency on oil was no longer a necessity as other power sources were readily available. The promised nuclear plants had appeared in many locations and were being commissioned and coming online all over the States as well as in parts of Europe and Asia. As a further incentive to strive for a better way of life, Lana, with the assistance of a small team of scientists from the mother ship, had dealt with a number of common medical problems that had plagued the human race for centuries—measles, tuberculosis, cholera, and many others—although a cure for the common cold still evaded them!

After a period of one hundred years, it became apparent that the human race was less productive or fertile than it once had been. People wondered if this was intentional or some natural phenomenon; perhaps it was the cause of the decline of the Zellian population so long ago. Jon was not prepared to speculate on this question, but he thought it a welcome solution to the world's population problem. Furthermore, it had occurred without any distressing actions needing to be taken to curb the pleasures of men or women!

By this time, all the original friends of Jon and Lana had long since departed this life on Earth to be replaced by others of a less intimate nature. Jolan was now a grown young man, who appeared to have inherited the physical perfection of both his parents, and was currently training in all the sciences that would be of benefit to humanity and possibly the Zellian race as well. Rega, of course, was looking forward to spending an extended holiday at Buccaneer's Point so that he could enjoy being with his family, and to make it a happier occasion, he was planning to persuade Lana's mother to visit Earth for the very first time.

Epilogue

In all, life was looking good for the ambassador of Zel and his family. And Buccaneer's Point was now the most famous island in the Caribbean, if not the world.

Review Requested:
If you loved this book, would you please provide a review at Amazon.com?
Thank You